Slowly and methodically, Strasser began to make his way toward her. She looked around frantically for something, anything, to help. But there was nothing. He was going to grab hold of her and throw her out the door. And Simon would be sure to follow.

She would be damned if she was going to give up without a fight though.

Strasser stalked her around the car, a predator playing with his prey. Finally he cornered her, and Elizabeth reached behind her to hold on to the handrail for all she was worth.

Strasser closed the distance between them and she kicked and kicked. He fended off her blows until he was right in front of her.

"This game is over," he said, smugly.

"Simon Cross is so smoking that it turns off my higher cognitive functions...Adventuring through time with these two characters is a real treat, and I would happily follow them for another twelve or so books."

SM Reine, author of *Death's Hand*

Other Books by Monique Martin

Out of Time Series

Out of Time: A Time Travel Mystery (Book #1)
When the Wall Fell (Book #2)
Fragments (Book #3)
The Devils' Due (Book #4)
Thursday's Child (Book #5)
Sands of Time (Book #6)
A Rip in Time (Book #7)
A Time of Shadows (Book #8)
Voyage in Time (Book #9)
Revolution in Time (Book #10)
Expedition in Time (Book #11)

Out of Time Christmas Novellas

In Time for Christmas
Christmas in New York
The Christmas Express - coming winter 2019!

Saving Time Series

Jacks Are Wild (Book #1)
Aloha, Jack (Book #2)
Nairobi Jack (Book #3)
Book #4 - coming soon!

The Blaze Series

The Blaze (Book #1)
Mirror (Book #2)

Hollywood Heroes Series

The Frame (Book #1)
The Curse (Book #2) - coming soon!*

Monique Martin

Expedition in Time

Out of Time Series
Book #11

Cover Photo: Karen Wunderman
Cover Design and Interior Layout and Formatting: Terry Roy

ISBN-13: 978-1-09-644150-2
ISBN-10: 1-09-644150-0

For more information, please contact
writtenbymonique@gmail.com
Or visit: www.moniquemartin.weebly.com

For George and Marion

Acknowledgements

As always this book would not have been possible without the help of many people. I would like to thank Michael, Eddie & Carole, Mom & George, Dad & Anne, Cidney, Gillian, Andra, and especially Laura for everything she did to make this book possible.

I'd also like to thank the thousands of people who help preserve the past through books, websites, museums, and sheer will.

Expedition in Time

(Out of Time Book #11)

Monique Martin

Chapter One

1936, Somewhere in the Brazilian Jungle

THE JUNGLE AROUND HIM vibrated with life. Gaspar had lived his whole life in Brazil, and those years had taught him great respect for both the jungle's beauty and its danger.

He paused to wipe the sweat from his forehead. The damp heat of the rainforest pressed down on him like hands upon his shoulders. His handkerchief was already soaked, but he mopped away the perspiration and took a deep breath of the cloying air.

He'd been journeying for weeks and without his native Guarani guide, Moacir, who led their small party deeper and deeper into the heart of Brazil, he would be lost, swallowed by a jungle that subsumed everything that did not keep moving. Gaspar was Brazilian, but not native to this place, not to the jungle. Few were.

In the distance, tree frogs and cicadas sang their songs to the river, and a hundred birds chirped and squawked in the dense canopy above. A small, bright green snake slithered over the toe of his boot as if to remind him not to remain still for too long. A large mosquito stabbed his neck and he slapped at it, crushing it beneath his palm. When his hand came away a small smear of blood covered it.

The jungle always takes a bite.

He wiped it away with his sodden handkerchief.

"*Por aqui!*" Moacir called out from not far away. "*Por aqui!*"

Stuffing his handkerchief back into his pocket, Gaspar hurried to catch up to his guide.

Moacir, a small man with a bowl haircut and a belt made of feathers and leaves, jabbed his machete toward a large twining of vines draped like a curtain over a rough outcropping of rock that rose up from the jungle floor.

Gaspar assessed the area Moacir motioned so vehemently to with guarded anticipation.

"Are you sure?" Gaspar asked.

Moacir nodded and pulled away a few of the vines. "*Aqui.*"

"*Meu Deus,*" Gaspar whispered under his breath as he realized why Moacir was so adamant. The rock outcropping beneath the vines was not natural. It was a series of large stones set upon the other, each carved by human hands. Etched into the side of the stone were symbols Gaspar had never seen before.

Briefly, reverently, he ran his fingers over the runes. *Could this be it? Have I really found it?*

He knew it wasn't the city itself, but the guidepost to it and more treasure than he'd ever dreamt of.

His heart surged at the thought. Professor Mendoza had been so sure, but Gaspar never believed him. He was just happy to take the professor's money, certain this trek was as useless as the rest had been. But now...

"*A tigela?*" he asked, remembering the purpose for his journey. "The bowl?"

Moacir pointed his tip of his machete toward a gap in the stone as the rest of their small party gathered to see what he would find.

Gaspar tried to control the excitement that surged inside him. Carefully, he pulled aside more of the vines. There was an inset in the rock, but it was too dark to see what was inside.

Quickly, he shed the pack on his back and rummaged around for a flashlight. He turned it on, but the batteries sputtered and the light dimmed. He slapped it against his palm and the light came back to life. Stepping back toward the opening, he pulled the curtain of vines away from the entrance and shined his light inside. It was a small alcove just large enough for a man.

Tamping down the fear that rose in his throat, he stepped inside. Leaves and debris covered the floor; however, there was an unnatural pile of them at the back of the small cave. He reached to brush some of the leaves aside when a huge tarantula crawled out from between them. Snatching his hand away, he thought better of his plan and unclasped the knife from his belt. Using the tip of it, he flicked away the spider then the top level of leaves, then the next. His excitement had begun to wane as the pile was nearly gone when his knife hit something solid.

He shined his light toward it and a bright yellow reflected the beam.

"*Sim, sim,*" he said to himself as he carelessly brushed the rest of the leaves and twigs away from his goal.

His breath caught as he saw it for the first time—a large, shallow bowl made of pure gold with an ornate, golden snake undulating around the outside.

Almost hysterical laughter bubbled out and his eyes gleamed as brightly as the metal before him.

"*Bela.*"

Finally, he picked the bowl up and brushed away the last bits of dirt. It was magnificent and he'd found it. He, Gaspar, had found it!

He reached to caress the cool metal when sounds outside of the alcove drew his attention away. The howler monkeys in the trees above began to whoop and bark. Of course, he'd heard this many times before but never so insistent, never so many.

Putting the bowl into his knapsack and hefting it over his shoulder, he emerged from the small cave to ask what was wrong. Moacir and all of his men stared up into the thick canopy above as the howling grew louder and louder until it seemed to shake the very ground upon which he stood.

Suddenly one of Moacir's men, then another, turned quickly, spears at the ready, staring out into the jungle.

Then the howling stopped and an eerie silence filled the space where it had been.

"*Que*—?" Gaspar began, but Moacir held up a silencing hand.

The quiet was more unnerving than the monkeys' screams. Gaspar strained to see something, anything, in the thick undergrowth that surrounded them.

The arrow whizzed past his head so closely he could feel the wind from it. It embedded itself in a crevice in the rock behind him.

Moacir's dark eyes went round and he grabbed at Gaspar's sleeve, pulling him away. It was a good thing he had; the second arrow would not have missed if he hadn't.

The monkeys screamed again.

One man and then another emerged from the forest as if they'd come from the bark of the trees themselves. They wore necklaces of bone and long sharp fangs pierced their lower lips curving up like a second set of teeth. Moacir yelled something in Guarani that Gaspar

4

didn't understand and his men charged. As the two tribes clashed, Moacir grabbed his arm and they ran.

He'd heard stories of these people but like the lost city, he'd never believed. Now, he did.

He ran as fast as he could, following close behind Moacir, who led the way and hacked at the jungle ahead of them like a madman, his machete swinging wildly as they tried to escape.

Branches scratched his face and arms as they ran headlong into the jungle. In the distance, the screams of their attackers mingled with the anguished cries of Moacir's men as they were cut down.

He didn't know how long they ran, only that his lungs burned. When they reached the rope bridge, Moacir motioned for him to cross and stood guard ready to fight off whoever followed, for surely some had.

Only one man could cross the bridge at a time and Gaspar wasted no time arguing. Fear pulsed through his veins. Crossing was precarious under the best of circumstances and now his footing was less sure. He stumbled once, barely catching himself with the rope railing to keep from falling into the rocky gorge below. He heard a scream behind him, but didn't dare look back. After what seemed an eternity, he managed to make it to the other side. He turned back to motion Moacir across, but he was gone. Gaspar scanned the other side of the gorge for him, but there was no sign of the man nor of the tribe that had attacked them.

He knew he should press on, but he needed to see the bowl, to be sure. He shed his backpack and looked inside, worried it had all been a dream. But it wasn't; inside was the glorious golden bowl, the key to so much more. Professor Mendoza would pay him well for it, more than promised, and he would be set for life.

It took him several days to find a friendly tribe to help him and several more weeks to return to civilization. Clean and fed and finally free of the jungle, he went downstairs in his hotel in São Paulo to make a phone call. It took several minutes to make the connection to the United States and he held the backpack to his chest as he waited. It was never out of his sight.

Finally, the call was put through and he heard the professor's voice across the thready connection.

"I have found it," Gaspar told him. "I have found it."

PRESENT DAY, SANTA BARBARA, CALIFORNIA

"LET'S GO, GO, GO steady!"

SIMON WINCED AS ELIZABETH and Charlotte sang along with the boy band du jour's most popular and inane song in an impromptu concert in their living room. He was supportive of his daughter and involved in all aspects of her life, save one—this music. Try as he might he could simply not find any common ground between Schubert and the Soldier Boys, the unfortunate name of her current favorite band. He wasn't sure which part he liked less: soldiers or boys.

As he sat at the dining table going over the tragedy that was his students' essays on elemental magic, Charlotte and Elizabeth broke out into a fit of laughter in the living room as Elizabeth misstepped in the choreographed routine the two had been practicing to the mind-numbing pop hit, "Let's Go Steady, Yeah?" While the title of the song was enough to make him shudder, it was the implications of it that made him truly uneasy. His daughter, his child, was not quite ten years old, and far too young for such ideas. Although, a traitorous part of him whispered, she was on the verge of puberty and boys would be more than just lyrics in a song soon.

The whole idea of it gave him indigestion.

"Simon?" Elizabeth asked, catching him watching them dance, and waving him toward them. He demurred, of course. Even so, he was a little bit jealous.

Despite loathing the Soldier Boys, their music, and in particular that floppy-haired, absurdly-named, Pony Boy, that Charlotte seemed far too enamored with, he wanted to understand, to be part of it. He didn't want there to be any part of his child's life he was excluded from, but he just couldn't find a way into this one. Elizabeth had no such problems and joined in naturally and gleefully.

Watching them together reminded him just how young Elizabeth still was. She wasn't the girl he'd met at university all those years ago, but she was somehow just as youthful as when he'd fallen in love with her. He, however, was not. His fiftieth birthday had come and gone and with it any semblance of the lie he told himself that he wasn't actually getting older, getting *old*. As he watched them dance and giggle, he felt it more keenly than ever.

He knew that having a child at his age would present challenges. He'd thought he was up to them. He usually was, but today he felt out of touch with her, with them both, the two most precious people in the world to him, and he knew it would only get worse. Time would not yield. As they continued to blossom, that occasional ache in his knee would grow more frequent, the grey hair at his temples would spread, and those reading glasses he pretended he didn't need would become a necessity.

He was so deeply entrenched in his self-pity that it took him a moment to realize the music had, blessedly, stopped. Gathering himself, he gave them a round of applause. Charlotte took a bow and Elizabeth blew him and the rest of her imaginary audience kisses. The sight of the two of them lifted his sagging heart.

"One more time?" Charlotte asked, bouncing on the balls of her feet in anticipation.

"I only do two shows on Sunday," Elizabeth answered with faux pomposity.

Charlotte's face fell in disappointment but rebounded nearly as quickly with a bright smile. "Can I invite Jenny to come over?"

"May I," Simon corrected reflexively.

"May I?" Charlotte amended quickly.

Simon caught Elizabeth's eye. She merely shrugged *why not?*

"Yes," he said finally, earning a squeal of delight from Charlotte who ran toward the hallway and her room, only to stop suddenly and rush to her father's side.

"Thank you," she said and kissed his cheek.

She beamed up at her mother before running off to her room to call her best friend.

Elizabeth came to stand behind him and slid her arms around his shoulders as she peered down at his work. "That bad?"

"Hmm?" Simon asked before realizing that she was talking about the papers. "Oh, no worse than usual."

Elizabeth stood and came around from behind him to look him in the eye. "Something wrong?"

He felt foolish now for even harboring his morose thoughts. He was the damn luckiest man alive. Old or not.

He took her hand, shifted in his chair to make room, and tugged her down onto his lap. "Nothing at all."

Elizabeth's eyes searched his face for the truth. She was far too perceptive and knew him far too well.

To stave off questions he wasn't prepared to answer he leaned in and kissed her. It was a brief but promising kiss and one he knew would divert her attention for now.

"Mmm. You taste like tea. Me likey," she said, earning a chuckle from him, and she moved in for another kiss.

Just as his worries were all but forgotten, the telephone rang.

"Maybe it's Jenny's parents," Elizabeth suggested.

He didn't care who it was and leaned in to kiss her neck.

"Simon," she chastised lightly as she wriggled out of his grasp and answered the phone. "Cross residence . . .Oh, hello." Her eyes rounded with surprise and intrigue. "Yes," she said, "I see."

Simon joined her by the pass-through to the kitchen where the phone's base was.

"I understand," she said, "Yes, yes, I'll let you know. Thank you." Then she hung up.

"Who was it?" he asked, although he had an inkling. Her eyes didn't sparkle like that for home room duty.

"The Council."

As he'd surmised. "And?"

"They have an assignment for us," she said.

"I see."

It had been some time since they'd gone on a mission for the Council for Temporal Studies, and Simon found he was enjoying the respite and the normalcy of life without time travel. But he knew his wife and her heart. Each call from the Council was a call for help and she'd never turned away anyone who needed it.

"We don't have to take it," she offered, as if sensing his thoughts. "I don't even know the details."

He knew that the details didn't matter to her. She would go anywhere, and any time. Not that she was reckless about it, not with Charlotte in their lives now, but it was who she was. Who they were, he had to admit. As idyllic as their lives in Santa Barbara were, she *needed* more. If he was honest, he loved what they did as well, but he did not love the risk.

"It's okay," she began, reading his unease. "I'll call them back and—"

"I'll make the necessary travel arrangements," he said, conceding the argument before it began. For security reasons, all meetings took place at Council headquarters in San Francisco, and that meant flying up there and usually spending the night.

"Really?" she asked.

"Really."

Her arms slid around his neck as she pulled him toward her. His arms encircled her waist, resting comfortably around his wife.

"Simon Cross, Man of Action," she said. "Very sexy."

"Man of Consideration," he corrected. "I've only agreed to hear what they have to say. Nothing more."

He was willing to help the world, within reason.

"Still sexy," Elizabeth said and leaned up to kiss him.

A gagging sound from the hallway brought them up short. Charlotte eyed them with open distaste.

"Yes?" Simon asked, used to, although not always pleased with, his daughter's impeccable timing.

"Jenny's mom said yes."

He and Elizabeth exchanged looks. "About that..."

"Good afternoon, Mr. and Mrs. Cross."

"Hello, Rhys," Elizabeth said.

The young man smiled up at her as she and Simon entered Travers' outer office. Rhys was Peter's latest secretary. Ever since Peter had married Grace, he'd gone through a series of unfortunate assistants. She liked Rhys a far sight better than Peter's previous assistant, Mrs. Fletcher, who had a whole Nurse Ratchet vibe going. Rhys was just the opposite. He was young, maybe thirty, but seemed quite nice and was very good at his job. "Is Peter in?"

Rhys cocked his head to the side. "No, I . . .I thought they told you."

"Told us what?" Simon asked in that clipped way of his that augured trouble.

"Mr. Travers is, well, currently indisposed. Mr. Hewitt requested you."

They'd dealt with Hewitt a few times before, but only casually. Actually, she realized, they'd never said more than a few words to him. He seemed nice enough though.

"Hewitt?" Simon said, clearly displeased not to be dealing with Peter. Even though they'd worked with the Council for a dozen years, Simon's mistrust of them stood the test of time. He trusted Peter Travers and precious few others. The Shadow Council might be long gone, but Simon's wariness remained.

"Yes," Rhys said, rising from behind his desk. "He's waiting for you." He gestured toward the inner office.

Simon's mood sufficiently soured, Rhys ushered them into the director's office.

Their arrangements to come to San Francisco had been made quickly. They were lucky that the sleepover had been easily swapped to Charlotte staying at Jenny's house instead, so their daughter was looked after while they were away.

Elizabeth preceded Simon into the office.

James Hewitt was a kindly looking man, tall, balding, and with a soft oval face. He looked like the high school principal everyone wished they had. Slightly befuddled, but trying.

"Where's Travers?" Simon asked without preamble.

"Simon," Elizabeth chided.

Hewitt didn't seem to mind Simon's abruptness and merely chuckled as he rose from his seat behind the large mahogany desk at the far end of the room. "He's ..."

"Indisposed?" Simon finished for him. "Precisely what does that mean?"

"I'm afraid I can't say exactly. You know how it is," he added amiably.

Simon grunted in reply.

Elizabeth ignored her husband's mood and smiled. "Good to see you again, Mr. Hewitt."

"Please." He gestured toward the two leather club chairs opposite his desk. Once they were seated, he perched himself on the edge of the desk in front of them. "Thank you for coming on such short notice. I guess we might as well get right to it."

He handed them each a mission dossier.

Elizabeth flipped hers open. Paper-clipped to the top of a stack of papers was a photograph of a man in his mid-sixties, graying, balding, with a mustache and a kindly academic look about him.

"Doctor Emil Mendoza," Hewitt began. "Professor Emeritus National Autonomous University of Mexico, and Distinguished Visiting Professor Universität Berlin and Cambridge, among others. Dr. Mendoza is a renowned archeologist and historical linguist and, without meaning to, we think, he presents a grave threat to the timeline."

"How so?" Simon said without looking up from his quick scan of the report.

"An object of great concern will come into his possession. Have you ever heard of the Staff of Life?"

"Bread?" Elizabeth said, offering the only definition she knew.

Hewitt fought down a smile and shook his head.

"There have been many mythical artifacts with similar appellations—Khatvānga, Caduceus, even Merlin's staff have all been considered the Staff of Life at one point or another," Simon said. "Perhaps you could be more specific."

Hewitt grinned and pointed his finger at Simon. "I knew you were the right man for the job. Spot on. Now, frankly, we don't know if it's one of those or all of those or something else entirely."

12

"That's rather vague," Simon put in.

Hewitt shrugged. "When the timeline's in flux, getting a clear picture is . . .challenging. Hard to put your finger on things sometimes."

Elizabeth knew that was true, but she was confused about something. "This staff. It may or may not be Merlin's, which by the way, would be awesome."

Hewitt's expression brightened; he clearly enjoyed her enthusiasm. "Agreed. But we simply don't know if all of those are names for the same object or different objects. Our staff has tried to narrow it down, but the mythology is a little murky and well, time is..."

"Wiggly?" Elizabeth supplied, winning another broad grin from Hewitt.

"It's not uncommon," Simon said, as if he were addressing his students, "for a myth to spread even across continents and be adopted by various peoples along the way, each of whom claims it as their own."

"Right," Hewitt agreed. "To be honest, our actuaries aren't quite sure what it is or just what it's capable of—destruction, creation. But they are certain of one thing—it's potentially very powerful and very, very dangerous in the wrong hands."

Simon's expression darkened at that bit of news, not that it was surprising. They were never sent after mythical balloons and lollipops.

"That's where you come in," Hewitt continued as he stood to move and sit behind the desk. "You're to travel back in time, if you accept the mission, and take possession of the staff and bring it back here."

"Steal it?" Elizabeth asked.

Hewitt thought for a moment. "I suppose that's one way to look at it. Regardless of how you view it, or how you do it, frankly, the staff must be brought back to the Council for safe keeping."

Simon snorted at that.

Hewitt ignored him. "It needs to be removed from the timeline at all costs."

He sat back in his chair. "Even though the staff itself is quite dangerous, the mission itself should be rather easy, as they go. The professor appears to be no threat on his own. We think he has no idea just what he's about to come in contact with. And 1930s Miami is hardly the fall of Pompeii. All you have to do is follow him and take possession of the staff. Simple really."

Simon grunted. "Simple. Have you ever time traveled, Mr. Hewitt?"

"No, I've never had the chance."

"There's nothing simple about it."

Simon was right, of course, but going to Miami wasn't exactly the same as going on the Titanic or surviving the Blitz. They could do this. They *should* do this.

"No, of course not," Hewitt added quickly. "I didn't mean . . . I just meant that compared to some of your other missions this one should be relatively easy."

Just when she though Simon was on board, that crease between his eyes popped as he closed the dossier.

"Why us?"

"Pardon?"

"Why send us? Why not send another team, or Jack? You haven't called on us in some time. Why now? Why this?"

"While not every trip back in time requires a working knowledge of the occult, occasionally . . . Well, we need someone like you, with your expertise. You should be able to stay close to Mendoza, and if need be, speak his language. Precious few of our operatives possess your proficiency in mythology and history. Considering the subject matter, it seems wise to send someone with prowess in both."

Not one to be buttered up, Simon was still clearly suspicious, but Elizabeth could tell that he also saw the logic in what Hewitt said. If they had to get close to Mendoza, Jack or someone else wouldn't have the knowledge necessary to do so.

"And of course your wife brings ineffable skills to every assignment she takes part in. I cannot imagine anyone else worthy of the task. So," Hewitt said, rubbing his palms together. "What do you say?"

Simon turned to Elizabeth, a question in his eyes, although she could tell that he already knew how she felt. His small acquiescing smile told her all she needed to know.

She sat straight in her chair and turned to Hewitt. "When do we go?"

No matter how many times they'd done this, Simon would never grow accustomed to saying goodbye to Charlotte. How firemen and policemen did this on a daily basis he did not know.

At first, they'd wondered if it was best to even tell her they were going at all. After all, they'd be back before she even had a chance to miss them. It was one of the quirks of traveling in time via the watch. Although they might spend weeks or even months in the past, when they returned to the present, only a few seconds would have passed there. It seemed pointless to worry her needlessly when they'd return almost instantaneously. But there was always the chance that they would not return at all. And on that off chance, he and Elizabeth had decided that she had a right to know. They all had a right to say goodbye in case it was the last time they saw each other.

Simon's chest tightened at the thought as it always did.

"Okay, so that's the cutter," Jack told Charlotte as they sat together on the sofa. He held a baseball in one hand, showing her the proper grip. "You try it."

He handed her the ball and she tried to mimic what he'd done.

"Good. Get your thumb under it a little," Jack instructed, nudging her hand into the proper position.

Jack, when he was available, always came over for the goodbyes. If anything were to happen to them, it was some solace to know that Charlotte would be well cared for. Jack loved her as if she were his own.

Jack silently urged Charlotte to toss the ball back to him.

"It seems that this is a thing one man should not have to say to another man," Simon began, "but no ball in the house."

"Spoilsport."

Carrying a small travel bag, Elizabeth came downstairs to join them and placed the bag on top of the small mountain of luggage she'd packed. Between the clothing they'd acquired on their various trips to the past and those they'd borrowed from the Council, they were prepared for nearly any eventuality.

Elizabeth looked beautiful, as always, and pleased not to be wearing a corset for once. Her dress was a simple knee-length floral pattern with slightly puffy shoulders and a fitted-waist. She put her hat and clutch purse down with the luggage.

Simon walked over to join her. "Ready?"

She puffed out a breath and nodded. She was anxious, as he was, but beneath that he could feel her excitement at another adventure.

"You look nice," she said, smoothing out the lapel of his cream white linen suit, de rigueur for Miami in the thirties.

"Shall we?"

Together they walked over to Charlotte and Jack.

She looked up from her pitching lesson. "Is it time?"

Elizabeth nodded and Charlotte mimicked her, and then stood to come over for a hug.

"We'll see you in a few minutes," Elizabeth said. "Be good."

When it was Simon's turn, he knelt down to hug her and held on a moment longer. "We love you, darling," he said, unable to keep the emotion out of his voice.

"I love you, too," Charlotte said, bravely. "Be safe."

She held out her hand to Jack who took it and gave it a squeeze. "We'll see you in a bit," he said as he and Charlotte moved toward the doorway.

They'd quickly discovered that while Charlotte was quite sanguine about what her parents did, she did not like to see them go. Simon could hardly blame her. The memory of the time he'd had to stand by and watch Elizabeth and Charlotte travel without him still disquieted him.

They had decided that they would say their goodbyes and Charlotte would go to her room or they would go to theirs so she didn't have to see the moment they disappeared. Then, a few moments later, they'd return and walk into her room as if nothing had happened.

"Now the splitter, that's a little tricky," Jack said as he opened the front door. Charlotte glanced back one last time at her parents before going outside with him.

"Will that ever get any easier?" Elizabeth wondered aloud.

Simon took her hand. "I doubt it."

They both stared at the front door for a moment before Elizabeth shook off her momentary ennui and tugged on his hand. "Ready to save the world?"

They walked back over to their luggage, which Elizabeth kept one hand on while the other held on to his arm. Simon took out the watch and inserted the key. He turned it and the world shook itself apart.

CHAPTER TWO

FEBRUARY 1936 - FLORIDA

Elizabeth looked out of the window of their room on the eighth floor of the Roney Plaza, a massive 500-room hotel in South Beach. There was a slight chill in the breeze that came off the water, the first of many surprises about Miami.

She was embarrassed to admit that she hadn't realized South Beach wasn't just a beach but a barrier island. When Simon turned their rental car onto the Venetian Causeway—a nearly three-mile long bridge that traversed Biscayne Bay—she'd been surprised. That's what she got for leaving the map-studying to Simon.

She'd never been to Miami and had only a vague image of sultry beach resorts, Cuban food, and rows of palm trees in her head. That much was true, but it wasn't nearly as hot as she thought it would be, even for February. It wasn't cold exactly, but seventy-two degrees wasn't Miami-ish. While their hotel was huge, the island wasn't nearly as built up as she'd expected. But then, Miami was still a baby, relatively speaking. The city was only incorporated forty years earlier with a whopping population of about three hundred hardy souls. By the mid-1930s the population shot up to about 150,000. A few clever entrepreneurs managed to convince people that a malarial swamp was a great place to live and convince them they did. Nicknaming Miami the "Magic City" they sold a getaway from the cold north with sandy beaches and swaying palms. Just ignore the giant flying Palmetto bugs that buzz past your head like a B52.

Despite several catastrophic setbacks—the economic hardship from the Great Depression and major hurricanes—the city made its own magic and grew into its nickname. It was still a far cry from the tourist mecca it would become, but it was well on its way. She saw plenty of construction underway on their drive to the hotel.

"All set?" Simon asked as he came up behind her, his panama hat already in one hand silently signaling his impatience to get started.

Elizabeth had just finished unpacking their suitcases, an old habit she'd had since she was a girl traveling with her itinerate gambler father. A hotel room was just a room until she unpacked; then it was home.

They'd gotten a room in the same hotel as Professor Mendoza, so now all they had to do was find him, follow him, and steal one of the world's most powerful mythical artifacts from him. Easy peasy lemon squeezy.

The lobby was spacious and elegantly decorated, but also not the Miami she envisioned. Built too early to embrace the modern lines of Art Deco or Art Nouveau she associated with the 1930s, it seemed more turn of the century than modern resort. That certainly didn't stop anyone from coming. Even now, the hotel was busy and the Bamboo Room, where everyone from Walter Winchell to J. Edgar Hoover would hold court was sure to be filled to capacity that evening.

Simon rang the bell at the long front desk and was promptly greeted by a clerk. "Is everything to your satisfaction, Mr. Cross?"

"Yes, fine, thank you. I was wondering . . .an old acquaintance of ours is staying here. Could you possibly tell me his room number."

"Of course, sir," the clerk said and moved toward their registry. "What is the party's name?"

Elizabeth jabbed Simon sharply in the ribs just as he was about to answer.

"Jiggers," she said under her breath, turning away and pulling him with her.

"What on earth was that for?" Simon asked.

"Shh." She jerked her head to the side and widened her eyes with silent urgency. Simon looked over her shoulder and saw what had caused her to react as she did. Professor Mendoza stood not five feet from them, returning the key to his room as he went out for the day.

If Simon had blurted out his name, and their "old acquaintance" was standing right there . . .well, it might have been hard to explain away. And their chance at covertly following the professor would have been ended before it even got started.

"I see," Simon said quietly.

"Is something wrong, sir?" the clerk enquired.

"No, we . . .we'll find him later. Thank you," Simon said handing the clerk their key, and quickly escorting Elizabeth a few feet away.

Business finished, Mendoza put on his hat and started for the door.

"That was close," Simon said. "We can find out his room number later."

"Forty-seven," Elizabeth replied as they started after Mendoza. Simon looked at her curiously and she grinned back. "I saw the clerk put his key in its cubbyhole."

20

"Clever girl."

"I have my moments."

He looked at her in a way that spoke of admiration for more than just her observational skills. "You certainly do."

"Flatterer."

ELIZABETH SHIFTED SIDEWAYS ON the bench seat of their Ford Roadster convertible, and eased up the hem of her dress just enough to reveal a little more leg.

The movement pulled Simon's attention away from the office building they'd been watching. "What on earth are you doing?"

"The sun feels good."

"Elizabeth," he chided, then refocused on the entrance to the building.

Reluctantly, she covered back up, but the sun did feel good. Mostly, though, she was bored and just trying to find something to occupy herself with. She'd already stared at the burled walnut dashboard for so long that she started seeing faces in it. The car was, thankfully, very comfortable. Huge, but comfortable. She was really glad Simon was doing the driving. Even though it was a two-door roadster, it was still easily over twelve feet long. How people maneuvered these behemoths she didn't know. And you could forget parallel parking. She still missed her Bug.

Simon stared dutifully toward the entrance to the building where Mendoza's cab had brought him. Eager to get back in the game, Elizabeth had watched the building along with Simon for the first hour. When it rolled into the second, her mind had begun to stray. So far they'd been sitting there doing a grand total of nothing for two hours and twenty-seven minutes. She was antsy to get into the action, to *do* something. When they'd followed Mendoza from the hotel, the old adrenaline had kicked in as she anticipated excitement and adventure on the horizon. All she'd gotten for her trouble was a numb backside.

She settled back into her seat. "What do you think he's doing in there?"

"I don't know," Simon said, the same impatience she felt clear in his voice.

"Maybe he's—"

"Coming out," Simon said as he sat up straighter, eyes fixed on the entranceway.

Mendoza emerged from the building, a document tube in one hand.

A tingle of anticipation made Elizabeth's heart beat faster. "Do you think that's it? In the tube? The staff."

"It's awfully small for a staff."

"Maybe it's a staff for pygmies?" she suggested, earning a snort from Simon. "What? You don't know."

Simon turned the car over, the engine catching in a loud grind that grew into what sounded a little like an airplane propeller before settling into a chugging hum.

The professor hailed another cab and they set off to follow it. They trailed along behind until it pulled over on Collins Boulevard a block from their hotel.

"What's he doing?" Elizabeth asked.

"Walking the rest of the way, it appears," Simon said as he quickly scanned the area for a parking space. Of course, there weren't any.

They assumed he was going back to the hotel, but they couldn't afford to lose him or risk, if that really was the staff, that someone else might get ahold of it before they did.

"Stop the car," she said.

"What?"

"Pull over. I'll follow him and you can catch up."

Simon didn't look too pleased with the idea of separating, but he knew it was their only option.

He pulled off to the side. "Be careful."

Elizabeth gave him an answering nod, then slid out of her seat and hurried to catch up to Professor Mendoza.

Luckily, he was in no hurry, seemingly content to enjoy the afternoon sunshine in the park. He strolled along the crisscrossing paths until he came to a food vendor's cart. Elizabeth stayed back, lingering under the shade of one of the ubiquitous palms that lined every part of the city. The professor bought a hot dog and made his way to one of the benches in the dappled shade of the palm fronds above.

Curious thing for a man carrying a priceless artifact to do.

He certainly didn't seem in any rush to get back to the hotel or even the least bit concerned with the document tube he carelessly laid on the bench next to him and proceed to ignore as he admired the park.

He took a large bite of his hot dog and Elizabeth's stomach gurgled. She could get one, too, she supposed. It was a perfectly normal thing to do and far less suspicious than lurking out by a tree by herself. Besides, she was hungry.

Careful not to lose sight of Mendoza, she approached the vendor's cart. The hot dogs were only a nickel! She might have two. Maybe surveillance wasn't so bad after all.

She was nearly halfway to the cart when she heard Simon behind her.

"Elizabeth, what are you doing?" he said in a low, tight voice. He came to her side and slipped her arm into his, veering her, sadly, away from the cart. "We're supposed to be keeping a low profile."

"I was, just with food."

23

He led her to the far side of the open expanse of the center square of grass opposite Mendoza and tucked them behind a tree where they could keep an eye on him.

"I can't help it if I'm hungry."

"We'll get you something after we're sure the professor and his . . .whatever that is are safely back at the hotel."

"About that, the whatever it is," she clarified, "Pygmies aside, I don't think whatever is in that tube is all that valuable."

"No?"

"Look at him," she said as she watched the professor idly eat a truly delicious-looking hotdog . . . *Is that relish?* "If you'd just picked up a priceless artifact would you stop for a dog in the park? Not you, but you know what I mean. And look at him. He's not even paying attention to it. I'd be holding onto it tight."

"Which would only serve to draw attention to its value," Simon proposed.

"I guess so. But either way, wouldn't you make a beeline for the hotel where you could at least lock it up in your room or something?"

"Yes," Simon said, the wheels turning in his mind so loudly Elizabeth could practically hear them.

A few minutes later, the professor finished his hot dog, crumpled up the paper it came in, and wiped away a bit of stray mustard that singed the fringe of his mustache.

As he began to walk toward the hotel, Elizabeth started after him, but Simon's hand on her arm held her back.

"He's leaving," she said, not understanding why Simon had stopped her.

"He's not the only one." Simon inclined his head toward a tall man in a dark suit who stood on the opposite side of the park, closer to Mendoza. It was obvious that he wasn't just some random person in the park, but that he was following the professor, too.

"I saw him earlier this afternoon," Simon continued, as he escorted Elizabeth along the path behind both men—a couple simply out for a stroll. "He circled the building the professor went into, twice. I thought he was merely looking for parking, but now that he's here..."

"Who do you think he is?" she asked.

Simon's arm tensed under her hand. "Trouble."

THEY STAYED BEHIND THE man trailing Mendoza, careful not to give themselves away. The professor entered through the front of the hotel, the other man close behind. When Simon and Elizabeth joined them in the lobby, she got her first good at look at him. He was a little strange-looking actually. There was a blockiness to his face, his features almost not quite fully made, as if a sculptor had shaped stone into a semblance of a man and walked away. He was big and thick, as tall as Simon but probably at least twenty pounds heavier. His jaw looked hard and his meaty hands flexed at his side as he watched the professor with dark piercing eyes. He stood by one of the columns in the lobby, but didn't even pretend to be casual about it. He was so intense that she wasn't sure if he was capable of being anything else.

Mendoza slowly made his way through the large and moderately crowded lobby to the front desk as Simon and Elizabeth took a place by the sitting area off to the side where they could see both men.

Mendoza put the document tube down, leaning it against the counter. As soon as he let go of it, the man watching made his move, and instinct drove Elizabeth to make hers.

"Elizabeth," Simon's quietly strained voice came from behind her, but she ignored him. She knew that the man was going to steal the tube and she couldn't let that happen.

She weaved between the hotel patrons on an intercept course, having no idea what she was going to do when she got there. The man lengthened his strides and she had to practically run to keep pace. But she did, and a few feet from the front desk, she stepped right in into his path. He collided with her, catching her arms with those big, thick hands of his.

"I'm so sorry," she said quickly. "I'm so terribly clumsy. I was looking for my husband. Tall, British, scowly," she added as she caught sight of Simon coming her way.

The man's dark eyes glared at her then shifted to the document tube just as Mendoza picked it up again.

Seemingly angered at missing his opportunity, his jaw tightened, and so did his grip until it was actually painful. Elizabeth couldn't keep from wincing.

"I really am sorry," she said, feigning confusion at his anger. "I was just—"

He glowered at her again then released her with a grunt and stalked away just as Simon arrived.

"Are you all right?" he asked, glaring after the man as he headed out of the lobby and toward the street.

Elizabeth rubbed her upper arms. "Yeah." She was fine, but she wouldn't forget the look that man gave her, the unbound hatred in his eyes. It seemed to come as naturally to him as breathing.

"That was somewhat reckless," Simon said, bringing his attention back to her.

"But effective," she replied.

Simon inclined his head, reluctantly admitting that it had been.

His key retrieved from the front desk, Mendoza walked over to the bank of elevators, tube safely in hand.

"So, what do we do now?" Elizabeth asked. "Break into the professor's suite and liberate the tube? Vive la tube!"

Simon couldn't keep a laugh from escaping. "No, Sticky Fingers. No breaking and entering. We can find a way to discover what's in the tube without resorting to committing felonies, I should hope. Besides, I sincerely doubt the tube contains the staff."

"It's something important or else Stoneface wouldn't have wanted it so badly."

"Stoneface?"

Elizabeth wiggled her fingers in front of her face but gave up trying to explain before she'd even started. "Never mind."

"Perhaps you're right or, perhaps like us, he doesn't know and can't exactly ask."

"Well," she said, "let's hope he's as averse to breaking and entering as you are."

Simon stared at the busy front entryway to the lobby. "Yes. Let's hope so."

ELIZABETH YAWNED, COVERING HER mouth with the back of her hand and blinking sleepily.

"Sorry," she said. "Need more coffee."

Simon poured her another cup from the small silver pot the waiter had left at their table at his request. They'd managed to have their room changed to one next to the professor's and had listened for signs of a struggle that never came.

Early the next morning, they'd taken breakfast in the small cafe section of the restaurant that adjoined the lobby and remained lingering over coffee as they waited for Mendoza to come down.

Elizabeth huddled over her cup and took a sip. "Nothing like a steaming cup of joe."

She knew Simon didn't quite agree. To his mind, tea was far more civilized, but a strong cup of coffee did have its uses.

Just after eight, the professor appeared and went straight to the concierge. Simon and Elizabeth left their table and took up a position near a rack of sightseeing brochures. The small fold-out pamphlets offered everything from a ferry ride to Musa Isle Indian Village where one could see real live alligators and real life Seminole Indians at the entrance to the mysterious Everglades to an afternoon spent at the Miami Beach Kennel Club where you could gamble your worries away by betting on the dogs at the track. *Something for everyone.*

"Yes," Mendoza was saying behind them. "I just wanted make sure that my travel arrangements were all in place. I'm quite anxious to get started."

Travel? Where was he going?

"Of course, Doctor Mendoza. Your plane is scheduled to leave tomorrow at 10 a.m. and your accommodations in Rio are arranged. I've written it all down for you." The concierge handed him a piece of paper.

"Rio?" Elizabeth whispered. "As in de Janiero?"

"South America," Simon said, obviously not pleased with this turn of events. "I should have known it wouldn't be so easy. Damn that Council."

Mendoza thanked the concierge, tucked his itinerary into his pocket and headed toward the restaurant for breakfast.

Simon waited a moment and then approached the concierge desk. "Is there a telephone I can use? I need to make an international call."

The man gestured toward the corner of the front desk. "They can accommodate you, sir."

"Who are you calling?" Elizabeth asked as she trailed after him. "The bank."

The bank meant only one thing—the Bank of England and the Council's very special account there. The account had been established at the same time the bank was in 1694 and had virtually unlimited funds in it. One of the perks of being an organization of time travelers was that money was seldom a problem. As one of the bank's first and most generous depositors, the Council enjoyed a special relationship with them. Basically, anything they asked for, they got. No questions asked. Access to the account had come in quite handy for Simon and Elizabeth in the past and it looked like they'd need every string they could pull if they were going to keep up with Mendoza. Travel to South America in the 1930s wasn't something someone often did on a whim and she guessed it wouldn't be cheap. Before the war, commercial air travel was still in its infancy and generally reserved for the wealthy.

One hour and several phone calls later, everything had been arranged. They had two seats on the same PanAm clipper as Mendoza, leaving from Dinner Key, Florida tomorrow morning. The bank contact had also made arrangements for them to have a full line of credit at the Banco do Brasil for any additional expenses they might incur. Additionally, he'd arranged for a "cancellation" at the Copacabana Hotel in Rio, a rare thing with Carnival just around the corner, and a suite would be awaiting their arrival in six days' time.

"Wait a minute?" Elizabeth remarked. "Six days? I thought the plane left tomorrow."

"It does," Simon said, less than happy about the whole thing. "The trip to Rio apparently takes five days."

"Wow." She'd never considered that it could take so long. Brazil was a long way away, but five days?

"Just a quick jaunt to Miami," Simon groused. "Bollocks."

"I think it's kind of exciting." They were like Fred and Ginger—Flying Down to Rio! "South America. Rio. It all sounds so exotic."

"And potentially dangerous. Here, at least, I could fool myself into thinking I had a modicum of control, but there..."

"I don't know, I think it sounds romantic," she said as she placed her hand on his chest and played with the lapel of his jacket. He looked at her skeptically, but she saw the light in his eyes. "Who says we can't have a good time while we save the world? We can do anything as long as we're together."

His brief pique melted and she could see from the darkening of his eyes that he wanted to kiss her, and would have if they hadn't been standing in the middle of a busy lobby. He straightened to keep himself a proper Englishman, but his eyes still held hers and spoke the things he would not say here. "As long as we're together."

CHAPTER THREE

DOZENS AND DOZENS OF cars parked around the circular drive at Dinner Key, home of Pan Am's International Airport. It was a small airport, just one building, and Elizabeth didn't understand why there were so many cars parked there. As their cab pulled up to the front of the terminal, she noticed a rather large crowd of people gathering along the shore and wondered if there was a boat race or something going on.

Simon and the cabbie wrangled their luggage out of the car and onto a small trolley to bring it inside.

"What's with the crowd?" Elizabeth asked.

The cabbie followed her gaze. "Oh, they come to see the planes. Don't see what the big deal is myself."

Air travel was new, but surely the novelty of seeing a plane had worn off a little.

Confused, Elizabeth thanked him and walked with Simon toward the terminal building. It wasn't until they were almost there that she realized what spectacle had really drawn the crowd. A plane was coming in for a landing and seemed to lose elevation over the water. She thought for a moment it was going to crash and gripped Simon's arm tightly.

"It's all right," he said.

She was about to argue the point when she realized the plane wasn't crashing into the water; it was landing on it, to the applause and pleasure of the crowd. It wasn't until then that she realized there was no landing strip at all.

"Wait a minute. Are we …?"

"Flying boats, they call them," Simon answered.

The large four-propeller plane sloshed to a slow pace and then taxied to the docking area.

"There aren't very many airports yet," Simon explained, "and fewer still where we're going. Just not enough need yet."

"Why build a landing strip when nature provides one?" Elizabeth said. The thought made her uneasy. Landing should have land involved. It was right in the name. However, as it always was with her, mixed in with the fear was excitement. Her adventure just got a little more adventure-y.

"Let's see if we can find the professor," Simon suggested.

The terminal was modern and spacious with a large high-ceilinged central room. Banners hung from the rafters detailing the history of flight, from Da Vinci's glider to a four-propeller job that looked like the one that had just arrived with a splash. But what really got her attention was the enormous ten-foot diameter globe in the center of the room. It sat slightly sunk into the floor and slowly rotated. Each country that passed seemed to offer the dream of a far-off locale. It not only sparked travel but the imagination and tempted travelers to see themselves in all the far-flung places of the globe. Adventures big and small surrounded them. "Fly down to Havana for just $35," a sign said. "Always wanted to go to Buenos Aires? No time like the present." One advertising banner invited travelers to have "breakfast in Miami, lunch in Havana, and dinner in Jamaica." The world was literally at your fingertips.

"There he is," Simon said. The professor and his luggage stood waiting at the Brazilian counter ready to check in for the flight. The document tube sat safely at the top of the pile of bags and Stoneface was nowhere to be found.

They stood in line behind Mendoza at the counter and Simon readied their papers. Not that much was needed. Although they brought period-appropriate passports and myriad other forged documents with them just in case, passports weren't required for travel outside of most European countries.

Their arrival drew the professor's attention and he offered them a polite smile in greeting, his gaze lingering briefly, curiously, on Elizabeth. Then he gathered his ticket from the clerk and, touching the brim of his hat politely, he walked toward the rear exit of the terminal and the docks where the plane would be boarded.

Their plane, a Sikorsky S-42 also known as the Brazilian Clipper, was massive for a seaplane. Or at least, it seemed so to Elizabeth. Designed by aviation pioneers Charles Lindbergh and Igor Sikorsky, it was 68 feet long with a wingspan of 118 feet, according to the brochure. Four absolutely enormous turbine engines and their propellers were attached to the wing that was affixed on top of the fuselage. The plane could hold thirty-seven passengers or be configured to fourteen sleeper births. Its maximum speed was a whopping 188 miles per hour, which partly explained why the over four thousand mile trip to Rio took so long. The rest of the delays, Simon had explained last night, were because the planes could only fly during daylight hours. So, they'd fly four to six hours then set down somewhere, then rinse and repeat in the morning. It was a little like taking a sky cruise.

MONIQUE MARTIN

Their luggage stowed except for small carry-ons, the passengers lined up on the dock to board the plane. Their flight was just over half-full with only twenty passengers today, so there would be plenty of room to stretch out.

The crew wore what looked a lot like smart navy-like dress white uniforms and greeted each passenger as they came aboard. They weren't the only ones dressed for the occasion. Every man wore a suit and every woman a dress. Travel was a luxury and people dressed appropriately. No sweatpants and tennis shoes here. Flying was still a novelty and one still fairly exclusive to the wealthy. It wasn't until after the Second World War that air travel would become more commonplace and even then it was still an exciting adventure until everyone became too cool for school in the eighties.

Elizabeth was all for comfortable clothes. Lord knew she'd worn her share of corsets, but she wondered if the world hadn't lost something along the way by having every day be casual Friday.

"Welcome aboard," the steward greeted them as they reached the gangway. It was really more like boarding a yacht than a plane. The crew looked like they were straight off the Queen Mary and every aspect of the journey felt more like they were setting out on an Atlantic passage than a plane trip.

They walked down the dock toward the rear of the plane and the large twin vertical stabilizers on the tail. A short arched gangway led to the top hatch where rubber mats had been laid out for traction on top of the plane's fuselage.

"This way, miss," one smart-looking attendant said as he ushered her toward the stairs leading down into the cabin. Simon held onto her elbow as she reached for the railing and then descended the stairs into the plane.

The interior felt even more like a ship than the outside. The cabin was divided into four compartments with a long companionway

34

running the length of the plane. Rich walnut veneer covered the walls and seats were plush and large. The compartments were set up like a dining car on a train. Two sets of seats on either side of the aisle sat facing each other on opposite sides of a narrow removable table. Two passengers sat playing cards and smoking cigarettes as they waited for the rest to board.

Simon and Elizabeth made their way toward the front of the plane where they found Dr. Mendoza sitting alone at one of the tables.

"Do you mind if we join you?" Simon asked.

The professor cleared away some paperwork from the table and gestured to the empty seats across from him. "No, no, of course not," he said as he stood as much as the table would allow in deference to Elizabeth.

"Thank you," she replied.

She took the window seat and briefly gazed out of one of the large round porthole windows—another very steamship-like feature.

Simon took off his hat and ran a quick hand through his hair. A steward appeared almost instantly at his side to take his hat and stow it safely in the back.

Simon held out his hand before he sat down. "Simon Cross, and this is my wife, Elizabeth."

"Dr. Emil Mendoza. Very pleased to meet you both." His voice was deep and melodious.

Once again, his eyes lingered on Elizabeth. He frowned slightly, chagrined when she noticed. "Forgive me. Your smile reminds me of my daughter, Aurora."

"Beautiful name. Is she joining us?" Elizabeth asked, making a show of looking for her, although there hadn't been any mention of a daughter in Mendoza's dossier. It wasn't all that odd for personal details to be left out no matter how often Elizabeth asked for them to be included.

"Possibly later," Mendoza said.

"Aurora," Simon repeated. "Roman goddess of the dawn, I think."

Mendoza's eyes brightened with delight. "Yes, that's right. Have you studied mythology?"

Elizabeth snorted, earning a look from Simon, although he couldn't hide his smile completely. "He teaches it. Well, that and history and folklore."

Mendoza's pleasure grew. "A kindred soul. Wonderful! I've always found history fascinating. I'm an archaeologist myself."

"Really?" Simon said, convincingly surprised and as delighted as Mendoza. "So fascinating, and not so different from what I teach. I doubt there's been a single discovery in the last one hundred years that wasn't steeped in mythology of one sort of another."

"So very true," Mendoza said, leaning forward with excitement. "Take the Malinalco site."

"Aztec, isn't it?"

Mendoza looked like he would have proposed to Simon on the spot if he could have. "Yes. Oh, this is a delight! I'm good friends with José Payón, you know. Have to admit I do envy him his discovery."

"I'm sure you've had your share," Simon said kindly.

Mendoza chortled. "Nothing of true consequence. Yet," he added with a secret smile.

Neither Simon nor Elizabeth showed any outward reaction to that but inside she was buzzing. They knew just what he'd find, if only they knew when and where.

The stewards walked through the cabin and announced that cocktails would be served as soon as they were in the air and that everyone should prepare for take off.

What preparing meant, Elizabeth didn't know. There weren't even any seat belts.

The plane's engines roared to life and the whole plane vibrated. Surprisingly, it was not as loud as she thought it would be. The padded bulkheads and cabin did a decent job of quelling the roar.

The pilot navigated the plane away from the dock and out into the relatively calm waters of the channel. The soft hum of the engines grew as they taxied across the water, gaining speed. No matter how smooth the water looked though, it was still a bumpy ride. Everyone jostled about inside the cabin as they got up to speed, which frankly didn't seem fast enough to take off. Elizabeth was used to modern jet travel where a plane would reach 160 miles an hour or more as it took off. They couldn't have been going half that. The plane felt heavy and sluggish in the water and she wasn't sure they would ever have enough speed to lift off.

As if sensing her feelings, Simon's hand slid over to hers and gave it a comforting squeeze. Of course, he was calm.

Just when she was sure the nose would come back down and they'd have to abort, they somehow found enough speed and lifted from the water. It seemed as though a restraining hand had let go of them and she felt as buoyant as the plane as it soared into the air.

Out of her porthole window she could see the hundreds of people who watched from the shore of Dinner Key as the plane rose up from the ocean below. Now, she knew why they came. It was damn exciting.

The plane turned and set its course toward the southeast. Their adventure had finally truly begun.

"*WEETZILOPCHI*?" ELIZABETH SAID, earning a chuckle from Simon and a patient smile from Mendoza.

Simon was sure she was playing her role as a struggling but eager student just to make Mendoza feel at ease. Idly, he wondered how often she'd done that with him.

Her quick hidden smile told him that the answer was more often than he wanted to admit.

"Very close," Mendoza said encouragingly, despite her intentional butchering of the name. "*Huītzilōpōchtli*. The Aztec language is very complex although not altogether foreign," Mendoza went on. "Tomato, avocado, and chocolate are all English words with a Nahuatl origin."

"Really? Chocolate?"

"It's quite fascinating," Mendoza went on, warmed to his subject and immediately falling into his academic posture. "Did you know that there are as many classical texts in Nahuatl as there are in Ancient Greek?"

"I had no idea," Elizabeth said honestly.

"Forgive me," he replied, ducking his head. "I often find myself carried away by my own enthusiasm for history."

Elizabeth cast a quick glance at Simon. "I wouldn't know anything about that," she said with a straight face, earning a laugh.

"She was my assistant at university," Simon explained.

"Before getting promoted," she added, holding up her wedding ring.

Simon took her hand in his and gently rubbed her ring finger with his thumb. Despite it not being conventional until after the war for a man to also wear one, he always wore his wedding ring when they traveled. It was one concession he refused to make.

Mendoza seemed to genuinely enjoy their banter, but there was an undercurrent of sadness that accompanied it now. The jovial air around them seemed to collapse like Elizabeth's ill-fated attempt at a soufflé for their last anniversary.

Simon wasn't sure what had caused the subtle shift of Mendoza's mood, but they needed him to feel relaxed and at ease with them if they were going to ingratiate themselves enough to be close to him when the staff appeared.

Simon lifted Elizabeth's hand and took over the professorial reins in an attempt to buoy the conversation again. "Did you know that the ancient Egyptians and Greeks believed that there was a vein in the fourth finger of the left hand, the *vena amoris*, that ran from the finger straight to the heart?"

Elizabeth wiggled her finger. "Really?"

"Either that or it's all a marketing ploy from jewelers."

"Oh, Simon!" she said as she tugged her hand away with a laugh.

"Pardon me," the steward said as he arrived at their table to set up for lunch. He held up a white linen tablecloth. "If I may?"

He laid out the tablecloth while another steward arrived with place settings for lunch. They'd already had morning tea and coffee. The tableware was a far cry from the pseudo-TV dinner accoutrements so common in modern air travel. Even in first class, the settings weren't this elegant. This was akin to going to a fine restaurant. Attractive glassware, china, and silverware were laid out as the menus were given to each passenger. The meal was divided into several courses and included tropical fruit cocktail, cream of tomato soup, broiled chicken in wine sauce, wax beans, Delmonico potatoes, and Boston cream pie for dessert. He could practically hear Elizabeth's stomach's cry of joy at the prospect.

The meal was surprisingly good considering the constraints the crew had in preparing it. After the dishes were removed and they were left to linger over coffee, the professor pulled out a pipe.

"I must say," he said, "I'm awfully pleased you two are along for the trip. These journeys can get rather lonesome."

"You travel a lot?" Elizabeth asked.

He lit his pipe, puffing to make it come to life before answering. "More than I should. But I hope this will be my last trip."

"That sounds a little ominous," she said.

"Does it?" he replied with a chuckle. "I don't mean it quite that way, but I'm hopeful that, well, that this will allow me to spend more time with my family. Do you have children?"

"A daughter," Simon said. "Ten."

"Ah, a wonderful age."

Simon sensed again that slight clouding over of the professor's mood and filed the moment away to talk with Elizabeth about later.

Perhaps she noticed it as well because she immediately sought to change the subject.

"We miss her, of course, but it's nice to get away, just the two of us once in a while. And speaking of, our first port of call is Puerto Rico. Have you ever been?"

"Not in many years, but it's a wonderful country."

"I know we don't have long there," she said. They would only have what was left of the afternoon and evening when they arrived. "But if you have any suggestions on places we should see..."

Mendoza brightened again. "The Spanish forts are magnificent. Castillo de San Cristóbal and El Morro must be seen. The history, well ..." He puffed on his pipe before continuing and gauging their reaction to what he was to say next. "Some say they're haunted as well. Not that I believe all of that, but ..."

He let the question of it linger between them allowing them to set the tone moving forward.

Simon and Elizabeth shared a look before she answered. "There are more things in Heaven and Earth..."

His eyes lit as a broad smile lifted his face as he leaned forward. "Precisely. I would love to show you around a bit if you're amenable to an old man taking over."

"We'd be most grateful, Doctor."

"Please, call me Emil."

DESPITE HER BEST EFFORTS to "feel" something, Elizabeth didn't see or hear any sign of the ghost soldier or a mourning widow at the haunted sentry box at El Morro. Even so, she had a wonderful time. San Juan was tropical and beautiful but with an old school Spanish flavor. Of course, most conquerors left a little "flavor" behind, not all of it pleasant. But the architecture and the cathedral and Casa Blanca, the mansion built for Ponce de León, were wonderful. And Emil was a delightful tour guide.

After an afternoon of sightseeing, they all retired to their hotel for dinner and a quick night's sleep before setting off again in the morning.

"And of course the statuette was Etruscan and not early Roman," Simon said with a laugh as he finished his story.

Emil joined his laughter. "Can you imagine such a mistake?"

"I really can't," Elizabeth said, which was true, mostly because they'd lost her somewhere around 600 AD. "I followed you to Byzantium but then you zigged when I thought you were gonna zag."

Emil laughed again, a rich hearty sound. "She is wonderful."

Simon reached for her hand. "You have no idea."

"I'm afraid I've been a terrible host," Emil went on, "Monopolizing your husband's time this way."

"Not at all," she said. She didn't mind, in fact, she was thrilled to see Simon talk with such enthusiasm with someone about the subjects he loved. She tried to be a good sounding board for him, but she just wasn't knowledgeable enough to carry a conversation the way Emil could. The two of them had been swapping stories for the last two hours and she couldn't have been more delighted.

Simon had precious few friends, not that he coveted more, but she wished he could spend more time with like-minded people. Working for a top secret society half the time made that more challenging, and those in the academia of Santa Barbara weren't quite at his level. There were a few colleagues scattered around the world he could talk to, but it wasn't the same over the phone. And Jack. Well, Jack was Jack.

"I'm more than content to sit and listen to you both," she continued.

Simon snorted. "That would be a first." After her slightly wounded look, he quickly amended, "I mean that my wife is a woman of action. I'm not sure I've seen her sit still this long in years."

"I understand," Emil said. "History is fascinating, but there's nothing quite like getting your hands dirty with it. Do you know what I mean?"

They most certainly did. "I think so."

Emil sat back in his chair, the dinner long over and the coffee cold. "You know, I never did ask why the two of you are going to South America in the first place. Business? Pleasure?"

"Pleasure. I thought it sounded exciting," Elizabeth said. "Exotic."

"She grows restless for adventure now and again," Simon added honestly.

"Well," Emil said, looking at them both carefully. "I might be able to provide a little excitement to your journey. If you're amenable."

"I'm amenable all over the place," Elizabeth said, then tried not to look too eager and schooled her features to what she hoped was mild curiosity. Was this where they learned about the staff?

Emil glanced at Simon who remained silent but clearly interested.

"I told you earlier that I was traveling to Rio on business and that's not entirely true. It's not untrue, but the nature of my business is rather unique." Emil clasped his hands on the table and looked at each of them in turn. "What do you know about the Lost City of El Dorado?"

Elizabeth felt Simon tense next to her. He'd been worried about their detour to South America, and if this was going where she thought it was going, he might have been right.

"El Dorado? Just the usual," she said, "lost city of gold, Sir Walter Raleigh, Pizarro, and the usual conquistadors passing out small pox and coming up empty."

"Because it is a myth," Simon interjected.

"Is it?" Emil asked.

Dear God, has he really discovered where El Dorado is? She certainly didn't remember hearing about that in the history books. The idea of it sparked her already-vivid imagination.

Simon, however, remained skeptical. "El Dorado was originally a man, a chieftain of the Muisca people in Colombia, who, as the legend goes, covered himself in gold. Years later, the myth and the man were transmuted into a city of gold. As the centuries wore on and the legend grew, so did the city, which eventually became an entire empire all made of gold. But there is no practical evidence to support any of it."

Emil leaned in and spoke quietly, "Until now."

Simon's eyes shifted to Elizabeth briefly and then back to Emil. She could sense his skepticism but also his interest. "What do you mean? You've found something."

"A map," he said. "I hope it's the map; I haven't seen it yet, but I believe it is."

Simon's skepticism overrode his curiosity. "You haven't seen it yet."

"It's not just about the map. That was the final piece of the puzzle I've been putting together for the last ten years. Forgotten manuscripts, misidentified artifacts, the clues were always there if you knew where to look."

"And you know?" Simon asked, and Elizabeth could hear the worry in his voice. Not that Emil was mad, but that he was right.

"Yes. I do and I have. Others came close. I'm sure you've heard of the Fawcett expedition."

The worry lines around Simon's eyes crinkled as they narrowed in thought. "Yes. He and his party, including his son, disappeared searching for a lost city he called Z in the Brazilian jungle in 1925."

"Z is El Dorado, and he was right. It's there. He was just looking in the wrong place."

Elizabeth had heard of the book and the movie made from it, *The Lost City of Z*, but she hadn't read or seen it. It looked kind of dark. Maybe that was just as well.

"You really believe you've found a way to El Dorado? That it's real?" Elizabeth asked.

Emil was gauging their reaction to the news as much as they were trying to gauge his truthfulness. "I do."

She believed him. And why not? Finding a mythical lost city of gold didn't seem strange when held up against the things they'd done, the things they were doing.

A tingle of excitement sent goose bumps sweeping across her arms. What she wouldn't give to be part of a discovery like that. *Indiana Jones, eat your heart out. Although not literally, there was that guy that tried.*

Simon, however, was less enthused at the prospect and more than a little dubious about the professor's claims. Emil might as well have said that he'd found a way to the moon and back in a canoe for the way Simon drew out his response, "Really?"

Emil chuckled. "I don't blame you for being skeptical. I was as well."

"It's just that's quite a claim," Simon said.

"Indeed, and not one I make lightly. I'm no fool nor do I wish to be seen as one. But this . . .this is my life's work and more important to me than I can say. I believe with every fiber of my being that I'm right."

Elizabeth could see that it was important to him in ways that transcended professional curiosity. And why not? Finding something like that would be life-changing.

"Most people find it hard to believe," Emil went on, "and I understand their reticence and yours. I did not come to this blindly. But it is true. I believe I know where the lost city is and in it are treasures beyond imagination."

And world-changing. If the staff was hidden among those treasures, and Elizabeth knew it was, they had to go with him to find it.

She could almost feel the anxiety coming from Simon now. He really hadn't even wanted to go on the mission and had only agreed, she knew, because it appeared to be a relatively easy assignment. Now, they might be tasked with delving into the depths of the Brazilian jungle. Hardly the milk run advertised.

"If it's true," Simon said, "and you really have found it, it will be the most remarkable discovery of the millennium."

"You believe me?" Emil asked, evidently used to people thinking him deluded at best and mad at worst.

Simon looked at the professor for a moment before he replied, "I do."

A weight seemed to be lifted from the professor's shoulders at this admission. "I wasn't sure if I should tell you. Tell anyone, frankly, but . . . I'm glad I have. I sensed you'd understand."

The light in his eyes dimmed briefly. "My wife used to be my partner and I find I miss the camaraderie. I'm pleased to have someone of a like mind to share it with."

"It's remarkable."

"It will be if we can get there. Sadly, nearly as difficult as finding the place itself is finding the money to fund the expedition. It took over a year of searching and quite a lot of convincing to find someone to underwrite it."

"I can imagine. Funding isn't easy to find under the best of circumstances," Simon said sympathetically.

"These are hardly those. Ever since Fawcett's disappearance and the resulting ballyhoo with so many coming to try to find Fawcett and the lost city, Brazil has placed an embargo on all future expeditions."

"That kind of makes it hard to go, doesn't it?" Elizabeth asked. He didn't seem the type to try to circumvent the government.

"It does, however, my benefactor, a young Spaniard named Vega—good man—is a rather convincing fellow when he wants to be. And he's as anxious as I am to prove my theories. I have no doubt he'll find a way to get the permission we need from Minister Correia of the Department of Antiquities and Cultural Heritage."

"Then all you have to do is find the city," Elizabeth said.

Emil chuckled. "That's all." He sobered and added very seriously. "I've placed a great trust in you, revealing this. If word got out, well, you can imagine how many people would descend upon a city of gold."

"We understand, and we're honored that you shared this with us. It will never go beyond this table. On that you have my word," Simon said, clearly hoping to assuage any fears the professor might have that they might have their sights set on a few million dollar trinkets for themselves.

The professor appeared more at ease. "Thank you."

"It makes my find of that twelfth century reliquary seem rather insignificant," Simon said.

"My dear boy, it makes *everything* insignificant."

"CAHN YOU IMASHEN?" ELIZABETH said loudly, her mouth full of toothpaste before spitting it out into the sink. "A city all of gold?"

From the bedroom, all she heard was a grunt in response.

Ever since they returned to their hotel room, he'd been in a mood. She had a pretty good idea why.

"Don't you believe him?" she asked, shutting off the light in the bath and joining him in the bedroom.

"I do," he admitted, sounding anything but pleased at the prospect.

While she'd gotten changed and ready for bed, Simon had barely managed to take off his shoes and untuck his shirt. He sat in a chair staring off in thought.

Elizabeth slipped her arms around his shoulders and kissed his cheek briefly as she passed. She sat down on the edge of the bed and waited for him to start. When he didn't, she did it for him. "Should we have the argument now or in the morning?"

"Hmm?" he asked, pulled himself again from his reverie.

"About whether we stay or go."

He smiled wanly, stood, and began to unbutton his shirt. "We haven't had that conversation in a very long time."

It was true; they'd stopped having the "Do we stay or do we go now?" discussion years ago because it always ended the same way. They stayed. That would always be the case, and there was no point in going through the motions of debating it any more. They weren't sent on frivolous missions. Every time they used the watch the stakes were too high to give up, so they never did. But she knew he never stopped worrying. They might not have the argument over whether it was too dangerous to press on, but she had no doubt he still felt the same way and he always would.

His instinct, above all else, was to protect her, and she knew that the thought of tromping through the jungle, the same jungle that had killed far more experienced explorers than they were, ate away at him.

"I can say 'it'll be easy' and you'll give me that look and tell me ten very good reasons why it won't be. I'll pout a little—beautifully, I might add—then you'll point out that doesn't work on you anymore, even though it does. And eventually, you'll agree to stay and I'll know you were going to all along."

"You don't even need me," he said, jokingly, but there was whisper of something else in his words.

"Don't ever say that," she said, coming over to him and sliding her hands under the loose sides of his shirt and up his chest. "I'm lost without you and you know it."

He smiled in reply but there was definitely something wrong. It wasn't always there and it was difficult to pinpoint, but she'd sensed a feeling of, she wasn't sure what, maybe ennui, about him on occasion lately.

"What's going on?" she asked.

He looked like he was about to say something when he sighed and turned away. "It's that damn Council. I'm sure they knew about this and didn't tell us." He shed his shirt and turned back to her. "I find it hard to believe that they had no idea this staff was lost in the middle of the bloody jungle."

"True," she conceded. Although she didn't give the Council quite the perpetual side-eye Simon did, they had withheld important information from them before.

"I don't like being a pawn in their game."

"I don't either," she admitted, "but the game needs to be played. If the staff is half as powerful as they said it is—"

"Yes, I know," he said.

Elizabeth sat down on the edge of the bed. "Maybe it won't be as bad as all that. If the professor—"

"It's not one of your movies, Elizabeth," he snapped. "The jungle isn't a studio backlot."

The sharpness of his tone caught her off guard and hurt mingled with annoyance in her response. "I know that."

"I'm sorry," he said. "I know you do. I'm just not sure we're . . . *I'm* fit enough for what's ahead."

She wiggled her eyebrows. "You were certainly fit last night."

He tried to scowl at her, but his smile won out. "You know what I mean."

"I do, and we'll face whatever comes, together. We don't really have a choice, do we? If we have to follow Emil into the heart of the darkness, I promise I won't let you go all Kurtz on me."

"That was the Congo."

She shrugged. "Same difference."

She knew he was about to remind her that the rivers were on different continents when he stopped himself, realization dawning. "You're baiting me."

She fought down a coy smile. Simon abhorred "same difference" almost as much as "anyways."

"Maybe a little," she confessed.

She got off the edge of the bed and moved to turn down the covers. "We don't even know if we'll have to go. The professor doesn't even have permission yet. Maybe the staff comes into his hands in some other way."

"And if it doesn't?"

She slid beneath the covers. "We'll do what we always do."

"Save the world?"

"At least our little bit of it."

He gazed at her for a long moment. "How do you do that? Always believe?"

The answer was simple and true. "Because I have you."

He was her anchor. She could afford to believe in the unbelievable because he was there to catch her if she fell.

With an almost shy smile he went into the bathroom to finish preparing for bed. A few minutes later he joined her wearing the pajama bottoms to the tops she wore. He lay down, folding his arms behind his head to glare up at the ceiling.

"Maybe it won't be so bad," she said.

He rolled his head to the side to give her a frown.

She ignored it and she folded hands across his chest and rested her chin on top of them. "Maybe."

His expression was unchanged as he looked back up at the ceiling. Undeterred, she moved slightly up his body and began to kiss his chest, making her way to his collarbone.

"I'm brooding," he said.

"I know," she said between kisses. When she got to his jaw and he didn't react, she pulled back. "I'll leave you to it then."

She began to move back to her side of the bed when his hands caught her arms and gently pulled her back on top of him. "Don't you dare."

And she knew he meant it. Meant it in ways that went far beyond wanting her to kiss him again. Despite over a decade together, left to his own devices he would still always find the silver thread among the gold unless she was there to stop him. And he'd always cherished her all the more for her ability to shine light into his darkness.

He lifted his head and kissed her, then waited for her to determine what came next. And she did, and they held each other and shared both their darkness and their light.

CHAPTER FOUR

THE NEXT MORNING FOUND them back on the plane and flying
down to Trinidad. Simon hated to admit that he knew very little
about the island nation off the northeastern coast of Venezuela. It
was the larger of two islands—Trinidad and Tobago—currently
under British rule. Part of the West Indies, it was, like so many others
countries, colonized by the Spanish, then the French, and finally
the British before winning its independence in the mid-twentieth
century.

"They call it the Dragon's mouth," Emil said as they passed over
a series of straits and descended toward the calm bay waters of Port
of Spain.

The bay was busy with traffic, from luxury liners to sloops and
schooners, yachts and freighters, fishing boats and even several
battleships representing a variety of nations.

A lovely Caribbean island, Trinidad had all the charm of a small
tropical island but with a strong colonial footprint in its sand. Old
provincial dwellings dominated the architecture.

As their cab took them through town, they passed a royal
botanical garden and several open-air marketplaces where breadfruit

and guava could be had for a few cents. It was surprisingly diverse. There were Catholic churches, Hindu temples, and even Muslim mosques all mixed into a rather small area. There was a notably high population of East Indians, most brought here for labor.

Giant bamboo grew on the sides of the road and rippling streams glistened in the afternoon sun. Grapefruit, cocoa, and sugar cane fields spread out in the distance.

They visited the Angostura bitters factory with its centuries-old casks and even indulged in a taste or two. Despite Elizabeth's sudden fondness for Old Fashioneds, which she blamed on a Mad Men marathon, she didn't enjoy the samples.

After their drinks, they decided to walk back to the hotel, having their luggage sent along and kept safe until they arrived to check in. It was late afternoon and the heat had diminished somewhat, although it was still fairly humid. Despite the fact that it was still warm and a hot wind seemed to blow constantly, it felt good to stretch their legs after a second day on the plane.

They turned up a road lined with large mora trees, their enormous, sprawling trunks like thick planes of muscle gripping the earth. They walked past a woman making a stew with green leaves and the sweet cloying smell of boiling coconut milk.

"It's callaloo," Emil had said. "A traditional meal that is a mixture of many things and different on every island. Here it is mainly okra, taro, crab meat, onions and peppers boiled down with the coconut milk. The country is very much like its food. Eclectic."

Just as the sun was sinking below the horizon, they arrived at their hotel and retrieved their day bags from the front office. They'd learned early on to prepare one bag for the hotels and to leave the rest in the hold of the plane.

The hotel was really more in the style of a motel—two stories with outdoor entrances to each room. The three of them walked from the main office to their respective rooms, bags in hand. Simon noticed that the professor had brought the document tube with him this time. They reached Mendoza's room first. It was only a few doors down from theirs.

"Dinner in an hour?" he asked as he set down his burdens to key into his room.

"Sounds perfect."

Simon and Elizabeth continued under the covered walkway to their room and had just reached it when they heard the professor call out. "What are you doing?"

A man wearing a dirty white khurta and loose fitting pants wrestled with the professor over the document tube.

"Let go of that!" Mendoza cried as he tried to pry the tube away from the stranger.

"You there!" Simon called out as he dropped their bags and sprinted toward them.

The man turned, his eyes widening with fear that someone else was now becoming involved. He shoved Mendoza to the ground, wresting the tube away from him, and ran.

Simon could hear Elizabeth's footfalls behind him on the concrete pathway and looked over his shoulder.

"Go!" she urged. "I'll look after him."

Simon ran past Mendoza, who didn't seem hurt, just shocked, and tried to keep pace with the thief. He dashed away from the hotel and across the two-lane road that led to the hotel and into the thick bamboo forest on the other side. Simon wedged himself between the trees and tried to keep up, but the man was smaller and younger and knew the terrain. It wasn't long before he disappeared into the thick undergrowth and Simon lost sight of him completely.

"Damn."

He turned back for the hotel, defeated. By the time he returned, Elizabeth had Mendoza resting comfortably inside his hotel room.

"Are you all right?" he asked as Elizabeth opened the door for him.

She nodded quickly and glanced over at Mendoza. "No worse for the wear," she said, and then focused on Simon's arm. "Are you hurt?"

Only my pride.

His jacket was torn, but he wasn't injured. "I'm afraid he got away."

"Oh dear," Mendoza sighed.

"I hope it wasn't too valuable," Elizabeth said, coming to sit on the edge of the bed with him. "It wasn't a map, was it?"

"Yes," he said, seemingly surprised they knew that.

Wonderful, Simon thought. *And I let them get away with it.*

"To you-know-where?" Elizabeth added.

Mendoza laughed. "Oh, no, no. Nothing like that. Just a set of antique maps of the Colorado territories and few vintage wanted posters from your Old West."

Simon could hardly believe what he'd heard. "What?"

"I have a friend at the library in Rio who collects them. Oh, Tiago is going to be so disappointed."

Elizabeth began to laugh but stopped herself as Mendoza looked at her with concern. "I'm sorry. I thought it was *the* map and your expedition was lost."

"Oh, my dear, not to worry. The map is safe and sound in Brazil, waiting for us to arrive."

Thank God.

Whoever stole the document tube was in for a rude surprise. It was a relief indeed that the map was safe, but the theft was a potent reminder that Simon had let his guard down, something he could not afford to do again. Either the man who'd stolen it worked for Stoneface or there was more than one interested party. Whichever was the case, he'd been a fool to grow even the least bit complacent on their trip south. It was a mistake he vowed not to make again.

ON THEIR WAY TO Belem, their next stop, Elizabeth gazed out of the large porthole window. The waters of the Atlantic buffeted the coast of South America as they hugged the shoreline and continued south. They'd already passed Venezuela, Spanish, British, French, and Dutch Guyana—apparently everyone had a Guyana—and the northern tip of Brazil when she saw what looked like the mouth of a mighty river. She realized what it was—the Amazon—mythic, shrouded in mystery, and frankly, terrifyingly enormous.

It was a potent reminder of what lay ahead for them. The jungle seemed to stretch out as far as she could see.

She was just about to point it out to Simon when Reg, one of the stewards, came down the aisle of the plane. After several days in the air she was on a first name basis with the entire crew.

Today, however, Reg was sporting a fluffy white beard and a crown jauntily perched on his head. Helpfully pinned to his chest was a nametag that read simply, Neptune.

"What on earth?"

"Ah, we must be crossing the equator!" Emil said, joyfully.

Reg bowed stoically and held out a hand.

"What's he doing?" Elizabeth asked.

"He wants your hand. It's a cleansing ceremony. Nothing to worry about. All in good fun."

Reg tugged down his beard. "Don't worry, miss. It won't hurt."

Elizabeth gave Reg her hand, and he proceeded to rub it gently with a bar of soap.

"The line-crossing ceremony started with sailors and commemorates a person's first time crossing the equator," Emil explained. "Initially, it meant to test a young sailor's resolve, or pollywog as they were known. They were given a series of good-natured but rather arduous tests, and if they passed, they were welcomed as shellbacks to the crew. The idea was that if they passed the test, Neptune cleansed their sins and accepted them into his kingdom."

When Reg finished rubbing the soap on her hand, he gently cleaned it with a wet cloth. He turned to Simon next who extinguished the idea that he would endure such a thing with a single look.

"Fine," Elizabeth said. "Stay a pollywog."

"Happily."

THEY SPENT THE NIGHT in Belem, Brazil and another in Recife before starting on the final leg of their journey to Rio. There had been no other incidents. Whoever the man was in Trinidad, a local hired out by someone Simon supposed, neither he nor anyone else bothered them again.

It had been a long five days of travel, and even though they'd had afternoons and evenings to explore, Elizabeth was anxious to arrive in Rio. That afternoon, they did.

CHAPTER FIVE

THE HARBOR AT RIO de Janeiro was known as the most beautiful harbor in the world and as their plane began its descent, Elizabeth could see why. The setting was breathtaking. The blue waters of the large bay were surrounded by the deep green of the jagged and cascading mountains.

The broad white sand crescent-shaped beaches of Ipanema and Copacabana curved along the edges of the shore while a tall promontory known as Sugarloaf stood sentinel at the entrance to the bay. She thought she could just make out the 130-foot-tall statue of Christ the Redeemer perched on one of the mountaintops overlooking the city as they turned north to land in the calm waters of Guanabara Bay. The inlet looked like the mouth of a river, but it was just the opening of the gorgeous balloon-shaped bay.

Glad to have finally arrived, they were eager to disembark. The luggage sorted, they shared a cab with the professor to their hotel, the Copacabana Palace. It was situated directly across the street from the broad expanse of Copacabana beach. Built in the 1920s, the hotel was the premiere destination in Rio at the time and looked every inch of it. Smart, modern, whatever-came-before-jet-set since there weren't any jets yet. It reminded her a little of the Winter Palace Hotel in Luxor, Egypt—tall, broad, gleaming white in the afternoon sun and the height of luxury. Eight stories of extravagance in an extravagant setting. Large street lamps lined the lower patio where people enjoyed the last of the day's sun with a cocktail, while across the street the black and white tiled Portuguese sidewalk with its intricate mosaic patterns wound its way along the beach that stretched for over two miles from the hotel.

The lobby was lavish and felt almost French in design. Nearly everything except the exotic tropical plants was clean and white. White marble covered the floors, and imposing columns rose up to the high ceiling where ornate crystal chandeliers dangled.

It was warm outside, but not too hot, yet it still felt comfortably cool inside. It seemed strange that February was later summer, but welcome to the Southern Hemisphere.

Simon and Emil went to the front desk to check in while Elizabeth lingered by the windows catching a glimpse of the pristine beach beyond. Maybe, if they had a chance tomorrow, they could spend a little time there. It would be a crying shame to come to Rio and not spend at least a few hours on one its world-famous beaches.

She turned to head back to the front desk and bumped right into someone. For a moment, she had a flashback to Miami and thought she'd see Stoneface when she looked up to see whose chest she'd run into. It wasn't old Stoneface, but someone just as disconcerting. He was good looking or would have been if he hadn't seemed so severe. He was tall and well-dressed in a cream colored suit, but there was something positively forbidding about him. His hair was light blonde, verging on white, his skin sallow, and his eyes a blue that was as clear and as cold as ice.

"Pardon me," she said.

The corner of the man's mouth turned up in an appraising half-smile, giving Elizabeth the shivers. He tipped his hat and politely stepped aside to let her pass. Even the way he moved seemed unnatural, a contrived grace that made her uneasy. She could feel his eyes following her as she walked away and hurried her steps.

When she reached the desk, despite the heat, a shiver overtook her.

"Something wrong?" Simon asked, looking over her shoulder to see what had caused such a reaction.

She turned but the man was gone. "Nothing."

"Professor!" a man called out across the lobby.

Emil turned toward the sound of the voice and broke into a grin as the young man approached. He was handsome, perhaps in his twenties, with dark skin and warm brown eyes. He smiled back broadly at the professor.

"Good to see you have arrived safely," he said with a slight Latin American accent she couldn't pinpoint.

The two men shook hands, obviously pleased to see each other. "And you are well, Raul?" Emil asked.

"Yes, and the package is secure, but I am not sure Gaspar is."

"What do you mean?"

"I was to meet him yesterday as per your instructions, but he was not home and has not telephoned."

Emil's always-pleasant face darkened with worry. "That is concerning."

Raul's gaze shifted uneasily to Simon and Elizabeth, who stood back while the two spoke.

"Forgive me," Emil said. "Mr. and Mrs. Cross. This is Raul Navarro, my assistant."

Raul inclined his head politely. "Pleased to meet you," he said, as he extended his hand to Simon. "Mr. Cross."

"Mr. Navarro."

And then he extended his hand to Elizabeth. "Mrs. Cross."

"Elizabeth, please."

He flashed his smile and amazingly white teeth. "Then you must call me Raul," he said, speaking his name almost as a purr.

His hand held hers a moment too long causing Emil to clear his throat. Raul got the message, quickly dropped her hand, and turned back to his employer who gave him a stern look. Raul accepted the silent censure but couldn't keep his eyes from darting back to Elizabeth before giving the professor his full attention.

"I am afraid I have some things to attend to," Emil said to the Crosses, "but perhaps dinner later? Seven?"

"We'd be delighted," Simon replied.

"Wonderful." Emil bowed slightly then put on his hat as he and Raul excused themselves and began talking again in earnest.

Simon stared after Raul and would have continued to do so if the bellboy hadn't arrived with their luggage cart, ready to escort them to their room.

"Raoool," Simon grumbled under his breath in a mock imitation as they walked to the bank of elevators, earning a giggle from Elizabeth.

When they reached the top floor of the hotel, the bellboy led them down the broad hall and unlocked the door to their room. He handed Simon the key and waited for them to precede him inside.

But it wasn't a room, it was a suite, and not just any suite, but what looked an awful lot like the penthouse suite. The living room was elegantly decorated with dark wood tables and a contrasting white sofa and chairs. A gold framed mirror hung on one wall, while still life paintings and various pieces depicting tropical landscapes adorned the rest. The bellboy took their luggage from the cart and carried it into the massive bedroom. He put their suitcases down

61

and pulled back the long, sheer curtains to reveal their own private balcony that ran the length of the suite.

She wondered just what the Council contact had done to get whoever had booked this room previously to cancel on such short notice. Then again, maybe it was better she didn't know.

The bellboy gestured to a large black phone on a side table in the living room. "The telephone to the front desk is at your disposal should you require anything."

"Thank you."

He bowed smartly and started for the door. Simon followed him, giving him a generous tip, before closing the door.

Elizabeth stepped out onto the balcony through the French doors in the living room. All of Copacabana beach spread out before her, and the waters of the Southern Atlantic beyond. The undulating wave pattern of the Portuguese pavement, a mosaic of tile that served as the sidewalk running the length of the beach, was almost hypnotic.

"Not too shabby," she said to herself. If they were going to risk their lives at least they were going to do it in style.

Simon joined her, carrying an ornate silver bucket with a bottle of champagne cooling on ice inside it. He put it down on the small bistro table on the balcony. "Compliments of the management."

"Oooh," Elizabeth cooed.

"Would you like some?"

"I don't see why not. We made it."

"This far," he cautioned.

She knew his thoughts had already strayed to what lay ahead and the dangers they would invariably face.

"We're halfway around the world," she countered. "That's pretty far in my book."

A slight smile touched his eyes.

"But we can save it for a special occasion if you want," she offered.

"Every moment with you is a special occasion."

From anyone else it would have sounded silly, but he meant it. Truly meant it. Her heart never tired of hearing him say things like that. How in the world did she get so lucky?

She stepped forward and slipped her arms around his neck. "Who needs champagne when I have a husband who says things like that?"

"So, no champagne then?"

"Let's not go crazy." She kissed him briefly and he released her with a laugh, then set about opening the champagne. Somehow he always did it without making a huge mess. Jack had to wear an eye patch for a week the last time she'd tried.

"The manager also invited us to the Gala Masquerade Ball on the first night of Carnival," he said as he handed her a glass.

She'd completely forgotten about Carnival. She'd seen bits of it on TV a few times and always wanted to go, although who knew what it would be like in 1936.

"Wait? Masquerade?" she asked, realizing all of what he'd said. "As in costumes?"

"Yes, but most attendees wear only ornate masks."

"*Only* masks?" she asked with a sly grin.

"Elizabeth. It's apparently quite an elegant affair. If we're not hopelessly lost in the jungle by then we might even attend."

"Here's hoping."

Simon raised his glass. "To a safe and successful mission."

That was a toast Elizabeth was more than happy to drink to.

PROFESSOR MENDOZA ROSE FROM his seat as Simon and Elizabeth neared his table in the hotel's restaurant. At his side young Raul Navarro, who'd been distracted by something, belatedly found his manners and stood at Elizabeth's approach flashing her that same appreciative smile he had when they met.

"Did you get some rest?" she asked the professor.

"No rest for the wicked," he said. "Raul and I had some arrangements to see to and I was hoping to catch Alex before he went out for the evening, but I seem to have missed him."

"Alex?"

"Vega. My benefactor."

Part of Simon was uneasy about Vega. The last time they'd met a mysterious benefactor was in Cairo and it turned out to be Catherine Vale who very much wanted he and Elizabeth dead. Hopefully, Vega was less so inclined.

Once they were seated, the waiter came to take their drink orders. Simon allowed himself one scotch, but with the way Raul kept ogling Elizabeth, a second might be in order.

In spite of Raul's enthusiasm for his wife, dinner was pleasant enough. And Simon could hardly blame the man for his affliction. She was stunning in her green and gold silk dress. Her hair was styled in what she called a "Veronica Lake." The result was a smooth wave of hair that cascaded seductively down one side of her face and stopped to caress her shoulder. His fingers itched to ease it away from her neck and kiss her until she forgot why they were both there. He made a mental note to do exactly that later. For now, they had roles to play and relationships to nurture.

They'd been lucky to get into the professor's good graces, and it seemed, judging from the attention he paid to Elizabeth, winning over his assistant wouldn't be difficult.

"You were *his* assistant?" Navarro said, landing with incredulity on the idea that Elizabeth had worked for Simon.

Perhaps when all was said and done Simon could cap it all off by throwing Navarro into the bay?

"Before we were married, yes."

"That is something else we have in common."

"Are you and Emil planning to run off together?" Simon asked.

Navarro laughed. "No, no. I simply meant that your beautiful wife and I share the burden and privilege," he added quickly, "of working for an older but brilliant mind."

Maybe it wasn't too early to throw him into the bay?

Emil dramatically puffed out a burst of air in false injury. "I'm not that old."

"Notice that he did not argue about the brilliant part," Navarro said with a wink toward Elizabeth.

The table dissolved into laughter. While Navarro and Elizabeth shared horror stories of working for their professors, Simon found himself drawn into an esoteric and frankly fascinating discussion with Emil about the Mesoamerican mythology. But the attention Navarro paid to his wife as they spoke did not go unnoticed. The very last thing his somewhat fragile ego needed at the moment was a young rival unabashedly flirting with his wife. However, years of being married to Elizabeth had taught him how to suppress his outward reaction to such provocation, even if that time had done little to dull the way it made him feel.

As if she sensed his inner turmoil, Elizabeth caught his eye and gave him a private smile, one that was separate from the rest of the world and meant only for him. It was a salve for any wound real or imagined.

"It must be very exciting," she said, turning back to Navarro, "to work on this expedition with the professor."

"It is the best education I could have ever hoped for. I am most grateful to him for the opportunities he's given me. I come from a poor family in Colombia, the first to graduate college. I would be nothing without the professor's belief in me."

Emil waved off his praise with a humble shake of his head. "He is exaggerating."

"I am not," Navarro said in earnest. "He is a great man."

Emil clasped his hand over Navarro's briefly, and Simon could see the genuine affection the professor felt for the young man.

"It will be an honor to assist him in this great undertaking."

"Assuming we get to go at all," Emil said with a sigh.

"Worried about convincing the minister?" Simon asked.

"That, and I am concerned about something else." He glanced at his assistant, silently urging him to explain. Navarro hesitated. "I trust the Crosses, Raul. Speak frankly."

Raul looked them both over briefly before acquiescing to the professor's wish. "I was to meet yesterday with a man named Gaspar. He had recently unearthed a very valuable artifact. Something that the professor has been searching for, for many years."

Simon had an idea what he referred to. "The map?"

"Yes, but so much more than that," Emil said, the light of discovery in his eyes. "But yes, a map. It is hidden in the base of a golden bowl."

Gold? Simon had little doubt he knew what had happened to both the bowl and Gaspar.

"I thought the existence of the bowl was a myth," Navarro admitted. "But the professor, he always believed. I was to meet with Gaspar yesterday to retrieve it, but it seems he has gone missing."

"Missing?"

"He was not at home when I went by for our appointment, and he has not telephoned to explain his absence," Navarro said. "It is not like him."

"Do you think perhaps," Simon suggested carefully, "that he's . . . run off with it? It is gold, after all."

Emil and Navarro shared a look, and Navarro replied, "No, I do not think he would do such a thing. He is a good man and has done work for us before. I cannot imagine why he has not contacted us, though."

"Maybe he can't," Elizabeth said carefully, speaking aloud what Simon was thinking and earning a worried look from Emil. "If it is as valuable as you say, maybe someone else found out he had it."

"Do you think he's come to harm?"

"I don't know," Simon said honestly. "But I think perhaps we should find out."

WHILE THE PROFESSOR WAS sure that there was a perfectly logical explanation for Gaspar's absence—he trusted the man implicitly—it was agreed they would to go Gaspar's home tomorrow at midday after the professor's meeting with Minister Corriea in the morning.

As the group left the dining room and moved to the bar for a nightcap, Raul excused himself. He bid them all a goodnight, especially Elizabeth, who he lingered over indulgently before finally bidding her a goodnight as well.

"I'm amazed he could tear himself from your side," Simon said quietly to her as they followed Emil into the bar.

She knew it irked Simon, but it was flattering and harmless. Raul was just enjoying himself. There was no actual heat behind any of it. She'd known plenty of men like him who simply enjoyed the chase. And it was a safe one with her husband sitting only feet away.

The bar was crowded and tables scarce.

"Why don't you two find a table," Simon suggested, "and I'll put in our order with the bartender."

"A tawny port, if they have one," Emil said.

"Just some madeira, my dear," Elizabeth added.

She definitely needed a digestif. Her eyes had been bigger than her stomach, a rare feat, and she was starting to regret those last few bites of steak. A little help in the digestion department was welcome and a little fortified wine was just the ticket. After all, it was fortified! With brandy! That was the kind of fortification she could get behind. It was sweet and nutty and the perfect end to a perfect meal.

She and Emil searched for a table in the large, dark bar.

"Seems to be a popular spot," Emil said as they maneuvered through the tables looking for an empty one.

"Maybe we should—" Elizabeth began, but Emil interrupted her.

"Ah, perfect. This way, my dear."

He led her to a small table in a corner where a man sat reading a book.

"I was wondering where you'd gone off to," Emil said to him. "I see it's into the pages of a book again."

The man looked up from his book, a smile coming to his face. He stood and held out his hand. "Good to see you again, Emil." His eyes shifted to Elizabeth.

"May I present Mrs. Cross. Mrs. Cross, Alex Vega."

Vega bowed slightly at the waist. "Mrs. Cross."

"Elizabeth, please."

"I met Elizabeth and her husband on the plane down. Delightful companions."

She wasn't sure what she'd been expecting, but the young, handsome man in front of her wasn't it. He was about her age with brown hair, a slightly olive complexion, and soulful hazel eyes.

He seemed surprised and a little unsure of her presence but recovered quickly. "Won't you all join me?"

He politely held out a chair for Elizabeth, who noticed the book he'd been reading.

"*Lost Horizon*!" She loved that book, and the movie, although she couldn't remember when it came out so she was sure not to mention it.

"Have you read it?" he asked.

"I liked it even better than *Goodbye, Mr. Chips*. But don't tell my husband."

"Don't tell me what?" Simon said, appearing at their table.

Emil made quick introductions.

"We were just discussing my book," Vega said. "Your wife expressed admiration for it."

"It suits her," Simon replied, seeing the book's title. "She's a dreamer."

"'People make mistakes in life through believing too much,'" Vega recited, "'but they have a damned dull time if they believe too little.' You will forgive the colorful language, it is not my own."

"Yes!" Elizabeth said, excitedly. She loved that quote from the book and believed it to her core. "Are you a dreamer, as well, Mr. Vega?"

"I suppose I am. After all, what a dull existence it must be to be a skeptic in a world filled with so much wonder."

Skeptics had their place, she knew. She'd married one, but she was a dreamer down to her toes.

"'A dreamer can only find his way by moonlight, and his punishment is that he sees the dawn before the rest of the world,'" Elizabeth replied.

Vega tilted his head in acknowledgment and appreciation of the quote. "Oscar Wilde."

Oh, she liked him!

"This one's a keeper," she said to Emil as Vega fought down a shy smile.

Simon cleared his throat. "Yes, well. It's a pleasure to meet you, Mr. Vega, and I suppose your book is apropos." When he didn't seem to make the connection, Simon continued, "You and Emil are searching for your own Shangri-La, as it were."

If he'd seemed surprised at their presence, he was doubly so at their knowledge of the coming expedition.

"No need to be concerned, my boy," Emil assured him. "I trust the Crosses implicitly."

"I see." He demurred with a dip of his head. It was clear that he was not quite as convinced as Emil but would keep his own counsel for the time being.

"They've already been an immense help. Chasing down thieves and such."

"Thieves?"

Emil told him about the incident in Trinidad and he looked troubled.

"You think it was simply a random act?"

Emil did, although Elizabeth knew Simon didn't and she had her own doubts.

"Either way," Emil said, "it's of no real consequence. Our troubles lie elsewhere. Have you made any progress with Minister Correia?"

Vega shook his head. "He is a difficult man. Arrogant, drunk with both alcohol and power, both of which he enjoys in abundance. I am not sure he will be convinced through . . .conventional means."

"I don't follow," Emil said.

"I think I do," Simon said. "He might be *induced* to change his mind?"

Vega nodded.

"A bribe?" Emil said, a little too loudly.

"Compensation," Vega said. "It is not uncommon for functionaries to exploit their positions for personal gain. I have no doubt Minister Correia is quite adept at this."

"Oh, dear."

"Do not worry, Emil," Vega said. "We have not come so far to let such a thing stand in our way. What is a few thousand more pesetas?"

"I'm sorry."

"It is not your fault and do not worry. We will see what we can do tomorrow, yes? We shall see just how 'convincing' we need to be."

"Thank you," Emil replied just as the waiter arrived with their drinks.

"So," Simon said, after taking a sip of his cognac, "Emil tells us you're from Spain."

"I am."

"Your accent is unique."

"You are very observant," Vega replied. "I have lived in many places. Madrid, Paris, London. Even your New York," he added to Elizabeth. "I enjoy traveling."

Elizabeth shared a quick look with Simon. "So do we."

"Good for the soul," Emil chimed in, "to see how others live."

"Is that what has brought you to Brazil? To see how others live?"

"I was looking for a bit of adventure and my husband was kind enough to humor me."

"A wise man," Vega said. "And it seems in Emil you have found it?"

Elizabeth could sense his unease and even suspicion at their abrupt friendship with Mendoza.

"We don't mean to horn in—"

"Nonsense," Emil said quickly. "Cross here is probably even better well-versed in mythology than you are, Alex."

"Are you a professor as well?" Elizabeth asked.

"No, I merely enjoy the subject."

"He's being modest. He's quite the Renaissance man. History, art, music. He even draws."

"I sketch," Vega said, dismissing the praise as unworthy.

"I'd like to see your work some time," Elizabeth said.

Vega hesitantly, almost shyly agreed. "You are most kind."

There was something about him. Something stirring beneath the quiet exterior that intrigued her. Maybe it was the vague sense of melancholy that seemed to surround him. He was polite and attentive, clearly very bright and accomplished, but there was something missing. Some ineffable sadness that clung to him.

She'd always been drawn to wounded things. Heck, that's how she'd fallen in love with Simon. He carried his wounds from the past around like pieces of armor. She couldn't help but wonder what lay beneath Vega's still waters.

"Another drink, Alex?" Emil offered.

"I am afraid I should call it a night. It has been a long day." He stood and addressed Emil. "I will meet you downstairs at nine?"

"I'll be there."

He bowed politely toward Simon and Elizabeth. "It has been a pleasure to meet you both. Until tomorrow."

"Lovely man," Emil said as he sipped his port.

"Damn."

Alex Vega nearly threw his hotel room key across the room in a fit of pique, but controlled himself. Barely. Instead, he tossed it onto the table of his suite and took a deep calming breath.

This would not do. What was Mendoza thinking? The old fool.

The woman was, he had to admit, intriguing, but the man would be a problem. He was far too perceptive. If it had only been the woman, he could have enjoyed her company and dealt with her when the time came, but the pair presented problems. And he did not like problems.

His mission was complicated enough without outside interference. And what of the event in Trinidad? Alex had no doubt it was not mere coincidence. He knew there would be others seeking what he sought. He would be damned if he'd let anyone else get their hands on it, though. He had worked far too hard and far too long to be where he was to allow that. That included the attractive Mrs. Cross.

Mendoza was clearly taken with them both, though. He'd have to tread carefully not to arouse suspicion. If he were to put his foot down and force Mendoza to push them out, it could upset the delicate trust he'd achieved with the professor. He could not afford to destroy that now. Not when they were so close. Not when what he desired was nearly within his grasp.

He tugged on his tie and slid it from around his neck, tossing it carelessly onto the bed. He unbuttoned his collar and unconsciously rubbed the thin scar that marred his throat.

He sat down on the foot of the bed and calmed himself. He could deal with this. He had dealt with far worse before. He was still in control. He just had to be smart about it.

He would find a way. He always had and he always would.

Chapter Six

"I MIGHT EVEN DO A little frolicking," Elizabeth called out from the bathroom. "Just shy of cavorting. Well, maybe a little cavorting. But absolutely no capering. That is where I draw the line."

Simon snorted and put down his teacup as he walked over to their open balcony doors. The view was lovely, but he was anxious to discover what had happened to Gaspar and the golden bowl. However, he would have to wait for Emil's meeting with the minister to be over first. Emil had insisted that he go with them to Gaspar's today and that meant they were left to their own devices until noon. With Copacabana beach so enticingly near, that meant only one thing for Elizabeth—beach day, or at least morning.

Simon loved the ocean, especially the cold forbidding Atlantic that surrounded England or even the slightly less forbidding Pacific near their home in Santa Barbara. He was not, however, what anyone would call a "beach person." He preferred a wool jumper to a swim suit and a hot toddy to a piña colada.

Elizabeth, though, could not get enough of the sea. She blamed it on being landlocked in the heart of Texas for most of her life.

There was no force on heaven or earth that could keep her from the beach this morning, and all he could do was try to enjoy it. Perhaps it wouldn't be so horrible. The beach was pristine and not too crowded yet. Besides, if Elizabeth was happy and by his side, he could ask for little more.

"What do you think?" she asked, posing in the doorway of the bath, one arm up-stretched and holding onto the door jam and the other on her hip.

The bathing suit she wore was, by any modern standard, modest. It was a one-piece made of some sort of shiny deep emerald green material and was slightly loose fitting except across the chest where a seam cut into an X accentuating that particular portion. The suit showed far less skin than her swimsuits at home, yet the effect of the modest cut and material made this look more like a piece of lingerie than swimwear and the result was impossibly provocative. It felt far more intimate than even the bikini she sometimes wore. Perhaps it was because it looked like she was in a state of undress, rather than suited for the beach, but the prospect of her going out in public like that made him distinctly uncomfortable.

"It's . . .very nice," he managed.

Either ignoring or unaware of his actual reaction, she grinned and grabbed a small cover-up. "And it comes with this, in case the sun is too much."

She slipped on the short, yellow-hooded cape that finished the ensemble. When she flipped up the hood, she could not have looked more alluring if she'd tried.

She cocked her head to the side. "Something wrong?"

"No," he said. "You look beautiful."

"Do I?" she asked coquettishly, batting her eyelashes for effect. "I have to admit," she went on seriously, "I kind of love it. Now, are you going to get ready or not?"

"I am ready." He was wearing trousers, absurdly high-waisted, but that was the fashion, and a short sleeve polo shirt.

"You're not wearing your suit."

"Nor shall I be."

"Oh, come on," she said, picking up the offending item from the bed where she'd laid it out for him and holding it up.

It was a tragedy—an unholy marriage of briefs and boxers, but sharing none of the best qualities of either. It was uncomfortable and ill-fitting, and he'd be damned if he would ever wear it.

"You don't like the belt?" she asked with a laugh.

The coup de grace of the abomination was the white belt that was worn high on the waist to keep the whole accursed thing from falling off.

"No," he said.

She stifled a laugh. "I didn't think you'd wear it, but I had to try." She looked at it one more time. "I don't think anyone can make that look good. Not even you."

She tossed it on the bed and picked up her outrageously large hat, oversized sunglasses, and a purse the size of a small car. "Ready?"

He wasn't. "Of course."

Just as they'd found a pair of lounge chairs under the shade of two large umbrellas and away from the growing crowd, a voice called out to them. Well, to her.

"Elizabeth! Mrs. Cross!"

Raul Navarro bounded over to them, jogging through the deep sand, his white teeth flashing.

"Hello!" he said, his naturally tanned chest rising and falling from the effort.

"Raul!" Elizabeth said with enthusiasm, which was more than Simon could muster.

It wasn't bad enough that the man was quite obviously taking in Elizabeth's figure, but he was wearing the same damned suit Simon was supposed to wear, and looking quite fit in it. The whole thing set Simon's teeth on edge.

"We were just playing a little football," Navarro said. "Just kicking it around really."

One of his equally fit friends called out to him, and Simon noticed the small group kicking a ball back and forth across the sand.

"Would you like to join us?" Navarro asked.

"No, that's all right," Elizabeth said. Even though she sounded quite sincere, Simon knew that she would love to, but wasn't for his sake.

"Go ahead if you'd like," Simon said.

She looked at him in question, but he could see the light in her eye. "You don't mind?"

"I'll manage."

A beautiful smile graced her face as the leaned over to kiss his cheek. "I won't be long."

"Just remember," he said, "no capering."

With a laugh, she joined Navarro and the others in their chaotic game of football. She wasn't the only woman, and some were quite pretty, but he couldn't help but think she was by far the most beautiful among them.

She chased down the ball with the same eagerness she did everything, but Navarro deftly maneuvered the ball away from her causing her to stumble and fall into the sand. Instead of feeling foolish, she delighted in it, laughing until someone gave her hand up. It was Elizabeth in microcosm—adventurous, open, and unafraid.

And here he sat on the sidelines, too vain, too stuck in his ways, too old to join in. He'd always been content to sit and watch her, but he'd begun to wonder if she was content with that. A soft traitorous voice had started to whisper doubts in the back of his mind. She was in the prime of her life and he past his. Was that fair to her? Did she deserve more than he could give?

Forcing his mind and his gaze away, he turned his thoughts to more immediate problems. He was anxious to discover what had happened to Gaspar and the bowl. If they didn't have the map, how could they possibly find the staff? For a fleeting moment, he thought that perhaps they might be spared having to trek into the ungodly Brazilian jungle, but he'd been doing this long enough to know there was no easy way out. They would have to find the bowl, one way or the other, and the map it held. If, of course, Emil was right about it. He was very knowledgeable and they wouldn't have been sent back to take the staff from him if the Council hadn't known with some certainty that it would come into his possession. It was a little troubling, however, that despite his apparent trust in them—he had disclosed the truth of his expedition, after all—that he had not mentioned the staff even once. It was possible that he was unaware of it and was truly in search of El Dorado. However, considering the power of the staff, it would be foolish to assume it wasn't his goal. Gold, even a city of it, paled in comparison to the powers of the Staff of Life if it did even half of what it was rumored to do. Life from death, untold destruction.

While Emil did not seem the sort to covet such power, it was possible. It was also possible that Simon had been so pleased to find a man of like-minded passions that he missed something, some tell about the professor's true intentions. He would have to redouble his efforts to be observant and not take anything or anyone at face value.

Elizabeth tired of the game after a half an hour and rejoined him. She was flushed and pleasantly exhausted as she sat down next to him.

"Running in that sand is impossible. I'm getting too old for this," she said jokingly. But Simon knew exactly how she felt.

ELIZABETH TAPPED SIMON ON the leg.

"Is Emil here?" he asked, lowering his newspaper and scanning the lobby. They'd changed from the beach and were waiting for the professor and Raul so they could all go to Gaspar's.

"No, that's the man I told you about," she said, drawing his attention to the tall, slender man who'd so unnerved her the day they'd checked in.

Simon quietly observed him as he walked past them across the lobby.

A bellboy met him partway. "I found the paper you were looking for, Mr. Rasche."

"Very good," he replied. The man took the newspaper and handed the young man a few coins, and then continued on his way.

"I don't see anything unusual about him," Simon said.

"Trust me. There is. I don't know how to explain it, but he gives me the willies."

Simon looked at her dubiously. "The willies?"

"Yes," she said, firmly. She wasn't making it up. There as something wrong with that man.

"Well, then we'll have to keep an eye out for him."

She loved that he didn't question it. She said there was something wrong with him and he accepted it. Between her guts and his brains, they made an awfully good team. And she was going to tell him so when he spotted Emil coming toward them.

He stood to greet him. "How did it got with the minister?"

Emil shook his head. "Not as well as I'd hoped, but Alex thinks it will simply take time. He said the minister is 'playing hard to get,' but that we'll win him over in time. I certainly hope he's right."

"I'm sure—"

"Emil Mendoza, you old horny toad!" a man bellowed across the room.

Emil's always kind face crumpled into displeasure. "Bridges," he muttered before forcing a smile to his face and turning to the man who approached.

He was tall, almost as tall as Simon but a little thicker and a lot rougher around the edges. He took off a tan Stetson to reveal hair that was on the long and scraggly side as was his beard. Both were streaked with gray.

He dressed like a cowboy who'd struck it rich, down to the fancy bolo tie and alligator skin boots.

"Funny meeting you here," he said, although his tone and smirk implied just the opposite.

"Yes," Emil said, clearly not pleased to see him.

"Come for the Carnival, did ya?" the man asked, his voice a little too loud.

Two more men, dressed like a hundred cowboys she'd known in Texas, lingered behind him. One had the fat-lip look of a dipper, and he confirmed her suspicions when he leaned over and spit his tobacco juice into a potted plant.

"Something like that," Emil replied.

The man grinned, a cocky, knowing grin. "Me, too," he said and then turned his attention to Simon and Elizabeth. "Ain't you gonna introduce me?"

Judging from his accent he was either Texan or Oklahoman. Either way, he was the very stereotype of the loud American.

"Mr. and Mrs. Cross, this is Clay Bridges," he said reluctantly. "An old acquaintance."

"Is that what I am?" Bridges said with a laugh. "All right." He held out his hand to Simon to politely shake it and touched the brim of his hat for Elizabeth. "Ma'am."

"What are you doing here?" Emil asked. She'd never seen him so edgy.

"Just visitin'," he said. "Always wanted to come down this way. Thought the time was right."

He said everything with a smile but it was as insincere as he was. She'd known a few men like him before—bullies. Big, brash, bullies.

"I'm sure," Emil said, tightly. "If you'll excuse us, we have business to attend to."

"You go attend to your . . .business, Emil. And I hope you don't mind if I, uh, keep an eye on you," he said, pointing a finger toward his eye to emphasize the notion as he smiled. "I'm sure we'll run into each other again."

With another tip of his hat, he and his men walked away.

"Who on earth was that?" Simon asked once they were gone.

Emil ran his fingers across his eyebrow as if he had a headache coming on, then he let out a deep breath. "A competitor, as it were. He is an archaeologist."

"*He* is?" Simon asked incredulous.

"What he really is, is a thief. He conveniently appears at other people's discoveries to either ride on their coattails or worse yet, steal the credit for the discovery entirely. I've had the displeasure of knowing him for many years."

"He steals other people's finds?"

81

"If he can. If he can't, he steals a few artifacts and sells them to the highest bidder," Emil said with distaste. "He is a scoundrel and thief."

"And I'm assuming it's no coincidence that he's here now," Simon said.

Emil closed his eyes briefly. "No. We must be very careful. Don't let his brashness lead you to think he's a fool. He is far from it. And he will stop at next to nothing to get what he wants."

Wonderful, Elizabeth thought. *That is all we need.*

"Come," Emil said. "The sooner we find Gaspar, the better."

Navarro drove their car out of the city and up into the hills surrounding it toward the favelas, the growing slums of Rio. Elizabeth was uncharacteristically quiet and Simon knew why. Her heart bled for everyone, and especially for the poor and disenfranchised. The favelas had both in spades.

Simon knew only a thumbnail sketch of the history of Rio and this particular area. Some attributed the growth of the favelas to soldiers, who with no more war to fight needed places to live in the late 1800s, while others pointed to the influx of impoverished former African slaves brought here by the Portuguese looking for a place to call home when none was to be found in the city itself. The truth was probably a mixture of both.

Whatever the genesis, the result was all too familiar—a slum growing in both size and squalor. It would grow worse with time, Simon knew, as they drove up the hill toward Gaspar's apartment. In the mid-1930s it was just becoming the tangle of small colorful tenements that so defined this part of modern Rio.

With no city planning, the streets, such as they were, and buildings were haphazard. From the random strings of electrical wiring to the mix of materials used to build the homes themselves, there was no semblance of order and the chaos was more than just skin deep.

Gaspar's apartment was in one of the nicer buildings in the neighborhood, made of brick and stone instead of wood scraps and daub. The two-story building was constructed directly into the steep hillside, with two of like construction on either side. As they parked, a woman strung laundry on a line stretched across the vacant lot between them. Soon all of the empty spaces would be taken up by more buildings as the population of the favelas expanded.

"Gaspar's rooms are upstairs," Navarro said.

"He lives here?" Emil asked, obviously surprised by his surroundings.

Navarro, who seemed to better understand the realities of poverty and life in a city for those without means, was sanguine about it. "It is better than some," he said as he started inside.

Their little company followed him up the rickety steps, Elizabeth followed by Emil, with Simon cautiously bringing up the rear.

When they reached the second floor, Navarro knocked loudly on Gaspar's door. They all waited anxiously.

When there was no answer, Navarro said, "You see."

Elizabeth's eyes narrowed and she leaned close to the door.

"What is it?" Simon asked as her face paled.

"Don't you smell it?"

He leaned in close and after two breaths, he smelled it and winced. The odor of death was vile and putrid, and not a smell one ever forgot. The lack of proper sanitation in the apartment had masked it, but it would not for much longer.

"What is wrong?" Emil asked.

"I'm afraid something has happened to Gaspar," Elizabeth said.

"Perhaps you should wait in the car, Emil," Simon suggested.

"What do you mean?"

"We need to get in there," Elizabeth told Simon.

He agreed. He knew Elizabeth could pick the old lock, but that might result in questions they did not want to answer. A more blunt form of entry was required.

"Stand back," Simon said.

"What are you doing?" Navarro asked.

Simon ignored him and put his shoulder against the door. He took half a step back and then shoved his body against it. The door was old and brittle and gave way easily. As soon as the door was open the smell became apparent.

Emil covered his mouth. "Dear lord, what is that?"

Simon walked into the small apartment and found what they knew they would. "Gaspar."

"What do you—Oh, Dios mío," Emil uttered as he saw Gaspar lying face down in the living room.

Navarro gagged but moved to Gaspar's side and announced, rather needlessly, that he was dead.

"Very," Simon added.

If the smell hadn't given that away, then the blood caked on the back of his skull did. Not to mention his hands were already starting to turn slightly greenish as putrefaction had already begun, no doubt hastened along by Rio's warm, humid weather.

"He's been murdered," Emil said, still in shock.

Elizabeth squeezed his arm to comfort him. "I'm so sorry."

Knowing they couldn't linger long, Simon quickly took in the room. There had obviously been a struggle. Aside from the injury to Gaspar, a chair was overturned and several magazines and a lamp lay on the floor. But nothing else was disturbed. It had been brief and violent.

A half-dozen cigarette butts sat in an ashtray, one snubbed out with force enough to crush what remained as if done in anger. An open bottle of beer sat on an end table and another bottle, its contents soaked into the rug, lay near the body.

Two bottles. Two people.

"He knew whoever did this," Simon announced, adding when Emil seemed confused by his announcement, "There's a second beer bottle, and the door was locked from the inside."

"Who could do such a thing?" Emil asked.

Simon knew the answer was far too many people, especially when there was something of value at stake.

"You're sure he didn't tell anyone about the bowl?" Simon asked Navarro.

He nodded, but Simon knew he couldn't be sure. Judging from what had happened here, Gaspar possibly told someone about the bowl. Something so rare and valuable; it must have been difficult for a poor man like Gaspar to keep it to himself. Perhaps he told a friend, invited them over to show them, and had gotten killed for his trouble. Or, perhaps he was selling the bowl and the deal turned sour.

However it had happened, Simon had no doubt the bowl was gone and with it their chances to intercept the staff.

"We need to . . .report this," Emil said, struggling to accept what he saw.

"Yes," Simon agreed, glad for once that there was no telephone. As soon as they told the police about the missing bowl, any chance of Minister Correia agreeing to let them go would be gone with it. An anonymous tip later would have to do. It was hardly enough, but if they became involved in any official inquiry, they would doom their mission before it had really begun. And the price for failure was too high.

Gaspar's fate was a painful reminder of just how dangerous that mission was. Someone had already died for it.

"I don't see the bowl," Navarro said. He quickly checked the bedroom to no avail. "They must have taken it."

"The bowl?" Emil said. "What does it matter? A man is dead."

"Professor, without the bowl, his life, all of this, will be for nothing," Navarro countered.

"Yes, but..."

"If we find who took the bowl, we find his killer," Elizabeth interjected.

"We should go," Simon announced. The longer they remained, the higher the risk that they'd become involved in something they could ill-afford to be. He began to usher the others out.

"Maybe someone saw something? One of the neighbors?" Elizabeth asked quietly as they left the apartment.

Simon hoped so, but had his doubts anyone would be willing to talk to them. Places like this did not share their secrets with outsiders easily. But they had to try.

Once they were outside, Emil leaned against the car, still recovering from what he'd seen. Navarro, to his credit, seemed to understand the situation they were in.

"Without the bowl . . . I will ask around to see if anyone saw anything."

Simon and Elizabeth joined Navarro on what ended up being a fruitless quest. As he suspected, no one saw anything or if they did, they weren't talking. Navarro spoke to the neighbors who were willing to talk, translating the Portuguese for his and Elizabeth's benefit.

"What about that woman?" Elizabeth suggested. "The one who was putting out laundry."

"There was no answer at their house," Navarro said.

"Try again," Simon suggested.

They went back to the woman's door and rapped again, loudly. Finally, a woman in her early thirties answered it, and Simon recognized her as the one they'd seen when they arrived.

Navarro asked if she'd seen anything and she quickly shook her head and tried to close the door.

"*Por favor?*" Elizabeth asked. "Please?"

The woman was clearly more comfortable talking to a female and seemed as though she was going to reply when a noise came from deeper inside the house.

"*Sinto muito,*" she said with a rueful shake of her head. She was about to close the door again when her husband appeared and stopped her, demanding to know what was going on.

Simon could smell the liquor on his breath and didn't need to see the woman's flinch to know the truth of their relationship.

"We just wanted to ask a few questions," Simon said, stepping forward and trying to draw the attention away from the woman. "Can you help us?"

The man barked something in Portuguese that Simon did not need a translator for and then shoved his wife aside and went back into the house.

"Thank you for your time," Simon said to her, which Navarro translated, and then the two of them started back to the car. Elizabeth lingered by the door. The woman clung to it for a moment before disappearing back inside.

"We'll go back to the hotel," Simon said, "and report what we've found, but I think it would be wise to do so anonymously."

Emil, still somewhat in shock, looked at him blankly.

"If we become embroiled in a murder investigation, I sincerely doubt any amount of money will convince Minister Correia to allow the expedition to proceed."

Emil nodded slowly.

"Do you think that fellow Bridges could have anything to do with it?" Simon asked. "You said he'd do almost anything to get what he wants."

"Clay?" Emil asked, surprised by the question, but he shook his head. "No, no. He's many things, but a murderer? No."

Elizabeth joined them at the car and Simon opened the door for her.

"What's the point of getting permission now?" Navarro asked. "If we don't have the bowl, we don't have a map."

Elizabeth paused before getting into the car and turned to Navarro. "What does sesta-fighta mean?"

He looked confused at the non sequitur and repeated what she said aloud, finally realizing what she meant. "Sexta-fiera. It means Friday."

"I don't understand. What does that mean?" Emil asked.

Elizabeth glanced back over her shoulder. "I hope it means that we still have a chance."

Simon looked at her curiously. "She said it to me, the woman, before she closed the door. I think she wants to talk but can't right now. Not until Friday, I guess. Maybe her husband will be away."

It was something. Slim, but something.

Simon glanced back at the door and hoped it would be enough.

Chapter Seven

I T TOOK THE REST of the day for Emil to recover from the shock of seeing Gaspar. It appeared to be his first dead body. Sadly, it was not Simon's nor Elizabeth's.

They anonymously reported the incident to the police, but left out any details of their involvement or of the missing bowl. Simon had no doubt the police would do little about it other than write a soon-to-be-forgotten report. Sadly, another death in a favela was probably not high on the police's priority list.

If Emil had been struck by their calm in the situation, his own shock muddied the entire experience for him and, thankfully, he didn't ask any questions. Unfortunately, Emil and Navarro knew very little of Gaspar's life in Rio and could offer no tangible leads. All they had now was the hope that the woman next door would be able to provide them with a lead to follow in two days and hope that the trail wouldn't be impossibly cold by then.

In the meantime, there was still work to be done to prepare for the expedition, should it ever happen. There was a chance, too, that a recently discovered manuscript might contain a few clues to help them, should they be unable to find the map. The following morning they arrived at the Biblioteca Nacional.

The National Library was housed in a magnificent old building about a half an hour from the hotel up the coast. It was immense and grand enough to rival any of the great libraries in the States.

Raul stayed behind to see if he could learn anything more about what happened to Gaspar without the entire retinue along. In his place, Vega decided to accompany them.

A small man with round spectacles waited for them at the base of the stairs of the main entrance hall.

"Tiago!" Emil cried and the two men exchanged a heartfelt handshake. "It has been too long."

"Good to see you, my friend."

Quick introductions were made and then Mr. Tiago Da Silva escorted them to a private room upstairs.

"I had a gift for you, Tiago," Emil said, as they climbed the grand double staircase. "Maps of the Colorado territory, but I am afraid they were stolen en route."

Da Silva shook his head. "So many thefts. The museum lost the Chancay pre-Columbian ceramic figure I told you about not two weeks ago."

"The one with the little hands?" Emil asked, mimicking what Simon assumed was the figure's pose.

"Yes," Da Silva said sadly. "There are thieves everywhere."

He had no idea how true that was.

Da Silva led them into a private reading room where delicate and rare manuscripts could be viewed.

"I still can't believe you found it," Emil said, staring at the large leather folder as Da Silva dismissed the guard.

"In the basement of all places!" Da Silva moved the large folder that housed the manuscript labeled 512-A to the center of the table.

"I imagine the world's greatest treasures are actually sitting right beneath us if we only had time to go through it all."

"You found this in the basement?" Vega asked, moving to the other side of the table for a better view of the papers.

"It was mislabeled. The original piece, Manuscript 512, was purportedly written in 1743 by a Portuguese expedition into the interior. As I understand it, it was what set Colonel Fawcett off on his little adventure."

"If that's little, I'd hate to find out what you think qualifies as big," Elizabeth quipped.

Da Silva laughed. "Yes, well. The manuscript was found by bandits, as the legend goes, and eventually made its way to the library. Somewhere along the line parts of it must have been separated."

"Hence Manuscript 512-A," Vega observed noting the label on the leather folder.

"Precisely. As near as I can discern, this is the second half of 512 and, if I may be so bold, even more extraordinary. I knew of Emil's theories and called him as soon as I found it. It is well beyond my areas of expertise."

He began to open the folder but paused. "No one else has seen this yet."

"I am in your debt, Tiago."

The little man dipped his head in acknowledgment. "I shall leave you to it then. I hope to hear of all your magnificent discoveries from it soon."

"Thank you."

Da Silva laid open the folder and left them to study it.

"Remarkable," Emil whispered as he scanned the first page.

The manuscript was yellowed with age and tattered and torn, and some parts of the page had been eaten by worms, but much of the text and the drawings were still legible. Or would have been if Simon could read Portuguese.

"What does it say?"

Emil put on a pair of white gloves. "It's talking about a group that left the main expedition and traveled further east. They, too, found furnas, caverns in the ground, covered by flagstones. Manuscript 512 detailed such things. Great holes in the ground, so deep, they could not plumb the bottom with their ropes. In addition to descriptions of grand plazas of a long-abandoned civilization."

He turned the page to reveal a series of drawings. There were totems with inscriptions carved into them and great doorways over which more symbols were carved.

"Do you have any idea what those mean?" Elizabeth asked.

"I'm not certain. They're curious," Emil said. "Some of them seem to be Malian."

"Malian?" Simon asked in surprise. "As in Mali? Africa?"

"Yes, and these," Emil continued pointing to a series of glyphs, "These appear to be from Vai, West African, as well."

"They're not dissimilar to some I have seen from Ceylon," Vega added.

"Precisely. And even the Cherokee in North America."

It all seemed impossible. An ancient language with fragments in Africa, North America, and Sri Lanka? How was it possible for one language to seed so many around the globe in a time before sailing ships could traverse the seas?

Emil turned the page and nearly gasped out loud.

"What is it?" Elizabeth asked.

Simon might not have been able to read Vai syllabary, but he recognized several of the symbols on the page.

"These are runes. Germanic runes," Simon said, in awe of what he was seeing. "Impossible."

"And yet ..." Emil said, gesturing toward the page.

The symbols were unmistakably runes. They were predominately a series of staves, almost like arrows with various pieces of the fletching missing.

"Can you read it?" Elizabeth asked Simon. He was familiar with the language but was hardly proficient.

"Only the unblemished may pass," Vega read softly.

"You can read Germanic runes?" Simon asked in surprise.

"Bit of a hobby," he replied distractedly as he continued to scan the document.

"I told you. Renaissance man," Emil added.

"What does unblemished mean?" Elizabeth asked. "No pimples allowed?"

Vega kept his eyes down but laughed. "Not quite. It could mean only the pure or the worthy."

He and Emil exchanged excited glances and then he read on. "He who is . . .worthy, will become Master."

Elizabeth leaned in so far to get a better look she brushed against Vega. "Sorry. So what does the lucky winner get if he passes Master muster?"

Emil turned the page and Simon's heart stuttered in his chest. "This."

A detailed drawing of a staff filled the page. It wasn't overly ornate. It was long and rough as if made from twisted vines. At the top of the staff, the hardened vines rose up like fingers to make the headpiece and within them sat a stone about the size of his palm carved into the crude shape of an eye with little shards of light emanating from it.

"It's true," Emil whispered.

Simon recovered himself. "What is?" he asked.

"I'd read legends of such a thing but didn't dare believe. It is the Staff of Life." He clasped Vega's arm in shared victory.

Simon and Elizabeth exchanged looks of both relief and concern. That answered one of Simon's questions, anyway. The professor was aware of the staff's existence.

The staff seemed to be embedded within the stone. "It looks a little like Excalibur, doesn't it? All sword-in-the-stone-y?"

She was right. It did.

"It's possible this is a version of the Arthurian legend," Simon suggested. "After all, that particular myth, the legend of worthiness, transcends any one culture. Odysseus, the quest for the Holy Grail. Demonstrations of worthiness are commonplace."

"Same song, different verse?"

"Precisely."

"What does this say?" Elizabeth asked, pointing to a series of runes and glyphs hewn into what looked like a pedestal upon which the staff rested.

"This part reiterates the need for purity or worthiness and those who will be tested. The rest? I am unsure. It is a mixture of runes and glyphs and symbols. This is staff and this is life, but this ..."

"Is 'death'," Emil supplied sending a chill through the room.

"So is it the Staff of Life or Death?" Elizabeth asked.

"Both it would seem."

"That's vague."

"Perhaps and perhaps not," Emil said. "The staff is rumored to have great power—the power to both give life and take life. It is powered," he read on, "by the energy or elixir of the source of life itself."

Simon's stomach dropped at the description. He knew something else that went by that name.

"And the eye-thing?" Elizabeth asked. "The stone?"

Emil reached out a trembling finger to hover above the stone set into the headpiece of the staff. "It's a gemstone. Its purpose isn't known; it could merely be decorative. However, legend says that it is the heart of the staff. That it can see into the soul." He seemed suddenly far away and then came back to himself. "The symbol of the eye is common to many cultures."

He sounded distracted and Simon could hardly blame him. He'd found evidence of something he'd spent years searching for; his mind must be racing with possibilities. But that wasn't what distracted Simon. It was the large symbol on the base of the pedestal—an ancient and all-too-familiar depiction of the sun—that chilled him to his core. It was not just any sun, but one Simon had seen before and hoped never to see again.

"And this?" he asked, prompting the others to confirm his fears, although he had doubts they would know about the truth of the symbol in 1936.

"Hmm," Emil said, his lips pursed as he studied it. "I'm not certain."

Vega stared down at the paper, lost in thought.

"Mr. Vega?" Simon prompted. "Do you know what this is?"

"Some representation of the sun, clearly, but beyond that, I'm not familiar with it."

Either they didn't know or weren't saying, but Simon knew. It was the *Schwarze Sonne* or Black Sun. He'd seen it himself on the side of a castle in Germany owned by Heinrich Himmler himself, commander of the SS and one of the most powerful men in Nazi Germany.

Once they were back in their hotel room, Elizabeth took off her shoes and sighed with relief. They were cute as heck—little two-tone t-straps—but they pinched. And they weren't the only thing. Simon looked a little pinched himself. She must have missed something.

She set them aside and sat down on the sofa in the living area of their suite to briefly massage her aching feet. "I thought today went pretty well."

"If you can call Nazis going pretty well."

"Wait. What?"

She'd definitely missed something.

Simon paced across the room, shaking his head. "I should have known. 1936. Of course they'd be involved. They're involved in bloody everything."

It was an understatement, but Nazis were never good. "Involved how?"

Simon heaved a heavy sigh and turned back to her. "What do you know about vril?"

"Let's see. Vril, vril . . .yeah, I got nothin'."

He managed a small smile, but she could see that he was truly worried, and when Simon was this worried, there was usually something to worry about.

"I suppose I should start at the beginning."

"That might be best," she said, tucking her feet beneath her.

"Have you ever heard of Edward Bulwer-Lytton?"

"I get the feeling I'm gonna fail this pop quiz."

Simon chuckled and sat down next to her on the sofa. He held out his hands in a silent offer. Elizabeth untucked her feet and laid them in his lap. He gently began to massage one with his large, warm hands while he spoke. It was heaven. "He's most famous for, 'It was a dark and stormy night.'"

"I thought that was Snoopy."

He laughed and pressed on. "He was quite popular in the mid-1800s. None of his works really stood the test of time save one, and for a very troubling reason. Like so many other authors of the period, he grew interested in the occult and the birth of the

96

science fiction genre. He wrote a book called, *Vril: The Power of the Coming Race.*"

The "coming race" paired with any mention of Nazis set off alarm bells. "I don't like where this is going."

"In it a man discovers a subterranean alien race. Their advanced society is powered by an 'all-permeating fluid' that gives them the power to create and destroy. He called this substance vril."

That sounded familiar, Elizabeth thought. "Emil said that the staff was powered by 'the energy or elixir of the source of life itself.'"

"Yes. Vril was thought to be nothing more than a fiction created by Bulwer-Lytton. However, some occultists of the time took it literally, including our old friend Helen Blavatsky."

Elizabeth shuddered. She had no good memories associated with the theosophist, considering one of her students had turned out to be Catherine Vale.

Simon squeezed her foot gently in solidarity. "I know."

He didn't need to say more. They both remembered how close they'd come to losing each other, thanks to that woman.

"Don't tell me she's going to show up again."

"No," he said. "God, I hope not. Regardless, the legend of vril's existence and the story's representation of the Hollow Earth theory inspired others who are far worse."

"Worse than Catherine Vale?" That didn't seem likely.

"Nazis."

Okay, worse.

"The occultists in the party latched onto the idea of vril and this supposed superior society and believed it was evidence that the Aryan race was descended from these people or ones like them. Chief among the believers was Heinrich Himmler himself."

Okay, a lot worse.

She knew Himmler was an occultist and had even formed a division of the SS called the Ahnenerbe to promote the racial ideology of the party. It was the inspiration for the Nazis in *Raiders of the Lost Ark*. Now, she was going to meet a few of them herself. But the idea that all of this came from a book?

"That's a bit of stretch, isn't it? Basing it all on a story? A piece of fiction?"

"Mythology and fiction have always intertwined with fact. Sometimes it's difficult to discern where one ends and the other begins, and what inspired what. Most believed, of course, that the idea of a subterranean super race was pure science fiction. But to those searching for proof of their 'ancestry' it was considered a written legend based on historical fact."

"But it wasn't," she countered. "It was just a story. Written not that long ago, all things considered. It's not some ancient manuscript."

As soon as she said it, she realized the problem. Manuscript 512-A wasn't ancient, but it was several hundred years old. "The manuscript we saw today talked about caverns and underground rooms," she said.

"Yes."

"And the elixir of life. Vril?"

"Possibly. Even if it is not as powerful as you fear, you can only imagine how the Nazis will twist it to further their narrative."

"And if it *is* as powerful?" she asked, already knowing the answer. The prospects were truly horrifying.

He'd stopped massaging her feet now and just held them in his hands.

"There's more, though, isn't there?" she asked. "I mean it could just be some other legend of the elixir of life. Even I know that's an oldie but a goodie in mythology. China, India, Japan. Harry Potter."

Simon's eyebrows rose in surprise.

"What? I pay attention sometimes."

"Yes, it is somewhat commonplace, as you say, but there was something else that gave me pause. And it could add insurmountable fuel to the Nazi's fire. The emblem on the base of the pedestal in the drawing of the staff. It's called the Black Sun and is made of twelve radial sig runes circling a central disc."

"Sig?" She didn't know many runes, but that one she knew, unfortunately. The SS emblem was a double sig rune. She'd seen enough of them to last a lifetime. "That's not good."

"No," he agreed. "If this lost city and the staff are somehow related to these Nazi legends, all hell is going to break lose when we find it."

She noted but didn't comment on the fact that he said when and not if.

"So you think the Nazis are going to be going after it as well."

"It stands to reason."

Elizabeth lifted her feet from Simon's lap. "I hate Nazis."

They'd had their share of fighting them and it was always terrifying. There was somehow something so much worse about a human who could do such horrible things than any creature.

"Welcome to the club."

She scooted closer and leaned against his shoulder. He lifted his arm and pulled her to his side.

"Do you think they're already here?"

"I wouldn't be surprised."

Suddenly, she sat up. "I think I saw one. Maybe. I'm not sure."

Simon patiently waited for her to make sense, as he always did, knowing it would come eventually.

"I think I might have actually met one."

Simon pulled away. "What?"

"Not really met, but ran into." She envisioned the cold, hard look in the man's pale blue eyes. "Remember that man I pointed out in the lobby yesterday?"

"Rasche?" Simon recalled.

"I know I'm judging a book by its cover and all, and I might be wrong, but if I were Central Casting, he'd be playing Lurking Nazi in the Lobby in my next film."

Simon grunted in thought. "That is troubling."

"I'll say. Hey, I wonder if old Stoneface is one, too?"

"Possibly," Simon allowed, visibly growing more concerned by the moment.

"Or maybe we're wrong on both. I mean, we don't know that they're Nazis. We don't want to start seeing Nazis hiding behind every bush."

"No, but after what we saw today at the library, we'd be fools to ignore the possibility."

"And we're no fools," she said, causing him to smile slightly in spite of his worry.

"No." He eased her back against his side.

"Do you think they even know about the expedition?"

"We know. That boor Bridges knows. I'd venture to say yes. Besides, the Ahnenerbe was formed for precisely this sort of thing. I think it's safe to assume that they will be searching for the staff, if they aren't already. We need to be very careful, Elizabeth. Not in just what we do but what we say."

"Trust no one!" she said, lifting a finger into the air dramatically and feeling his chest rumble beneath her cheek with a laugh.

He grasped her hand. "Almost no one." He kissed her wrist.

She snuggled back into his side and tried not to worry, but it was easier said than done.

ALEX VEGA PACED BACK and forth across the floor of his hotel suite. He could hardly believe it. He'd been right! He knew there was a connection. Finally, he would be vindicated.

He scrubbed a hand over his mouth in barely restrained elation as he paused by the window, almost unable to stop from smiling. Years of work, years of being shunted aside would be over. He would be hailed a hero.

He let out a short laugh. His father would finally have to acknowledge him again. He would have no choice. Oh, and how rich that moment would be.

He walked over to the table where he'd placed the bottle of scotch he'd ordered from room service the other night and poured himself a celebratory glass.

He raised it in salute to himself and drank down the liquor in one go.

A knock on the door interrupted him as he began to pour another.

He fully expected to see Professor Mendoza, wanting to talk over all they'd learned at the library, so he was brought up short by the man who stood at the threshold.

His joy of a moment earlier evaporated. "What are you doing here?" he asked.

Erik Rasche raised one of his pale blonde eyebrows with such sharpness, Vega was sure he'd practiced in the mirror. "Aren't you going to invite me in?"

Having little choice, Vega stepped aside to let him into his suite. "What if you were seen?" Vega asked as he checked to make sure the hallway was empty.

"No one saw," Rasche said in that condescending way he had. "No one knows who I am."

"They know who I am," Vega insisted. "Your being here puts everything at risk."

"That is exactly what I told the Reichsführer about you, Herr Dietrich, or should I say Vega, hmm?"

Vega was fuming, but he would burn in hell before he'd let Rasche see it. "I am sure you did." Rasche's disapproval of his appointment to the mission was no secret. After all, he'd actively campaigned against him, making no bones about his personal distaste for Vega.

"Vega?" Rasche mused aloud. "How you can answer to such a name, I do not know."

He'd become used to it. After all, he'd been undercover for nearly two years.

Rasche walked to the table where the bottle and glass sat. "Drinking already, I see?"

He would not rise to the bait. "What do you want?"

Rasche picked up the glass, appearing so calculatedly casual it would have been funny if it wasn't so infuriating. "To make sure the mission is a success."

"Then we want the same thing."

Rasche couldn't keep the smirk from coming to his face; it was practically grafted there. "We shall see."

"What's that supposed to mean?"

Rasche sniffed the glass and wrinkled his nose. "I will not mince words," he said, putting down the glass.

"When have you ever?"

"I do not believe you are capable of completing the mission Herr Himmler has given you."

"And there are others who feel this way?" Vega asked, knowing the answer.

Rasche lifted his bony shoulders in a diffident shrug. "I would not be here otherwise."

"I am as committed to the cause as any," Vega vowed. "More so."

"Impossible."

Vega clenched his jaw and tried to resist enjoining the same argument he'd had all of his life.

"Do not feel badly," Rasche said with mock sympathy. "You cannot help your dirty blood."

Vega's hands flexed at his side at the provocation; he quickly loosened them but not before Rasche noticed, his persistent smirk growing.

"You see? You are incapable of controlling yourself. You are a liability."

Vega had been antagonized in the same manner since he was a boy. He'd grown proficient at hiding his reaction to it, but Rasche knew just what buttons to push.

Vega was also aware of his opponent's weakness, however. "Then why is it the Reichsführer sent me and not you?"

Rasche's expression remained unchanged except for a slight narrowing of his eyes. He'd hit his mark.

Vega walked over to pour himself another drink, knowing it would bother Rasche. "That's right," he mused aloud. "It is because you don't have any idea what we're searching for or how to find it. You lack the expertise. *Any* expertise as far as I can tell."

He drank his scotch, enjoying it and Rasche's impotent anger.

"Perhaps," Rasche said, taking a step closer. He was considerably taller, but size had never bothered Vega. He'd cut down much bigger men. "But I will always enjoy the party's favor and you will not."

It was true. But if he returned with the staff and the gold, then the tables would turn. Rasche, his father, Himmler, perhaps even the Führer himself, all of them would respect him, perhaps even fear him if his suspicions about the staff were true.

Rasche leaned in a little. "But that's what comes of having a gypsy whore for a mother."

Vega chuckled. He'd not let such schoolyard taunts bother him since he was a small boy when he'd been put through hell for it and he had the scars to prove it. But scar tissue was stronger than normal flesh, taut and unfeeling. He'd learned to use them. He'd needed to.

His mother was a Spanish gypsy who his father had married in a moment of weakness that he quickly overcame. Their son, the shameful reminder of his lapse, was promptly sent away to boarding school. All the best schools, though, of course.

The taunts and jeers there meant to break him only made him stronger, showed him who he really was. He was destined to transcend the stain she'd left upon him. This, this mission, was his chance to finally take his place in the party and by his father's side.

For now, he knew he had to tolerate Rasche's presence. He was well-seated within the Reich and, for reasons he didn't understand, a favorite of Herr Himmler's. He would humor him such as he could and avoid him as much as possible. Rasche was a blunt instrument in a delicate operation.

Rasche moved around the room, inspecting it coolly. "What progress have you made, or have you wasted the Reichsführer's time as well as his trust?"

Vega briefly sketched out what he'd discovered, knowing it would be relayed back to Germany.

"That is quite promising. You are sure of what you've seen?"

"I am."

Rasche walked over to the window and eased back the curtain sheers. "And the couple? The Crosses. Why have you not eliminated them? At worst, they are American or British spies and at best an unnecessary nuisance."

"Emil trusts them."

"Oh, Emil does, does he?" Rasche said, derision dripping from each syllable.

Vega was not dissuaded. "Yes. And we can't afford to upset him. Not yet. Not when we're so close. We need him. And I think the Crosses might be helpful in other ways."

A leering grin tugged at Rasche's lips. "She is very beautiful."

"Not like that," Vega said. Leave it to Rasche to find the crudest of reasons. Elizabeth was attractive; there was no denying that. He was, after all, a man. She did appeal to him, although he would never admit as much to Rasche or anyone. But his reason for wanting to keep her near was something else entirely. Call it intuition or instinct, but he had a feeling she would be necessary to the mission's success. How, he was not quite sure.

Rasche waited for further explanation, but Vega had no intention of offering one that would be merely ridiculed.

"Leave it to me."

Rasche stared at him with the cold eyes he'd hewn over decades of a soulless life. "For now."

He walked toward the doorway and stopped as he put his hand on the doorknob. "Remember, though. I will be watching and waiting."

"For me to fail, no doubt?"

Rasche answered only with a grin.

Vega walked over to him and stood a little too closely. "Just stay out of my way."

Rasche snorted and pulled open the door. "With pleasure."

Once he was gone, Vega strode over to the scotch and started to pour another, but stopped himself. He would not let Rasche antagonize and manipulate him. He was better than that. And there was far too much work left to do.

CHAPTER EIGHT

"Do you think there'll be music?" Elizabeth asked.

"I would imagine so." Vega and Emil had invited them to join them that evening at Cassino da Urca, a fashionable nightclub and casino on the bay. Vega learned that Minister Correia would be in attendance tonight and thought meeting with him outside of the office might afford a more affable atmosphere in which to convince him to sign off on their permit. Simon had his doubts, but a night out might do them all good.

He rapped sharply on Emil's door.

Next to him, Elizabeth wriggled slightly in anticipation. "I feel the need to dance."

Once their work had ended, one way or the other, he was more than happy to oblige.

A few moments later the door opened, but it was Navarro and not Emil who stood there. His eyes flicked to Simon's then landed firmly on Elizabeth. He could hardly blame him. She was stunning. Her dress was floor-length violet silk satin and what she described as "slinky." The halter top revealed the creamy skin of her shoulders and the low-cut back dipped down to her waist. The bias cut material clung to her figure in all the right places, although he was disconcerted that the design meant she had to forgo wearing a brassiere. It wasn't that the dress was indecent or that her "going commando," as she put it, was salacious in any way. It was just that *he* knew, and he found that knowledge . . .distracting.

It was the sort of dress that made heads turn, and turn they did. Navarro's practically snapped off his neck.

"Hello," he said, staring at her like an idiot.

"Hi," she said, then added after he did not move, "Is Emil here?"

"Yes, sorry." He stepped aside and let them enter. Simon put his hand on the small of her bare back to guide her in ahead of him.

"You look . . .beautiful," Navarro said, as if knowing the word was inadequate. Upon that Simon agreed.

"Thank you. Are you coming with us?"

His face fell with disappointment. "No, I am afraid not."

"Pity," Simon said, earning a half-snort from Elizabeth.

"I have work to do. If you are successful, there is still much that needs to be organized for the journey."

"Ah, don't you look lovely, my dear," Emil said as he came out of the bedroom struggling with his bow tie.

"Let me." Elizabeth moved toward him and began to fix his slightly askew tie.

"I never could get the hang of these," he said. "Isabel always has to do this for me."

Emil seldom spoke of his wife. He had mentioned her but not in any detail. The dossier said that he was married but not much more.

"That should do it," Elizabeth said, patting his chest once she'd finished.

Emil took hold of her hand and looked at her the same way he had when they'd first met. "Your smile is so much like Aurora, I ..."

Embarrassed, he dipped his head and let go of her hand. "Shall we? Alex will be meeting us there."

Simon drove them out onto the northern side of a small peninsula that marked the entrance to Guanabara Bay. In the shadow of the mountain peak Sugarloaf, they pulled under the vast porte-cochère of Cassino da Urca.

Duesenbergs, Rolls-Royces, and Benzes expelled tuxedo-clad gentlemen. Women wore mink stoles to brave the twenty-foot walk from the car to the cloakroom in the bracing seventy-degree weather.

Simon's rental car was suitable but quickly whisked away to be parked elsewhere. They passed through the entry hall and directly into the main theatre where a floor show was just ending. The room was much larger than he'd imagined and packed with tables, save for the dance floor directly in front of the grand stage. Smoke drifted up toward the high ceiling and a long, narrow semi-circular gallery on the second floor housed additional tables. The settings were as high-end as the crowd, adorned with white linens upon which sat intricate silverware, crystal, and Limoges porcelain. It was as fine as any nightclub he'd ever been to.

"Look," Elizabeth said, drawing his attention to the stage. As the band finished their set, the stage opened up and they were lowered into a pit, parts of the stage floor rotating to cover them as an orchestra on a bandstand rolled out from deep backstage to take over. The unmistakable rhythm of a Samba started.

"I half-expect to see Carmen Miranda walk out," Elizabeth said.

No sooner had she spoken than a voice over the loudspeaker announced just that.

"Holy cow."

She was everything he'd imagined except that she wasn't wearing her iconic fruit hat. The crowd broke out into rousing applause as she began to sing. Showgirls danced out from the wings wearing plumed feathered headdresses. It was Las Vegas before Las Vegas.

Elizabeth stared in wide-eyed wonder. He tried to usher her along.

"But, it's her!" she protested. "Chica chica boom."

"We'll come back to enjoy the show after we find Vega, all right?"

Reluctantly, she agreed and they continued past the bar and into one of the three casinos. They found him lingering off to the side in the main room.

"Is Correia here?" Emil asked, looking around.

Vega's gaze shifted toward a crowded craps table. "He is busy at the moment."

"Which one is he?" Elizabeth asked.

"Dark hair, next to the shooter."

He was a handsome man in his late thirties with jet-black hair and a dark complexion. He put his arm around the woman next to him, a rather vivacious-looking brunette crammed into a too-small dress, and pulled her close after he placed his bet. She kissed his cheek leaving a smudge of her fire-engine red lipstick behind.

"Is that his wife?" Simon asked.

"No," Vega replied. "He apparently doesn't bring her to places like this."

The woman giggled and took a handkerchief out from her ample and apparent bosom to wipe the lipstick away.

"I can see why."

"Yes," Vega said, sounding as if he disapproved. "I've been waiting for him to lose and walk away, but his luck has not yet run out."

"Is that Nuno Almeida over there?" Emil said, his attention drawn to another part of the casino. "He's the foremost expert on Olmec iconography. I'd love to ask him a few questions."

"I will wait for the minister," Vega offered.

"You don't mind? Cross, maybe you should come, too. I'd love for you to meet him. Saville's and his continuity theories on the jaguar votive axes as the key to nearly all pre-Columbian Mesoamerican mythologies are fascinating."

Simon looked toward Elizabeth in question.

"You go," she said. "I'm better with craps than . . .what he said."

He knew her eyes would have glazed over after a few minutes, but he was, admittedly, interested and had a few lingering questions about some of the figures they'd seen in the manuscript. But he hated to leave her alone.

"I'll be fine," she said, anticipating his concern. "I have Alex."

That was not much comfort. While Vega had the good grace not to drool over her the way Navarro had, Simon had noticed him noticing her. However, Elizabeth was certainly capable of taking care of herself and he could not blame the man for admiring a beautiful woman.

"If you're sure?" Simon asked.

"Go. We'll be fine."

"We won't be long."As Simon and Emil wandered off to talk to Mr. Almeida, Elizabeth turned to Alex. "So, what do we do? Just wait?"

"That is what I have done so far."

As she watched the table, an idea came to her. "Tell me. Do you gamble?"

"I have on occasion, but—"

"Good," she said not waiting for the rest, slipping her arm through his as she started toward the craps table.

If she could go on a lucky run, they might soften up the minister a little; if she didn't, they were no worse off than they were now. And she was feeling lucky. They watched politely until the round ended.

"Seven out! Sete fora!" the stickman called, causing a groan of disappointment from the table. "New shooter. Nova atirador."

She'd carefully taken up position near the shooter's right where she knew the task would soon fall to her. The next person in line declined and it was her turn to be the shooter.

"Oh," she said, feigning surprise as the stickman offered her three pairs of dice to choose from. She made her selection and nudged Alex. "Make a bet," she said softly.

He seemed confused but did as instructed, getting chips from the boxman and placing a bet on the Pass line, mimicking Correia.

The minister finally noticed him. "Mr. Vega."

"Minister."

She'd always been a good gambler, far better than her father. Games like craps, though, weren't about skill but luck. Maybe it would be on their side tonight?

Elizabeth shook the dice and then tossed them across the table. She rolled a seven on the come-out eliciting a cheer from the table and earning all pass line betters double their money. Correia was impressed, and from the way his eyes dipped down to her chest, he was impressed with other things as well.

He slid his bet from the Pass line to the Don't Pass line, essentially betting against her ability to make her point.

"Are you sure you want to do that, Minister Corriea?" she asked.

"No one is lucky forever."

"Suit yourself."

She rolled again, setting the point at four. Corriea must have known the odds of hitting her point and rolling another four were slim, and he enjoyed what he hoped would be his victory.

But fate and Elizabeth had a different idea. She hit a four on the next throw.

A dealer picked up Corriea's chips and paid out the winners.

"I did warn you."

He bowed slightly and placed another bet, this time on the Pass line.

Luck was on her side and she rode it as far as she could. She hit point after point until the table was nearly swamped with onlookers. Finally, though, her luck ran out and she sevened out.

"I suppose you're right, Minister, no one is lucky forever."

But she had been very lucky and those that backed the shooter had made off like bandits, including the minister. Alex, a little shell-shocked from the experience, gathered his chips as the dice were passed on to the next shooter.

The minister took the opportunity to take his substantial winnings as well. Now that he was happy and a little wealthier, it seemed the perfect opportunity to address the issue of the permit.

"Minister Corriea," Alex called, getting his attention.

"You should have brought your wife along the first time you came to see me, Vega."

"She is not my wife."

Corriea's smile grew. "She isn't? Then you *definitely* should have brought her along."

His meaning was lost on no one.

Vega cleared his throat. "You misunderstand."

"She is not your latest offer?" the minister asked, having apparently checked his decency as well as his coat at the door.

"No," Vega said, firmly. "And I think—"

Alex was clearly about to defend her honor when Elizabeth stepped in now that her plan had gone belly up.

"It's all right. I think the minister and I understand each other," Elizabeth said, trying to smooth things over before Vega said something they'd all regret.

Corriea leered at her. "Not so well as I would like."

She squeezed Alex's arm to stop him from responding. She could live with a little lewd innuendo; they needed the minister on their side. She'd dealt with men like him before and they did not handle outright rejection well. Better to ease out of it gently.

"I'm afraid my husband might not like that."

"Husband? Pity."

"We would like to talk to you about the permission for our expedition, though."

His eyes widened. "Your expedition? A woman? You must be joking."

"No, if you'd just give us a few minutes of your time—"

One his toadies appeared and whispered in his ear and his attention was instantly elsewhere. "Perhaps another time. Come by the office, and do bring your husband, won't you? I'm sure it'll be most amusing."

"Please, Minister Correia—" Alex began, but he was already walking away.

"Well, that was a bust," Elizabeth said.

"I am sorry."

"So am I."

"He is a boor and a profligate."

"And kind of a jerk," Elizabeth added causing Alex to laugh and easing some of the tension. "I really thought that might work. And now I think I might have made things worse."

"It is a game to him. I am afraid it is one we will have to keep playing for now."

"Keep rolling the dice. Metaphorically speaking, of course," she said, earning another smile. "I suppose we should go find Simon and Emil and give them the bad news."

She and Alex searched, but because the casino was so large and crowded, they ultimately decided to split up to cover more ground, agreeing to meet in the entry hall in half an hour.

Elizabeth wove her way through the crowd wishing, not for the first time, that she was taller. Even with her heels, she was barely scraping five foot seven. She thought she saw him off to her right and started to pivot when she nearly crashed into someone.

"I'm sorry," she said, reflexively, until she looked up and saw who it was. Rasche.

An ember of life tried to spark and then died in his cold smile. "Ve must stop meeting like this."

And how. If she had any doubts about his nationality before, she had none now. He was definitely German.

She smiled and tried to escape as quickly as she could. She looked back and saw him turn to another man.

"Strasser?" he said. The man turned around at the sound of his name, and Elizabeth felt her face flush as she saw who it was—Stoneface.

Both he and Rasche looked at her, their smiles oddly knowing and very unnerving. She felt an instinctive rush of fear down to her toes. She hastened away as quickly as she could without looking like it.

She stepped outside and onto the large balcony that overlooked the bay. Several people stood along the low balustrade enjoying the magnificent view. She breathed in the cooling night air to sooth her jangled nerves. It was clear the two men knew each other and it seemed they recognized her. That was not good. So very not good.

Everything about those two men made her stomach sour. And she'd manage to make a mess of Alex's negotiations with Correia. All in all, not the best night.

She looked out at the view of Guanabara Bay and tried to calm down. Taking a deep breath, she stared out at the smooth water, the lights of boats passing by and the glow of homes along the shore. In the distance, she could just make out the outline of Christ the Redeemer standing high on a mountain top. It was beautiful and soothing.

She was just calming down when a hand touched her shoulder. She spun around with a gasp, nearly falling backward over the low balustrade.

Simon gripped her arms to keep her upright. "Elizabeth?"

"Oh, am I glad to see you."

"What's wrong?"

"Everything."

ELIZABETH FELT MARGINALLY BETTER about things the following morning. A generous helping of Eggs Benedict always did wonders for her mood. Alex assured her that she didn't sabotage his progress with Correia, as there was little already made. He still believed he could convince the minister to allow the expedition, but it would take time. Simon was outwardly calm about her revelations about Rasche and his friend Strasser, but she knew he was as worried as she was. Having Nazis in the mix was always trouble.

By 1936, Hitler's true power was just becoming known. In the three years he'd been Chancellor, he'd already broken the Treaty of Versailles, passed anti-Semitic legislation, and begun the expansion of Germany by re-occupying the Rhineland. It would be several more years before the world would see what was truly in store for them, but the seeds had been planted and the rotten fruit was already beginning to grow. The world was on the precipice, although most didn't know it yet. It was one of the benefits and burdens of being a time traveler, knowing what was coming. And, in this case, knowing what losing the staff to the Nazis would mean.

Emil, unaware of the devils in their midst, was happily occupied by thoughts of the expedition. "I thought we might revisit the library this morning. Take another look at 512-A. I'll admit it was a bit overwhelming. There are certain aspects I'd like to review."

"I agree," Simon said. "It's quite possible there are things we overlooked. Or some connection with 512 you haven't made yet. No offense."

"None taken. You're quite right. My eyes are open but perhaps I have not seen."

Simon took a sip of tea. "Do you think it's possible that there's more to it than what we see? Some hidden text?"

"Like the Codex Zacynthius?"

"Possibly."

Elizabeth was already lost. "What's that?"

"It was a palimpsest where the original text had been washed off or erased and new writing put in its place," Simon explained. "But I didn't really mean that so much. I meant in the pictograms and in the symbols and glyphs. Perhaps their placement has as much meaning as the symbols themselves."

Emil brightened visibly at the idea. "Yes."

"Maybe there's some valuable information about the location of the city we missed. Or the staff."

"Oh, that's intriguing. We should go as soon as possible," Emil said, gesturing for the check.

Simon, too, seemed enamored with the idea. "Perhaps we should examine Manuscript 512, as well, if that's possible. There might be some connection between them that we've overlooked."

"Yes. Wonderful idea. Just wonderful."

Emil signed the check charging the meal to his room and stood. "The sooner we start the better."

"Elizabeth?" Simon prompted. "Are you ready?"

"Let me freshen up. Give me two minutes." She held out her hand for the room key, which Simon handed her.

"I wonder if the pedestal is a key somehow," Emil mused.

"Possible. Or the archways or pillars outside."

"Oh, that's intriguing, yes."

Elizabeth left them to it, knowing they'd still be at it when she came back. She wasn't as knowledgeable as they were about glyphs and iconography and the rest of it, but she did love a good puzzle. And sometimes having an outsider's view of things helped.

The elevator deposited her on their floor and she made her way down the hall, glad she'd have a chance to freshen up before they left. She'd never mastered the art of eating without destroying her lipstick.

She put the key into the lock and stepped inside, digging around in her bag for her lipstick when she stopped in her tracks. The cushions for the sofa were on the floor, the console cabinet doors open, and even the door to the patio was open. The room had been ransacked.

As much as she wanted to investigate, she knew discretion was the better part of valor having been through this before and turned to leave and get Simon. But she had barely started to turn back when she was shoved hard from behind. The force and surprise of it sent her stumbling across the room, tripping until she crashed into the coffee table, falling on top of it, then rolling off onto the floor in an unceremonious pile. She got ready to defend herself against another blow, but none came. Cautiously, she sat up, just in time to see the door swinging closed.

117

She got up and hurried to the door to look out into the hall, but whoever had been in the room was nowhere to be seen. She stepped back inside and glared at the offending door. He must have been hiding behind it when she came in.

It wasn't until then, until the initial rush of adrenaline started to wane that she felt the numbing pain in her elbow and her head. She must have hit them on the coffee table when she pirouetted across the room. She rubbed her elbow a few times and the strange feeling started to abate.

The shove had scattered the contents of her purse across the floor. Her favorite lipstick had been crushed into the carpet beneath her own big, clumsy feet.

"Nuts."

"You could have been killed," Simon said.

She knew he needed to get it out of his system and so she let him pace and worry. He was quite gifted at both.

"But I wasn't."

He gave her a sour look and resumed his pacing. "What the hell were they looking for?"

"I don't know." Her head had begun to throb a little, although she wasn't sure if it was from bopping it on the coffee table or watching Simon wear a hole in the carpet.

"I should have come with you."

"And help me put on lipstick?" she said as she rubbed the small knot on the back of her head and winced.

Simon immediately put his pace on pause and tuned his impressive fierceness upon her.

"What's wrong? You *were* hurt," he accused her.

"It's nothing." It really wasn't even worth mentioning, hence the not mentioning. "I hit my funny bone."

"Last I checked that was in your elbow and not in your head."

"I have two?"

He heaved a deep sigh. "Elizabeth."

"I'm fine."

He didn't quite believe her and came to sit next to her to reassure himself. Again.

"Did you lose consciousness?" he asked, tilting her head so he could look into her eyes.

"I only misplaced it," she said, trying to leaven the mood. Judging from the look on his face, he didn't think her joke was all that funny, though. She laid a placating hand on his knee. "Really, Simon, I'm all right. I wasn't knocked out; it's just a small bump."

He probed it gently, earning another wince and renewing the lease on his worry.

She touched his cheek. "I'm all right."

The emotion was thick in his eyes as he covered her hand with his and moved her palm to his lips before kissing it.

"I'm not going to win any medals for grace, though," she said. "Should have seen me do a half-gainer off of the coffee table. The judge from Finland was not impressed."

That managed to tug a smile from the corner of his mouth. "You were lucky."

On that she had to agree. Resisting the urge to rub her elbow, which still felt a little tingly, she looked around the room. It was a fairly sloppy job. She had, sadly, some experience with having her room tossed and this felt amateurish. They hadn't even torn open the cushions, which everyone knew was Quality Room Searching 101.

She was about to comment on that to Simon when there was a knock on the door.

"That had better be the manager," Simon said, and Elizabeth felt a pang for whoever it was. Simon's anger and frustration would find an outlet eventually.

But it wasn't the manager, it was Emil. After her close call, she'd telephoned down to the front desk and had them send Simon and Emil up. Emil had immediately gone to find the manager for them.

"Where's the manager?" Simon asked, looking behind Emil as if he was somehow hiding him.

"He'll be here soon," Emil said, but he seemed distracted.

"I can't imagine what they were looking for," Elizabeth wondered aloud.

"I am afraid I can," he said.

Simon's expression grew hard. "What do you mean?"

Emil worried the fleshy part of his left hand with the thumb and forefinger of his right. "On my way to find the manager I thought it wise to check my own room. It, too, had been searched in a . . .similar fashion, but they did not find what they were looking for."

"How can you be sure?" Simon asked.

"Because what they were searching for is in the hotel safe."

"And just what were they looking for?"

Emil hesitated. "The Eye."

Chapter Nine

"The eye?" Simon echoed. "What do you mean the eye?"

"The Eye of the staff."

"The stone of the headpiece?" Simon asked, trying to make sense of it.

"Yes."

So, the professor was not as forthcoming as they'd thought. What other secrets had he kept? Had they badly misjudged him?

"I don't understand," Simon said, giving him the chance to explain before he squeezed the truth out of him. They were risking enough being here without important information being withheld. Hell, Elizabeth could have been seriously hurt, or worse. His anger and impotence at being unable to stop what might have been still twisted his gut.

"The Eye of the staff came into my possession quite accidentally nearly ten years ago."

"Ten years?" Elizabeth asked.

Emil looked contrite. "Yes. I didn't realize what it was at first, and it didn't even occur to me that having it might put you in any danger. I'm so sorry, my dear."

He came toward her and she took his outstretched hands. "It's all right."

She was far more forgiving than Simon was at the moment.

Emil squeezed her hands and then let them go. "I wasn't even certain of it until yesterday when we saw that sketch. I found the stone quite by accident in a collection of items up for auction—the estate of an amateur antiquarian who had passed. Most of his pieces were only marginally interesting. This one was intriguing, however. I'd only heard rumors about the staff then. Something quite similar to the stone had been described as part of the headpiece, but it seemed so unlikely that I would find it in Mexico City. I bought the stone and started to investigate the legends more carefully. One thing led to another and, well, here we are."

As angry as Simon was for being kept in the dark, he was in no position to force the issue; they were involved solely because of Emil's generosity. They weren't partners. Simon hated having vital information kept from him, but to be honest, if he were in Emil's shoes, he would have been far less forthcoming.

"And you really think it's the Eye, the actual Eye of the staff and not just some other random eyeball?" Elizabeth asked.

"Well, I can't be certain until we find the staff itself, but yes, I think it is. As you can imagine, I've done a tremendous amount of research into it. Most of which was no more than legend or pure fiction."

"Who else knows you have it?"

"Alex, of course, Raul, quite a few others, I'm afraid. Before I realized the import of what I had, I was quite garrulous about it. I was not as circumspect in my research as I would have been otherwise."

That didn't bode well. Clay Bridges, Rasche, and who knew who else could know of its existence.

It was a miracle it hadn't already been stolen, Simon thought. "And you had this with you all along? During our plane trip?"

"No. I mailed it to Raul weeks before."

"Mailed it?" Elizabeth gasped.

"Yes, it seemed strangely safer than carrying it on my person. Considering what happened in Trinidad, I think I was right."

It wasn't unprecedented, Simon knew. Harry Winston's of New York sent the infamous Hope Diamond, worth roughly $350 million dollars, in a nondescript package through the mail. It was outrageous and it worked. And apparently it had for Emil as well. Although this package might end up being worth far more.

"And it's in the hotel safe now?" he asked.

"I wanted to go back to the library to look again at the sketches before I told you about it. I'm sorry."

"It's all right," Simon said, actually meaning it. He understood Emil's reservations all too well. "I probably would have done the same."

"Thank you. I really had no idea my having it would put you in any danger. If I had—"

"Say no more."

"I should have known Clay might try something like this."

"Bridges? You think he's responsible for the break-ins?"

"Yes. He's definitely not above a little breaking and entering. He'd steal the shirt off your back if he thought he could sell it for a profit."

Simon looked forward to having a little chat with him about that. Assuming, of course, he was the guilty party. It could just as easily have been Rasche or Strasser or even someone else, God help them. Elizabeth hadn't gotten a good look, or any look really, at the perpetrator.

"I'll have a talk with Clay, you can be assured," Emil said.

Simon didn't tell him about their other suspects. Emil wasn't the only one withholding information. For a moment, Simon debated telling him what they suspected, but he wasn't even certain himself who Rasche and Strasser were. But keeping secrets would eventually lead to more problems.

Elizabeth looked at him in question, and he knew she was going through the same considerations. He shook his head briefly. For now, they would keep their suspicions about Rasche and Strasser to themselves.

"After I speak with the manager," Simon said, "I think we should ensure that the Eye is safe and, if possible, I think it would be wise for Elizabeth and me to see it before we return it to the vault."

"Of course, of course," Emil agreed.

Simon had a "chat" with the hotel manager who assured him that the lock on their door would be replaced with one far superior and that security throughout the hotel would be increased. Simon didn't harbor any illusions that a new lock would keep someone out should they be determined enough, but it would have to do. Once he settled his business with the manager and head of security, he and Elizabeth went to Emil's room and were greeted at the door by Alex Vega.

KURT DEITRICH HAD BEEN honest, truly honest, so infrequently over the past two years that he felt an odd sort of vulnerability when he actually was. It was as if the act lifted the curtain and anyone looking would see the truth of him behind it.

When going undercover, it was always best to use as much honesty as possible to create a believable persona, but that was not always possible and rarely so for Kurt Deitrich in the guise of Alex Vega. He did not need to manufacture enthusiasm for the quest for the lost city and the Staff of Life; that was genuine enough. But the rest of his pretense, being deferential to a man like Mendoza, tolerating others he would not have otherwise, was a trial. One he would gladly withstand for the cause, but one that tested him nonetheless.

When Emil told him about the break-in into the Crosses' suite, he was . . .angry. He told himself it was because he suspected Rasche was behind it, going against his orders, interfering, and making his mission more complicated. However, there was more to it than that, he was ashamed to admit. That lapse was the second in so many days. He'd felt the same flush of anger at the casino when the minister was so disrespectful to Elizabeth. He had been, however briefly, willing to derail his efforts to court the minister's favor in defense of her honor. It was a shameful failure on his part that he did not quite understand. He was never so easily provoked before. These unwelcome feelings were weaknesses he would have to control.

Putting aside Rasche's potential interference—and that would be dealt with—he should not care one way or other about the Crosses' wellbeing. They were immaterial. They served a purpose only to keep Emil happy and nothing else. They would be discarded at the first opportunity when they became too much of a nuisance. Perhaps this incident would frighten them away. Had Rasche unwittingly done him a favor? It would certainly make his job easier if they were not so attached to the professor nor he to them.

And yet when he opened the door to let the Crosses into Mendoza's suite and he saw her, he felt that same rush of emotion before he was able to control it.

"Emil told me what happened," he said. "You are unharmed?"

It was perfectly within character to be solicitous. They would expect him to be.

"Only my ego was bruised."

He didn't understand and looked to her husband for clarification, but Cross merely shook his head.

"Please, come in." He stepped aside to let them enter.

They joined Emil in the sitting area of his suite where he stood holding a modest-sized cherry wood box. "Ah, there you are. All settled?"

"As much as can be hoped for," Cross said.

"Good, good." Emil waved them closer. "Please, sit."

The men waited for Elizabeth before taking their seats, her husband close to her side on the sofa, and then Emil placed the box on the coffee table between them all. The box appeared commonplace, but what was in it was anything but. Or at least Emil and he hoped so. Their research had been filled with tantalizing promises, none of which were fulfilled until yesterday.

"First," Emil began, "I want to apologize again for not telling you about the Eye earlier. I—"

Impatient, Cross interrupted him. "It's all right. We understand."

"Good. Well, then." Emil opened the box and took out a small bundle wrapped in linen. He unfolded the wrappings to reveal an amber colored gemstone roughly the size of his palm. It was almond-shaped, as in the drawing at the library, and roughly resembled an eye. It wasn't nearly as elaborate in design as the Eye of Horus or Anubis, but there had been remarkable skill in creating it nonetheless. The material was deeply faceted like a diamond and it gave the stone an innate vibrance. Light seemed to catch inside the crystal, making it appear almost alive.

"What's it made of?" Elizabeth asked.

The professor turned it over in his hand. "Citrine. It's a type of quartz not uncommon to Brazil."

"I doubt there are a lot of these lying around, though."

"No."

The Eye was perfectly cut like a precious jewel and the result was compelling. Vega could clearly remember the first time Emil showed it to him. He'd been drawn to it immediately. He knew of the legend of the Eye. It was the soul of the staff and the sole arbiter of who was worthy to remove it from its stone prison. It was alleged that the stone would "recognize" anyone who was pure enough of heart to free the staff and release its power. He could still remember the disappointment that washed over him when he held the stone for the first time and it gave no outward sign of recognizing him or his worthiness.

Of course, why would it? He was many things, but pure of heart was not one of them. He had no illusions about that.

Emil had searched for nearly a decade for any sign that the stone was the Eye, that it might react in some way to someone it deemed worthy. Vega had joined him in the last two years, but to no effect. In the end they were forced to conclude that either it offered no outward sign of its acceptance when apart from the staff or there was no one worthy of it. Vega was inclined to believe the latter. He certainly had not met anyone remotely pure of heart. He was sure no such creature existed on this planet or any other.

"The design is very unusual for the region, is it not?" Cross asked, once again a little too observant and knowledgeable for Vega's tastes.

"Yes," Vega replied as he took the stone from Emil. "The Tupi and Guarani, the two main indigenous tribes of the area have nothing like it. There are dozens of others native peoples, small tribes, but none have any written language or significant iconography that predate colonization."

"Making the sketches depicting the languages we saw in the manuscript all the more unusual," Cross reasoned.

"Precisely. How any of it came to be in the heart of the Brazilian jungle is a mystery."

Vega handed Cross the stone.

"How old do you think it is?"

Emil shook his head. "Impossible to say. Hundreds? Thousands?"

"That's quite a variance," Elizabeth added, moving closer to Cross on the sofa to get a better look at it.

"I'm afraid there's no way to be certain."

"It's really quite beautiful. May I?" Elizabeth asked Emil, who gave his assent. Cross handed her the stone. "I wonder if—"

The rest of what she was about to say died on her lips as the stone began to glow. Small shards of light shot through the facets of the crystalline structure. Vega's breath caught in his throat. Could it possibly be?

Cross tore the stone from his wife's hands and as soon as he did it fell dormant again. He placed it on the table and turned to Elizabeth. "Are you all right? Did it hurt you?" He took hold of her hands to examine them for injuries.

Elizabeth shook her head, stunned but unharmed.

"What the hell was that?" Cross demanded.

"I'd given up hope," Emil said before turning to Vega and sharing a look of barely restrained joy.

"Hope of what?" Cross bit out.

While his anger had taken control of him, Elizabeth seemed oblivious to it and merely stared at the stone in rapt curiosity.

"We, that is, I believed that the Eye was far more than a decorative headpiece," Emil began, the light of discovery bright in his eyes, "that it was the heart of the staff, so to speak."

Cross looked skeptical and still quite angry. Elizabeth had yet to look away from the stone.

"Legend said that the Eye would literally 'see into the soul' of those who possessed it and recognize whoever had the purity of heart to remove the staff from the stone. I searched far and wide for the right person. But no matter how many held it, it showed no signs of recognition."

"Until now."

"Yes, until now," Emil agreed. "Are you certain you're all right, my dear?"

Elizabeth pulled her attention away from the stone. "Yes. I'm fine. Really. But I'm not worthy."

"The Eye seems to have different ideas on the matter."

"You can't be serious. Simon?"

"It's possible," he conceded reluctantly. "I have to admit I've seen things in my life I cannot explain, and you are . . .the most worthy person of any sort I've ever known."

"Worthy of what? I'm just a girl from Texas."

"It's not about where you're from," Emil explained, "but what's in your heart."

"I'm sure it was just static electricity or something," she protested.

Vega could hardly believe it was possible. Could she really be the one?

"Try it again," Vega suggested.

Cross was reticent but he clearly knew they had no choice. Cautiously, he picked it up from the table. It remained inert. "If you feel the slightest discomfort," he cautioned her.

She nodded and he handed her the stone. As soon as she held in her hands the light came again, brighter than before. It lit her face in a golden glow, catching her eyes and her hair. She was magnificent.

"Are you all right?" Cross asked.

"Yeah. I don't really feel anything, just a slight tingle, but nothing bad."

She set the stone down and it fell quiet again. A single touch from her finger was enough to light it from within again. She turned it on and off like a light switch with just the merest touch.

"That is strange," she muttered under her breath.

Strange wasn't the term Vega would use, world-changing was.

"BLOODY HELL." SIMON STRODE across their hotel suite to the drink cart and poured himself a scotch.

"A little early for that, isn't it?" Elizabeth said, trailing behind him and closing the door to their rooms. "It's not even noon."

He glared down at the half-full glass in his hand and knew she was right and knew it wouldn't have helped anyway. He put the glass down and turned back to Elizabeth. "How can you be so calm?"

"I'm the Chosen One?"

He scowled. "That's not funny."

"No, it's not."

Her reply gave him pause. She might have seemed to take the entire absurd incident in stride with her usual élan, but she was worried. And with good reason.

After the revelation of the Eye and its reaction to Elizabeth, he'd begged off, saying they needed time to process everything. The problem now was, he had.

"You do realize that you're now indispensable to the expedition? That, in their eyes, you alone are capable of retrieving the staff?"

"Yeah, I got that part."

"And that anyone else who wants the staff will need you to do it?" She obviously hadn't thought of that. "As if the danger you were already in wasn't bad enough."

"The danger *we're* in."

The danger he faced was irrelevant. "I'm not necessary for the trip."

"The hell you aren't. I'm not going without you."

"Which might be the only thing that keeps me alive."

"Wait a minute, what?" She came over to him. "What do you mean?"

"*You* are required. I am not. To someone like Rasche or possibly even Bridges, I'm merely an inconvenience."

"Well, if anyone thinks I'm going without you, they need to have their heads examined."

"And if they force you?"

"They can't."

He knew, and she knew, that wasn't true, but he appreciated her bravado on his behalf.

"Maybe we're getting ahead of ourselves," she said. "All we know is someone broke in looking for the stone. No one's graduated to kidnapping or murder."

"Yet."

"Except for Gaspar."

"Yes," Simon agreed, "although I don't think any of our current players had a hand in that."

"Yeah, probably not. Hopefully, we'll find out tomorrow when we go see that woman and pray that the trail for his killer and the bowl haven't gone cold."

Simon nodded, but his thoughts began to turn. "Maybe it would be better if it has."

"We need the bowl to find the staff."

"Exactly. Without it, there might be no expedition at all. No one finds the city or that damn staff."

She took hold of his hand, so small in his. "We've been over this."

"Yes, but that was before you were the bloody Chosen One."

"Daddy always said I was special."

"Elizabeth."

She let go of his hand. "Don't you think I'm frightened? I am seriously freaking out."

"You don't seem it."

"Because if I don't keep it together right now, I'm going to dissolve into a giant puddle of self-pitying goo."

Simon stepped forward and took hold of her arms. "You don't have to be strong for me."

"Says the man who wrote the book on it."

He gave her a wan smile. He wanted to be strong for her, to protect her from everything and anything that could harm her, but that was becoming harder and harder to do. It didn't help that he felt less up to the task than usual as well. So far, he hadn't been able to protect her at all. And now, the fate of the world rested upon her slender shoulders. And he could not do a damn bloody thing about it.

She slipped her arms around his waist and rested her head on his chest.

"I hate this," he said, holding her close and wishing he had the power to change what he could not.

She lifted her head. "Maybe the Eye's on the fritz? I like to think I'm a good person, but I'm not anyone special."

He couldn't stop the laugh that rose in his chest. "You are."

"You're biased."

"Perhaps, but I cannot imagine anyone else—Damn it all to Hell!"

He turned away, briefly ignoring her surprise at his outburst. He was too furious to even speak for a moment.

"What?" she asked. "What happened?"

"The Council happened," he said. "That bastard Hewitt. He knew this all along. That's why we were sent here, not because I'm an expert in the occult."

"I think a couple pages are stuck together because I missed something."

"Don't you remember?" he asked. "When I asked Hewitt why send us? He gave me some song and dance about my expertise and then he said the truth, finally, although I didn't realize it at the time. He said, 'And your wife . . . I cannot imagine anyone else worthy of the task."

"That could just be coincidence," she offered.

"With the Council? Nothing is coincidence. They knew. I don't know how, but they knew you were the One and didn't tell us."

"Maybe they had a good reason."

"They're pillocks."

"That, too," she said. "But maybe if we'd known we might have behaved differently. If I'd known, it would have colored everything I've done so far."

"And if I'd known, we wouldn't be here."

They both knew that wasn't true, but he wished it were.

"A little knowledge of the future can be a dangerous thing," she said.

"I wish you would stop being reasonable."

She laughed and took his hand, rubbing his knuckles with the pad of her thumb. "I don't like being in the dark any more than you do, but I have to admit being in the know isn't that much better."

She really was frightened.

He drew her closer, laying her hand on his shoulder as he pulled her against him. "No, it's not," he said. "But we will see this through. Despite being the Chosen One, you are not alone. For what little it's worth, I will always be at your side."

She cupped his cheek. "That's worth everything."

CHAPTER TEN

ELIZABETH STOOD WAITING IN the lobby for Raul while Simon had "another word" with the hotel manager about security.

"Elizabeth," Raul called out, waving as he approached her.

Today they were going to see Gaspar's neighbor in the hope that she could provide them some lead about who might have killed him and taken the bowl. Raul had volunteered as interpreter.

"You are looking well," he said as he neared. "I feared the worst when the professor told me what happened. You are sure you are unharmed?"

He looked her up and down.

"I'm fine."

"Why was your husband not with you? If you were my wife, I would never leave your side."

"Which is just one of the reasons you are not her husband," Simon said, his light tone defying the look in his eyes.

He had never been fond of men's attention toward her. Heck, she'd never thought she was the jealous type either until that Prussian countess tried to sink her Teutonic claws into him. For the most part, Simon handled the situations cleverly. After ten years of marriage, he'd

134

become adept at deflecting, intercepting, or even sometimes ignoring the occasional come-ons she endured. It was strange to see him angry about it, even if he didn't put it on full display. With someone like Raul, young and basically a twenty-something boy who drooled over everything in a skirt, he usually paid it little heed. But lately, he'd been more like the Simon of old. A little tetchy about it.

For his part, Raul seemed oblivious to the undercurrent in Simon's words and mood and merely grinned.

"I think perhaps—" Simon began.

"That we should go," Elizabeth added, sure he was about to say something that might put the kibosh on their only good lead.

He looked ready to say something else, but instead gave her a deferential nod and they started toward the door.

After the revelations of the gem and her leading role in the coming drama, they went back to the library to go over the manuscript more carefully. She and Simon had been hoping for some loophole, something that might get her off the hook as the only one who could remove the staff, but all they found was more of a muddle and more potential problems. Not only was there a worthiness clause but a series of glyphs that Simon, Emil, and Alex argued over for nearly half an hour seemed to imply that there was also a trial codicil. What that meant was still up for debate. Emil believed the proper translation was the word "test" and that it was just another reference to the Eye. Vega, on the other hand, believed that "trial" was the appropriate term. Elizabeth and Simon didn't like the sound of that.

She'd seen enough movies to know that trials for things like the Staff of Life usually involved poison darts and giant rolling boulders. Elizabeth wasn't in bad shape but she had skipped Pilates for the last forever. Running for her life and leaping over gaping chasms filled with vipers wasn't her forte.

But for now, she decided not to worry about it. It would be what it would be and Simon would do plenty of worrying for them both in the interim.

She was looking forward to doing some good old-fashioned Nancy Drewing. And besides, without the bowl and the map it supposedly contained there would be no expedition at all.

They returned to the favela that Friday just after noon. As they got out of the car and started toward the house, Elizabeth paused.

"Maybe you should wait in the car?" she suggested to Simon, who merely rose a questioning eyebrow. "She seemed a little afraid of men and you can be a little intimidating. To those that don't know you," she added quickly.

He didn't take offense, but his focus shifted to Raul. Obviously, he had to go with her or they'd be stuck in the world's worst game of charades all day long. But that didn't mean he liked it.

"Very well," Simon agreed.

Elizabeth and Raul knocked on the door, hoping the woman's husband was gone.

The woman opened the front door and looked anxiously about before waving them inside. Raul made quick introductions. The woman's name was Belmira.

She nervously offered them some yerba mate tea which they politely declined. Elizabeth sat down on the small sofa, moving aside a pillow to discover a spring pushing up through the torn fabric.

The woman looked mortified, but Elizabeth smiled and waved off her remorse, putting the pillow back. "It's fine. *Tudo bem*."

The woman seemed surprised at her knowledge of the language and launched into a stream of sing-song Brazilian Portuguese.

It was Elizabeth's turn to be embarrassed. "I only speak a little." She held up her thumb and index finger. "*Poquito*. Um…"

"*Pequeno*," Raul corrected.

"*Pequeno. Perdão*," Elizabeth apologized.

The woman nodded her understanding. Phrasebook Portuguese only got one so far.

"Ask her what she saw," Elizabeth said.

Elizabeth waited patiently while Raul and Belmira spoke. There was a some back and forth as Raul asked for details or clarification before translating.

"She saw a man climbing out of Gaspar's window."

Oh, that was good. "Was he carrying anything?" Elizabeth couldn't help but pantomime her question, cradling something in her arms.

"*Bebê?*"

"No, no *bebê*." Maybe she should just let Raul translate.

"She is unsure. It was dark. But there was definitely no baby," Raul added with a small grin.

"Ask her if she saw his face. Did she recognize him?"

Raul relayed her questions and Elizabeth didn't need a translator to see the reluctance in Belmira's face. She was taking a risk talking to them, and pointing a finger at someone was an even greater one. Finally, she nodded.

"His name is Cadú," Raul explained after they spoke. "She's seen him around before and sometimes with Gaspar."

"Does she know where we might find Cadú? Does he live close by?"

Belmira shook her head when Raul asked her.

A name was something but it wasn't much to go on. For all Elizabeth knew Cadú could be the Brazilian equivalent of John.

Elizabeth stood and thanked her for her time when Belmira tapped her arm to get her attention.

"She thinks he might work with horses."

"How does she know that?"

Belmira winced and pointed to her nose. "*Mal cheiroso.*"

Elizabeth understood that well enough.

"He was always dirty and smelled of manure," Raul said. "She isn't sure but she thinks he might work at the Jockey Club in Gávea."

Elizabeth held out her hand. "Thank you so much for speaking with us. Can we offer her anything for her time? Some money?"

Raul asked but the woman shook her head. "Doing the right thing is its own reward," he translated.

"*Obrigrada.*"

They found Simon leaning against the car, arms crossed, impatiently waiting. "Well? Anything?"

"A lead."

He opened the door for her and she slid across into the passenger seat. "And where does it lead us?"

Elizabeth couldn't help but grin. "To the races."

RACE TRACKS ALWAYS REMINDED Elizabeth of her father. He'd gambled and lost at nearly every one in Texas and more than a few in Oklahoma. Despite them never hitting the trifecta, it was a day out with her father and a heck of a lot more fun for a kid than the dingy backrooms of the gambling halls where they spent most of their time. Some kids went to Disneyland on holiday; she went to the track.

The Jockey Club was a hippodrome built near the former marshlands bordering the area of Rio known as Lagoa that encircled a picturesque lagoon. The new grandstands were oddly romantic and mixed beautifully with the old colonial buildings courtesy of the King of Portugal. He'd been a keen racing enthusiast, and when Portugal relocated the capital of the empire to Brazil as part of a "strategic retreat" from Napoleon, he and 15,000 of his closest court-y friends made Rio their home. The magnificent buildings at the Jockey Club were just part of that legacy.

Although there were no races scheduled that day, the setting was still spectacular. Elizabeth could just envision the horses racing along the far straight, the calm waters of the enormous lagoon stretching out behind them. But they weren't there to sightsee and made their way to the stables.

After speaking to a few workers, they finally came across one who recognized the name Cadú. He apparently worked on and off for a Colonel Pickering, which sent Elizabeth immediately into her best and worst *My Fair Lady* impressions. Raul had no idea what she was on about but laughed each time she did it.

They found the stable master who told them that Cadú had not been in to work for the last two days and if they found him to tell him not to bother coming back at all. They managed to get Cadú's home address in Santa Marta.

The hillside of the Santa Marta favela rose up before them at a dizzying angle. Elizabeth was sure their car wasn't going to be able to make it. In the end, it couldn't anyway as the roadway ended and they were left to hoof it the rest of the way through the narrow warren of alleys and pathways to Cadú's.

Raul asked for directions to the address and led them up the steep hill to one of a hundred cracker box-style homes that were built one on top of the other. None of them were painted with the vivid colors she'd seen in modern photographs. In the 1930s, they were dull and dark and depressing although an improvement over the favela where Gaspar had lived. This area seemed to be one rung up from the bottom of the social ladder.

"I'm so glad you're here, Raul," she told him. "We would have been lost without you."

Raul beamed at the compliment and offered her his hand to step over an uneven bit of pavement. Behind her she could have sworn she heard Simon grumble, but when she turned back to look at him, he merely offered her a not overly-convincing smile. She'd have to talk to him about that. Raul had been a little flirty, but he'd also been a godsend. They wouldn't have had a chance in heck to find Cadú without his help. Simon was usually more gracious about that sort of thing.

Finally, Raul stopped in front of a two-story brick building. "This is Cadú's."

Simon knocked on the door to the upstairs apartment, and a few moments later a woman carrying a toddler on her hip answered it. Inside, a baby cried and two little boys about seven or eight were having a tug of war over a shirt. The woman smiled embarrassedly. The toddler slowly and methodically pulled strands of hair down from the woman's updo bun. One of the boys shrieked and she turned back to scold the boys but they ignored her.

"*Boa tarde*," Raul began.

"*Com licença*. Excuse," she said, holding up a finger and begging off for a moment.

Striding back into the small house, she yelled at the two boys and ripped the shirt from their grasp, finally getting their attention. She scolded them again and handed off the toddler to the bigger of the two before returning to the door.

She tried to straighten what was left of her bun. "Desculpa. I am sorry. The children."

"You speak English?" Elizabeth asked, excited at the prospect of being able to speak directly with someone.

"Some."

"We're looking for Cadú. Is he your husband?"

The woman's face turned hard. "Idiota."

That needed no translation.

"What he do now?"

"We were hoping to speak with him," Simon offered. "Is he home?"

She shook her head. "Not for two days. He..." She looked at Raul for help and spoke to him in Portuguese for a moment.

"Ah," Raul said, "he is off to drink, what is the word? On a bender, I think you call it."

Wonderful.

"Do you know where?" Elizabeth asked.

"No, and I no care. *Fihlo da puta.*"

"This is not good," Raul added needlessly. They'd come so far only to come up empty.

Raul and the woman spoke again briefly in Portuguese.

As they did, a little girl of no more than five appeared at her mother's side and clung to her skirts with one hand and held onto a raggedy doll with the other. She looked up at Elizabeth with big brown eyes. Elizabeth smiled down at her but the girl hid her face in her mother's dress shyly, finally peering back up and letting a tiny smile sneak out. She didn't look anything like Charlotte, but instantly that was all Elizabeth could think of.

"*Olá,*" Elizabeth said to her.

Before the girl could respond, her mother shooed her back inside.

"I am sorry, that is all I am knowing."

"Her husband came into some money it seems," Raul explained. "Rather quickly. Not the first time that's happened. She doesn't know how or where he's gone, but it's not uncommon for him to disappear for a few days at a time like this."

Simon took out several thousand real and handed them to the woman. She hesitated to take them, but he insisted. Raul scribbled down their hotel information and gave it to her, asking that she let them know when Cadú returned, but Elizabeth had little hope she would. For now, all they could do was wait, again. *Waiting for Cadú*—a new play by Samuel Beckett.

By the time they returned to the hotel it was late afternoon. Elizabeth walked out onto the balcony to watch the ocean.

A few moments later, she felt Simon come up behind her. "You were awfully quiet on the ride home. Is something the matter?"

She looked out at the waves gently tumbling onto the shore. "No. Just thinking."

Simon moved to stand beside her and leaned against the railing. "About?"

"Charlotte," she confessed. Ever since she'd seen the little girl at Cadú's she hadn't been able to get their daughter out of her mind.

"Ah," he said. "The little girl."

Elizabeth nodded. "It's silly, but—"

"It's not silly," Simon said, standing and easing her around to face him. "And right on schedule."

"What do you mean?"

"Every time we go away, you put on a brave face for a week then on day six or seven, you stop pretending you don't miss her."

Elizabeth blushed. "Do I really?"

"Like clockwork," he said with affection.

"I didn't realize I was so predictable."

"I'm grateful that there's at least one area in which you are." He caressed her cheek and then turned to look out at the view. "I miss her, too, you know."

Every time she was away from Charlotte, she felt a pang of loss. When their trips sometimes went on for weeks at a time, it was particularly difficult. She knew she was doing the right thing in going, though. They weren't just saving the world, they were saving the world *for her*.

"I think I miss her laugh the most. The one when she sort of giggle-snorts and then laughs even harder."

Simon chuckled at the thought of it. "She gets that from you, you know?"

They stood in silence for a long moment before Simon spoke again.

"I miss kissing her goodnight, convincing myself she isn't growing up as fast as she is. And I always sleep better when the three of us are under the same roof," he added with a quick look toward her, admitting his one true vulnerability—his love for them.

She moved closer and he tucked her under his arm.

"I suppose that's a solace—that while we're away we aren't missing anything. She's not aging or getting any older. Unlike us."

Simon's arm tightened almost imperceptibly around her and then released her as he stepped back.

"You're probably hungry," he said.

The shift in the mood and in topic surprised her. There was definitely something going on with him. She'd been patient, waiting for him to tell her in his own time, but patience was not her strong suit.

In the years they'd been together Simon had gone from closed off to open on weekends, emotionally speaking, at least with those close to him. He was still often distant with people he didn't know and his students still feared him. But he'd been kind too many times over the years, even with them, to keep up the pretense that he was Big Old Meanie Professor Cross of old. He still nurtured the legend now and again, but his hard edges had softened over the years. Love will do that.

Despite his willingness to be open with her, there were still times when he withheld a little part of himself. It was usually out of fear of hurting her or Charlotte, and she'd invariably get it out

143

of him. This felt different though somehow and she couldn't quite pinpoint why.

He always let her work things out in her own time. She was determined to do the same for him, even if doing so went against her natural inclination to "help" everyone, even if they didn't know they needed it.

"Would you like to go out for dinner or eat at the hotel?" he asked, whatever was bothering him buried deep again.

"Whichever you prefer."

He nodded and went inside to make arrangements, leaving Elizabeth with one more mystery to solve.

DINNER AT THE ELEGANT, French restaurant had been a quiet affair. Between sips of a fine Bordeaux, Simon could convince himself that they were simply out for an evening, as usual. Of course, there was nothing usual about what lay ahead and over much of dinner, each was lost to their own thoughts of what might come next.

They'd agreed to meet Emil in the hotel bar after dinner for a drink. Simon wasn't in the mood, but it wasn't late and he had no valid excuse to beg off.

He held the door open for Elizabeth and both immediately heard Clay Bridges' loud and slightly drunken voice.

"And I took out my six gun and shot that snake right between the eyes. And I don't mean the governor," he said to a small entourage gathered around him at the hotel bar. "Although he deserved it, too."

Simon hoped they could make this visit a short one. They found Emil sitting alone in a corner booth.

"Ah, good to see you," Emil said, standing for Elizabeth and waving for one of the waitresses to come over.

Emil continued to nurse his gin and tonic while Simon ordered a scotch and Elizabeth decided to try *caldo de cana*, a sweet drink made from pressed sugarcane juice.

"Raul told me about your visit to the favela today," Emil said. "It sounds as though we might have better luck finding the bowl than the man at this point."

Simon had to agree. The money that Cadú had come into had a likely source. Someone without knowledge of the bowl's true worth would surely see it only as gold. And for someone like Cadú, selling a stolen object left him with few options.

"I think tomorrow we should visit some of the local pawnshops and the like," Simon said.

"Agreed," Emil said.

"We can cover more ground if we split up. Perhaps Navarro can advise us about the best locations, and Elizabeth and I can take our share."

"Very kind of you."

"We're part of this now," Simon said. "Like it or not."

Emil nodded thoughtfully and turned his attention to Elizabeth. "How are you feeling about it all, my dear? I realize it's quite a lot to take in."

"Honestly, I'm having a little trouble accepting it."

"I understand. I—"

"Well, look who we have here," Bridges said, appearing at their table. "You've been a busy boy," he added, poking a wavering finger at Emil. "But so have I."

He wobbled slightly on his feet. "Went to the library today for some verrry interesting reading, if you know what I mean?" He sloppily touched the side of his nose.

"If you'll excuse us," Emil said, "we're enjoying a drink—"

"Don't mind if I do," Bridges said, insinuating himself into the seat next to Emil, forcing him to move to accommodate the larger man.

"Do you often go where you're not invited?" Simon asked.

Bridges laughed. "As a matter of fact, I do."

Simon was about to lose his temper when Elizabeth placed a hand on his arm and shook her head. She was right. Making a scene would solve nothing, except perhaps ease the ache Simon had to wipe that smug grin off the man's face with his fist.

"What do you want?" Emil asked.

"Just a little information. Just a tiny bit," Bridges said, holding his fingers up to emphasize it. He drank down what was left in his glass and set it down on the table. "A little bird told me about Manuscript 512, A, B, C, whatever they are, all of them. Very interesting reading."

"You said that," Simon said.

Bridges snorted. "You don't like me much, do you?"

"Not even a little," Simon answered honestly.

That seemed to amuse Bridges even more. He swung his glassy-eyed gaze toward Elizabeth. "He's funny. I like him."

"What do you want, Clay?" Emil prompted, clearly hoping to get to the point soon.

"Right. Well, I know you've got the Eye," he said. "No need to pretend, everybody knows it."

Emil sat straighter in his seat. "And I suppose you or one of your hooligans went searching for it the other day?"

"Oh, I heard about that," Bridges said with mock disapproval. "Broke into your room. Both of your rooms, I think. "

Simon's hand slowly closed into a fist.

Bridges looked at Elizabeth. "Heard you got roughed up a little. That's a shame."

"I ought to break your neck," Simon said, having had enough.

Bridges seemed to like the threat and grinned back, welcoming a fight.

"I try not to hurt ladies," Bridges said, "especially when they're so pretty."

Simon's patience was quickly reaching its expiration date.

"If you have a point, Mr. Bridges," Elizabeth said, "I suggest you get to it."

He grinned, enjoying his moment. "I only have one question." He leaned in closer to Emil. "Does it work? Does the Eye actually work?"

"I don't know what you're talking about."

Bridges studied him keenly, a small smile coming to his lips. "It does, doesn't it? You bastard. You finally got the damn thing to work, didn't you? How'd you do it? That whole thing about it being some sort of gatekeeper to the staff is just hokum. No one's *worthy*."

"I wouldn't expect a man like you to understand," Emil said. "You can't even imagine a world that isn't as petty and selfish as you are."

"That's true. But that's because I'm right. No one's pure of heart. Not even you, Emil," he said.

Emil didn't respond but his eyes inadvertently shifted toward Elizabeth, a movement which was not lost on Bridges, who shifted his gaze to her with startling clarity. Simon was beginning to think Bridges was not nearly as drunk as he pretended to be.

"Her?" he said loudly. "The Eye responded to *her*?"

Emil shifted nervously in his seat. "I never said that." But his unease gave it away.

147

Bridges laughed. "Oh, Emil. I never thought you were the type to fall for that old racket. She's got you fooled, doesn't she? Bats her pretty eyes at you and—"

"That's enough," Simon said feeling an odd calm come over him as he finally reached the end of his tether. "I suggest you get up from this table and walk away, or I'm going to help you do it."

Bridges chuckled but held up a placating hand. "All right. I'm going."

He stood on legs far less wobbly than before. Drunk or not, Simon was ready to break his jaw if he said one more word. The two of them sized each other up and for a moment Simon thought he might get the fight he wanted, but instead Bridges turned back to the table.

"It's been an education. Ma'am," he said, and then walked away.

Simon watched him go, his adrenaline reluctantly receding. He retook his seat and looked at Emil.

"I'm sorry," Emil apologized. "I'm not very good at this sort of thing."

"It's all right," Simon said, trying to appear nonchalant about it. "At best he doesn't believe it and worst . . .he knows."

"And he's not the only one," Elizabeth said, staring off toward the corner of the bar.

Simon followed her gaze and his blood ran cold. He'd been so distracted by Bridges he hadn't even noticed anyone else. Strasser sat at the bar and had clearly overheard the entire exchange.

CHAPTER ELEVEN

S IMON PAUSED TO READ the street sign and consult the map they'd gotten from the concierge. They'd already hit two pawn shops and one antique store, and number four on the list wasn't far.

He squinted down at the paper and moved it a little farther away to read it properly.

Elizabeth didn't say anything. She knew he needed reading glasses. Heck, *he* knew he needed reading glasses. They'd "discussed" it before, but he'd always downplayed the need. She didn't see why. Half her friends needed them. Besides, Simon would look even sexier with a pair of glasses. In her mind, it was a win-win.

Normally, she would have gently teased him about it, but considering the revelations of the last few days she decided discretion was the better part of valor. So instead, she merely nudged a little closer to his side and read the map herself.

"This way, I think," she said, tracing out the path with her finger and then turning in a southerly direction.

"Right," Simon said, folding the map and tucking it back into his jacket pocket.

Elizabeth found it a tiny bit adorable that he was too proud for his own good about all of it and slipped her arm through his as they weaved their way through the thick pedestrian traffic. A sea of boater straw hats stretched out as far as she could see. She was glad Simon stuck with the panama-style, though. There was something about straw hats that made her think of the 1920s and brash college frat boys wearing raccoon coats in summer and saying "twenty-three skidoo."

They turned the corner and headed toward the next pawnshop on their list. So far, the morning's search for the bowl had been a complete bust. They knew it was a long shot, but they had to do something. The bowl *was* out there somewhere, but until Cadú dried out enough to come home, they wouldn't know where. And even then Elizabeth doubted he'd talk. He had, after all, killed someone to get it. But until they had a chance to talk to him and find out for themselves, all they could do was look in the places where it might be.

It wasn't all bad. She was getting to experience Rio in a new way. They'd walked block after block and come across shops offering virtually anything anyone could want. Rio, Simon had explained, wasn't a manufacturing city so nearly all goods were imported. British, French, American? It was available here. Priceless golden bowls? Not so much. Not yet, anyway.

The city was really quite lovely. Aside from the practically perfect tropical climate, the Portuguese pavement with its intricate mosaics made the sidewalks a work of art. The city was a wonderful mix of classical old world and modern metropolis. From the neo-Gothic to neo-Classical, making the old new again seemed to be the watchword of the day. Rio was an old city, nearly five hundred years old, but it felt fresh and modern. The old world poked through, but it was definitely a city striding toward the future.

Mixed in with stores selling radios and other contemporary electronics were street vendors with trained monkeys or beautiful scarlet and blue macaws resting on their shoulders. One man's little marmoset plucked people's hats off as they passed by. There were also a few things that were purely Brazilian, including a store that sold nothing but souvenirs created from butterflies. The iridescent wings were pressed under glass and used to create everything from wall art to commemorative ashtrays. Elizabeth wasn't sure she'd ever seen anything so beautiful and so tragic at the same time.

The next shop on their list turned up no leads for the bowl, although they did offer a pair of Fred Astaire's tap shoes from *Flying Down to Rio*. Somehow Elizabeth doubted he wore a size seven.

"Another one bites the dust," she said as they left.

Simon surveyed the street. "Yes. Chances are he sold the bowl to someone in a back alley somewhere. There's no telling where it might be now."

"It's here somewhere," she said firmly. He merely arched an eyebrow. "I feel it in my gut."

On cue her stomach gurgled, earning a chuckle from Simon.

"Talkative, isn't it?"

"That was a plaintive cry for sustenance."

"We had breakfast four hours ago."

"Exactly. I'm practically wasting away." She spied some vendor carts down the street. "Come on."

Elizabeth loved street food. Simon was a bit more cautious about it, but was still willing to give a few things a try. She bought a little of everything and had trouble holding the paper cones each delicacy came in. There was coxhina, small crunchy croquettes stuffed with chicken, pão de queijo, fluffy little cheese bread balls, and finally bacalhau, salted cod balls, which were a lot better than they sounded.

It was basically the Brazilian version of fish and chips and she happily tucked in.

Simon, always more circumspect in his food choices, especially those from the side of the street, tried some picanha, skewered barbecued meat, and cassava chips. They washed it all down with two bottles of Guaraná soda which tasted a little like sweet apples.

They continued on a few more blocks to walk off a little of what they'd eaten before driving to the next shop on their list, which also came up blank. With nothing to show for it and the day nearly over, they returned to the hotel to compare notes with Raul and Emil. Elizabeth hoped they'd had better luck than she and Simon, but one look at Emil's face told her the story.

She sipped her tea as they sat on the veranda of the hotel overlooking Copacabana beach. The ocean breeze was picking up as the sun began to set. The mood was somber.

"There are still many places for us to try tomorrow," Raul said. "I will make another list."

"Thank you," Simon said.

"We'll find it," Elizabeth said, hoping her positivity would shake the bowl loose from wherever it was hiding.

Emil managed a weak smile. "Yes. I am sure you are right."

"She usually is," Simon said affectionately before excusing themselves to go to their room to rest and change before dinner.

Elizabeth looked around the lobby idly while Simon got the key from the front desk.

"A message was left for you, Mr. Cross," the clerk said, as he handed Simon both the key and a slip of paper.

"Thank you."

"What is it?" Elizabeth asked as he opened the note and read it.

He led her a few paces away from the front desk. "It's from Cadú. He wants to meet us tonight."

"Really?" That was unexpected but good news. "Where?"

Simon's brow knit together. "Sugarloaf."

"That mountain thing in the bay?"

"Yes, and I don't like it. It says, 'come alone.'"

Nothing good ever followed that, but it was to be expected. Secret meetings never had caveats like "come as you are" or "bring a friend!"

"It could be a trap," Simon said, folding the note up and putting it into his breast pocket.

He was right, of course, but they had little choice. They had to go. "I guess we'll find out when we get there."

"Why there?" Simon wondered aloud as they started toward the elevators.

Elizabeth remembered seeing the promontory when they'd flown into the bay and again when they'd driven to the casino in Urca. The only way to the top was via a suspended cable car. "It's isolated. He is on the run after all."

Simon grunted. She could see his mind turning over the dangers and the possibilities. But in the end, they had to go. It was the only lead, real or not, that they had and they had no choice but to follow it.

THE RENDEZVOUS WAS SCHEDULED for eight o'clock that night. Simon and Elizabeth drove in silence to the base station of the tramway in Urca. These were the moments she hated the most—the ones cloaked in dread. She knew something was coming but just didn't know what. Dollars to donuts it wasn't going to be easy. Cadú, if the note really was from him, had already killed someone. He might be frightened and remorseful or he might be looking to snip off loose ends.

Simon parked the car and reached into his jacket pocket. He rechecked the cylinder of the revolver again before slipping it into the back waistband of his pants. Elizabeth still didn't like guns, but it would be foolish to go without one.

Simon didn't ask her if she was ready. He didn't tell her she should stay behind. He didn't do anything other than look at her, leaving all the rest unsaid. It didn't need to be spoken. They both knew. They'd both shared what they thought were their last moments together too many times to count. The experience had taught them to treat every moment that way. But there was no way to duplicate the tension and fear that coursed through her body at moments like this. She reached out and squeezed his hand once before getting out of the car. Time to get this show on the road.

They bought their tickets for the last tram of the day. The sun had just finished setting, giving the sky that ethereal look stuck somewhere between day and night. The horizon glowed orange and yellow against the near black sea and above that the blue ombré of the night sky went from light to midnight blue. It was eerily beautiful.

The tram was fairly large; it could probably hold about twenty people, although they were its only passengers. It was strange being alone inside the car. It seemed solid enough, even if it was just made of wood. Well, as safe as anything can be that's about to be dangling hundreds of feet in the air suspended by a thin cable.

She tried to distract herself from the danger they might face at the top with the view of the bay. It was breathtaking. From so high up it looked like all of those picture postcards or travel posters she'd seen.

"All right?" Simon asked, coming to stand next to her at one of the many windows that covered the upper half of the tram.

She nodded and even managed a small smile. The car moved along at a slow but steady clip toward Urca mountain's peak where they'd disembark and get on a second car to the summit of Sugarloaf.

The world around them seemed to get darker by the second as they steadily rose higher and higher. The car reached the second station and slowed to a halt as it was carried inside the small building meant for boarding and disembarking.

Simon opened the door and they stepped out onto the platform. The second car to the summit waited for them in a small circular loading area. They waited for an attendant to open the door for them but none came.

"Maybe he took off early?" Elizabeth suggested. It was the last tram of the day.

Simon looked around carefully and then cautiously escorted her to the waiting car. There was a small control room where a man operated the cars. Simon waved toward him to come out, but the man inside just gestured them toward the car.

"I suppose we should just let ourselves in," Simon said.

Simon opened the door to the second car and let Elizabeth inside first. She'd only taken a few steps inside when she heard a voice behind her, and it wasn't Simon's.

"Do not move."

Stoneface Strasser stood behind Simon. She knew from Simon's ramrod posture that there was a gun in his back.

The only thing worse than a Nazi was a Nazi with a gun.

Strasser quickly patted Simon down and found his gun. He tossed it out of the car and shoved Simon forward. So much for being prepared.

Strasser stepped inside after him and closed the door to the car. Then he gestured to the man in the control booth and the tram started. Elizabeth nearly lost her footing as it did, but Simon's hand steadied her.

He turned toward their captor. "Who are you? What do you want?"

155

How he could sound so in control in moments like these she would never know.

Strasser grinned. "You are about to have a terrible accident."

He waved them to the far side of the car with his gun. They had little choice but to comply. The car left the confines of the station house and began the steep climb to the peak nearly 1,300 feet above sea level.

Strasser stood calmly, which was a lot easier at that end of a gun, and waited.

Elizabeth took hold of Simon's hand and he gripped hers tightly. Her heart raced as fast as she knew Simon's mind must be. They'd been in worse fixes before and found a way out. They would now, too. They simply had to.

"We don't even know you," Simon said.

"But I know you. You have ingratiated yourself to Doctor Mendoza and have filled his head with lies."

"What are you talking about?"

His gaze shifted firmly to Elizabeth. Her stomach dropped. Being the Chosen One really wasn't all it was cracked up to be.

Next to her, she could feel Simon tense. He started to step forward. "This is all a mistake. We haven't—"

Strasser's dark eyes flared and he took a meaningful step toward him, gun ready. "Do not move again, unless I tell you to. Do you understand?"

Simon stood straight, half in defiance and half in at least temporary acquiescence. "Whatever you think we've done, you're mistaken," Simon tried again.

Strasser looked mildly curious. "I don't know how you managed to trigger the stone, but it is of no matter in the end. No *Untermensch* will touch it. Only a true patriot, a man of pure Aryan blood can wield the staff. Rest assured, one will soon."

Any hope they had of talking their way out of this evaporated. Zealots have no room for logic.

Elizabeth swallowed and tried to think positive thoughts. They'd fought Nazis before and won. They'd find a way this time, too. She looked around the car for anything they might be able to use as weapons, but there was nothing. That left them only one thing—each other.

The car crept along, every creak and groan magnified in the tense silence. When the car suddenly stopped, the abrupt movement making it sway slightly back and forth as it dangled from the cable.

Strasser opened the door and then stepped back away from it. "This is where you get out."

Elizabeth's already upset stomach threatened a full revolution.

Simon edged her slightly behind him. "Shooting us won't look very accidental."

Strasser looked at the gun. "This? This is merely for persuasion."

"We're not going to do what you want," Simon said. Their defiance was their only leverage. Simon had clearly reasoned out the same thing she had. If Strasser wanted to shoot them, he could have already. He wanted this to look like some sort of accident.

"I think you will," he said, pointing the gun at Elizabeth, his leverage becoming clear.

Simon would jump or she would be shot.

"No," Elizabeth said, tightening her grip on Simon's hand and arm.

Strasser cocked the gun.

Simon looked down at her with such pained love that her heart clenched in her chest. She knew he would do anything for her. Including this. But there was no way she was going to let him. Strasser wasn't going to let either of them live and she would damn well go down fighting.

157

She shook her head and held on tightly to his arm.

"Then you can jump or I will shoot him." Strasser moved the gun toward Simon. "Your husband was cheating on you and you killed yourself in despair. Very tragic."

Neither she nor Simon moved and Strasser's patience began to wear thin. He took a forceful step forward. "I could just shoot you both."

"No," Simon said, stepping away from Elizabeth.

"Simon!" She felt sick at the thought of what he was about to do and reached out to grab onto him. There had to be another way. "He's going to—"

Simon cut her off by grabbing her arms and holding her firmly. "Sometimes the only way to stay together is to be apart," he said intensely.

"Very poetic," Strasser said.

But the way Simon looked at her made her think. He was trying to tell her something and it took her a moment to realize what it was. She nodded once.

"I love you so very much," he said, and gently cupped her cheek as he pulled her in for a kiss.

Elizabeth fought to keep her tears back as Simon rested his forehead against hers.

"On my signal," he whispered softly.

"All right," Strasser said once they'd separated. He stood near the door and waved Simon forward.

With each slow step he took, Elizabeth edged a little farther away. The more distance between them the better. Strasser kept his eye on Simon but his gun trained on Elizabeth. That split focus was the key to their plan.

As long as they were standing next to each other, Strasser had them both in his sights. But if there was distance, his attention would be torn between them and maybe, just maybe they could find an opening.

Simon took another step forward and another. Elizabeth's heart raced in her chest. He was nearly to the door now.

"You won't get away with this, you know?" Simon said.

"I believe I already have."

"Have you?" His confident defiance drew Strasser's full attention toward him. His gun hand moved slightly away from Elizabeth. And as soon as it did, Simon called out, "Now!"

Elizabeth knew she had only a split second to react, to draw Strasser's attention back to her and hope she didn't get shot in the process. As soon as Simon called out to her, she screamed and dove to the floor. Strasser was caught off-guard and turned toward her in surprise. Out of the corner of her eye, she saw Simon lunge, and then the gun went off.

The gunshot sounded like a cannon in the confined space of the tram car. Elizabeth hit the floor hard as the bullet dug into the wooden panel just beneath the handrail that circled the car only a few feet above her.

Simon collided hard with Strasser, sending them both tumbling to the floor. Simon managed to get on top of Strasser and briefly pin his gun hand to the floor, but Strasser was bigger and stronger than Simon and quickly rolled them over.

Elizabeth got to her feet and dove onto Strasser's back. She tried to pry him off Simon, but he was far too heavy. Simon struggled to keep the gun pointed away and had to use both hands to do it. Strasser's free hand wrapped around Simon's neck and began choking him.

Elizabeth was in a frenzy to try to get Strasser off of him. She tried hitting him, but the angle was impossible and he was far too big and strong for it to have any effect.

"The gun," Simon gasped.

Elizabeth tried to pry it out of Strasser's hand but his grip was too tight, so she did the only thing she could think of and bit his hand with everything she was worth. He cried out in pain and the gun fell to the floor.

Elizabeth tried to reach it, but Strasser grabbed her and threw her aside. She collided hard with the side of the car before righting herself. Strasser and Simon continued to grapple with each other, the gun somewhere beneath them. Suddenly it slid out onto the floor. Strasser reached for it, but his inattention to Simon left him open and Simon caught him with a strong right cross. He turned back to return the favor and the ensuing scuffle sent the gun skittering across the floor and right for the still-open doorway.

Elizabeth lunged and then dove after it. It seemed to be crawling away from her as it remained just outside of her reach. Her fingertips just managed to touch the edge of the handgrip as it tipped over the threshold, falling until it disappeared from sight.

She'd been so close! But there was no time to worry about it now. She pushed herself back up onto her feet just in time to see Strasser's enormous fist collide squarely with Simon's jaw. His head snapped to the side and he stumbled, only keeping himself from falling by grabbing on to the handrail. He shook his head to clear it, but Strasser was on him again before he could. He grabbed Simon's head with both of his hands.

"Simon!" Elizabeth cried, but he couldn't hear her. He was nearly out on his feet.

Then Strasser smashed Simon's head down onto the handrail with a horrible sound Elizabeth would never forget. She started to run toward him as he slumped down onto the floor unconscious— *Please let that be all it is*—when Strasser turned to face her.

She stopped in mid-stride and knew she was their only hope of getting out of this alive. Slowly and methodically, Strasser began to make his way toward her. She looked around frantically for something, anything, to help. But there was nothing. He was going to grab hold of her and throw her out the door. And Simon would be sure to follow.

She would be damned if she was going to give up without a fight though.

Strasser stalked her around the car, a predator playing with his prey. Finally he cornered her, and Elizabeth reached behind her to hold on to the handrail for all she was worth.

Strasser closed the distance between them and she kicked and kicked. He fended off her blows until he was right in front of her.

"This game is over," he said, smugly.

"Not quite."

She brought up her knee and hit him in the groin as hard as she could. His eyes popped open wide with shock and pain and he stumbled back, half-doubled over. She leveraged herself on the handrail and did her best Rockette high-kick and hit him squarely in the jaw. It stunned him and it felt like she might have broken her foot.

He staggered again but didn't go down. When he regained his footing, he lunged for her. She kicked at him again, but he caught her ankle and pulled. She was suspended between her hands clinging to the handrail and his hold on her leg.

With a roar of anger, he jerked her toward him and she lost her grip. The sudden loss of resistance sent them both hurtling toward the open doorway. Strasser hung half-in and half-out of the car and reached for anything to pull himself back in. Elizabeth tried to scramble away, but he grabbed her leg again, dragging her with him to the very edge.

Channeling her best Captain Kirk, she kicked at him with her other leg and finally struck him hard in the face, then again and again. He lost his grip on the side of the door, but not on her leg. He slid out of the door, pulling her out with him.

She was going to die. The world seemed to both slow down and speed up around her and a scream was torn from her throat as she slipped over the threshold, clawing desperately for something to grab hold of.

She managed to dig her fingers into a gap in the threshold and held on for dear life. Strasser's weight tugged on her leg briefly, and she nearly lost her tenuous grip, but his hands slipped off her calf. She heard him yell something in German as he flailed helplessly in the air, plunging toward the rocks far below. Dangling from the side of the car, she looked down to see him grow smaller and smaller as he plummeted hundreds of feet down to the ground.

Before he hit, she looked away and tried to catch her breath. Her entire body shook as she dangled from the edge of the car. Her fingertips were curled tightly into the small ridges of the threshold, but she knew she couldn't hold on for long.

She tried to pull herself up but wasn't strong enough. She hung on to the side of the car, willing herself not to look down. But it was like telling yourself not to think of pink elephants and seconds after swearing she wouldn't, she looked down. The ground seemed impossibly far away. A wave of nausea overcame her.

"Oh, God," she breathed and closed her eyes. "You can do this. Elizabeth, you can do this."

She swore by all that was holy and a few things that weren't that if she lived, she was going to the gym, and not just to ride the bike and watch reruns of Friends on the TV.

She knew she couldn't hold on for much longer and tried again to pull herself up. She managed to make it about halfway before her arms gave out. The resulting drop made her lose her grip with her right hand. She cried out and somehow managed to keep hold of the groove in the threshold with her left hand. But it was growing weaker by the second.

Desperately, she tried to swing her body enough to get the second hand back on the lip, but she was quickly running out of strength. *Just one more try,* she told herself.

She swung her weight from side to side to create enough momentum for her to reach the lip with her right hand. Her fingers touched the edge of the threshold, the tips of her fingers finding the groove. *Almost got it.* But she couldn't get a strong enough grip and her fingers slid off. She started to fall back, knowing her left hand would not be able to hold her now. She could feel the fingers of that hand beginning to slip.

She said a silent prayer as her last two fingers slid from the groove and she began to fall. Suddenly, a strong hand gripped her wrist in an iron vise. She looked up to see Simon leaning out of the car, holding onto her. All she could think was that he was alive.

He grasped her wrist in a grip that would not let go and then with sheer will pulled her up, dragging her back into the car. He helped her to her feet and she clung to him as he moved her away from the open doorway.

He didn't say anything. He just cupped her cheeks with both his hands and kissed her and kissed her. Her knees were skinned, her hands and shoulders ached. Blood streaked down his face but neither one cared. They were alive. Somehow, they were both alive.

Chapter Twelve

Simon woke with a start. His heart raced as he sat up suddenly, turning quickly to make sure Elizabeth was alive and by his side. She lay next him, sleeping soundly, one arm curled under her pillow and the other tucked close to her chest. He watched her for a long moment, letting his heart slow and his breathing even out as the remnants of his nightmare receded. When he felt marginally in control again, he let his hand brush gently against her cheek. She nuzzled the pillow in response and the cold grip around his heart began to lessen. A little.

Careful not to wake her, although little could—she was the soundest sleeper he'd ever known—he got out of bed and shrugged on his robe. He went into the next room to stare through the closed glass patio doors at the dark ocean beyond.

The events after he'd pulled her back into the tram car were a blur. He'd been so certain he'd lost her he could think of little else in the hours afterward. The car had started to move again shortly after Strasser's death. They'd ridden it in near silence, simply holding each other. It had felt an eternity until they were finally back at the ground station. He didn't even remember looking at the man in the control booth along the way. Whether it was bribery or coercion that made him and the other employee do Strasser's bidding, Simon didn't care. At that moment, he didn't care about anything other than the fact that Elizabeth was alive and in his arms.

There was sure to be a police inquiry, but at least they would not be involved in it. The men, if they ever returned to work, would no doubt have little to say about the matter. It was supposed to be an "accident," after all.

He closed his eyes and an echo of the fear he felt in the car when he regained consciousness flashed across his mind. He'd been fighting Strasser and losing, badly. He remembered Elizabeth calling out his name. Then nothing. Nothing until he woke to an empty tram car and the belief that his world had come to a sudden end. She was gone. Elizabeth was gone.

Then he heard a soft grunt and saw her small hand trying to find purchase in the open doorway. He'd never been so grateful for anything in his life. He had been so certain he'd lost her that he wouldn't let himself believe she was alive until he held her in his arms and kissed her.

But the feeling of that first moment, of the despair of waking and being so certain she was lost to him forever still pained him. And it was made all the worse by the fact that he'd failed so miserably to protect her.

Every fear he'd ever had, every insecurity, coalesced in that moment. He'd been right to worry, right to think he wasn't up to the task. His failure had nearly cost Elizabeth her life. He loved her with every fiber of his being and wanted nothing more than to be by her side, but was that what was best for *her* now?

What good was he on these missions, in her life, if he could not protect her? A younger, stronger man could have fought Strasser off. He could have saved Elizabeth from all she had to endure. And it would only get worse with time. What if she wasn't strong enough or clever enough to fight off whatever he let past next time? What if he lost her? That, he could not endure.

He opened his eyes again and saw her reflection in the window glass. She looked ethereal and so achingly beautiful that for a moment he wondered if she was a dream. But she stepped closer and laid her hand tenderly upon his back. He turned away from the darkness and toward her. She looked up at him with such love and warmth and understanding that it nearly undid him.

She didn't say a word. She just stepped forward and slid her arms around his waist and pulled him to her. His arms encircled her. He held her tightly, and wondered if he'd ever be strong enough to let her go.

It had taken Vega all night to calm down. That fool Rasche had nearly ruined everything. He'd wanted to throttle him the moment Emil told him what had happened. It was lucky for Rasche that their being seen together was a risk. In other circumstances, he would have marched to Rasche's room and put a bullet in his head.

The delay in their meeting had allowed Vega to control his anger. Early the next morning he drove to a small cafe in Joá, far enough away from the others to ensure that they would not be seen or recognized.

Rasche was already sitting at a small table reading the local paper when Vega arrived. The headline of the paper read, "Death at Sugarloaf." And if Rasche persisted in his idiocy there would be a second.

At Vega's approach, Rasche lowered the paper, offering him that smug smile of his. How he yearned to wipe it from his miserable face.

"Good morning," Rasche said in German.

"Is it?" Vega answered in kind.

Rasche shrugged and made a show of looking around the picturesque local. "It is not Berlin, but..."

Vega sat down and tried to calm himself. Just the sight of Rasche inflamed him. He'd thought about what he wanted to say, needed to say, all morning. Now that he was here, all he wanted to do was wring Rasche's neck.

"Explain yourself," Vega said.

Rasche feigned confusion. "About?"

Vega tapped his finger on the front page of the newspaper. "This."

"Ah, well, Strasser. He was a fool, ardently devoted to our cause, of course, but a little hot-headed."

"You're saying that—" Vega began, only to be interrupted by a waitress bringing coffee.

"She does not speak German," Rasche reminded him. "Do you, my dear?" he asked her in their mother tongue.

The woman just smiled in confusion, clearly not understanding.

"You see," Rasche said, with a smile as he took a sip of his coffee. "You worry too much."

"And you not enough. Do you expect me to believe that your dog Strasser did this on his own? He wouldn't take a piss without your permission."

"No need to be crass."

Vega leaned forward and spoke in hushed and angry tones. "Do not play me for a fool."

"Then do not act as one. Why should you care what happens to the Crosses, unless you have become . . .attached."

Vega bristled at that, but covered it. "It is not an attachment, but one of need."

Rasche's eyebrow shot up lasciviously. "Need? Are you so—"

"You really are a pig. The woman, she might be helpful."

Rasche evidently thought of another tawdry remark but instead of making it, seemed to consider the possibility before a curious smile came to his face. "The Eye?"

Vega tried not to let his surprise show, but didn't do a very good job of it.

Rasche clearly enjoyed being the cat with a mouse. "Oh, I know a great deal about it. About everything you have been doing for the last two years. Surely, you did not think you were unobserved."

Vega hated the idea that Rasche, or anyone, had been watching him, but it was foolish to expect otherwise. Regardless of who observed what, he was in control.

"It is none of your concern," he said. "None of this is. This is my mission."

"And mine is to make sure you do not fail."

"And so you try to sabotage it?" Vega demanded.

"I am trying to save it. Worthiness? I expect such foolishness from Mendoza, but you, how can you believe that a person, a woman, no less, like that Cross creature could possibly be the one to free the staff?"

Rasche was the worst kind of fool, an overconfident one.

Vega wasn't about to admit his own previous doubts about the Eye. He was sure now that Elizabeth Cross was the only one capable of retrieving the staff. "I saw the truth with my own eyes."

"Your eyes deceive you," Rasche said. "Or is it some other part of you that sways your thinking?"

Vega bristled at the illicit implication. He was not attracted to Elizabeth. She was objectively attractive, of course, but his interest in her lay solely in her ability to help him achieve his goal. He was furious last night when he'd heard what had happened, but that was only because she was necessary for the success of his mission. "The Eye has chosen her," he said simply.

Rasche snorted. "An Untermensch? Impossible."

"She is not German, but she—"

Rasche's eyes flashed. "Only one of pure German blood will wield the staff."

"Once it is removed from the stone—"

"You misunderstand me. *I* will remove the staff from the stone. I will bring it to the Führer along with untold riches."

Vega laughed, lightly at first and then with growing fervor. "You?"

"This is not amusing. You question the purity of my blood?"

"Oh, but it is amusing," Vega said. "Not your blood but your soul. You have not been pure of heart since the day you were born. Possibly not even then."

"You cannot truly believe that sophistry. Only one deemed worthy? Who else would the creators choose to give the power of vril to other than a true Aryan?"

"The Eye has chosen."

"A trick of light," Rasche dismissed the idea.

"It was not. I was there."

"You see what you want to see."

"I see what is. The staff can only be removed by one the Eye deems worthy. And that is Eliz—Mrs. Cross. Your idiotic plan to eliminate her could well have destroyed any chance of our retrieving it. I can only imagine what Herr Himmler would say to that."

"You cannot possibly believe that the Creators would have left such a thing for someone like *her* and not—"

"Someone like you?" Vega finished for him. "Yes. And when she removes it from the stone, *I* will be there to take it. *I* will be the one to return it to the Fatherland."

"You and your mongrel blood are not worthy to touch it," Rasche said, the venom in his voice clear.

Vega knew he was more worthy than a thousand Rasches. Blood or not. He was more German than someone like Rasche could ever hope to be. It wasn't just blood but soul that made a man. And his was dedicated to the Reich in a way Rasche could never understand.

"And yet I was tasked with this mission. I'm starting to wonder if you were even sent here or came because of some delusional fantasy you've concocted with yourself as the hero."

"Remember yourself, Deitrich," Rasche warned.

They might be of similar rank, but Rasche did hold far more influence in the party than he. He could not afford to cross him openly. Not yet. But he needed to stay out of his damn way or they would never have the staff.

Sadly, it was clear that Rasche was too stupid or close-minded to see the truth of that.

"The Eye was held by hundreds of people," Vega explained with forced patience, "many of them well-placed within the Reich; I saw to that, I assure you. And it responded to no one. In the ten years Emil has had it, it awakened for only one person. One."

"I have not held it," Rasche said, sitting up like a petulant schoolboy.

"Would you like me to arrange that?" Vega offered, knowing what Rasche's reaction would be. "We can see once and for all if you are worthy?"

"It would draw attention if the stone were stolen now," Rasche replied uneasily, and Vega knew the source of his discomfort was not fear of being caught but fear of the truth being known.

"I'm sure I could find a way to borrow it temporarily without Emil's knowledge."

"It is too risky," Rasche said. "When the time comes I will show you who is worthy and who is not."

Whatever glory Rasche thought he would claim would not come to pass.

"I look forward to it."

SIMON WAS IN NO mood for a party. He had let himself be convinced that going was better than staying in at the hotel, but as he watched Vega help Elizabeth out of the car, his glance lingering just a moment too long, he was already beginning to regret it.

The party was hosted by opera singer Gabriella Besanzoni and her husband, industrialist Enrique Lage, at their rather palatial estate at the foot of Corcovado, the mountain upon which the statue of Christ the Redeemer stood. Simon had to admit that the setting was beautiful. The lush grounds were every bit the tropical paradise, and yet carefully curated and shaped into expansive lawns, paths, and fountains. The home itself was impressive. Mighty pillars and soft grey brickwork gave it an old school elegance of a palazzo in Milan, although the architecture was eclectic, complete with a facade with a portico, a grand pool in the central patio, and Italian frescos adorning the interior walls.

Under different circumstances he would have been pleased to spend time appreciating its beauty, but even now, a day later, his head still throbbed on occasion and he felt more on edge than ever before.

After the incident at Sugarloaf, they had no choice but to tell Emil about their suspicions. He had been mortified at what they'd endured and ready to call off the entire thing. Simon was tempted to let him, let someone else deal with this misadventure. But, as Elizabeth reminded him, there was no one else to do it. She had to go. And where she went, he went.

"Your dress is most becoming," Vega told Elizabeth as she waited for Simon to come around from the other side of the car. "I am so pleased your unfortunate experience has not kept you away tonight."

Despite, or perhaps because of his fears that perhaps Elizabeth deserved something more, he was on edge around her inevitable suitors. Worrying she might be better off with someone else and seeing her with someone else were entirely different things. And he felt a surge of proprietary jealousy that he could not quash.

Knowing better than to voice it, he merely walked over to his wife and escorted her away, giving Vega what Elizabeth would call "the stink eye." He wasn't one for marking his territory, so to speak, but he was compelled to do so tonight. He wanted to make it clear that it was he was the one she came with and he was the one she would leave with. It was petty and needless, but he did it nonetheless.

The ostensible reason for coming to the party was once again to try to curry favor with Minister Correia. If the experience at the casino was any indication, this, too would be a waste of time. He would have much rather stayed in, but Elizabeth insisted they come.

"Have to stay in the game," she'd said.

And so they did.

"I think I could use a drink," Simon announced once they were inside. "Anyone else?"

"I could use a bit of a fortifier myself," Emil said, still shaken by the events of the past day.

Both Elizabeth and Vega declined the offer. Simon was reluctant to leave her side, but knew she would not appreciate being smothered. Even if his concern was warranted.

"We'll be back shortly," he said before he and Emil went to find the bar.

As a string quartet played in the corner, Elizabeth and Alex enjoyed a canapé as they waited for Simon and Emil to return.

"What is this song?" Alex asked. "It is quite lovely."

"It's a ballata from *Rigoletto*," she said as she surveyed the room, looking for the minister.

"You are an aficionado of opera?"

Elizabeth laughed. "No, but I'm married to one. It rubs off. Despite my best efforts to fall asleep during all of them."

Alex smiled, amused. "Your husband does not appear to be in very good humor this evening."

"He's in no humor at all."

"It is understandable, after what you have both endured."

It was, and Elizabeth didn't blame him for being testy. Nearly getting killed will do that to a person. But she knew there was more to it than that. There was something off about him even before Sugarloaf.

"He's worried."

"About you, of course," Alex said.

"Yeah, but I can't …" She wasn't sure it was wise to talk about, but since Jack wasn't around to spill her guts to, she needed someone as a sounding board. Emil wouldn't understand. Raul would probably try to make a move if she confided in him. That left Alex. "Honestly, I think there's something else bothering him. I don't know. He's been funny lately."

"About?"

"Little things. I don't know. Like needing reading glasses. Everyone does."

"As they grow older," Alex agreed.

And as he said that the pieces slowly started to fall into place. Was that what was worrying him?

"You do have quite a difference in your ages," Alex observed.

"It's never bothered him before." And it hadn't. They were so different in so many ways that the difference in their ages seemed irrelevant. At least it was to her.

"I knew a couple once with a large disparity in age. She was thirty and he nearly sixty when they met. He was quite worried that it would be an issue."

"See?" Elizabeth said, trying to push away her worries about Simon's worries.

"It did not work out between them, sadly, but I am sure that will not be the case for you."

So much for not worrying.

VEGA WAS SURPRISED BY Elizabeth's confession about her husband. She was far too open for her own good. And that might be to his advantage. While Rasche was wrong about her—she was the One—he was not wrong about the inconvenience that the Crosses presented. Vega had been willing to tolerate them for as long as necessary to keep Emil happy, but now that Elizabeth's participation in the expedition was all but required, that relationship could not be severed. Her husband, however...

He was still too keen, too observant for Vega's comfort. While he had little doubt in his skill to maintain his facade as Vega, it would be far less taxing without Simon Cross around. Not to mention that he would undoubtedly present a problem once they retrieved the staff. Not an insurmountable one, to be sure, but a problem nonetheless. If it was possible to keep her and eliminate him, all the better.

He could not be as clumsy as Rasche in his attempt to divest himself of Cross. It would require delicacy and finesse. Elizabeth would not continue on if he were injured, he was sure of that. But there were other ways of separating them that did not require violence or brute force.

A man's insecurities could be more destructive than any weapon. Elizabeth may well have given him all he needed to drive a wedge between them. And if she happened to end up needing a shoulder to cry on, he would not resist. She was comely, after all.

SIMON'S TEMPERAMENT DID NOT improve over the course of the evening. As he had suspected, the minister was content to merely toy with them again. It was growing tiresome, and Simon was growing tired. His head and his jaw ached, and he wanted nothing more than to catch up on the sleep he'd missed last night. Although, he knew he would not sleep soundly again until they were home.

"It was a wondrous sight, as you can imagine," Emil went on next to him in the back seat. "Each day at Pueblo Bonito was a revelation."

Under normal circumstances, Simon would have loved to discuss the discoveries in Chaco Canyon, but tonight he was more interested in the conversation Vega and Elizabeth were having in the front seat. Vega had offered to drive and, given Simon's headache and lack of knowledge of the area, he was happy to relent. But he was beginning to regret it.

Vega's and Elizabeth's conversation was innocuous enough, something about time at university, but it was the way he looked at her that kept Simon's attention. It wasn't the prurient way Raul admired her, but something more troubling. It was difficult to put his finger on, but there was a light in Vega's eyes occasionally when he glanced over from the driver's seat in her direction that made Simon distinctly uncomfortable.

He was about to mention something to the effect that Vega should perhaps keep his eyes on the road when the car's engine sputtered. It coughed several times, misfiring. It had been driving rough all night, but Simon had written it off as merely a symptom of being an older car in a tropical climate. But when the coughing and the wheezing became a sputter and then silence, he knew it was more.

"Oh, dear," Emil said as Vega pulled them over to the soft shoulder of the dark road.

Vega tried to start the engine again, but it wouldn't catch.

There were no houses around and considering where they were, it would be unlikely any would have a telephone regardless.

Vega opened his door. "Let me a take a look and see what I can do."

"Would you open the trunk?" Elizabeth asked. "I think I saw a flashlight in there."

They all exited the car and Vega opened the hood.

Simon found the flashlight and shined it on the engine.

"Check the leads first," Vega said to himself and leaned over the car. "Can you shine the light there?"

Simon knew a great many things, but his knowledge of cars was limited to working the GPS and calling AAA.

"Here, let me," Elizabeth said at his side as she reached for the flashlight.

Reluctantly, he gave it to her and stepped back.

She and Vega leaned in together to search for the source of the problem.

"Looks okay," she said.

"You are knowledgeble about automobiles?" Vega asked in surprise.

"Some. I had an old car that liked to play dead. Learned a lot keeping it going."

"Opera and autos?" Vega said. "If I am a Renaissance man, then you are indeed Renaissance woman."

Simon had always hated that damn Bug of hers and now he hated it even more.

The two of them huddled close together as they tried to diagnose the trouble. "Might be the fuel filter," Elizabeth said. "Mine was always getting gunked up."

"Good idea," Vega replied. "Can you shine the light just there?"

They both leaned over, their bodies touching, as Vega reached down into the engine and Elizabeth held the light for him. They worked well together, laughing and joking as Vega removed some sort of glass jar from the inside of the engine compartment. Together, they cleaned the filter and reattached it.

"That should do it," Vega announced.

"Well done, my boy," Emil said. "Well done, both of you. You two make a marvelous team."

Simon gritted his teeth as he got back into the car, hating beyond reason that Emil was right.

CHAPTER THIRTEEN

"**D**AMMIT!"

"You all right?" Elizabeth asked from their bedroom as she finished buttoning her blouse. All she heard in reply was angry muttering and went in to see what was the matter.

Simon arched his neck to get a better look at the small cut he'd carved in his neck with the straight razor. The injury was slight, but a trickle of blood was already dripping down his throat.

He'd grown quite adept over the years at using one, but occasionally, especially when he was tired or distracted, he managed to cut himself.

Elizabeth tore off a bit of tissue and applied it to the cut.

Simon huffed out a breath. "Thank you."

She ran her hand up his arm. "Are you all right?"

"Fine," he said tersely and returned to shaving.

Elizabeth didn't ask again. It was clear whatever burr was under his saddle, he wasn't ready to talk about it yet. Instead, she observed him silently for a moment. His eyes were slightly bloodshot. She knew he hadn't slept well or much at all the last few nights. That would make anyone cranky. But she also knew there was more to it. At first, she'd chalked it up to their near-death experience in the tram, but his mood pre-dated that extravaganza. Last night he'd been quiet and withdrawn and even almost rude to Alex.

She had the worrying thought that maybe his head injury was worse than he was letting on.

"Are you sure you're okay?"

"I told you I was fine," he said.

They didn't fight often, but she felt one coming on. He was being closed off and that was one thing they'd both promised each other they wouldn't do. They might disagree, even argue, but they tried not to keep things from each other. Not important things anyway. And he was doing just that.

She turned to leave, trying valiantly not to pry, but she was worried and, honestly, a little hurt. Being pushed away like that wasn't something he did to her often anymore. And when he did, when the old Simon, the one who built walls to keep people out, built a wall to keep her out, it was painful.

"Okay," she said trying to sound neutral, and started to leave.

"I'm sorry," he said, looking at her in the mirror before turning to face her. He looked ready to say more but didn't and turned back to his reflection. "I'm just tired."

Another brick in his wall.

She nodded, accepting his apology, but still feeling the sting of rejection. "I'm going to go down early and get a table."

With Carnival just a few days away, the hotel was filling up to capacity and finding a good table at the restaurant was becoming a challenge. Leaving early also gave her an excuse to take a breather and try to talk herself out of getting too wound up over things. Maybe he was just tired.

"All right," he said, not looking at her anymore.

She hesitated in the doorway for a moment but then left. She grabbed her purse and headed for the elevator, telling herself to let it go. She had more pressing things to worry about.

The elevator doors opened to reveal Clay Bridges leaning against the wall. He was the only one inside. She considered not getting in; she didn't trust him and was fairly certain he was behind the break-in into their rooms, but she'd be damned if she was going to let him intimidate her.

"Mornin'," he said, pushing the brim of his Stetson up slightly.

"Mr. Bridges," she said politely, pressing the lobby elevator button even though it was already lit.

The doors closed and that awkward elevator silence ensued, but only for a moment.

"Heard about your little adventure on old Sugarloaf," he said.

They'd not told anyone other than Emil and Vega about that, but Bridges apparently had a way of finding things out. "I don't know what you're talking about."

She kept her eyes forward, but out of the corner of her eye saw him push off from the wall and take a step closer, so she turned to defiantly face him.

"Now, why would you want to go and lie to me?" he asked.

"Because I don't trust you."

He snorted with laughter. "Fair enough. I appreciate your directness."

"And I would appreciate it if you would leave Dr. Mendoza alone."

"No can do, I'm afraid. And besides, if this is what he thinks it is, and the old man's usually right, there's more than enough to go around."

"Do you ever do anything yourself or do you always steal someone else's work?" she said, letting her simmering emotions from earlier get the better of her.

His smile remained, but the good humor behind it died. "You should be careful, Mrs. Cross. This can be . . .dangerous work."

"Is that a threat?" She knew it was.

"Just a bit of friendly advice, ma'am," he said as the doors opened.

He touched the brim of his hat and exited the elevator, leaving her feeling like she'd only managed to make things worse. She'd really thought, maybe, possibly, since they'd survived Strasser's attempt on their lives, that they might at least get a break, but apparently not. Rasche was still out there and Bridges couldn't be ignored either.

A few minutes later, Simon joined her at the small table she'd manage to wrangle at the restaurant, but he didn't sit down and join her.

"We'll have to skip breakfast, I'm afraid," he said.

"What is it?"

"I received a call. It seems Cadú has returned home."

SIMON RAPPED SHARPLY ON Cadú's door. Elizabeth wished they had Raul or Emil with them to translate, but neither was around and Simon didn't want to wait and possibly miss Cadú. So they'd gone on their own to meet with him.

Behind the closed door, she could hear the children screaming and playing and then a man's voice yelling. A moment later, the door opened. The man on the other side was about forty years old, not quite fat but working on it, and with a dark complexion and impossibly black hair. Slightly greying stubble covered his chin and cheeks, and he scratched it as he looked at them.

"Cadú?" Simon asked.

The man's eyes narrowed warily.

"We'd like to speak with you."

He eyed them up and down, suspicious but also curious. "About what?"

"Gaspar."

The name was like a gunshot. Cadú slammed the door shut, or tried to, but Simon was too fast and a strong hand kept it from closing all the way. He pushed the door open and they stepped inside. The living room was just off to the right and they entered just in time to see Cadú dive head-first through the open window.

Elizabeth gasped as they ran toward it. He hadn't plummeted to his death; they were, after all only on the second story, but he instead landed on a nearby rooftop, shoulder-rolled and kept on running.

"Oh, hell," she muttered. Her dress and shoes were not designed for Jason Bourning, but they couldn't afford to let him go. She started to climb out of the window.

"Don't be absurd," Simon said, taking hold of her arm. "Come on." He pulled her back toward the front door and down the stairs.

"He's getting away," she protested. If they lost him now they'd surely never find him again.

"What goes up must come down," Simon said, and then she understood. Cadú might be able to jump from rooftop to rooftop, but eventually he'd have to come down.

The buildings in the neighborhood were built in roughly aligned rows with slender alleys between them and narrow walking paths running on either side of the row.

"This way," Simon said, pointing at the pathway in front of them in the direction Cadú had run. He started down the path, but Elizabeth paused.

"We should split up," she said. "Be on either side, cover more ground."

Simon was about to argue, but she didn't let him. There wasn't time. She dashed between the buildings to cover the other side.

She ran up the narrow alleyway trying to keep pace with them both. Her heels were low, thank God, but her little pumps were definitely not track shoes. The leather soles were slick and she found herself constantly slipping on the pavement.

As they passed the gaps between buildings, she caught glimpses of Simon on the other side of the row. Above her, Cadú leapt over the small chasm between buildings.

For the first few buildings her little alleyway was clear and straight, but the higher up the mountain they climbed the more of a warren it all became. The buildings were like a giant game of Jenga gone wrong and she had to climb steps, make sharp turns and duck under clothes lines.

Before long her legs and her lungs began to burn. She seriously needed to hit the gym when they got back. Piles of empty and half-empty crates blocked her path and she clambered over them, tearing her dress.

"Fiddle."

The snag slowed her down but she caught up enough to see Cadu running on the roofs above her much faster than a man his size should be able to.

Eventually, she found a strange rhythm to it all and moved gracefully around each obstacle. She pulled off what she thought was a pretty sweet Barry Sanders-esque spin move to miss a man coming outside to toss his garbage and was just wondering if she'd missed her calling when she tripped and face-planted right in front of him. He looked at her in mild curiosity as if people did this sort of thing all the time here.

183

"*Ola*," she said as she picked herself up and brushed off bits of gravel that left red, raw divots in her palms.

The man dumped his garbage and went back inside.

Elizabeth pushed on, but knew the delay had cost her and worried that she'd fallen hopelessly behind when suddenly Cadú leapt over the chasm in front of her.

"Simon!" she called out. "He's here! This way!"

Cadú made a sharp right and Elizabeth turned to follow.

Behind her she heard Simon calling out her name. In the maze of buildings Cadú's sharp turn had made it nearly impossible for him to track where she was.

"Here!" she called out, but didn't dare stop running.

The cramped alleyway she was in suddenly intersected with a wider street, at least fifteen feet across. The gap was too wide for him to traverse and on the rooftop above her Cadú tried to skid to a halt, but lost his footing and slid over the side. He clung to the side of the building briefly and she ran over to him. But like her, he couldn't do a pull-up either and dropped like a sack of potatoes at her feet, crying out as his ankle twisted.

Elizabeth was sweating, filthy, and her dress was torn as she looked down at him. "It really would have been easier to invite us in for tea."

Cadú winced and held his leg. Several people stopped to stare, but only briefly and then stuck to their own business.

"Elizabeth!" Simon called from not too far away.

"Over here."

Simon arrived out of breath but looking no worse for the wear. "Are you all right? What happened?"

"What goes up..."

Simon glared down at Cadú, who was panting for breath and in obvious pain.

Simon knelt down next to him and Cadú shrunk away.

"What happened with Gaspar?" Simon demanded.

"It was an accident."

"He accidentally hit the back of his head?"

"I did not mean to hurt him. We fought and he hit his head."

"And the bowl?"

"I—I sold it. To—to a shop in Benfica near the hospital. I did not mean to harm Gaspar. You must believe me."

In the end, it didn't matter if they believed him or not. They couldn't afford to have the police involved any more than he could.

SIMON FINISHED CHANGING HIS shirt as he waited for Elizabeth to emerge from the shower. After they left Cadú they immediately went to the second hand shop where he'd sold the bowl, only to find out that it had already been resold, apparently to some collector near Ipanema.

They returned to the hotel to pick up Emil and for Elizabeth to clean up after her fall. She claimed that she was all right, but she was uncharacteristically quiet since the favela. While they still didn't have the bowl, they had made immense progress. Her distance worried him.

Finally, she emerged from the shower, a towel wrapped around her, her damp hair cascading onto her shoulders. Another scrape adorned her already bedazzled knee, fresh blood seeping to the surface after its cleansing.

"Are you all right?" he said coming toward her.

"Fine."

"Elizabeth."

"I told you I was fine," she said, imitating both his accent and his tartness from that morning and then fighting down a smile.

He felt both guilty and ashamed for his rudeness from this morning. "I'm sorry I was short with you earlier. Forgive me."

She looked at him with a warmth and understanding he was sure he did not deserve. "You've been fighting for your life, got a concussion, haven't slept in days, and the fate of the world as we know it is currently jigging on the head of a pin in the Brazilian jungle. I'd say you're entitled to being a little testy now and then."

He gently took hold of her arms. "An explanation, but not an excuse. I am sorry."

She nodded her acceptance, but he knew there was more bothering her than his earlier asperity.

"Sit," he said, as he maneuvered her to a chair in their bedroom. "Let me see to your leg."

She let him guide her to a seat and waited for him to return with first aid supplies. He knelt at her feet and gently disinfected the wound. It was red and angry but not deep.

He dabbed at it gently with gauze. "I wish you'd tell me what's wrong."

If she saw the irony in his question, she ignored it. "I just . . . I hate the idea that we have to do bad things in order to achieve the good things."

He was beginning to understand. "Letting Cadú go free?"

"He killed someone. It might have been an accident like he said, but Gaspar is dead and the man responsible won't face justice because we're playing God."

"We have no choice. Minister Corriea—"

"I know," she said with a heavy sigh. "If he found out, and he would, he won't grant us the permit and the mission would fail," she said, resigned to the truth but not liking it. "The needs of the many and all that."

It was a prickly ethical dilemma. Do the right thing and destroy any chance the mission might have for success and with it risk the future itself, or look the other way in this one instance and ensure they still had a chance to find the staff and save the timeline.

It wasn't the first time they'd had to make a choice like this. They'd even been forced to keep Jack the Ripper alive to preserve the timeline once. Simon was sure it wouldn't be the last time they'd face such a quandary.

He pulled out the Mercurochrome and hesitated.

"Is it going to sting?" she asked.

He read the bottle, although he knew what it would say. "Yes, but it also contains small amounts of mercury which is why it's no longer available."

"Oh. Well, I think we can risk it this one time."

She was undoubtedly right. The sanitation in the favelas was far from ideal. Better this than nothing.

He gently held on to her calf, applied a small amount, and then lightly blew on it to help alleviate the sting.

"You know, it's worth getting a scraped knee for that," she said, a playfully seductive smile coming her lips.

He ran his hand up the back of her leg to the knee, relishing in her reaction. "Is it?"

She leaned forward and gently grasped the front of his shirt to pull him toward her for a kiss. Their lips were almost touching when there was a knock at the door.

"Bugger."

It was probably Emil, ready to go with them to the collector's house.

"Remember where we left off," she said, giving him a small, promising kiss on the corner of his mouth.

He would not forget.

"Eep! I'm not even dressed yet!" she cried.

"No. Perhaps, you should put on something a bit more . . .more."

"Right." She hurried into the bathroom only to do a quick u-turn and grab the clothes she'd set out.

He watched her go, a familiar warmth spreading in his chest, until the knock came again, pulling him back to less enjoyable but more practical matters.

THE COLLECTOR, CIRANO INFANTI, lived in an impressive home in Gávea brimming with enough artifacts to fill a museum. Elizabeth didn't know much, or anything, about Mesoamerican art. Heck, she'd only recently realized that pre-Columbian meant before Columbus. So while Simon and Emil oohed and ahhed over small clay figurines and chipped bowls, she contented herself with admiring the paintings on the far wall of the salon where they waited for Infanti.

"Is this a Picasso?"

Simon joined her and inspected the signature. "I think it is."

"Well, well." The only collection she had growing up was the garnets she used to pick out of the gravel.

The collector certainly knew how to collect. The room was filled with art and artifacts, but there was no sign of the bowl. Yet.

A few minutes later a small gray-haired man with an olive complexion, a quick smile, and a fastidious demeanor entered the room. "I'm sorry, I was not . . .um." He clasped his hands together. "Forgive me, but who exactly are you?"

Emil strode forward, hand extended. "My apologies for coming unannounced. I am Dr. Emil Mendoza, Professor Emeritus National Autonomous University of Mexico, and this is Simon and Elizabeth Cross."

Infanti looked at them politely but cautiously. "And what is it I can do for you?"

"We've come about one of your pieces. A recent acquisition," Emil said.

"Ah, I see," he gestured for them to sit. "My collection has drawn quite a bit of attention."

"I've no doubt," Emil said.

Elizabeth took a seat but neither Emil nor Simon did.

"And what piece was it you were curious about?"

"A golden bowl with a snake wrapping itself around the outside, a jararaca to be specific."

"Ah! Yes, marvelous. I've only just obtained that. Days ago as a matter of fact. How is it you know of it?"

Emil said firmly, "Because it belongs to me."

Infanti straightened to his full, if unimposing, height, but his hands trembled and he clasped them more tightly than before. "I'm afraid you are mistaken."

"I am not," Emil said, bluntly. "The bowl was stolen from one of my men and sold to a pawn shop where I believe you bought it."

Infanti laughed, a slightly high-pitched sound. "I think perhaps you should go."

Emil did not budge. "I had thought at first that you were merely ignorant of its provenance, but having admired some of your 'collection,' I see now that you are simply a thief."

"I beg your pardon."

"That Teotihuacan mask and that Chinesco figure were stolen from Mexico City last year," Emil said and walked over to a bookcase where a small squat figure sat. "This Chancay figure was taken from the museum here in Rio not more than three weeks ago."

Infanti looked torn between denial and running for his life.

"Should I go on?" Emil asked.

Elizabeth was impressed. She'd never seen Emil so forceful before.

Infanti looked nervously from Simon to Emil. "What do you want?"

"For you to return all of these to their proper owners," Simon said. "You can do so anonymously or the Provincial Police can do it for you."

"And in return?" Infanti asked.

Emil held out his hand. "My bowl."

CHAPTER FOURTEEN

"I'D HATE TO BE that guy," Elizabeth said, "but I don't see any map."

After retrieving the bowl from Infanti they were joined by Alex Vega and retired to Emil's hotel room to study it privately. Emil had also retrieved the small Chancay figurine, planning on returning it to the museum himself.

"Don't get me wrong," she went on, "it's gorgeous, if a little creepy."

The golden snake wrapped along the outside of the bowl was so lifelike she thought it might come to life at any second. The head was very detailed and she could even see the small fangs as it bit into the edge of the bowl.

"Yes," Emil said, clearly perplexed. "The drawings I found and the literature described the bowl in rather basic terms—the shape, the general size, etc. The etchings here and here," he said as he pointed to a series of glyphs and esoteric writing that was far beyond Elizabeth, "were not relayed in any detail. All that was said about the map was that the bowl contained it."

"Contained it?" Simon echoed.

"Yes, exactly that—that the map was contained within the bowl."

They all looked at it again as if something would change from the last hour-plus that they'd stared at it, but nothing did.

"Maybe what's written on the side of the bowl is the map, directions," she suggested.

"No, I do not think so," Alex said. "I have not fully translated them, but they speak of a snake, many snakes actually."

"Rivers maybe?"

"Possibly," Alex said, admiration at her logic in his voice.

"What if the map is in the bowl?" Simon suggested. "Literally inside the metal."

"And we have to melt it down to find it?" Emil replied. "Let us hope that is a course of last resort."

That was true. There was no un-melting if they were wrong.

"The writing has to be key," Alex said.

"Maybe they're directions," Elizabeth said, "not to where the city is but how to find the map. I mean directions like on a bottle of headache powder or do-it-yourself kit. Maybe they tell us how to unlock the map?"

Emil's face lit at the possibility. "Very good, my dear."

"Not just a pretty face, ya know," Elizabeth replied with mock conceit.

"And so humble, as well," Simon said jokingly.

"So, what does it say?"

Alex picked up the bowl and studied the complex symbols. "It'll take some time. Perhaps we can all work on it if we copy down what's on the bowl and study it."

Between the three of them, Elizabeth was sure they'd have it solved in no time. No time ended up being three hours. She was stuffing her face with a ham sandwich when Emil cried out.

"I think we've got it!"

Elizabeth took one more bite of her sandwich and rejoined them at the table.

"Well?" she asked, covering her mouth as she finished swallowing.

"It's a bit vague," Simon put in.

Elizabeth was disappointed but not surprised. "What does it say?"

"Only 'that which brings darkness will light the path.'"

"That's all?" she asked, and the others nodded. "That is vague."

"I'm not sure what it means," Alex admitted. "What brings darkness?"

"Maybe there's bioluminescent material in the metal and in the dark the map is revealed?" Simon suggested.

"Possible."

They closed the drapes and shut off the light to test the theory, but nothing changed. The bowl didn't glow.

Emil turned the lights back on. "It was a good thought."

Elizabeth stared at the bowl. Maybe it was like one of those third eye thingies and you had to un-focus to see it.

The men continued to brainstorm ideas.

"Maybe we are being too literal," Alex wondered aloud. "What other kinds of light and dark are there?"

"Knowledge and ignorance," Emil said.

"Beginning and ending."

"Perhaps the translation is wrong."

Elizabeth stared into the beady little eyes of the snake as it took a bite out of the rim of the bowl.

"Possible."

"Life and death?" Simon offered.

"If one has to die to see the map, that might be a problem."

"Venom," Elizabeth said suddenly. "These jacarandas—"

"Jararacas," Emil corrected.

"That. They're venomous, right?"

Emil was confused but intrigued. "Yes, quite."

"At first, I thought the snake was taking a bite out of the bowl, but he's not. He's being, what's it called when you extract the venom?"

"Milked," Simon said.

"Really? That's gross." She turned the bowl toward her to demonstrate her idea. "I don't think he's biting the bowl at all. I think he's excreting his venom into it."

"Only that which brings darkness will light the path," Simon recited. "The venom could be the darkness. It's possible there are chemical properties in it that interact with the bowl somehow."

Alex turned to Elizabeth. "Very much more than a pretty face."

Had they actually figured it out?

Emil looked like he was trying not to be excited at the prospect but failing. "It is most definitely worth pursuing."

"Good," Elizabeth said. "Just one question—where on earth do we find enough venom to fill a bowl?"

ELIZABETH HAD HAPPILY LIVED her life until early today ignorant of the idea that there were snake farms. She wasn't a fan of snakes. Not that she hated them, they were just being snakes, but she'd much rather they do their thing in a place where she wasn't doing her thing. She'd had a few uncomfortable encounters and now she was on her way to an entire farm of them.

Alex found a snake farm only a few hours outside of Rio. It was a supplier to the Instituto Butantan just outside of São Paulo, a world-renowned biological research center that specialized in all things venomous including lizards, spiders, insects and, of course, snakes. The satellite farm was used to harvest venom to be sent for research in immunology and infectious disease.

She wasn't sure what she'd been expecting—it was hard to imagine snakes out to pasture and then slithering into the barn at night—but the snake farm wasn't like any farm she'd ever seen. It was strange and reminded her a little of miniaturized Tatooine—little domed huts sitting on a barren landscape.

The snakes were kept on a small man-made island surrounded by a wall and a deep moat with steep sides. The little island itself wasn't more than sixty or seventy feet long and half that across with a dozen or so two to four foot high clay huts scattered across the low grass. Small paths wound their way from hut to hut.

A man in a white coat walked from hut to hut with a long stick, poking and dragging snakes either in or out.

She took hold of Simon's hand tightly. He glanced down at her half-amused and half-cautious. Strasser might be dead, but Rasche was not. Not to mention Clay Bridges was still about and had all but openly threatened them. When walking past a snake pit, under the best of circumstances, it paid to be careful. Now, it was a requirement.

But no one bothered them and for the sweet price of over one million reis, a little more than one hundred US dollars, they purchased less than one ounce of venom. They tried to get more, since a paltry ounce was hardly enough to fill the bowl, but they were lucky to get what they did. Now, all they could do was hope her theory was right and that it was enough.

I<small>T WAS LATE BY</small> the time they returned to Rio, but Elizabeth wasn't tired; no one was. They retrieved the bowl from the hotel safe and went up to Emil's room again.

His hand trembled with excitement as he poured their small precious vial of amber liquid into the bowl. They all gathered closely as he swirled the venom around trying to coat the entire inner surface. It smelled vaguely like rotten meat to her although no one else seemed to notice.

And then they waited.

"You don't think we're supposed to drink it, do you?" she asked. It was in a bowl after all.

Emil grimaced. "Lord, I hope not."

"Some venom does have neurotoxins that could theoretically have psychotropic effects, alter brain chemistry," Simon mused. "But let's hold off on that, shall we?"

The four of them stared at the bowl, willing something to happen. The seconds ticked by with no change when slowly, ever so slowly, an image began to emerge in the inner shell of the bowl.

"Look," Emil said, breathless with anticipation as line after line began to appear.

Alex quickly retrieved his pad and pencil and began to sketch out the image.

It looked a little like an inset from a map in her old copy of Lord of the Rings—mountains were tiny little carets, rivers squiggly lines, and lakes dark blobs. There was no writing on it, though, only a few symbols and one that looked a little like a caduceus, which she realized might represent the staff.

"Do you know where this is?" Simon asked.

Emil stared at the emerging map, enraptured.

"Emil?"

He looked up in confusion until Simon repeated his question. Emil went to the desk and pulled an old-fashioned paper map out of the pile of papers and laid it next to the one Alex was drawing. The similarities were obvious.

Emil tapped his finger onto the map. "Here."

"That's a large area," Simon noted.

"Yes, but this. You see this little bit," Emil said, gesturing to a section of the map in the bowl. "This is a particular stretch of river. You see how it bends back and forth and back and forth in quick succession."

"Like a snake," Elizabeth realized aloud.

"Yes, exactly." Emil gathered more papers. "There was a mention of that in one of the journals I found and this, this here. This flat-topped peak, you see, it's like a butte. You see how this one's different from the others? The city and the staff must be between the river and the mountain."

"Remarkable."

Alex studied his sketch to make sure he hadn't missed anything and then began to grin and laugh. "It is unbelievable, and yet . . . I think we have actually found it."

"I must dispatch Raul to make final preparations immediately," Emil said.

"We have not secured our permit yet," Alex reminded him.

Buoyed by their success, nothing could put a damper on Emil's enthusiasm. "We will, my boy, we will."

SIMON CAME AWAKE AS he felt the bed shift. It wasn't the first time that night. The tables had somehow been turned and Elizabeth was the restless one.

He rolled onto his side. "Are you all right?" he asked in a voice groggy with sleep.

"Did I wake you?"

He shook his head. "What's wrong? Are you worried about the expedition?"

Now that they'd found the bowl and the map, it was all becoming that much more real. The entire mission's success lay upon her shoulders.

"No. I've got 'The Girl from Ipanema' stuck in my head."

His brain was still foggy. "What girl?"

Elizabeth pushed herself up onto her elbow. "You know." She hummed a few bars of the famous bossa nova.

"I saw a sign that said Ipanema," she went on. "That's all it took. I can't get it out of my head now."

Relieved it wasn't something serious, Simon closed his eyes and rested his head against the pillow again. "Just try to think of something else."

"Why hadn't I thought of that?" she said tartly.

He opened one eye to sleepily glare at her.

"Sorry," she said. "Go back to sleep."

He settled in again only to hear her softly humming the song.

"Elizabeth."

"Sorry."

Silence came again and he was just starting to fall back asleep when the earworm took root and the song began to play of its own volition inside his head.

"Dammit," he grumbled, opening his eyes again. "Now, you've got me doing it."

She laughed and managed a weak, "Sorry."

Misery did love company, after all.

She moved closer, her hand resting on his bare chest. "But, now that you're awake..."

He tucked a stray tendril of hair behind her ear. "You have an idea of how to pass the time."

She leaned in and kissed him, and then said softly, "Let's play cards."

Simon laughed as she feigned getting up, and he dutifully pulled her back toward him so that she lay half on top of him.

The playfulness dissolved into something more serious as they simply looked at each other. He gazed up at her in the dim light, amazed as always that she was his wife. He pulled her down for another, deeper kiss, and soon the song and everything else in the world was forgotten.

CHAPTER FIFTEEN

ELIZABETH HELPED SIMON AFFIX his mask for tonight's Carnival Masquerade Ball. It seemed a fitting way to celebrate their finding the map. Even though they had yet to convince Minister Correia to give them the permit, she had faith that Alex would soon. Then they'd be traipsing through the jungle in the mud and the muck and the snakes. A night out wearing a designer gown, drinking champagne, and dancing with her husband was the perfect distraction for what was to come.

"I look ridiculous," Simon said as he looked at his reflection in the full-length mirror in their bedroom suite.

"You look handsome and mysterious." And he did. The mask wasn't as ornate as others, but it suited him. It was black with gold filigree. "You look like an extra hot Phantom of the Opera."

In his tuxedo, he almost did.

"If I recall correctly," he said, taking off the mask, "he lost the girl."

"He gave up the girl," she corrected. "So unless you have plans to hand me over to another man, I wouldn't worry."

He looked at her oddly for a moment and then put on his mask again.

She admired them both in the mirror, making sure they were ready to go downstairs. They were a handsome couple. She loved her dress. She'd been saving it for just an occasion like this. It was made of floor length, cobalt blue silk and was slinky in all the right places. It had a low back and a somewhat low front, lower than she was used to anyway. But it was too gorgeous to be self-conscious in.

She put on her mask, careful not to mess up her hair. It had taken forever and a day to get right. Her mask was more ornate than Simon's, although not nearly as fanciful as some. It was the same blue, or nearly, as her dress. The left upper section of the mask rose up into a cresting wave with a plume of blue feathers alongside it.

"Ready?" she asked.

"We could celebrate here," he suggested. "Alone."

"And miss all the free booze?" she said, turning to him and placing her hand upon his chest. "Do you really want to stay in?"

He didn't answer at first but finally said, "It would be a crime to deprive the world of your beauty."

"It's a masquerade ball," she reminded him.

"No mask can hide it."

She moved closer still. For a stuffy Englishman he was the most romantic man she'd ever met. She slipped her arms around his waist and he instinctively followed suit. "Maybe we should stay in."

His thumb gently traced the contour of her mouth. "Perhaps some things are better for the waiting."

The idea and the way he said it roused her passion. If he wanted to play, she was more than happy to play along. She slid from his grasp and said coyly over her shoulder, "I suppose we'll find out."

She paused to smooth the fabric over her hips and she heard him swallow hard.

"What have I done?"

"You look lovely, my dear," Emil said as he greeted them in the ballroom.

"Thank you."

The ball was everything she had hoped it would be. She'd never been to a Venetian ball, but this was pretty much how she envisioned them. Women were in exquisite gowns, men in striking tuxedos, and nearly everyone was wearing a mask, except Emil.

"You're not wearing your mask," she said, seeing his peeking out from his jacket pocket.

"I feel a bit foolish. An old man in a mask."

"You're hardly old and never foolish," she said.

Emil nearly blushed and reached to pull out his mask and put it on. "She is very convincing."

"You have no idea."

"Is Raul here?" she asked.

"He has traveled to Mato Grosso to complete the necessary preparations for the expedition."

"I'm sorry he's missing this."

"I am afraid you are stuck with me." Emil put his mask in place. "How do I look?"

"Dashing."

"Enough to earn a dance?"

Elizabeth held out her hand. "I'd love to."

Emil took her hand and began to lead her out onto the dance floor. "I'll try not to trod on her feet too badly," he called back to Simon.

The band was already playing "Did You Ever See A Dream Walking" as they found a spot.

Emil was shy at first and a bit of an awkward dancer, but they soon found a comfortable rhythm. They danced in silence, content to enjoy the music.

After a few moments Emil began to stare at her, so long in the face that she wondered if something was wrong. As if hearing her unvoiced question, he shook his head. "I'm sorry. But your resemblance to my daughter is striking."

"I'm flattered."

"Your smile and something about your eyes. Your kindness, I think, that was very much Aurora."

Elizabeth noted the use of the past tense. She was hesitant to bring it up, but couldn't stop her curiosity. "Was?"

The haunted sadness brought on only by profound loss came to his eyes. Looking embarrassed at his show of emotion, he stared off into the crowd as he spoke. "She . . .died several years ago."

"I'm sorry."

His eyes flicked back to hers. "As am I."

She had no idea that his daughter had passed. The mere thought of it brought back memories of her own she'd done her best to bury.

"I'm sure she'd be very proud of you," Elizabeth said. "Of all you've accomplished."

The sadness in his eyes was joined by something else, something she couldn't quite identify. "We shall see. I mean to say, we still have a great deal left ahead of us."

That was true enough. "But for tonight, we dance."

On cue the music segued from the gentle jazz standard to a more upbeat song. Emil hesitated but Elizabeth didn't let him stop. "Tonight, we dance," she reminded him.

He was far less sure in the steps of the Fox Trot than the pseudo-waltz they'd been doing, but Elizabeth was having a ball as they bounded around the floor.

SIMON WATCHED THEM DANCE and had to chuckle. Emil was quite literally trodding on Elizabeth's feet. He knew she would be a good sport about it and not let anything stop her from enjoying the evening.

He wished he could feel the same as Vega approached. He had no reason to dislike the man. In fact, he had every reason to the contrary. He was knowledgeable, helpful, and had acted in no way inappropriately. And yet, Simon found himself on edge around him. He didn't like to admit that it was perhaps that he saw in Vega the sort of man that might suit Elizabeth if circumstances were different.

Vega removed his mask as he neared. "Distracting, aren't they?" he said by way of explanation.

Vega's removal seemed to give him silent permission to do the same. "Very."

They stood together for a moment looking around the ballroom before Vega spoke again.

"And where is your wife?"

"Dancing with Emil."

"Being danced upon, you mean," Vega said. "I have seen him dance before, if that's what it can be called. The man has not two but apparently three left feet."

Simon chuckled.

"I saw the minister earlier," Vega continued as they stood on the periphery of the party watching the dancers.

"And?"

"He has invited us to his home for a party."

Simon thought that was promising. "Has he?"

"In three days' time."

Blast. Would this mission never end? "Well, at least it's an overture." He glanced at Vega. "Do you think we can convince him?"

"Every man has his breaking point."

It was cynical but accurate. And Simon hoped it was true in the minister's case.

Emil and Elizabeth flowed past them in the crowd.

"Your wife is looking exceptionally beautiful this evening."

Simon couldn't argue. "Yes, she is."

"But I am not sure she will survive," he added as Emil stepped on her foot again. Too chagrined to continue, he led her back over to Simon and Vega.

Emil mopped his brow with his handkerchief and said to Simon, "I don't know how you keep up with her."

Old to man to old man, eh?

Simon managed a polite smile.

"I'm afraid I must beg off of more dancing," Emil said. "For my sake as well as yours."

Simon knew Elizabeth wasn't ready to stop. "Dance with me?" she asked Vega.

Vega looked uncertainly at Simon, who deferred to Elizabeth. Who she danced with was her choice. Although he knew she bypassed asking him because he far preferred dancing to a more sedate rhythm, it still bothered him. If she'd asked he would have declined, and yet, the fact that she turned to Vega without hesitation irritated him.

"Come on," Elizabeth said, reaching for Vega's hand. "We have to celebrate finding the map."

Unable to resist her, Vega capitulated, leaving Simon and Emil on the sidelines to watch.

Vega leaned in and whispered something to her as they found a spot on the crowded dance floor causing Elizabeth to throw back her head and laugh. Simon clenched his jaw and watched as Vega took her into his arms, their bodies pressed together. He was, as Simon had feared, an exceptionally competent dancer and maneuvered Elizabeth effortlessly around the floor. She beamed as he led her through the steps.

Emil sighed, exhausted from his earlier effort. "Well, I think I could use a drink. You?"

Elizabeth and Vega passed by in each other's arms. "Definitely."

SIMON WATCHED ELIZABETH DANCE and tried to quash the growing irritation he felt. It was irrational. She enjoyed dancing and had found a willing partner when he was not one. There was no harm in it, and yet he felt an increasing sense of unease as he watched Vega dance with his wife.

"Champagne," Emil said as he held out a glass to Simon.

"Thank you."

Just as he reached for it someone bumped into Emil from behind and the contents of the glass sloshed out soaking the front of Simon's shirt.

"Sorry," the man muttered and hurried on his way.

"Oh, dear," Emil said, looking at the wet stain on Simon's shirt and jacket. "Terribly sorry."

Simon tried to blot the champagne away with his handkerchief, but it required more attention than he could give on the ballroom floor.

"You'll excuse me. I'm just going to clean up a little."

Simon made his way to the edge of the ballroom and the foyer that led to the restrooms.

"I seem to have ..." he told the attendant, gesturing to his wet shirtfront.

The attendant picked up a towel. "May I?"

"That's all right. I'll do it myself."

The attendant handed him the towel and Simon walked to the sink to get a bit of water to wipe away the champagne stain. He was making good progress on it when several men entered together. He recognized their reflections in the mirror immediately. Clay Bridges and his band of not-so Merry Men.

They quickly took stock of the room as the only other occupant finished washing his hands and left. Simon braced himself but continued cleaning his shirt and coat, surreptitiously searching for anything he might be able to use to defend himself.

Clay loomed over the small attendant. "Get out."

The man glanced nervously at Simon, but he was frightened of Bridges, and with good reason. Bridges stuffed a few bills into his pocket. "And make sure we're not disturbed. Need a private chat with the gentleman."

The attendant quickly fled leaving Simon alone with Bridges and his two men. Simon was fairly certain he could take Bridges. He was a little heavier than Simon but he looked slow. The other two were another matter. They were both easily Simon's height if not taller, and from the way they held themselves they were used to fighting. Part of Simon welcomed it. Ever since the incident on the tramway, he'd been itching to fight someone again. But three against one was seldom a winning proposition. All he could do was play along for now and wait for an opening.

All the while he continued to clean his shirt as Bridges stood by watching.

"Such a waste of good champagne," Bridges said.

So he'd orchestrated this? Probably paid the man inside to cause the accident to arrange this little tête-à-tête.

"It wasn't very good champagne," Simon said, setting down the towel and turning to face Bridges. His two flunkies stood close by. "What do you want?"

Bridges grinned. "Straight to the point, I like that. Your wife was very direct, too, when we had our little chat."

Simon's hand clenched into a fist. He'd wanted to punch Bridges in the mouth since he'd met him and should have after the way he'd threatened Elizabeth.

"Pretty little thing," Bridges went on.

Simon struggled not to rise to the bait, and it was a struggle.

"I thought I made myself pretty clear with her." He turned to his thuggish friends. "Don't you?"

They nodded gravely.

"See? But here I am having to deliver the message again."

"And what message is that?"

Bridges moved closer. Simon tensed, ready to fight, wanting to fight, but the other two men were ready as well. He would do Elizabeth no good if he got himself beaten into oblivion.

"Go home. Go back home. That's all I want," Bridges said, acting as if this were a reasonable request.

"And leave you to steal whatever Emil finds for yourself?"

Bridges shrugged. "That's about it."

"You're trash."

Bridges laughed and then took mock umbrage. "Well, that's not a very nice thing to say, is it, boys?"

He nodded his head toward one of the men who suddenly stepped forward and punched Simon square in the gut. The shock of it and the force of the blow knocked the wind out of him. He doubled over in pain, gasping for a breath that would not come, and fought to keep from sinking to his knees.

Bridges let him suffer for a moment then leaned over and whispered in his ear. "I'd hate to see anything happen to that pretty little wife of yours."

Seething with anger, Simon managed to straighten up and looked him in the eye. If he touched Elizabeth, he would kill him.

"Message received?" Bridges asked.

Simon wouldn't give him the satisfaction of a reply. It took all the strength he had not to wring Bridges' neck where he stood. No matter how satisfying the thought might be, he couldn't afford to, not yet. Not to mention, he'd probably be killed for his trouble. If he was going to try to protect Elizabeth, he had to stand there and do nothing. It made him sick.

Bridges grinned again and jerked his head toward the door. "Come on, boys, we've got a party to enjoy."

Discretion might be the better part of valor, but Simon felt anything but valorous as he watched them go, leaving him alone in the men's room. Intellectually, he knew he'd done the right thing— live to fight another day. But emotionally, he felt emasculated and ineffectual.

How could he hope to protect Elizabeth when he couldn't even protect himself?

"Lovely party."

Vega knew the voice and his gut turned cold. Rasche. He glanced at the man next to him. He wore a near full-face mask, but his eyes gave him away. Anyone who was paying attention could see him for who he was.

They couldn't be seen together. What madness was it that brought him to his side in public, at a party no less?

"What are you doing?" Vega demanded, careful not to look his way.

"I could ask you the same thing."

Vega glanced at him in anger before catching himself and pretending to casually observe the crowd.

"What do you mean?" he asked. "I am doing my duty."

Rasche stepped forward so they were standing next to each other. "Is that what it is called?"

Vega turned to glare at Rasche but noticed his attention was fixed across the room and followed his gaze. Elizabeth stood chatting with Emil. Even though he could not see Rasche's face, he knew the expression beneath the mask was a putrid mixture of lust and hate. It was what drove him.

"We've been over this," Vega said, as calmly as he could muster. "We need her."

"We? Or is it you that needs her?"

Rasche's cold blue eyes tried to dig into Vega's soul, but he'd been tested by men far better than Rasche. "You have grown far too attached to the woman. I am beginning to think it is clouding your judgment."

"I am merely playing my part."

"I saw you when you danced with her. I see the way you look at her even now. Should I report back to the Reichsführer that you are compromised?"

Vega's temper flared but with effort he controlled it. "I will complete my mission."

"*We* will complete it," Rasche said, turning his focus back to Elizabeth. "One way or the other."

Chapter Sixteen

"DID YOU KNOW THAT the roots of Carnival go back to the Roman festival of Saturnalia?" Elizabeth asked, as she read through a brochure she'd found in the lobby.

"Possibly," Simon said distractedly as he read the morning paper.

Elizabeth had been trying all through breakfast to snap Simon out of his funk. Ever since his run-in with Clay, he'd been all doom and gloom. She didn't really understand why. They'd both been threatened before. Heck, Clay had already threatened her, but so far he'd been all talk. And according to Emil that's all he usually amounted to, until he could swoop in and steal an artifact or two. Simon's reaction to it all seemed out of proportion. But then Simon's reaction to a lot of things had been a little out of whack lately. She was trying to give him time to deal with whatever was bothering him on his own, but she was going to have to intervene soon, especially if he kept in his current state of funkitude.

"Masters and slaves would trade clothes and enjoy a day of drunken revelry," she read on, hoping that his interest in history would spark something in him. She skimmed ahead. "Then the

211

Roman Catholic Church co-opted the event and made it into a festival preceding Lent."

She looked over the edge of their balcony where they'd taken breakfast and admired the people below. It was still early, with the real party not starting until that afternoon, but people milled about in costume, possibly just coming home from the night before. Four men in full Carmen Miranda drag, down to the fruit hats, sashayed up the sidewalk arm in arm.

Somehow she doubted that was quite what the church had in mind at the time. Regardless, that's what it had become—an all-out drunken party that lasts for a full three days. And here she was stuck in her hotel room with Eeyore.

"We should go out for lunch," she said.

A loud whistle sounded from the street. Several scantily clad women danced across the boulevard, stopping traffic, as the men traveling with them played drums, tambourines, shakers, and bells in an unmistakable samba beat.

Although the formal parade wouldn't be until tomorrow, it seemed that everyone was spontaneously practicing. It was a raucous block party that spanned nearly the entire city.

"We are definitely going out for lunch," she said. She wasn't going to miss this.

"I'm not sure that's wise," he replied, still behind his paper.

"Simon."

"Hmmm?"

"Please."

He finally lowered the paper and looked at her, almost warily.

"We can't stay in the hotel until the expedition."

He frowned thoughtfully. "No, but there's no reason to take unnecessary risks, either."

"Clay's just full of hot air. Emil said he hardly ever gets violent."

"Hardly ever? That's hardly comforting."

She reached across the table and took hold of his hand. "I know you worry. I love you for it. You know that?"

"But?"

"But you can't protect me by putting me in a cage."

It was a subject they'd struggled with throughout their marriage. Although he'd never grown accustomed to the danger she put herself in, he had grown to accept the necessity of it and that she could not be herself if she was wrapped in cotton wool. Her freedom, even if it meant occasional risk, was everything to her. He knew that.

He nodded thoughtfully and then let out a breath and looked down at his cold tea. "And what if I can't protect you at all?"

"You? The man who fought vampires, demons, and Jack the Ripper?"

"You did all those things."

"We did," she reminded him. "And we'll see this through, too." She could see his resolve weakening. "I honestly don't think we have to worry too much about Clay Bridges, but I promise to be careful. More than usual, I mean."

He snorted. "You've never been careful a day in your life."

She leaned in. "And you love me for it."

"In spite of it."

She began to lean back in a pout, but he tugged on her hand, pulling her from her chair and onto his lap.

A warmth filled his eyes as he brushed her cheek with his knuckles. "In terrible, terrible spite," he said softly as he guided her to a kiss.

"I DON'T SEE HOW we'll ever find them," Simon said, having to raise his voice over the din as they maneuvered around a particularly raucous group of partygoers.

Elizabeth craned her neck to try to see Alex and Emil. "We'll find them. Eventually."

Simon frowned but didn't contradict her. At least that was progress. Slim but something. He was still in something of a mood, but it seemed to be less clenched than earlier.

Although Carnival had officially started last night, the ball at the hotel had been a relatively sedate affair, threats and punches in the men's room notwithstanding. But this, well, this was what she imagined Carnival to be—streets teeming with people, some in costume, some not, but everyone having a good time.

She'd gone to Mardi Gras in New Orleans once in college. Sadly, all she remembered was getting so sick on Hurricanes that she couldn't even look at a bottle of rum for a year.

Carnival in Brazil was similar in many ways and yet wholly its own. It seemed like a mixture of Halloween, Mardi Gras, and a wild beach party.

Every small group of people seemed to be in their own private parade as they coursed up and down the avenue. Costumes ranged from homemade to extravagant, from a simple mask to an elaborate samba outfit complete with an enormous feathered headdress. Avenida Atlantica, which ran along Copacabana Beach, was filled with people simply milling about in search of a good time and most of them finding it.

A few samba bands were set up on the sand near the Portuguese pavement and drew crowds of dancers both on the beach and occasionally in the street itself. Casually decorated convertibles piled with people drinking and cheering cruised up and down the avenue.

"Now *this* is a party," Elizabeth said.

Simon grunted next to her. He wasn't one for raucous parties under the best of circumstances. It was hard to envision even a college-age Simon joining in some frat house keg party. Did they even have keg parties at Oxford? Surely, it wasn't all tea and scones. Making a mental note to ask him about that, she took his hand and led him across the street.

"We should wait here for Emil," he protested.

"Maybe they're over there listening to the music," she suggested.

Traffic was constant but slow and it was easy to navigate across the street to the beach side. They'd made arrangements to meet up with Alex and Emil and enjoy the late afternoon together before going to dinner.

The sun hadn't quite set, but Elizabeth could feel the tenor of the party shift as day began to turn to night. Everything became a little heightened. The music seemed louder and faster, the laughter a little more manic, the crowd a little more frenetic.

She was sure it wasn't strictly legal to drink on the streets, but everything seemed to be legal during Carnival. It wasn't quite a Roman bacchanal, but it wasn't the Disney Main Street parade either. Couples lay on the beach in ardent embraces and people danced with perfect strangers, as the rhythms of Brazil carried them all away.

It was a chance for the poor to mingle with the rich and the rich with the poor. Everyone was the same, a Carioca—a citizen of Rio. Carnival was the great balancer, if only for a few days.

The band closest to them began to play an irresistible samba and Elizabeth's feet began to move of their own accord. Her hips soon blindly followed. The mixture of African and Latin rhythms that created the samba felt like a celebration of life itself, not to mention slightly erotic.

She knew Simon wouldn't dance with her but that didn't mean she couldn't dance. She let the music move her. At first, it was just small steps in place and a swaying rhythm.

She'd been watching the dancers on the beach, and while she didn't know the formal steps, she had a good idea of the basics. It was a rare thing to be able to just dance in public, and for no one to bat an eye, and so she did. It wasn't strange or out of place, it was just Carnival.

"Elizabeth," he chided gently as she grew more daring and began to dance around him.

At first he seemed confused and perhaps even a little mortified. But soon curiosity and a little something else won out, and he stared at her as she moved her hips in the way she'd seen other dancers do.

She put her hand on his shoulder and ran it across his back as she danced behind him and around again.

"What? I'm just Carnivaling."

"That's not a word."

"It is today."

Despite his best efforts to remain a stick in the mud, a small smile began to tug at his lips.

"I see you're enjoying yourselves," Emil interrupted with a grin as he appeared on the sidewalk, Alex Vega at his side.

Elizabeth stopped, slightly embarrassed. "I was practicing my samba." She did a few little moves to show them, but their expressions were more confused than anything. "Maybe I need more practice."

"You are very . . .enthusiastic," Alex offered, earning a snort from Simon.

"I'll take that as a compliment," she said.

He inclined his head. "As intended."

"Why don't we walk north toward Leme Fort," Emil suggested. "I hear there are spectacles to be seen there."

"And all around us," Elizabeth added as a pair of men wearing coconut bras and grass skirts passed by.

Emil chuckled. "Yes." He gestured in the direction they were to walk.

As they made their way down the beach, Alex held out a book. It was Lost Horizon. "I thought you might enjoy rereading it before our own journey begins."

"Did you enjoy it?"

"Very much. Sometimes I feel 'a wanderer between two worlds' myself."

Elizabeth couldn't help but grin. "I know just what you mean."

THE FOLLOWING MORNING SIMON was in a better humor, comparatively speaking, at least. They didn't stay out late and there had been no sign of Bridges. The dinner, a Portuguese feast of oysters, caldeirada—a stew that's different from bouillabaisse or cacciucco, leitão—suckling pig, and arroz de pato or duck rice, along with one of the finest vintage ports he'd ever tasted, had been as pleasant as the company. Even Vega's occasional attention toward Elizabeth didn't bother him. A fine wine went a long way.

They decided to take brunch on the veranda overlooking the beach that morning. It was a relatively safe haven from the growing chaos in the street below and would afford Elizabeth a good view of the proceedings without being too close.

He knew she was right; he couldn't protect her by putting her in a cage. He'd honestly hoped he was beyond such things, but the stress of the mission combined with his own personal crisis of faith put him on the edge. His instinct was to protect her. Always and at any cost. But when that cost was her own happiness...

He'd reluctantly agreed to go to the parade later that day. His suggestion that they watch it from their balcony or even the hotel's veranda was brushed aside.

"That's like watching a parade on TV when you can be there instead," she'd said.

He did not mention that he'd rather not do either. Elizabeth was right, though, that it would be a shame to waste the gift they'd been given—to see history in person. However, he was more worried about the future, their future, at the moment than the past.

"I feel an éclair coming on," Elizabeth said as they walked out onto the patio where brunch was still being served, then she paused in thought. "Maybe a danish. I can't decide. What do you think?"

"I think you will ask me to get whatever you don't so you can eat half of mine."

She laughed. "Guilty."

He led her toward a table near the balustrade when they saw Vega sitting alone, sketching. Simon did not want to join him, but Elizabeth's prompting look forced him to admit that they should at least say hello.

He was drawing the view of the beach beyond in pencil as they approached.

"Good morning," Elizabeth said, catching his attention.

He stood politely. "Morning. Would you join me?"

"No," Simon replied before Elizabeth could. "Thank you. We don't want to keep you from your work."

"Ah. This is merely a diversion."

Elizabeth leaned over his shoulder to get a better look. "You're very good."

Simon was loath to admit it, but he was skilled. "Yes, quite beautiful."

"Thank you, but it is the subject that makes the art." He moved to close his notebook, apparently modest about his work. As he did so, a loose sheet fell out and fluttered to the ground.

It landed at Elizabeth's feet and she stooped down to pick it up. As she rose Simon noticed the shift in her expression, a smile coming to her face. "Is this me?"

That got Simon's attention. It was unmistakably her. Her hair was up in the style it had been during the ball. It was a remarkable likeness. It captured not only the way she looked, but the way she was. That more than anything disturbed Simon.

Vega shifted uneasily. "Yes, I . . . I was going to give it to you, but it felt presumptuous."

"It's amazing," she said, admiring it. "Is this how I really look?"

He nodded, his eyes shifting briefly to Simon trying to gauge his reaction.

Elizabeth held the sketch out at arm's length. "I'm kinda hot."

Vega laughed, the tension broken. At least on the outside.

Simon tried to hide his discomfort at not only another man drawing his wife, but doing it so very accurately. It wasn't just that he'd clearly studied her, intently, it was as if he saw exactly what Simon saw—not the outward appearance but something deeper. He'd always felt that there was some aspect, some intrinsic Elizabethness that was his alone to see. It was then that he noticed there was something other than curiosity in Vega's eyes; there was a challenge.

At first Simon thought he was imagining it; he'd been growing more irritable by the day and Vega was an easy outlet. However, as he returned Vega's gaze while Elizabeth marveled at her portrait, he definitely saw the spark of someone enjoying the reward of a provocation having reached its target.

Under other circumstances, Simon would have been content to ignore it, even feel pleased by it. Elizabeth was, after all, his wife, and happily so. But a perfect storm of emotional turmoil left him feeling raw and exposed in ways he was not accustomed to.

Simon took Elizabeth's elbow to usher her to their table. "We should be going."

"Hmm? Oh." Elizabeth handed the sketch back to Vega, but he shook his head.

"Keep it if you like. I had intended to give it to you, after all."

"Thank you. We'll see you later?" she said as Simon began to lead her away.

Simon didn't bother to look back for his response; he knew what it would be.

"That was nice of him," she said as he pulled out her chair for her.

Simon had all sorts of barbed responses poised on the tip of his tongue, but he kept them to himself.

"Yes. Coffee?" he asked as he gestured for a waiter.

He would only look a fool if he told her what he thought. She liked Vega, genuinely, and the man hadn't done anything overtly impertinent. A "look" hardly counted. But if there was one thing Simon had learned from his years with Elizabeth, it was to trust his instincts, and right now they were telling him that Alex Vega was trouble. A great deal of trouble.

CHAPTER SEVENTEEN

B Y THE TIME THEY went out to stake out a spot for the parade, a huge crowd had already gathered, many of whom were already as drunk as Cooter Brown as Elizabeth's daddy used to say. One man sat passed out, leaning against a wall, his boater hat tipped down over his eyes and a hastily written note pinned to his chest that said, "Return to Sender."

Simon gripped her hand as they tried to maneuver through the crowd behind Alex and Emil. The parade had just started and finding a spot near the curb was going to be a challenge. It wasn't all a loss; the crowd was nearly as interesting as the parade. People wore costumes and danced and sprayed each other with some perfume-ish substance.

"What is that?" Elizabeth asked Emil over the din.

"Lança-perfume."

"A bit of perfume mixed with ether," Alex explained.

"Ether?" Simon said, as shocked as she was. "As in ethyl chloride?"

That seemed like a dangerous thing to be squirting on people, but no one in the crowd seemed bothered by it.

"Yes, it is very common during Carnival. The effects are quite fleeting."

That was surprising. Drinking, she expected, a lot of it, but casual drug use, even something as seemingly innocuous as this stuff, surprised her. It shouldn't have, really, she realized. Cocaine and heroin were "medicine" for years.

As they wound their way through the crowd, Elizabeth realized the crowd was constantly shifting. This wasn't a "find a place and park it" parade like the Macy's Thanksgiving Day Parade or the Rose Bowl. This was fluid, constantly in motion, surging and moving and dancing. They weren't just spectators, they were part of it.

A large float appeared over people's heads and she could just make out a few women in large feathered headdresses standing on it. It had rows of fake palm trees on each side wrapped with little fairy lights. The people on the float threw confetti and serpentine streamers into the crowd. As fireworks both big and small went off over the beach, music floated closer over the roar of the crowd as one of the samba bands grew nearer.

The famous samba schools of Rio were still a relatively new thing in 1936. They weren't nearly as elaborate or competitive as they would become. But each school was like a club where the members trained and danced and performed. Carnival was the big show.

Finally, they found a spot at the curb just in time to see a group of men, wearing enormous and slightly terrifying papier mache heads, march ahead of the first samba school. Whistles blew and drums beat out a frantic rhythm that electrified the crowd.

The samba school danced in front of them briefly then moved forward to repeat the performance over and over as they slowly made their way down the boulevard. They were followed by another float with two enormous lighted wheels that spun hypnotically.

Many of the floats were wildly fanciful, with fairylands depicted or kings and queens in a lighted forest.

"Isn't it wonderful?" she said to Simon, who despite being something of a sourpuss all day, seemed impressed by the spectacle. "Aren't you glad I made you come?"

He offered her a smile and she leaned into his arm briefly until a roar from the crowd pulled her attention away. The next float was throwing candy and little toys into the crowd. And no one there was shy about wanting some. The whole crowd seemed to surge closer to grab a few of the goodies.

The swell of the crowd around them pulled her away from Simon's side. It all happened so quickly she lost sight of him immediately. She was caught in the tide of humanity, buffeted shoulder to shoulder like a human ping pong ball for a good ten or fifteen feet before she could step out of the tide. She turned to try to make her way to back to where she thought Simon was. As she did, someone sprayed her with lança-perfume. It stung and tingled where it hit her neck. She tried to wipe it away only to be sprayed again and again.

Immediately, her heart began racing in her chest, so quickly it frightened her. Her vision blurred and she felt dizzy. She turned around again, trying to get her bearings, but the world around her spun. She thought she might just throw up.

The sounds of Carnival grew distant and muffled, and all she heard was a roaring in her ears, when suddenly it stopped. She took a few panting breaths, as if she'd just popped to the surface after being submerged in water. She shook her head to clear it. The effects were fading.

In the distance she thought she heard someone calling her name. Poor Simon.

She realized it was probably her own sense of panic that had made things worse. Slowly she calmed but still felt slightly light-headed.

She stumbled forward and a strong hand reached out to steady her. She looked up to thank her rescuer when she found herself looking into the ice cold blue eyes of Rasche.

He grinned down at her and she tried to pull away, but he held tight. That's when she saw the gun in his hand. Everything else, the crowd, the music, the entirety of Carnival, faded away and it was as if they were the only two people there. The crowd danced around them, oblivious.

Elizabeth knew if she cried "gun!", if anyone even heard her, it could cause a panic. She couldn't risk that. Surely he wouldn't shoot her in the middle of a crowd, would he? As if in answer, a few random fireworks went off over the beach. Maybe he would.

He tugged on her arm and she knew if she let him take her anywhere she was as good as dead. She tried to wrench herself from his grip but it was no use.

"Let go of me!" she cried, but no one around her seemed to notice.

She struggled against him when suddenly the crowd roared again and surged en masse. The wave of humanity knocked into them both, pushing them along with it. But the surprise of it made him loosen his grasp, and she wrenched herself free and was somehow able to squeeze between people in her flight. She saw him for a fleeting moment, but soon the crowd engulfed him like quicksand and he disappeared.

She pushed her way against the tide like a salmon swimming upstream. She wasn't sure where Simon was, but she needed to get as far away from Rasche as she could and warn him. She was bumped and knocked from side to side as the revelers surged toward the street. Finally able to break free of them, she was birthed out into a less crowded portion of the sidewalk.

She gasped for breath, pushing away the fear and claustrophobia from moments earlier.

"Elizabeth!"

She heard Simon's voice long before she saw him. She turned, searching, and then saw him. He'd climbed up onto the base of a lamppost to get a better view of the crowd.

"Here!" she called out. "Here!"

"Over here," Emil's voice came from not far away. "She's over here."

Alex appeared at her side, taking her arm, Emil not far behind. "Are you all right?"

She nodded but didn't feel all right until Simon arrived and pulled her into his arms.

"What happened?" he asked once he'd eased her away to get a look for himself.

"I'm okay, but Rasche is here."

"What?"

"I got sprayed with that perfume stuff and I was a little confused. Then the next thing I know he's there. Rasche. And with a gun. I swear I thought he was going to kill me right then and there."

"You're sure it was him?" Alex asked grimly. They'd told both Emil and Alex what they knew and what they suspected about Rasche and the late Mr. Strasser.

"I'm sure," she said. "He tried to drag me through the crowd, but I got away." She looked back toward the throng of people. "He's in there somewhere."

Simon's already tenuous mood took a serious nose dive. "We need to get inside. Away from the crowd."

For once, Elizabeth wasn't going to argue with him. They hurried toward the entrance to the hotel and up the steps.

"I shall alert the authorities," Alex offered. "I will mention none of you. Just that a man with a gun was seen in the crowd. Perhaps they can find him."

Elizabeth certainly hoped so. The look in his cold eyes still echoed in her memory. Maybe the police could help, and they could definitely use all the help they could get.

"Good. I think we should all retire to our rooms and lock the doors," Emil said.

"Agreed," Simon said.

Once they were in the lobby, Elizabeth felt a lot better. It was busy, but nowhere near the press of people outside. She and Simon escorted Emil to his room first. There was no telling what Rasche might do next. Once they were sure he was safe and heard him lock the door, they made their way to their own suite.

They were alone in the elevator as they rode it to the top floor. Simon was at DEFCON 1, tense and anxious beside her. They rode in silence, the distance between floors seeming to be impossibly far. Finally, they reached the top floor and she heard the tell-tale ding signaling their arrival.

Simon stepped in front of her, fists clenched as the doors opened. A squeaky horn blew and Elizabeth nearly screamed in surprise. It took her a moment to realize it was a drunken man blowing a New Year's Eve style blowout party maker in surprise. He laughed sloppily and swayed into the side of his wife who was nearly as drunk.

"Happy New Year!" he slurred then giggled as he and his wife stumbled into the car.

Simon pushed out a breath. He looked like he'd nearly given the man a surprise of his own and clocked him.

"Come on," Simon said, taking Elizabeth by the arm and maneuvering them past the couple and out of the car.

Simon unlocked their suite door and let Elizabeth precede him inside. The room was dark with only a bit of moonlight filtering through the sheer curtains. Simon flicked on the light.

Sitting in the middle of the room, one leg crossed over the over, as comfortable as could be, was Rasche, gun in hand.

"Close the door," he told Simon.

Simon hesitated and she knew he was calculating the possibilities of pushing her back outside even if it meant taking a bullet.

"Simon," she said quietly.

His eyes shifted to hers briefly, but he relented and closed the door, but not quite all the way. He left it just the tiniest bit ajar. It might signal someone on the outside that something was wrong or give them a half-second's help if they tried to run. But for now, there was no running.

Rasche waved them forward with his gun. She was really hoping not to see it or him again, especially not so soon.

He stood and gestured toward the chair. "Sit," he ordered Simon.

Simon, wheels turning in his mind, did as he was told.

"Over there next to him," Rasche instructed her. "Tie him up."

"I don't have anything—" she started to protest when he pointed toward the sofa where four of Simon's ties lay.

"I borrowed them from your closet. I hope you don't mind," he added with a slight tugging smile.

Elizabeth looked at Simon, hoping for some sign he had a plan. They really, really needed a plan. But all she saw was a mixture of love and hate. They just had to buy time. Just time. An answer would come.

"Go on," Rasche insisted.

Elizabeth began to tie Simon's wrists to the arms of the chair, being sure to do it as poorly as possible, but Rasche wasn't fooled.

"Do it again. Properly this time."

She had no choice but to follow his instructions and bind Simon's hands to the chair with his ties. She could only hope the silk would slip somehow.

She stood up, ready to toss the other two ties back onto the sofa, but Rasche stopped her.

"Now, his legs."

She caught Simon's eye as she knelt down to follow her orders. She tried to drag the process out as long as she could, hoping against hope a miracle would happen.

"I'm surprised you were able to beat Strasser," he told Simon as Elizabeth worked. "I am impressed."

"He was a fool," Simon said. "And so are you."

Elizabeth glanced up at him, willing him not to antagonize the Nazi with the gun, but as she turned she suddenly realized what he was doing. Just over Rasche's shoulder, not more than ten feet behind him stood Alex Vega. He was slowly tiptoeing forward and Simon was doing his best to keep Rasche's attention toward them and away from the door.

"And besides," Elizabeth said as she stood by Simon's side, gripping his shoulder, ready to do whatever she had to do to save him, "I beat him."

"You? A woman?"

"Last I looked."

Rasche laughed. Vega was nearly behind him now. It took all of her strength not to look at him and instead stared into Rasche's cold blue eyes.

"He failed, just like you're going to," she said.

"Am I?" Rasche said cockily.

Just then Vega made his move. She hadn't noticed it before but he had something in his hand, not a gun but a thin white rope or cord. In one swift and fluid movement, he threw a loop of it around Rasche's neck and pulled the ends tight.

Rasche gasped and clawed at the cord choking him. His eyes bulged and his pale face blossomed red. He dropped the gun as he reached for the cord around his neck to vainly stop from being strangled.

Alex pulled the rope tighter and tighter, his own face red from the effort. Rasche bent backward in an effort to loosen the tension in the rope, but it was no use. Alex used his own body and back as leverage, slowly lifting Rasche until his feet were dangling just above the floor.

It was horrifying. She'd seen men die before but never like this.

"The gun," Simon urged her.

She managed to pull herself from the horror long enough to grab it, but couldn't look away.

Rasche's feet trembled and shuddered just inches from the floor as he hung lying across Alex's back. His feet twitched for a few moments, then they fell still as he lost consciousness.

The whole horrible thing took only ten seconds or so, but it felt like an eternity. Alex let Rasche's now limp body fall to the floor. Then he knelt down over him, and with a single swift and savage movement, he broke Rasche's neck.

Elizabeth gasped with shock, sure she'd never be able to forget the dreadful sound it made or the look on Alex's face as he killed a man.

Panting for breath, Alex slowly stood up again, the cord that was still entwined with his fingers and wrist slipping to the floor.

Elizabeth felt sick. Rasche was going to kill them; she knew that. But seeing something so brutal, so merciless shook her. Alex turned toward her, his face flushed with effort, his eyes wild, and then growing haunted as the shock over what he'd done slowly overtook him.

THE BLOODLUST STILL PULSED inside his body, a heady high of power. Vega knew he had a part to play now and did his best to regain some semblance of control. He prided himself on his control, but he'd lost himself to the primal pleasure of taking another life. Not to mention that he'd wanted to kill Rasche since the moment they'd met. Now that he finally had the pleasure, his mission hung in the balance because he had let his emotions, his true emotions show.

Despite knowing the revulsion he would see in Elizabeth's eyes when he turned to her, it struck him. But he quickly quashed his reaction. He had done what was required and for entirely logical reasons.

Admittedly, he had been furious when he heard of Rasche's attempt on her life. It wasn't that he cared for the woman, it was that Rasche was actively setting out to sabotage his mission. He'd told the fool that without her there would be no staff. But, of course, Rasche's conceit had blinded him to that truth. He had become a liability Vega could no longer tolerate.

Vega owned a gun, but shooting Rasche would draw far too much attention, even with the cover of Carnival. Not to mention, shooting led to blood and blood led to stains and stains led to questions. This had to be neatly done.

The alternative, it ended up, was poetic. Vega's own scars around his neck were a constant reminder of what could be. Although Rasche hadn't personally put them there, he was as guilty as those who had, those boys at boarding school who had tried to kill him, to rid themselves of his dirty blood. But he'd lived, scars and all.

Garroting, he discovered, was an incredibly simple and satisfying way to kill. He'd done it before and took pleasure in the idea of killing of Rasche the same way. Vega knew after his botched attempt to kill Elizabeth that Rasche would try again. And soon. With no other weapon at hand, he'd torn the cord from the curtains in his room and raced to the Crosses' suite.

He had planned on strangling Rasche to death, savoring the moment, but death by strangulation took several minutes. Witnesses made that impossible and so he'd done what he had to do. Quickly and neatly.

As he stood over Rasche's body and Elizabeth looked at him with fear and disgust, he felt a wave of shame, not for having killed but for displaying so little control while doing it. Once the act had begun he'd lost himself to his anger, to the roaring fire inside him. He had displayed a disgraceful lack of self-control in front of the Crosses, risking his very mission in the process.

But he could tell from the look on Elizabeth's face that his shame apparently read as contrition to her and touched her sympathetic nature. She had already forgiven him.

"Elizabeth," Cross said, pulling his wife from her fugue.

She gathered herself and untied him. Cross tossed away his bonds and took the gun from her hand and pointed it at Vega.

Careful not to react, Vega continued to wallow in his apparent shock over what he'd done, even as his mind worked furiously at how to diffuse Cross's anger and mistrust.

Elizabeth looked at her husband in surprised shock. "Simon, what are you doing?"

He ignored her, keeping his eyes locked on Vega. "Where did you learn to do that?"

Sure to maintain an outward appearance of shock at his own deed, Vega said, "In the army."

"The army?" Elizabeth asked surprised. The persona he'd presented of a poetic soul did not jibe with the military.

"Yes."

Knowing such an eventuality might present itself and violence would likely be required at some point, Vega had been sure to add a credible reason for it into Alex Vega's background.

"Spain has compulsory military service. I had no choice but to join. Believe me, I would not have if I had had a choice. They taught me how to do things like that, said I had an aptitude for it." He looked at Elizabeth, pleading with her to understand, to see him as the victim and not the perpetrator. "I left the military as soon as I could. I hated who I was there."

He ran a hand through his hair to emphasize his internal struggle. "I am not that man now, but it seems the lessons I learned were not forgotten."

"It's a good thing, too," Elizabeth said. "We'd be dead if you hadn't come in when you did."

Vega inclined his head, humbly accepting her praise. His eyes shifted to Cross. He knew her husband would not be as easily swayed. He clearly did not like or trust him. But that was of no consequence as long as Elizabeth did.

After a hesitation, Cross appeared to, at least temporarily, accept his explanation and tucked Rasche's gun into the waistband of his pants.

He looked down at Rasche's body. "We need to . . .remove him. Discretely."

They devised a simple plan. In addition to several suitcases, the Crosses had brought a large trunk with them and the body fit easily inside. After borrowing a luggage cart they brought the trunk down to the car.

The hotel and the city outside were still firmly held in the thrall of Carnival and no one paid any attention to them. They found a deserted location near an oceanside bluff and dumped the body over it. The cord Vega used to strangle him was discarded separately.

It was a neat and tidy end. He could tell headquarters any number of lies to cover for his deed. They would not question it. After he presented the staff to the Reichsführer, his loyalty, his abilities, would never be questioned again.

Chapter Eighteen

Simon closed the door behind them and turned the deadbolt, for all the good it had done them so far. Their room had been broken into not once but twice. Elizabeth knew Simon was clearly thinking along the same lines as he took a chair and stuffed the back of it under the doorknob as an extra precaution.

Elizabeth walked further into their suite and chill ran through her as she looked at the spot where Rasche had lain dead. Between what had happened and almost happened at Carnival, combined with what they'd just done, she felt dirty.

They'd needed to get rid of the body; they couldn't afford questions about it, but discarding someone, even someone like Rasche, like they were a piece of trash bothered her deeply. It had to be done, but it made her feel cold and unclean. The mission had to be completed; she knew that millions of lives could hang in the balance, but this sort of thing was a part of their job that she had never completely reconciled herself with.

"I need a shower," she said.

Simon didn't reply, but she didn't really expect him to. He'd been quiet ever since Vega had arrived in their room. Not that she blamed him. The night had been difficult for them both and they each had to process what they'd done, what they'd seen, in their own way.

For Elizabeth, that meant a long thinking shower. She scrubbed the ether from her skin, the dirt from her hands, and the memories from her mind. She went over everything they'd done, everything they knew, and saw no other outcome. They'd done what they had to do, and in order to keep functioning, she had to accept that as the truth and put the rest away.

Now that both Rasche and Strasser were dead, she hoped it would be the last of it. Of course, there was still Clay Bridges and the minor matter of surviving the expedition itself, but somehow facing snakes and spiders and all that the jungle had to offer didn't seem half so frightening as what they'd already faced.

Finally clean and at least somewhat more settled about things, she put on her pajama top and joined Simon in the bedroom, or tried to; he wasn't there.

"Simon?"

When there was no response, she walked into the living room. Simon sat forward on the sofa, elbows on knees, hands balled into a cupped fist resting beneath his chin, lost in thought. He didn't seem to notice she'd come in.

"Simon?"

He glanced up and offered her a smile that never touched his eyes.

She sat down next to him, putting a comforting hand on his back. "It's been a long day."

He nodded but still said nothing.

"We were lucky Vega came in when he did."

His eyes shifted to her and she was surprised to see anger in them.

"Or not?" she said, confused.

"He was very helpful," Simon said tightly.

"I thought so. Saving our lives and all."

Simon grunted in response. He was an eloquent man, although he would deny it. Whenever he reverted to caveman grunts, it was a bad sign. A very bad sign.

"What's wrong?" she asked.

"Other than you nearly being killed today? Twice?" he answered tartly. "Nothing. Everything is just peachy."

She leaned away from him, caught off guard by the tone in his voice.

His gaze slid over to hers. "Sorry. I'm just tired."

She had little doubt he was, but there was more to it than that. She'd been patient with him, waiting for him to tell her what was bothering him, but she couldn't stand it any longer. She'd given him space, but now it was a wedge between them.

"Tell me what's wrong."

"I told you—"

"Simon."

"It's . . .just as you said. It's been a long day." He looked at her with some semblance of the old Simon, but that was almost worse.

Marriages were full of small lies. Little white lies to spare feelings or lies of omission about things that weren't really important. But this was more than that. This was a true look-you-in-the-eye lie, and it made her heart clench a little. "You're lying."

He didn't deny it.

She reached out and took hold of one of his hands. "We promised we'd always tell each other the truth. Something's been bothering you even before we came here."

He shook his head, but his eyes gave him away.

She squeezed his hand. "Simon."

He swallowed and looked down at their joined hands. "You know that I only want what's best for you."

She did; he always had.

He struggled to find the next words. "I'm no longer certain that I am."

"That you're not what?"

"Best for you, dammit," he said, and suddenly stood.

"What are you talking about?"

He paced a few steps away from her and planted his hands on his hips, then looked up to the ceiling. "Nothing." He turned back to her. "Nothing. Go on to bed. I'll be in soon."

She stood her ground. "No."

"Please, Elizabeth. I'm tired and—"

She stood and faced him. "I need to know what's going on, Simon. Whatever it is, it's not the usual worrying. I know that look and this is more than that. You've been carrying something with you for weeks now. I wanted to know what it was, but you didn't want to tell me." The memory of those rejections hurt and she let it show. "But now you're scaring me. And I *need* to know what's going on. Have I done something?"

He took two long strides toward her before stopping just short of reaching her. "No. You've done nothing wrong."

"Then why are you pushing me away?"

His eyes filled with so many emotions she couldn't name them all—worry, fear, anger, love.

She closed the rest of the distance between them. "Let me help."

"Please, Elizabeth. Leave it be."

"I can't. One minute you're holding me so tightly I can barely breathe and the next you're pushing me away. Whatever is going on we can deal with it together."

He gave a short laugh, the sort that wasn't funny at all, but pained.

He looked away, his eyes falling on the sketch Alex had done of her. His jaw clenched and he turned away from it.

She had noticed he was uncharacteristically cold toward Alex tonight. Considering that he'd saved their lives, it seemed an odd reaction. And now that she thought about it, she'd noticed a similar reaction before with him. If he wasn't going to tell her she would have to start prying it out.

"Does it have to do with Alex?"

His expression hardened slightly and his eyes narrowed. "No," he said, but she knew it was a lie.

"We really were lucky he came in when he did, weren't we?"

"Very lucky," he said tartly.

She didn't understand. "Are you jealous? You know you have no reason to be."

"Yes, of course," he said flippantly. "Why worry about a man who draws a loving portrait of my wife. A man who saves her life?"

He really had lost the plot. "You're angry he saved my life?"

"No. Yes. A little," he admitted, then the dam broke and he paced across the room. "*I* should be the one to save you and I haven't. So far I've been nothing but a liability."

"That's not true—"

"A man tried to kill you, not once but *twice* tonight and what did I do? Nothing." He paused his long strides to emphasize the point. "All I did was manage to get myself bound to a chair by my own bloody ties! Since we arrived here you've been threatened, bullied, and nearly killed. And, as your husband, what have I done? Nothing."

"Simon—"

"And on that damn bloody tram I left you alone to fight for your life, for our lives. Every step of this journey, I've been too slow, too late, or too damn old. If I'm no good to you, what good am I at all?"

With that last sentence the whirlwind died away and he stood raw and revealed before her.

"What good are you?" she said, coming to him. "Oh my God, Simon. You're *everything* to me. You are the best man I've ever known. You're brave and fierce and wonderful."

"And if that's not enough?" he asked quietly, his fear laid bare. "What if I'm not enough?"

"Oh, Simon—"

"You're in the prime of your life. What if I'm holding you back? Or worse." He struggled to confess his feelings. "When I saw you on the beach with Raul and dancing with Vega, you looked so . . .right together, so happy. With them. Younger men."

She cupped his cheek, rough with stubble. "Simon."

"Our age difference didn't matter to me when we met, but now . . ."

"It matters even less," she said. He started to shake his head but she forced him to look at her. "I didn't fall in love with a forty-year-old man. I fell in love with *you*. And I'm still truly, madly, deeply in love with *you*. Nothing can change that."

He looked unsure, but she pressed on. "If I had an accident and couldn't walk, or I went blind or couldn't speak, would you love me any less?"

"Of course not," he said.

"Then what makes you think I could love you any less for a few gray hairs," she touched the bits of silver at his temple.

"It's more than that," he said. "What we do is dangerous. What if I'm not able to do what's needed? What if you need me and I'm not fast enough or strong enough or something enough to save you. I would rather you live without me than die with me."

"I'm not planning on doing either," she said. "I know this is dangerous work, but there is no one, no man, no woman, no superhero I want by my side. I want *you*. I trust *you* with my life, my heart, and my soul. And I will until the day I die."

He pulled her hand from his cheek and kissed it fiercely.

"You're stuck with me," she said.

A small smile came to his lips and he pulled her into his arms. "I don't know what I've done to deserve you."

"You're Simon Cross and that's more than enough."

CHAPTER NINETEEN

SIMON WATCHED ELIZABETH SLEEP and felt unburdened for the first time in far too long. His worries remained, but he felt a contentment with her by his side that he'd sorely missed. They'd woken together early in the morning, the first light of day filtering through their curtain sheers, and made love. Her touch said everything her words had not and he felt whole again.

He would still worry; he would always worry. But he had no more secret to hide and no more fear of her finding it out. Despite all reason, she loved him as much as he loved her.

She rolled over to nuzzle into his shoulder and he pulled her close. Even now, years later, he marveled at how right she felt next to him. He knew he would do whatever necessary to make sure she stayed there.

THE STREETS WERE JUST starting to come alive again as midday came and they drove to Minister Correia's party. Elizabeth basked in the sun in the back seat with Simon. She'd deferred Alex's offer to ride shotgun and happily leaned against her husband's side as they made their way up the coast.

Last night almost felt like a dream and so much further away than a few hours. It was easy to pretend none of it happened. Simon kissed her temple. Well, not all of it.

They'd gone through a crucible and come out the other side, stronger than before. Strasser and Rasche were gone, but they were certainly not out of the woods yet. They still had to convince the so far un-convinceable Minister Correia to sign off on their little adventure or they'd be stuck in Rio forever. Raul had finished making all of the preparations in the south for their trip. Now, all they needed was the go-ahead. Today, she was determined to get it.

Minister Correia's house was palatial. It wasn't quite as big as the Lage mansion, but it gave it a run for its money. Apparently, bureaucrats did okay in President Vargas's administration, but then they often did under dictators.

A valet took their car and they made their way toward the mansion. The party was centered around an expansive pool where a dozen or so children played. Waiters in white uniforms circulated canapés, and under the shade of a palm frond-covered hut a full bar was in full swing.

Simon was eager to find the minister, but they couldn't exactly bull rush him from the get-go. The four of them made their way to the bar where Elizabeth tried a caipirinha. It was the national drink of Brazil and she could see why. It was the perfect refreshing blend of ice, lime, sugar, and cachaça. It was a little like a mojito but better. She still had a little rum PTSD.

She happily sipped hers and enjoyed the atmosphere. It was just the sort of party she imagined someone in Rio might throw, with men in their white linen suits, women in colorful and easy flowing dresses and oversized sun hats. It was what those pool parties in old Hollywood aspired to be.

Simon was much more himself today. He was still on guard, but in a more normal Simon way. And the connection between them that had occasionally grown strained since their arrival felt as strong and as vibrant as ever. Her own fears about what might come seemed to fade into the background now that all was right between them again.

Of course, Simon wasn't exactly cuddly with everyone. He still treated Alex somewhat cautiously. For her part, she was still stunned by what he'd done, but she'd done things she'd never imagined she was capable of when the proverbial you-know-what hit the fan. Alex was slightly more subdued than before, while Emil grew conversely more nervous each day. She could hardly blame him. Aside from the fact that he had no idea what he was really getting himself into, his life's work was just beyond his fingertips. If she had her way, it would be in his grasp before the sun set.

They played the good party guests for half an hour, mingling and making what small talk they could. Her Portuguese hadn't improved enough to get much past "Thank you very much," and "Yes, I would love another fried cod ball."

Finally, they noticed the minister was alone and decided to make their move. He smiled a Cheshire smile as they approached.

"I am pleased to see you," he said, letting his gaze linger on Elizabeth.

Simon introduced himself, sure to use his title as he did.

"Ah, the husband. You do exist," Correia quipped.

"I do. You have a beautiful home," Simon said, as his look encompassed the grounds of his estate.

"And you have a beautiful wife."

Simon inclined his head, amazingly not rising to the bait.

"Mine is also beautiful," he said, looking off toward the pool where a lovely black-haired woman primped over a young boy before he dove into the water. "But troublesome. Is yours?"

"Very," Simon said, playing the game.

Correia enjoyed the repartee. He looked Simon up and down, sizing him and his pocketbook up. He seemed to like what he saw. "I wish you had enjoined the negotiations earlier. We could have had fun."

"And now?" Simon asked.

"Now I find myself bored with them."

Alex was right. It was all just a game to him.

"Surely there's an agreement to be made," Simon said. "I am not without means."

Corriea smiled. "I am sure you are not. But..." He shrugged and looked around. "What can you possibly give me that I do not already have?"

"Every man has his price. Name yours."

For a moment Elizabeth thought he was going to, but he shook his head, his smile never wavering. "It is impossible."

"Please, Minister," Alex interjected, but Corriea was having none of it.

"Enjoy the party."

"Please," Emil begged.

"I am sorry. It is as I said, impossible."

A woman's scream rent the air. A commotion at the pool got everyone's attention. It took Elizabeth a moment to realize what was happening. A dozen people converged at the edge of the pool, and women were screaming and crying. Then she saw the lifeless body of a boy being laid down onto the concrete.

"Aleixo!" Minister Correia cried and ran toward the boy which Elizabeth now realized was his son.

Aleixo lay still on the ground. A man knelt down next to him and pulled him into a sitting position. He slapped him on the back, but the boy remained unconscious. Another man slapped his cheeks to try to rouse him, but Elizabeth knew it would do no good.

"Lie him down," she said but there was so much panic, so many people that no one paid her any attention.

Simon stepped forward and tried to stop the two men, but they slapped his hands away as another tried to pull him back from the scene.

Elizabeth grabbed hold of Alex's arm. "Please tell them to listen to me."

He looked at her unsurely.

"Please?"

He turned to the crowd and began speaking in rapid Portuguese as he led her forward.

"I can help him. Please, lay him down," she said and Alex translated.

The men knew their methods weren't helping but only reluctantly stepped away, gently laying the boy's body down.

Elizabeth knelt down next to him and leaned over his face putting her cheek next to his mouth and nose to feel for breath. None came. A horrible sense of deja vu overcame her and she struggled to push down the instant panic she felt. Behind her, the boy's mother wailed. She pinched his nose and gave him two quick breaths and checked again. When she couldn't find a pulse she began chest compressions. As soon as she did someone tried to pull her away, obviously thinking she was hurting him.

"Alex, please. I know what I'm doing."

Alex spoke quickly and urgently. Although she had no idea what he said, it had the desired effect and the man pulling her back let go. She resumed chest compressions and Simon knelt by the boy's head. They alternated compressions and breaths for what seemed like far too long when suddenly the boy choked out a gush of water. The gathered crowd gasped and then cheered.

His mother cried his name as Simon turned him on his side to help him expel as much as he could.

Elizabeth sat back on her heels, panting for breath as he continued to cough and vomit up water. His mother knelt next to him and pulled him into her arms as she caressed his cheek and whispered to him.

"Hospital," Simon told Alex. "Tell them he must go to hospital."

Although he was breathing, the boy wasn't out of the woods yet. Far too many people ignored the dangers that were yet to come.

The mother nodded and kissed Simon's cheek before returning her focus to the boy. Simon stood aside to let Corriea join her. He cupped his son's cheek and kissed him.

Elizabeth and Simon eased their way out of the crowd.

"That was . . .remarkable," Emil said.

"Where did you learn to do such a thing?" Alex asked.

It would be another thirty years until CPR was taught. "Picked it up in our travels," she said, hoping they would leave it at that.

They both looked curious but were so overwhelmed by the moment that they didn't ask any other questions.

A few moments later, Minister Correia joined them. "Thank you," he said, wanting to shake both of their hands. "It seems you can give me something after all."

"Maybe the impossible isn't quite so impossible?" Elizabeth asked hopefully.

He glanced back at his son, who was sitting up now and alert. And alive. "It would seem so." He turned to Emil. "You will have your permit."

"Thank you, Minister. Thank you."

CHAPTER TWENTY

"GOOD MORNING," EMIL GREETED them brightly as Elizabeth and Simon stood in the lobby of the hotel. "Tomorrow's the big day."

"I can't believe we're finally going," she replied.

"Your plans for your last day in civilization?"

It was a little scary to think that was actually right. Tomorrow they'd be flying into the interior, into the jungle, into the unknown.

"Shopping."

Emil raised a cautionary finger. "We can only take the bare essentials. Because of the denseness of the jungle, we'll have no pack animals, you know."

"Understood. I just think it might be wise to have some better shoes for it," she said, lifting her sandaled foot off the ground for emphasis.

Emil chuckled. "Quite right. You do have that list I provided?" he asked Simon.

Simon patted his pocket. "We'll be prepared."

Emil grew serious. "I am sure you will. But once again I must warn you that—"

Clay Bridges interrupted him. "The gang's all here."

Emil noted Clay's two cronies were placing luggage by the front desk for a bellboy. "Going somewhere I hope?"

Clay smirked in reply. "Not yet."

Would he and his men really just follow them into the jungle? Could they even do that?

Clay's gaze shifted to Elizabeth, and Simon moved forward slightly. Clay laughed and put his toothpick back into his mouth.

"Going to breakfast?" he asked, as if her husband weren't ready to punch him in the mouth. She had a feeling he was used to that.

"You are not invited," Emil said boldly. "And you are not invited on our expedition. Should you try, I will have to take matters into my own hands."

Clay was not intimidated. "You do that, Emil." He put a patronizing hand upon his shoulder. "You just do that."

With a tip of his hat, he excused himself and then motioned for his men to follow him. The three of them walked across the lobby and out of the hotel.

"Will he really try to tag along?" Elizabeth asked. "Can he?"

"He has done so before. He is a leech."

"Then perhaps," Simon said thoughtfully, "we should pour salt on him."

Emil looked confused and was about to say something when Alex arrived, completing their foursome.

"I am starving. We should eat well today," he said. "Might be our last decent meals for a good long while."

That thought forced all others from Elizabeth's mind. "I hadn't thought of that."

"You will tire of canned meat and beans quickly."

She grimaced.

"It is not so bad. Provided we do not run out."

The reality of what they were about to do was slowly setting in. She'd thought about it, but it had remained something vague and distant, unreal. But now, tomorrow they were going into the jungle. This wasn't going to be like photo safaris in Africa. This was the real deal. The "people died doing this" deal. For a moment, she lost her appetite. But only a moment.

"I think I'm going to have the French toast and the pancakes. Pack it in."

Alex chuckled. "I do not know where you put it."

His glance at her figure was innocent enough but she felt Simon tense. His confession of his crisis of faith had alleviated the tension between them but that didn't mean it had magically gone away.

She moved closer to Simon and slipped her arm through his as she said, "I'm a bottomless pit. Just ask my husband."

"Indeed."

"I would like to make a quick call to Raul, if you don't mind," Emil said. "You go ahead and get started without me."

"Why don't you and Alex get us a table," Simon said, much to her surprise, as he disentangled himself from her.

Here she was trying to protect his fragile ego and he was handing her off to the man who supposedly had some sort of feelings for her. Color her confused.

"I have a few questions for Raul myself," he continued. "I won't be long."

Oookay.

"All right," she said, looking at him in silent question, but he just gave her his "later" face. She hated that face.

"We'll try to get a good table," she said when she realized that was all the explanation she was going to get for now, giving him one last "oh, we're going to talk later and it better be good" face. And it had better.

As the plane's engines revved up, so did the butterflies in Elizabeth's stomach. They were getting ready to board their seaplane—a smaller version of the clipper that had brought them to Brazil—to fly to an inland lake that would, presumably, take months off their journey. The fact that their journey needed months taken off it sent a chill up her spine. She was, honestly, excited at the prospect of what lay ahead, but also really and truly beginning to freak out. Spending weeks in the Brazilian jungle was not a picaresque romp. She could almost feel the bugs on her skin already. And speaking of pests...

"Well," Clay said as he and his two men walked out toward the plane. "Small world, isn't it? We're going to Mato Grosso, too."

"Are you?" Emil said tightly.

Clay answered with one of his smug smiles. "Just doing a little sightseeing," he said, half-addressing the steward standing nearby to help them board.

"I don't think you will be," Emil said, and waved someone forward.

Curious, Clay turned around to see a slender man approach wearing a military uniform and a pencil thin mustache. The officer bowed curtly toward Emil and then turned immediately toward Clay.

"You are Mister Clay Bridges?" he asked.

"I am."

"You are under arrest." He motioned for two other officers to step forward and take Clay into custody.

Clay fidgeted but didn't overtly resist as they took hold of his arms. "What's going on? Since when is it illegal to sightsee?"

"It is not," the officer said in clipped English. "You are under arrest for the possession of a stolen object of priceless cultural heritage."

"What are you talkin' about?"

The officer gestured toward a group of soldiers standing nearby and at the ready should they be needed. One of them came forward with a small duffel bag, removed something from it, and handed it to the officer.

"This rare Chancay figure that was recently stolen from the museum was found in your luggage at the Copacabana hotel this morning."

Elizabeth fought to keep a smile from coming to her face. It was a beautiful frame job. Simon and Emil had pulled it off perfectly.

"Do you deny the charge?"

"You bet your ass I do."

The officer nodded and handed the figurine back to his man. "Then you will have your day in court."

"But I—"

The officer, apparently done talking, waved for his men to escort Clay away as other officers carefully stood by to shuttle his two friends along with him. By the time they proved their innocence, if they could, they would have no chance of flying on their coattails.

"I didn't do it!" Clay protested. "I've never seen that thing before. Emil?"

Emil shrugged. "What can I do? I am just a doddering old man."

Simon watched dispassionately as Clay was led away, but she knew how secretly pleased he was. It was a far better revenge than a punch in the gut.

He turned to the others as if nothing at all had happened. "Shall we get on board?"

"I feel as though I have missed something," Alex said.

"I'll tell you all about it on the way," Emil offered.

THE PLANE MADE A sweeping turn over Guanabara Bay and turned inland. They flew over the plantations and ranches of the Old Republic that dominated the "coffee with milk" politics before the revolution in 1930. The old guard was still powerful, but their influence was fading, and so too would their land. Eventually, many of the plantations surrounding Rio would be swallowed once again by the rainforest they'd destroyed. But that was one of the few exceptions. As Elizabeth looked out of the window, she knew that much of the lush, dense jungle had vanished in the modern world, consumed by massive soybean farms and cattle ranches. The impenetrable canopy of trees beneath her would be gone. Man dominating nature. And, she knew, the farther inland they went the more that battle would be reversed. In the jungle, nature dominated man.

Although she already knew it, one of the things she realized on their six-plus hour plane ride was just how dang big Brazil was. They'd flown along its endless coast and now hours and hours across it. It wasn't all jungle either. In addition to the rainforests and the wetlands, there were plains and savannas, and valleys and mountains. It was one of the most beautiful and terrifying places she'd ever seen.

In all their years of time travel, she and Simon had been all over the world and all through time, but it wasn't often they left civilization and never so completely. Whether they were in nineteenth century

Paris or ancient Rome, there were buildings and houses and roads. No matter how different each time and place was, they were all the same in lots of ways, lots of familiar, comforting ways. But here, she thought, as she looked out at the jungle below growing denser by the mile, there would be none of that. The only familiar things would be those they brought with them and who they came with.

Simon leaned closer to get a better look and she gripped his hand. He looked at her curiously.

"Just glad you're here."

He didn't understand quite what prompted her to say it, but he didn't seem to care as the feeling was clearly mutual.

Finally, there was a break in the trees, and a series of small lakes and rivers appeared beneath them. The pilot brought them in for a landing and they taxied across the water to a small dock.

Simon helped her down the steps and across the pontoon. She was already glad she'd gotten a pair of comfortable boots and traded in her dresses for rather smart looking safari pants and a top.

A fisherman in a nearby dugout canoe watched them curiously.

The village was small, only perhaps a dozen or so buildings with thatched roofs and several smaller huts. It was oddly comforting to see.

A man in dirty white pants that were too short and a dirty white shirt that was too tight around the middle came toward them. Raul went forward to greet him. She couldn't understand what they were saying, but she could tell they knew each other and soon the man in white was beckoning them all forward.

He whistled and waved to a group of native men she hadn't noticed before. They were all squatting under the shade of a nearby tree and came alertly to attention when he called them. They were the first indigenous people she'd seen so far. It was silly, but she suddenly felt like she'd stepped into the pages of *National Geographic*. They were all on the short side with bowl-cut black hair, red and black face paint, and wearing nothing but a small thong to cover themselves.

They worked quietly and efficiently getting their luggage and supplies from the plane.

"This is Bira," Raul said, introducing the man in white. "He will be our guide."

Bira's English was sparse but he was fluent in Portuguese and several dialects spoken by the native tribes. He was constantly smiling and nodding his head reassuringly. He was deferential to them, but another man when it came to dealing with his men. His easy smile disappeared in an instant and he barked orders like a drill sergeant. His men didn't need much prodding as they went about their tasks quickly and silently.

The group set up camp in the shadow of the village. It was modest. There were two tents—one for Simon and Elizabeth and one for Emil, Vega, and Raul. The rest of the men, including Bira, slept in hammocks under the stars.

By the fire that night, they ate and drank as though they were on the veranda of the hotel and not at the clawed foot of one of the most dangerous places on earth. Everyone seemed to resist sleep, but they were leaving early in the morning and needed as much rest as possible.

Simon carried the lantern inside their small tent and hung it from a hook on the center pole. Elizabeth pushed aside a drape of mosquito netting and sat down on her folding cot, wondering if they could afford such luxury when they were hundreds of miles into the jungle.

"All right?" Simon asked as he began to unbutton his shirt.

"Just thinking."

"A little overwhelming, isn't it?"

It was, more than a little. Now that they were here, she felt entirely out of her element. She and her father had gone camping, but an RV park in Shallow Creek, Texas wasn't exactly the same. She'd convinced Simon to take Charlotte camping once. Once. It ended with them being caught in a deluge and spending the night in a local Howard Johnson's.

"A little," she confessed.

Simon held out his hand and she let him give her a hand up. He reached into his pocket and pulled out the watch. "We always have this."

"Which," she said, as she touched the case, "we can't use until we've done what we came here to do."

"Unless …"

"There's no other choice," she finished for him.

He didn't have to tell her to use it to save herself if necessary. He knew she wouldn't leave without him anymore than he would leave without her. They were, for good or bad, in this together until the end.

"We won't need it," she said, folding his long fingers back over the case.

He nodded once, but she could see the doubt and the worry clouding his eyes.

"I guess we should get some sleep," she said kissing him quickly and turning away. Her emotions were suddenly threatening to get the better of her. If she started, he'd just worry more and the endless cycle of shared worry would begin.

She took off her boots and slipped under the scratchy wool blanket before Simon shut out the light. She heard his cot creak under his weight as he got into it.

"Goodnight," she said into the darkness.

Then she heard a bit of rustling from his side of the tent. Her eyes hadn't adjusted to the dark yet and so all she could make out was a black shape against a charcoal background.

"What are you doing?" she asked.

She heard him bump into something and swear under his breath, causing her to laugh.

The lamp came back on. "I was trying to be romantic and move my bloody cot next to yours but I hit my head on the blasted pole," he said rubbing his forehead.

She couldn't help but laugh again. "Sorry."

She got up and scooted her cot over as close to the canvas wall as she could to make room for his. She'd be trapped by it, but she didn't care.

He maneuvered his next to hers and shut out the light again. He lay down next to her.

"Goodnight," he said softly as he leaned over to kiss her.

"Goodnight."

He lay back and she reached out for his hand in the dark. It was large and warm and strong and the only bit of home she needed. She held on to his hand tightly until she fell asleep and knew nothing else.

CHAPTER TWENTY-ONE

THERE WAS NO BAND to see them off, not even a group of curious local children. At dawn their little band of adventurers, which had grown to almost twenty with the tribal bearers and guides, set off without fanfare. Eight mules did the heavy lifting, carrying the bulk of their camp supplies, including lots of canned food and powdered milk, and several rifles. A small spotted dog trotted along with them as if herding them into the jungle.

They'd barely gone two miles through the fairly open forest when Elizabeth started to feel the effects of the heat and humidity. It wasn't as hot as it would get, or even as humid, but she felt the air around her now in a way she hadn't before. It wasn't unpleasant . . .yet.

Ahead of her and Simon, Emil and Alex chattered about this and that, studying the maps as they walked. Raul stayed near Bira, rifle slung over his shoulder and the little spotted dog jogging along at his side. They paused regularly to check their compass readings. Navigating through the jungle was an art that required a symphony of instruments including sextant, chronometer, glycerin compass, the seat of one's pants, and a whole lot of luck.

The forest so far wasn't particularly dense, allowing sunlight to break through the tops of the trees, casting long bright shards of light down onto the path. They followed the well-trod path for several more miles before stopping. It was the peak of the heat of the day and everyone needed a short rest and some water. They ate some of the fresh mango and pequi fruit they'd gotten in the village.

The pequi were strange, an odd mixture of citrusy sweetness and a strange cheesiness. They were cautioned about the pokey spines on the inner seed, and asked to save the seeds for later. They were apparently good roasted and they could afford to let nothing go to waste.

Elizabeth washed it all down with a few sips of water, grateful, not for the first time, for all of the scientific advances she and Simon were privy to. Whatever the Brazilian version of Montezuma's Revenge was, she really didn't want to get it here.

The little spotted dog came over to snuffle at the rinds of the fruit she'd discarded, and she poured a tiny bit of water into one for him to drink.

"What's his name?" she asked Bira.

"Mancha."

She gave him a scratch behind the ears. "Like that, Mancha?"

The dog licked her hand, probably trying to get the juice from them, but she liked to think it was a sign of affection.

"What does Mancha mean?" she asked. "Is it Portuguese?"

Alex smiled. "It means 'spot.'"

After a short break, they were on the move again. The deeper they went into the forest, the denser it became. And the louder. All around them she could hear sounds of life—cicadas, birds, frogs, and from a distance away, the unmistakable cry of the howler monkey. Even the trees seemed to be singing a song.

The denser the jungle became, the slower they traveled. The open woods and clear path were long gone. They didn't have to hack their way through the jungle yet, but judging from the size of the machetes that several men carried, she knew that time would come. By Emil's and Alex's best guess they had nearly two hundred miles to cover before they reached the lost city.

As the world around her grew more humid, the smells grew more pungent. It reminded her of some of the places back home after a strong rain—a kind of earthy dampness that hung in the air mixed with the occasional scent of a flower or something in mid-decay.

Their pace was moderate but steady. The mules plodded along and the rest of the party with them. By the time they stopped that first day, Elizabeth's feet ached and she was ready to stop. They'd made good time and, by Raul's reckoning, had traveled nearly ten miles. Progress would not be so easy to come by tomorrow, as they were about to step into the true depths of the jungle.

They set up camp again before the light faded. Around the campfire, the bravado of last night was gone, and in its place was a thoughtful wariness at the reality of what lay ahead. They woke at dawn and traveled on again. This cycle of camp, sleep, march repeated itself for several days. It was oddly comforting, the repetition. The more she did it, the better she felt, like she was getting her "jungle legs," or whatever the jungle equivalent of sea legs was. She and Simon set up their own tent on the third day, and while they weren't as fast as the other men, it felt good to do something other than watch.

On the fifth day, Elizabeth had the eerie feeling they were being watched. There was nothing she could put her finger on, just that tingling at the back of her neck and across the top of her scalp that faded as quickly as it came. She found herself looking off into the thickening forest around them more than at the path before them.

Until finally the inevitable happened and she tripped on an exposed tree root. Only Simon's quick reflexes and strong grip kept her from planting her face in the mud.

"All right?" he asked.

"Fine. Just tripped."

"Something wrong?" Emil asked. Any small problem could blossom quickly into something serious out here.

"No, I wasn't paying attention."

"Not recommended behavior here, I fear," Alex added.

"I know. I just..." She looked off into the woods around them and felt suddenly silly. "I'll be more careful."

Simon could read her too well though and knew something was up. He waited until the others had moved far enough away to speak to her privately.

"What's wrong?" he asked in a quiet voice.

"I don't know. I thought..." She shook her head. "I just had this feeling like we were being watched."

Surreptitiously, Simon scanned the area around them.

"It was probably just in my head. This place does bring out the paranoid in you, doesn't it?"

The jungle was full, quite literally, of unknowns. You could only see so far in any direction and beyond that anything could be lurking. It was too easy to let your imagination get the better of you.

Instead of poopooing her feelings, Simon said, "If you sense it again, tell me."

His response was both comforting and chilling at the same time. Maybe she wasn't imagining things after all.

The end of the first week brought with it a sense of accomplishment, growing hunger pains, and bugs. Lots of bugs. It was like they'd crossed some invisible bug line, and what had been a small annoyance before was now a squadron of B-52s buzzing around her head. Mosquitos, gnats, and small biting black flies called piums carried a lifetime supply of malaria and yellow fever with them. She and Simon didn't have to worry about those, thank God, but the bugs were very . . .buggy. Very, very buggy. They flew in small swarms that seemed to swamp a person for a minute, stabbing, biting, and annoying until moving on to the next.

"They have driven men mad," Raul said, pointing to one cloud of gnats.

Elizabeth believed it. She was wearing clothes of lightweight gabardine with long sleeves and pants and a bandana around her neck and she'd already been bitten a dozen times. This was not *Romancing the Stone*, for sure.

They slept with mosquito netting every night, but like little flying ninjas some always managed to get inside. The sleeves of her shirt had small smears of blood from those she'd managed to kill. Between that and the mud and the lack of bathing, the jungle wasn't the only thing beginning to smell. She and Simon did their best to have bird baths in their tent every day, and they would rinse out their clothes in the small streams they crossed frequently, but nothing was ever truly clean.

That night as Elizabeth was enjoying her tea, one of the few luxuries they were allowed, they were reminiscing about what they missed from civilization. When it came her turn she didn't answer truthfully; a bath seemed silly and somehow not appropriate to say in a group of men.

"I think I miss dessert," she said instead, and it wasn't a complete lie. "What I wouldn't give for an ice cream."

Suddenly, Bira looked at her sharply across the campfire. "Senhora," he said in a tight voice. "No move."

There's nothing that makes a person want to move, *need* to move, more than someone telling them not to.

She held as still as she could. "Simon?"

He started to turn toward her, but Bira held up his hand. "No move."

Slowly he stepped closer, his hand coming to grip the handle of his machete. Elizabeth's flight or fight instinct wasn't having trouble deciding and it took all she had not to run.

Bira kept a stilling hand up as his other carefully pulled the machete from his waist when suddenly he lunged forward and swung. Elizabeth squeezed her eyes shut and felt Simon's hand gripping her arm.

When she heard Bira let out a deep breath next to her, she opened her eyes. He stood up and held the body of a brown and tan mottled snake; its severed head remained on the ground at her feet.

"A jararaca," he said, holding it up. "Very dangerous. Man bitten bleeds from eyes." He signaled for one of his men to come over. He tossed him the snake. "Good to eat."

"Thank you," Simon said as he eased Elizabeth to his other side, closer to the fire and farther from the edge of the forest.

"Yes, thank you," she managed to finally say. She'd had enough of snakes to last a lifetime and bleeding from her eyes? Well, that was a pass.

The near miss did more than unsettle her, though. The fact that it was a jararaca, a viper like the one on the lip of the golden bowl, deeply disturbed her. It was silly to look for signs and portents when there were none, but when searching for a magical staff in a lost city in the jungles of South America, it didn't seem all that crazy. She half expected there to be Indiana Jones-style booby traps at the city guarding the staff. What she hadn't realized was that the whole jungle itself was one giant booby trap. She'd just sprung a tiny bit of it.

A few moments later when Simon suggested they make an early night of it, she didn't argue.

BY THE END OF the second week, the jungle had grown so dense, the canopy above them so complete, it felt like they might never feel the sun on their faces again. Simon knew this affected Elizabeth especially. She'd always said she grew sad at the mere mention of SAD, Seasonal Affective Disorder, and he was seeing the truth of it. She was like a flower that needed the sun to blossom. Day after day in the dark and damp had wilted her spirit. She was still Elizabeth, still amazing in every way, but he saw her struggle where others did not. To them she was still the same vibrant force of life she always was, but he saw the effort that took, when it usually came naturally. So when they finally broke out of the thick tangle of trees and vines and came upon a waterfall and a broad, fast-flowing river, he didn't look at it, but at her. The smile that came to her face was far more beautiful to him than any vista could ever be.

Everyone basked in the sun which, despite the heat, felt like life itself. The downside, of course, was that they had to cross the river, and managing that with pack animals was no small feat. They had to walk nearly two miles downriver to find a place suitable for the mules. Even then, it was touch and go. This tributary of some other major river was not the lolling and winding Amazon, but constant rapids with a series of waterfalls that made finding a crossing and then crossing it difficult. It took them hours to manage it, but manage it they did. The effort took not only time but energy, and everyone agreed that camping on the other side for the night was the wisest choice.

Everyone took turns washing their clothes and bathing. Simon stood guard while Elizabeth splashed about in a shallow pool, as happy as a bird. Once she was back in the relative safety of their tent, he allowed himself to do the same.

"Do you mind if I join you?" Vega asked.

Simon shook his head.

"Thank you. I fear I am making my own eyes water."

He unbuttoned his shirt and pulled his undershirt over his head, leaving his bandana tied around his throat. As he did, Simon noticed a small tattoo on the underside of his left arm between the elbow and armpit. It looked like the letter A. There was something about it that rang a bell in the dark recesses of his mind, but he couldn't put a finger on it.

The two men washed themselves and their clothes in relative silence, which suited Simon well. Vega had been nothing but polite and solicitous along their journey, but Simon had not forgotten the look in the man's eyes as he'd killed Rasche, nor the look in his eyes as he'd watched Elizabeth when he thought no one else was looking. No matter how cultured or how kind Vega appeared to others, Simon did not trust him. And the sooner he and Elizabeth had nothing more to do with the man the better.

"I'LL LEAVE YOU TO it," Cross said as he finished washing, and climbed up onto the rocks to head back to camp, leaving Vega alone. He'd not shaved in several days and remained behind to remove his beard.

As Cross left, Emil arrived.

"This seems to be the spot," Emil said, jovial as ever, even under the duress of the journey, which surely was taking a far greater toll on him than anyone else. He had noticeably lost weight and the bags under his eyes were fuller than before.

Vega moved his wet clothes aside to make room for Emil. "Please."

Emil waded into the water but instead of washing looked up at the waterfall and the thick green jungle that hovered over its shore.

"It is magnificent, is it not?"

Vega appreciated the aesthetic beauty of it, but his focus remained on the secrets it held. He wiped the blade of his razor on a cloth hung over his shoulder, pausing to give the view a cursory look. "It is impressive."

"It's making quite an impression upon me," Emil said, feeling his ribs. "I'm wasting away."

Vega eyed his still slightly plump body. "You have a way to go yet."

Emil laughed and scratched the sides of his belly. "I suppose I do."

He set about the task of washing his clothes and laid them out on the warm stones to dry. "Do you think we'll make it?" he asked quietly, a hint of doubt in his voice.

Vega didn't hesitate. "I do."

"Yes, of course, you're right. We will."

It was a pity he needed the old man, but he did. The straight edge in his hand caught the setting sun. In spite of all of Vega's study and knowledge, Emil was by far the expert. That expertise would be needed to retrieve the staff. And as long as that was the case, he would coddle Mendoza and coax him along.

265

"And you will be reunited with your daughter," Vega said, knowing it was what Emil needed to hear. "The staff's power knows no limits."

Emil stopped fussing with his shirt and stared down at the rock. "I have spent the last ten years hoping and praying I might find a way to bring her back to us. But now that the moment is nearly upon me, I find myself wondering if it's madness that drives me."

Vega regarded Emil, finding truth the best lie. "All love is madness."

Elizabeth hated leaving the river. The open skies and surging water felt like a reprieve after the weeks in the thick underbrush of the jungle. But the next morning they moved on. They traveled several more days into the jungle, the routine of walking, camping, and barely sleeping broken by new terrain. They'd reached what she guessed was the base of a mountain, although she could only tell by the sudden incline in the landscape. There was no sense of how big it was or far they'd have to climb. All she knew was the twenty or thirty feet in front of her went up, up, up.

Simon stayed steadfastly by her side and helped her over some of the rougher bits. She had no idea how the Indians managed to goad the mules up after them, but somehow they did. Their pace, however, had slowed to a crawl. The closer they got to their objective, the slower they seemed to be able to move. As each step became more difficult, she dug into her reserves and found a way to take it.

Simon remained quiet and ever-present, steadfast and comforting, her lifeline to sanity. The rocks beneath her feet might shift, the leaves and branches might give way, but Simon held fast, strong and reassuring, a constant in an ever-changing environment.

Somewhere along the way, she'd come to think of the jungle as a single entity, something that lived and breathed, pushing back against their incursion. It did not want them there. And if they stayed in one place too long, she knew it would eventually consume them. That thought alone kept her feet moving, one in front of the other.

She'd had that feeling again yesterday—that they were being followed. She told Simon about it, but it remained nothing more than a fleeting sensation. They neither saw nor heard anyone.

Ahead of her she heard Bira call out, halting their little procession. They'd reached a small clearing suitable for camp. Everyone set to their tasks without words. The day's climb had taken its toll and no one had any energy left for talking.

She dreamed a black panther ate the moon that night. It was a bit of folklore that Bira had relayed through Alex a few days before, a myth explaining the coming eclipse and it had seeped into her subconscious. That night before bed, she'd looked up through the break in the trees to see more stars than she'd ever seen before. The moon drifted past the opening, then dipped below the tops of the trees as the earth's shadow devoured it, blocking out the light and plunging the night into a darkness that seemed so thick and black that she could touch it.

Simon had checked their watch several times that night, worried that the humidity might gum up the works. And it might. That was, after all, why Bira had brought a chronometer. The damp got into everything.

The watch seemed to be working, but she had an uncomfortable feeling as the eclipse came and went. It felt like a door opening and closing, leaving them trapped in the jungle.

The next morning when Elizabeth went to relieve herself she paused at the edge of camp. They were faint, but she could clearly see two footprints in the mud. They could have been made by one of the natives, but they seemed too small. Not quite a child, but not quite a man.

She told the others and Bira knelt down to look at them more closely. He said nothing, but she could tell by the set of his jaw and the shift in his eyes to the thick woods beyond that he was concerned.

"I've had the feeling we were being followed for a while now," she said, although she and Simon had already mentioned it to the others. "I thought it was just my imagination."

Bira's grim face told her it was not.

Chapter Twenty-Two

"How close are we, do you think?" Elizabeth asked Emil and Alex as they paused yet again to refer to their compass and map and to make notes on their journey so far.

"Perhaps forty miles. Maybe less. About a week more I'd say."

She could do that. One more week. She could do one more week. She told the little voice inside her head that reminded her she'd have to do all of this again on the way back to cram it with walnuts. She couldn't think about that now. All she could focus on was moving ahead. One week.

"If we're right," Alex amended. "If not..."

If not, they were lost and, to put it succinctly, screwed.

Just when the cave of trees, that Elizabeth felt they were trapped in, seemed like it would never end, they came upon another river. She could hear it before she saw it—the raging rapids, the thrumming rush of a waterfall. Her spirits lifted immediately, only to be sunk again when they came to it. The dense forest ended abruptly at the edge of a cliff. Well over one hundred feet beneath them the river churned and roared. Upriver was a cascading waterfall, cliff after sheer cliff and impossible to pass. Downriver the chasm seemed to stretch out as far she could see.

"What now?" she asked.

"There should be a bridge. It should be here," Alex said, referring to the map he'd drawn from the etchings in the bowl.

The fact that it wasn't meant one of two things: the map was wrong or they were. Neither was comforting.

"It should be here," Alex said again, looking around and checking the compass readings.

"Lá!" Bira cried out, pointing downriver.

Elizabeth could barely make out what he saw, but sure enough, far down river there seemed to be a bridge. Relief coursed through her. She shared a look with Simon, who gave her a confident and comforting smile.

Their party backtracked away from the cliff's edge and made their way downriver. The jungle here was thick with trees, rocks, and vines. Cutting their way through was exhausting and arduous.

An hour later they arrived, and Elizabeth's relief at finding a bridge was short-lived. The bridge, if one could call it that, was no more than four ropes and a series of haphazard planks stretching out over the raging and boulder-filled river a hundred feet below.

"Surely there's another way across," Simon said.

Alex looked out at the chasm. "Maybe downriver or maybe not. This might be the only passage across for miles."

It had taken them an hour to go a few hundred yards. A few miles through this and with cliffs as a potential obstacle, they had little choice but to use the bridge. Or at least try to.

The ropes looked old and frayed and the planks worn and decaying. But they had to at least try.

"I will go," Bira said.

Elizabeth's heart was in her throat as he took his first tentative step across. The boards creaked under his weight, but held it. The ropes moved but didn't break. He walked half way across and then turned back. "It will hold."

They hoped.

Bira turned to the lead Indian bearer and gave him instructions. He quickly relayed this to several more men who began unpacking several of the mules.

"What's going on?" she asked.

"The mules cannot go across. Whatever we wish to take we will have to carry ourselves," Raul said and went to help sort things out.

That was a sobering fact. The journey so far had been difficult, but the mules and the men had done the bulk of the labor. She would have to pull her own weight from here on out. Literally.

A great many things didn't make the cut, including their tents. They would have to make due with hammocks and mosquito netting from here on out. The food, the guns and their personal possessions were crammed into heavy packs.

"Put that in mine," Simon said as he went over to help prepare the bags.

"I can carry my share," Elizabeth said, although she really wondered if she could.

"Don't worry, you will," Simon said, but she knew that he was taking on half her weight.

He helped her on with the pack to test it out. "How's this?"

It was heavy but manageable. "All right."

One of the bearers had already started across the bridge with one of the newly filled packs on his back. The added weight made the crossing even more perilous. Every step caused a greater shift of weight and the bridge swayed beneath his feet. But he never stopped moving. He was small but strong and agile. He and several others ferried the packs across to the other side. It was time for them to cross.

"I'll go first," Emil offered, trying to sound confident, but the worry on his face gave him away.

"Just go slowly," Alex offered needlessly.

Deliberately, Emil worked his way across. Near the middle his balance wavered and the bridge beneath him began to wobble and wobble.

"Easy!" Alex called out.

Finally, Emil regained his balance and made it the rest of the way across the bridge.

Bira looked for who was next. Elizabeth stepped forward.

"I'll go."

Simon moved to help her.

"One at a time," Alex reminded him. "It can only hold one person at a time."

Simon held on to her hand until she was forced to let it go and grab on to the rope railing. She could barely reach to hold both ropes at once. If she grabbed onto one too tightly it pulled her off balance, so she had to just graze her fingertips over the tops of both for balance. Sweat began to drip down into her eyes, blurring her vision, but she didn't dare try to wipe it away. She blinked rapidly and everything cleared.

She tried to keep her breathing smooth and even, breathing in through her nose and out through her mouth, focusing on each step as she made it. The key was not to stop. Just keep moving, slow and steady. Step after step. A board beneath her foot creaked and cracked loudly and she fought down her instinct to stop. She didn't dare look down. She didn't really need to. The image of the roiling water and jagged rocks were imprinted on her mind. Before she knew it, she was more than halfway and walking up the slight incline on the other side.

Emil reached out a hand to help her onto terra firma.

"Easy peasy!" she called back, swallowing her heart to force it back into her chest. Her heart made a U-turn and headed back into her throat as Simon stepped out on the bridge. Luckily, his arms were long enough to reach both ropes at the same time and he could steady himself more securely as he crossed. He walked slowly but purposefully across until one of the boards beneath him snapped in two.

His leg plunged through the bridge and Elizabeth cried out his name. Somehow he managed to steady himself on his right leg as his left dangled above the river. The bridge swayed back and forth beneath him as he fought to regain his balance and stand.

Elizabeth clutched at the knotted end of the rope on her side as if that helped somehow. It didn't. Finally, he managed to stand back up, two feet firmly planted on the board behind the now missing one. He glanced up at her before he lifted his leg to stride across the gap.

"Careful!" Elizabeth cried out.

Simon glared at her, stopping and then starting again.

"Sorry."

He tried again and with his long legs the gap was no problem. Once he crossed it, he continued the rest of the way without issue. When he reached Elizabeth, she practically yanked him off the bridge, pulling him into a hug.

"That was too close."

Although he only nodded and looked otherwise calm, she could feel his heart racing in his chest.

Alex, and finally Bira crossed. Little Mancha tried to follow him. Bira snatched up the dog and was forced to return to the far side, carrying the little dog with him. He put a rope leash on him and handed him to one of the men who were remaining behind.

Mancha cried and barked as Bira crossed without him.

"What's going to happen to him?" Elizabeth asked once Bira was on their side.

"The men will take him and the mules back to the village," Vega translated for him. Bira turned to look at the jungle ahead of them. "What lies ahead is not fit for a dog."

"Or man," Bira added.

"Remind me not to sign up for his motivational speaking class," Elizabeth said.

Simon chuckled and helped her on with her pack. She was fairly certain it had somehow gotten heavier in the last thirty minutes.

She turned back to watch the men on the other side of the bridge disappear into the jungle. Mancha barked a few more times and then all was silent except the river.

"Ready?" Bira asked.

She wasn't, but nodded as they started on the final leg of their journey.

They hadn't gone more than a mile when Elizabeth got that feeling again. The hairs on the base of her neck tickled and she had to rub the gooseflesh from her arms.

Simon looked at her with concern and she tried to smile it all away, but the feeling was unmistakable, like spiders crawling on her skin. She looked out into the thick undergrowth as they walked and was sure she saw something move. Then she looked toward Simon, but out of the corner of her eye something moved on the that side of them as well. Then there was movement like an animal rushing past them just out of sight in the jungle. Then another on the other side. They weren't just being followed; they were being surrounded.

She reached over and clutched Simon's forearm. "Simon."

"I see them."

They kept walking, hoping like a child it would all just go away like a monster under the bed.

But then she heard a thunk as an arrow embedded itself in a tree just in front of Bira. Everyone stopped. The jungle was still but the sounds around them grew in intensity. A howler monkey cried in the treetops above them, and the birds and cicada and the frogs all seemed to sing louder suddenly. And then a man stepped out of the jungle, a bow and arrow raised at the ready. And then another and another until they were surrounded.

Simon's mouth was suddenly dry. He eased Elizabeth closer and tried not to think about the fact that some Brazilian tribes were cannibals.

He slowly reached to his belt and gripped the handle of his gun. Alex had his gun out and pointed at who he believed was the leader. His face paint and adornments of feathers and beads were more elaborate than the others.

His bow still at the ready and flanked by two men on each side, he cautiously stepped closer. He looked at them carefully and then tilted his head to the side. "Raul?"

"Moacir?" came the cautious reply.

The little tribesman's face broke into a grin and Raul laughed as the two embraced and began speaking in a mixture of rapid Portuguese and some other language Simon didn't recognize.

"It seems they know each other," Simon said.

"Funny meeting you here," Elizabeth said under her breath.

Emil stepped forward and was introduced to Moacir. They shook hands, heads bobbing in agreement and delight at meeting.

"He's the fellow who guided Gaspar," Emil explained. Raul found him at that village near the lake. A remarkable man. I think these are his people."

"Come, come," Raul said. "We are safe with them."

They were taken to a small village. There was one large hut in the shape of a circle with an open center that served as a communal living space for the entire tribe. Everyone lived and ate and slept under the single roof.

That night they shared their food with the tribe and the tribe with them. Their meal consisted of nuts and berries, bananas and açaí fruit, and a dab of honey, which was a most precious delicacy.

Moacir, like Bira, had gone to a missionary school when he was a boy and had since straddled the lines between two worlds. He warned them of a neighboring tribe that would not be as accommodating as his. They saw all outsiders as a violation of the natural order and would not hesitate to kill them.

With that comforting thought, they strung their own hammocks amongst the Indians' and fell into a fitful sleep. Before dawn, Simon awoke to find himself being stared at. A small boy, no more than five, gazed at him with enormous dark brown eyes. Cautiously, the boy reached out and touched his cheek then checked his finger to see if the pigment had rubbed off. Simon shook his head and smiled at the boy who ran back to his mother. The experience triggered an instant and painful feeling of missing his own child. He hated being away from her. Even if she didn't have a sense of the passage of time, he did. And her absence in his life was felt acutely. He reminded himself that she was one of the reasons he was in this Godforsaken place, to find the staff before anyone else, to ensure the future remained the same and that she was there for them to return to.

By daybreak their party was ready to start off again. This time, they kept their guns at the ready. The little village disappeared quickly behind them, and more and more, Simon's worry began to grow. Not about whether they would find the city, but what would happen to them when they did.

Chapter Twenty-Three

Elizabeth's thighs burned and her calves felt like they were rubber bands about to snap. They'd come upon another hill, but this one gave and gave and gave. They climbed up and up. Somehow trees took root in the soil and sprung up between jagged outcroppings of rock. With each step, soil and small rocks cascaded down behind her. It was treacherous going, not just for her but everyone behind her. Raul and Bira helped Emil up while Alex and Simon assisted her. She had to take her pack off several times and hand it forward so she could climb over whatever obstacle was in their way, like this large boulder.

Once she was on top of it, she put her pack back on and they continued. She was determined not to slow them down, not much anyway. Everyone was slowing, especially Emil. The last few days had been even more demanding and challenging than the weeks before. The jungle had become a series of small and not so small hills. Traversing their way up and down them was backbreaking. But Alex and Emil agreed that they were "almost there." They believed that this most recent, and largest hill, would be the worst of it.

And so they climbed. One step forward and two steps back, literally, as their feet slid back downhill in the loose soil.

Finally, Alex gave her one final hand up as Simon shoved her unceremoniously from behind, and she reached the summit. It wasn't exactly Everest, but she didn't care. She couldn't believe she'd made it. Unlike Everest, however, this mountain flattened into a large semi-plateau at the top.

Simon climbed up behind her and they both turned to look at the view. It was amazing and terrifying. The hills they'd just spent days traversing lay before them along with dozens of others, and a green blanket of jungle seemed to stretch out as far as the eye could see in any direction. It was a potent reminder of just how isolated they were.

"I believe the entrance should be here somewhere," Emil said, breathless from exertion and excitement.

They took off their packs and quickly made camp. After an all-too-small ration of food and water, they began to explore the area, careful not to stray too far.

"What are we looking for?" Elizabeth asked.

"I'm not certain. A stone outcropping with writing on it, possibly. Or a hole of some sort. It might be well grown over, so look carefully."

They spread out to cover more ground but kept within shouting distance. They probably should have created a search grid or something equally brainy, but they were all too tired and too eager to bother. They'd come so far. If the city was here, they had to find it.

She and Simon stayed close enough to see each other as they walked through the woods. The undergrowth wasn't as dense here as it had been, so they could separate by thirty or forty feet and still be within sight. The ground was quite rocky and she paused every once in a while to brush away some dried leaves or vines to look for that mysterious writing. So far, all she'd uncovered was a giant millipede that was undoubtedly getting a starring role in her nightmares that night.

She saw Simon pulling leaves away from a promising looking rock formation. "Anything?" she called out to him as she went to see for herself.

"Not sure."

"Maybe if you—" The rest of what she was going to say disappeared with her as the earth beneath her opened up and swallowed her whole.

She cried out as she felt herself fall and then painfully stop falling as she crash landed about ten feet down. Dirt and debris rained down on her from the hole she'd fallen through.

"Elizabeth!"

After a moment to get over the shock, she realized that while her not-so-soft landing hurt, she wasn't injured. She pushed herself up and looked around at the small cavern. It was dark but there was enough light filtering down to see the walls, and they were walls, and there was writing on them.

"Found it," she said as she stood, rubbing her aching backside.

Simon's head appeared in the hole above her, sending more bits of rock and dirt down onto her. "Elizabeth!"

"I'm all right," she said, "but be careful up there. That first step is a doozy."

"Are you hurt?"

"Just my dignity," she said, sure she'd have a heckuva bruise to remember it all by.

Simon called out to the others and she could hear them gathering above her. Emil's head popped over the opening. "What have you found?"

Elizabeth walked over to one of the walls in the circular chamber and traced her fingers over the glyphs. They were just like the ones in the drawings at the library.

"You're gonna want to see this."

The end of a rope dropped through the hole. Simon climbed down it; his entrance was a lot more graceful than hers had been. He gave the room only a passing glance as he came to her side. "You're sure you're all right?"

"Nothing a massage won't cure," she said with a sly grin, then turned back to the stones. "This is it, isn't it?" she asked.

Simon pulled his attention away from her and seemed to see what she saw for the first time. "Good Lord. You found it."

"Better lucky than good."

Suddenly, a makeshift torch dropped down onto the floor and the room flickered to life.

Simon picked it up as Emil was hoisted down into the room, followed shortly by Alex and then another torch. The torch bathed the room in orange firelight. Simon held his torch close to the wall. The entire room was covered by writing. Now that she got a good look around, she realized that the room wasn't just round but a perfect circle, and carved into nearly every inch of available wall space were glyphs and symbols. The room was probably twenty feet in diameter and the ceiling ten feet high. It was a good thing it wasn't higher, she thought.

Carvings were made in the stone walls almost like the pages of a book; each was about four feet wide and divided into three horizontal sections. Carved into each panel was a series of the same sort of glyphs and symbols from Manuscript 512-A.

"Remarkable," Alex muttered as he scanned the walls, as overwhelmed as the rest of them.

Emil clapped him on the back and barked out a laugh. "I should say."

"There's just one problem," Elizabeth said.

"What?"

"If this is the entrance to the city, isn't something missing?"

"What, my dear?" Emil asked, too enamored with the discovery to see it.

"A door." The room was a momentous discovery, but the walls were solid rock. If this was the entrance to the city, one thing was missing—a way in.

THEY SPENT THE REST of the afternoon and most of the evening copying down the symbols to better study them. *At least that's something I can do*, Elizabeth thought. When it came time to translate them, she was about as useful as a screen door on a submarine. Simon, Emil, and Alex sat huddled by the fire staring at the sketches they'd made, laboriously working through each section.

Elizabeth brought Simon a cup of tea and sat on the other side of the fire with Bira and Raul.

"Heard any good jokes?" she asked.

Raul laughed and then translated to a confused Bira. It ended up that Bira had heard a few good jokes and proceeded to tell them until they got a little too off-color for Raul to comfortably translate.

"It just doesn't make any sense," Simon said, pointing at the page they had been working on for the last half hour. "This simply doesn't follow this."

Alex sighed. "No, it doesn't."

"It must," Emil insisted. "We must be mistranslating."

"It has been a long day. Perhaps we need to rest," Simon suggested. "Start again fresh in the morning. The room isn't going anywhere."

Emil started to argue, but when a yawn infiltrated his rebuttal, he gave in with a laugh. "All right. First light."

After the day's discovery, it was difficult to fall asleep, but Elizabeth finally did and found herself dreaming of a snarky millipede smoking a hookah and giving her odd directions to the City of Gold.

THE NEXT MORNING THE men were back at it and Elizabeth was back to feeling slightly useless. She suggested scouting the area for another entrance, but they were worried she'd "discover" something else and break her neck. But she couldn't just sit there while they did all of the work. She had to do something.

She liked puzzles, even if she wasn't always the best at solving them. Part of the problem was her impatience. Simon could study something quietly and contentedly for hours. She was just too restless. Methodically working through a problem like a Rubik's Cube was Simon's forte, not hers, but she was determined to join in.

Cuddling her cup of barely-tea in her hands, she stood behind them to look at the papers.

"This simply doesn't follow this," Simon said in exasperation. "It's nonsensical."

"No, but it could work with this," Alex said, pointing at a set of writing that was nearly on the other side of the room.

It struck her almost immediately. Excited by the idea, but worried she was wrong, she knelt down between them. "This goes with this, right?"

"Possibly."

"And what could this go with?" she asked, pointing out another section.

They all considered for a moment, studying their notes. "It could follow this," Emil offered.

And she knew she was right. She gathered up the pages.

"What are you doing?" Simon asked.

"I need a knife."

"Now I really want to know what you're doing."

"Never mind," she said and folded the papers horizontally.

When she began tearing them all three men cried out in protest.

"It's a Rubik's Cube or a Circle or something."

"What's that?" Alex asked, and she realized the reference was anachronistic since it wouldn't be invented for another forty years.

"A puzzle," Simon replied. "I'm not sure I follow though."

"Look." She aligned the parts she'd torn to match the sections they'd said followed each other.

No one said anything for an excruciating minute and she was sure they all thought she'd gone mad. When Simon hmm'd under his breath, she knew she was right.

"It is, isn't it?"

Alex looked both incredulous and impressed. "You do not cease to amaze."

"Oh my dear," Emil cooed, "I think you're right. Look here. This clearly goes with this."

He quickly slid the sliced pages until they all aligned in a new configuration.

"So can you figure out what it means now?" she asked.

"Quite possibly," he replied with growing excitement. "Quite possibly."

They lit torches and brought the pages back down into the chamber.

"This section," Alex said, as he ran his fingers over a bit of the wall, "talks of a direction or a path. That only the best or the most worthy will be able to see."

"He who allies with righteousness," Simon recited, and then walked over to another section of the wall. He turned to study it and then ran his fingers over the deeply etched symbols and down into the groove between the horizontal rows. "Does anyone have a knife?"

Alex pulled one from his belt and handed it to him. They all gathered around as he pried away the loose dirt that had filled the space.

"More light, please."

Emil moved the torch closer.

Simon pressed the tip of the knife into the wall and then pushed on the handle; the entire blade disappeared into the stone. He wiggled it back and forth and more dust and debris came away. Slowly, he revealed a gap between the horizontal layers.

"They're rings," Elizabeth said. "It really is a Rubik's."

"I think they move," Simon said, unable to hide his excitement. "Check other places."

They did, and the same result followed. The three strata of symbols were housed on three separate rings.

"How on earth can we move this much stone?" Emil asked.

"Here," Alex said, picking up a piece of timber strewn on the floor as he spoke. "I noticed holes before but didn't think anything of them at the time."

There were two holes that were around four inches in diameter just slightly larger in circumference than the wood in his hand; one in the upper ring and the second in the middle. He slipped his beam into the slot in the wall; it fit perfectly. He gripped it to demonstrate. "Like horses in a mill, we can rotate the rings."

Simon looked around the floor and found a similar piece of wood. He slipped it into the other hole.

"Surely the four of us won't be able to move so much weight," Emil said.

"If I'm right, there's probably a system of ball bearings or something similar in the walls to allow for the movement."

Elizabeth came to stand beside him, gripping the post he'd put into the wall. "There's one way to find out."

"Right."

"On the count of three. One, two, three."

Elizabeth put her full weight into it, but it didn't budge.

"Again," Simon said.

She pushed as hard as she could, and just as she was about to give up, it moved. The walls were rotating.

"Where do we stop?" she asked.

"The panel in front of you should align with that fourth one there," Emil said as he and Alex moved their part of the puzzle into place.

It took a little adjusting to get things lined up just right, like a combination lock, but finally they did and stood back to admire their work.

"So, what did we do?" Elizabeth asked.

Just then a deep rumbling came along with the sound of stone scraping against stone. Then the floor beneath them began to tremble slightly. Simon gripped her arm and they all looked around nervously, cautiously stepping backward.

In the center of the room, like a camera's iris, a hole opened. Alex pulled Emil back from the edge and they pressed themselves up against the wall until it stopped.

"I guess we did that," she said, answering her own question.

"Are you all right?" Raul cried from up top.

"We're fine!" Emil answered.

Cautiously, Simon edged forward, checking the safety of his footing as he went. Everything seemed solid, except for the gaping black hole in the middle of the floor. He held the torch out above it.

The light flickered upon a set of stone steps leading down into the dark.

"In for a penny, in for a pound," Emil said. Then looked up at Raul and Bira. "Bring me the satchel in my bag, would you, Raul?"

A few moments later, Raul returned with it and carefully tossed the bag down to Emil. He pulled out the Eye, briefly unwrapping it before stuffing it back into the bag.

Seeing it again was a potent reminder of what lay ahead and the responsibility heaped on her shoulders. Always attuned to her, Simon gave her an encouraging smile.

She could do this. She had to do this.

"Stay up there with the men," Emil told Raul and Bira, as he put the satchel over his shoulder. "We'll call out if we run into trouble."

Assuming they'd be able to.

Holding the second torch, Alex carefully took the first step, testing the ground beneath him as Simon had done. When it didn't fall away, he took another and another. All Elizabeth could see beyond him was darkness.

As Emil went next and then Elizabeth followed by Simon with the other torch, Alex said, "Stay to the left."

It wasn't until she was a few steps down that she realized why he'd admonished them to stay to one side. The left side was buttressed by the rough-hewn walls that the tunnel had been carved out of. The right side was . . .nothing.

Simon held out his torch to try to illuminate the staggering darkness, but all Elizabeth could see was the edge of the steps and then nothing.

"Dear Lord," Emil muttered.

"How far down do you think it goes?" she asked.

Alex paused and picked up a loose rock and then tossed it down the gap to the right side of the stairs. They never heard it land.

"Everyone, please step carefully," Alex said.

Elizabeth didn't need to be told twice. She kept one hand on the wall to her left, staying as close to it as she could. Thankfully, the steps weren't overly narrow—perhaps four feet across—but four feet between herself and oblivion seemed awfully small. Simon stayed right behind her as they descended.

Their footfalls echoed loudly in the cavern. The air was stale but surprisingly not humid. If anything, it was noticeably arid.

Step by step they made their way to the bottom, clinging to the left side wall. By her best count they'd gone down thirty-nine steps. Hitchcock would have liked that, she thought.

At the bottom of the stairs was a small landing that led into a chamber. No one wasted time on the landing and they all hurried into the safety of a room with four walls. The chamber was square, approximately twenty feet across and a ceiling about fifteen feet high. One wall was covered by a mural. On it a large man with dark skin and black hair stood above a group of men and women who bowed down before him. In his hand was the staff. The Eye glowed as it had for her and shafts of light reached out toward the people like rays of the sun. It reminded her of ancient Egyptian paintings except the style was different, more three-dimensional. No "walk like an Egyptian" motifs. But there were similarities as well, and she wasn't the only one to notice.

"Remarkable," Emil said softly as he studied the great painting. "So familiar and yet not."

"Professor," Simon said, pulling Emil's attention away from the mural.

Simon held up his torch above an arched doorway that led to a narrow tunnel. On the pediment above the door were several large symbols.

Alex and his torch joined them to shed more light. "The first is 'intelligence,' I think, or 'wisdom.'"

"Yes," Emil agreed. "The second is a little more complex. The first glyph in the compound is fear."

Elizabeth had a feeling that would show up.

"The second is, I think, the representation of without or lacking."

287

"So, without fear? Fearless?"

"Courage, perhaps, or bravery," Alex added.

Emil moved his attention to the third. "And third one is similar to faith, but perhaps trust or faith."

"Wisdom, courage, and faith."

"Not bad words to live by," Elizabeth said, feeling a little better about the mysterious creators of the staff.

They all stood at the entrance for a moment before Alex took the lead again. The tunnel was only wide enough for one person. They'd only gone a few steps when a light appeared at the end of it.

Everyone froze mid-step. Were they not alone here?

They paused but heard nothing, yet the unmistakable glow of a fire filled the far end of the tunnel.

They looked at each uncertainly.

"Hello?" Elizabeth called out, earning shushes from the others. "Well..."

There was no answering call. Cautiously, they continued down the corridor until it opened into another chamber roughly the same size as the first, but this room had no paintings. There was a lighted brazier shaped like a cauldron sitting on a pedestal in the center of the room and a single panel of glyphs in an otherwise featureless room. The only way in seemed to be the door they'd just come through.

"A dead end?" she asked.

"Possibly," Simon said as he and Emil went to study the panel. Elizabeth and Alex used the second torch to carefully examine the rest of the room, starting with the brazier. A large lid for the cauldron leaned against the pedestal.

"How did it light?" Elizabeth asked.

Alex looked carefully around the base of the pedestal the brazier sat upon. "I do not know. Our arrival must have triggered it somehow."

"Maybe there are pressure panels in the corridor?" she suggested earning a curious and slightly amazed look from Alex.

Not having any idea she'd only gotten the idea from a movie, he still looked impressed. "Possibly."

Other than the self-starting fireplace, there was nothing else in the room at all, other than the small section with the glyphs.

She and Alex joined the others at the panel. "What does it say?"

"Check our work, Alex, but we think it translates as, 'The path to knowledge begins with ignorance.'"

"So it's a giant fortune cookie," Elizabeth said.

Simon snorted before controlling himself. "Something like that."

"It's a puzzle," Alex said. "A test."

They looked around the room for inspiration but none immediately appeared.

"Well, so far we're acing the ignorance part. Or at least I am," Elizabeth said.

"It's not literal," Simon said. "It's a metaphor. What represents ignorance?"

Silence surrounded them again, except for the occasional sound of the flames from the fire.

Suddenly, Emil turned toward the brazier. "Darkness."

"I say, there is no darkness but ignorance," Simon recited what Elizabeth guessed was a line from Shakespeare.

"Precisely!"

"So, what does that mean? We have to put out the fire?"

"I think so."

Alex handed Emil his torch and started to pick up the lid to the cauldron but it was too heavy. Simon gave Elizabeth his torch and together they lifted the heavy iron lid and placed it over the fire, snuffing it out.

They all waited for something to happen, but nothing did.

"The torches," Alex said. "We should put them out as well."

Elizabeth wasn't too keen on the idea of no light at all, but the path to knowledge and all that.

They laid the torches down on the ground.

"I hope you can relight those," she said as Simon and Alex grabbed handfuls of dirt and sand to smother them.

"Don't worry," Simon told her with a comforting smile.

It was the last thing she saw as they were submerged into darkness. And it wasn't just dark, it was completely dark. Darker than the woods of Maine in winter dark.

"This is creepy."

And then lines in the floor began to glow, and on the walls and on the ceiling. Intricate designs glimmered in the stone. The lines seemed to draw themselves in glowing blues and greens. It was beautiful, like being amongst the stars.

"It must be some form of bioluminescence or phosphorescence," Simon said.

She could see him and the others now bathed in the strange light. The lines curled and curved in an almost mandala-like pattern until they converged on the floor and all ran straight toward one wall. Two handprints appeared about halfway up the walls roughly five feet apart.

"Think it's trying to tell us something?" Elizabeth asked.

Alex and Emil walked over to handprints and slowly raised their hands, pressing them onto the imprints. Elizabeth felt that same telltale shaking as she had in the entry room when the floor opened up. Sure enough, the wall between Emil and Alex split and a doorway appeared.

"Get the other torch," Simon said as he retrieved one and lit it with a match.

As soon as the torches were lit, the glowing designs disappeared again and they walked into the new corridor.

The next room was bare. There was nothing in it. No writing, no brazier, nothing.

"Okay. What are we supposed to do now?" Elizabeth asked.

Simon shook his head. "Look around, I suppose. There must be something we're missing."

They were about to feel along the walls for any seams, any hidden panels or writing, when one of the walls suddenly became a wall of fire. The whole thing was just fire. The heat was instantaneous and intense.

They all edged away from it.

"Are we supposed to put it out?" Elizabeth wondered aloud, wondering to herself how that would even be possible. She was already feeling like a rotisserie chicken.

"No," Alex said, sounding oddly sure. "We are meant to walk through it."

Emil chuckled then stopped. "You're serious."

Alex, his eyes nearly glowing with the reflection of the flames, said, "The words above the door. They're more than just a creed. They're tests. The first was wisdom, accepting the darkness to find the light. This is courage." He turned to face them. "We must walk through it."

"That's madness," Simon said, sweat beading on his forehead. "You'll be killed instantly, if you're lucky."

Alex started toward the flames. Emil grabbed his arm to stop him. "You mustn't."

"It's all right," he said with nearly preternatural calm.

"Alex, please?" Elizabeth beseeched him as he continued toward the fire.

He held up his hands to keep the heat from his face and Elizabeth had to look away. She couldn't watch him burn alive.

"Dear God," Simon whispered, and Elizabeth peeked back around just in time to see Alex step right into the wall of flame, and then disappear into it.

"Alex?" Emil called out.

There was a pause and then Alex's voice came to them. "I am all right. It is some sort of illusion." To prove his point his hand pushed through the flames from the other side. "Come."

Elizabeth and Simon looked unsurely at each other, but they knew they had to try. Emil cautiously walked forward into the flames and they followed.

The heat was nearly unbearable, but somehow they stepped through without being burned at all. They emerged on the other side to find Alex and Emil waiting for them.

Elizabeth turned back to look at the backside of the flame illusion and shuddered. There was something primally disturbing about it. She realized that was true of the first test, too. Fear of the darkness, fear of fire, these were basic survival instincts. A cold feeling balled up in the pit of her stomach at what fear the next room had to offer.

CHAPTER TWENTY-FOUR

"T HAT WAS DISTURBING," ELIZABETH said.
Simon couldn't help but agree.

"Wisdom, courage, and now faith," Simon said as they paused outside of the next room.

"Faith in what?" Elizabeth asked. "We don't even know what, if any, gods they worshipped."

"Perhaps it's a different sort of faith," Emil said as he took the lead and they stepped into what Simon hoped was the final trial. "More like trust."

The third room was similar to the others except for one very unique detail. There were dead bodies in it. The skeletons of two men, long since passed, and the floor nearest the entrance was also covered with dozens of arrows and darts.

"This is troubling," Emil said as he studied one of the men who'd passed this way and then . . .passed.

Their clothes were old and ragged. It was difficult to tell how long ago they'd tried to pass the test and failed.

So far, they'd managed to get through unscathed, but so had these two men, until this room. It was a harsh reminder of the stakes if they failed whatever test this room had in store. The dead men, as dead men do, made everyone tense. The earlier excitement was tempered to near nonexistence now, and all that was left was a sense of impending doom.

Simon found a panel with a single word inscribed on it. "Remain."

"Are you sure it isn't remains?" Elizabeth asked with a grimace as she looked toward the dead men.

Simon looked around the room carefully as Elizabeth picked up one of the darts from the floor.

"Be careful, my dear," Emil cautioned her. "Those might be tipped with poison."

She held it away from her by her fingertips. "Poison?"

"Curare."

Elizabeth quickly tossed it aside and failed to suppress another shiver. "What do you think 'remain' means? They remained and look what that got them."

"I'm not sure, but look at this," Simon said, beckoning them over.

There were three distinct squares on the floor. He knelt down to brush away some of the dirt and sand and found seams around each. Each square was about three feet across and spaced roughly the same distance from the next in the center of the room.

"What do you think they are?" Alex said, as he knelt down to run his fingers over one.

"Possibly more pressure pads."

"That trigger . . .what exactly?" Elizabeth asked.

"I'm not certain," Simon replied.

"But there's one way to find out?" she said, sounding nearly as excited by the prospect as she had when they started.

"How do we know that stepping on those isn't what killed those men?" Alex asked.

Simon arched an eyebrow. "We don't."

"But we must step on them anyway if we hope to unveil this room's secret," Emil said.

"I'm afraid so."

"Hate to be the party pooper," Elizabeth said, "but there are three of those and, unless I miscounted, four of us."

"You and I can share one," he said.

She gave him a smile. "Cozy."

They put their torches in sconces on the wall and all took positions behind their squares, Elizabeth in front of Simon. "I think it might be best if we all do this unison. On the count of three?"

The others nodded and be began the countdown. "One, two, three."

As one they all stepped into their squares and waited.

"I don't—" Elizabeth began but was cutoff by the all-too-familiar sound of stone scraping against stone.

At the base of the far wall, a three-foot width of floor dropped away and a large monolith rose in its place. Carved into its surface was a coil of serpents, each head carved in relief and facing them, ready to strike. The engineering of such a thing was remarkable, but his fascination dimmed as he realized that in each snake's throat was a hole. Suddenly, he understood—the meaning of the clue, the dead men and the test itself.

"No matter what happens," he said, "do not move from your square."

The first dart fired from the mouth of a snake before anyone could ask what he meant. It flew past Alex with a whooshing sound before colliding with the wall behind them and falling harmlessly to the floor. Then another fired and another.

Simon trusted his conclusion, but spun Elizabeth behind him to protect her with his body, just in case.

"Don't move!" he cried out as he held her.

The air around them buzzed with the sound of arrows and darts whizzing through the air, nearly hitting each of them. One inch outside of the safety of their squares and they would be killed. The instinct to move, to run, was powerful, but he fought it and prayed the others did as well.

Finally, the endless *thewp* and *thewp* stopped, and suddenly there was silence.

The deadly onslaught had lasted for less than a minute but felt like an eternity. Simon looked down at Elizabeth and asked if she was all right, although he knew she was. Hearing and seeing for himself calmed him.

"That was bracing," she said with a wry and then relieved smile.

He glanced over at Emil and Alex, who were also unharmed. The monolith began to lower itself back into the floor and a doorway appeared on the wall to their right.

"Faith to remain," Alex said. "Very clever. How did you know?"

"I wasn't sure, to be honest, but the men did die over there," Simon said, "and not over here."

"They ran."

Simon nodded.

"Is it safe to step off?" Emil asked, his voice slightly tremulous.

By way of answer, Alex did just that and when nothing happened, the others followed suit.

They retrieved their torches and continued on into the next room. It was just as it had been in the sketches they'd seen at the library. Embedded in a block of stone was the staff.

Elizabeth stood at the base of the platform and gazed up at it. "Moment of truth, I guess."

Simon laid a hand on her shoulder and she jumped at the contact. He gave it a gentle squeeze. "You'll be—"

"Fine," she finished for him. "I know."

"I was going to say magnificent." He tucked a finger under her chin. "But then you already are."

"Smooth talker."

The brief repartee did its job and Elizabeth was noticeably calmer. She walked over to Emil. "Time for the Eye, I think."

He took off his satchel and started to remove the bundle inside but stopped. "Before we go further, I must make a confession."

"Confession?" Simon asked warily.

Emil actually blushed as he dipped his head. "Yes. I hope you can forgive me for it, but I have deceived you. My interest in the staff is not purely academic."

Simon tensed. He knew this had all been going along too smoothly. "Meaning?"

"I am a selfish old man, but I hoped to use the staff to . . .bring back my daughter."

"Aurora?"

"When she died, the loss carved out a piece of my soul, tore my marriage apart, left us incomplete and unable to even look at each other for the pain of the memory," Emil said.

The anguish on his face went straight to Simon's heart. He and Elizabeth had nearly lost Charlotte, more than once. He'd endured months of anguish believing they were both dead. He'd been given a reprieve, but if he hadn't...

"I had hoped," Emil went on, "to use the staff..."

"To bring her back," Simon finished for him.

"For years I thought it folly. But the more I studied, the more certain I became that it was possible. And when you held the Eye," he said to Elizabeth, "I knew it could be so." He came closer to her, pain and hope filling his eyes. "It can be, can't it? You can do it. You can bring her back to me."

"Oh, Emil."

It was madness to consider, but having been in Emil's shoes even for a short time, he knew he would have done that and more to bring his family back to him.

"I can't."

"Can't or won't?"

"Emil."

"If it was your child?"

Simon knew she would do it in a heartbeat if she could. And that, in a nutshell, was what was so very wrong about the staff. No one should have that right, that power. If she could do that, what else would she do? What other "just" things would she change? They'd both been through enough with the Council to know that all changes have consequences. No matter how well-intentioned the original act might be, there was no telling what repercussions could result from it.

She took hold of Emil's hands and held them in both of hers. "It's wrong. We can't play God. When has anyone ever done that and not paid the price?"

"I will pay it," Emil begged.

"We don't even know what the price is," Simon said. "But it will be too high. You're a scholar, Emil, a student of history and mythology. Necromancy." He shook his head. "It is unnatural."

"You don't understand," Emil said.

Simon put a hand on his shoulder. "I do. I was released from it, but I understand the prison you live in. I know the pain you feel."

"Then you do understand?"

Simon's eyes shifted to Elizabeth then back to Emil. "Yes," he confessed.

Elizabeth reached out and touched the older man's cheek. "What would your daughter, what would *Aurora* say if she knew what you were asking?"

The pain in Emil's eyes doubled as shame filled them. Simon knew in that moment that the argument was over.

"She would tell me," Emil said in a trembling voice, "that I was being a selfish old fool," he finished with a tremulous laugh. "She was never one to hold back." Simon could see that he was envisioning his daughter in front of him and the agony of realizing that his need could never be filled. "She would tell me that I need to let her go."

Simon was filled with a newfound respect for Emil. He wasn't sure if he could have given up a chance to see his child again.

Emil sniffed back tears. "She always was annoyingly right."

"I don't know what you believe about life and death, but the things I've seen," Elizabeth told him, "I am certain that there is more to our existence than we know. This," she said, looking around the room, "isn't all there is."

Emil nodded blinking back the tears. "Yes. I believe that." He struggled to rein in his emotions but as he did, he seemed to realize how raw and exposed he'd been and grew visibly embarrassed by it. "I'm sorry. I..."

"It's all right," Elizabeth said.

"I should have told you before now."

"It's okay. Anyone else have any secret confessions?" Elizabeth asked, as if to lighten the mood.

Emil gave a small laugh and then cleared his throat. "Shall we get back to the task at hand? We were about to make history, I think. Or you were."

"We were," Elizabeth said.

Emil took out the Eye and unwrapped it, holding it out for her to take.

"Why don't you do the honors?" she suggested. "Put it back where it belongs."

Clearly moved at the honor and at the significance of the moment, Emil could only nod in reply. He walked over to the stone dais where the staff was confined and up a set of three stone steps onto the small platform.

"Are we ready?"

No one replied but then no one needed to.

Emil gingerly slipped the Eye into the cradle of the headpiece. Part of Simon expected some sort of reaction from the staff, but none came. Emil climbed down and gestured to Elizabeth that it was her turn.

She looked unsure for a moment, an expression Simon was not used to seeing on her face. His presence seemed to give her the final bit of assurance she needed, and she climbed the steps. He stood at the base of the dais, ready to help her if needed.

This was the moment they'd all been waiting for—some for years and years. Simon wasn't sure how they were going to steal the staff once it was freed, but they could worry about that later. He watched with apprehension as Elizabeth took her position next to the staff.

Emil stood wide-eyed with wonder and hope, while Vega stood stock still, his expression unreadable.

The hairs on the back of Simon's neck prickled and he fought against the urge to nervously smooth them down.

Elizabeth stood behind the staff, looked at each of them in turn and let out a deep breath. "Here goes nothin'."

She grasped the staff with both hands and then pulled. For a moment it seemed as though it was not going to give way, but then it slid up a few inches. Emil gasped and Vega took a step closer.

Elizabeth's brow furrowed with concentration as she slowly pulled the staff the rest of the way out of the rock.

"Well done!" Emil cried.

Elizabeth smiled back at him but there was something holding her back.

"Are you all right?" Simon asked.

She shrugged. "Fine. I was just expecting some sort of . . .woo. There was no woo."

There wasn't, and he, too, had expected something. Even the Eye didn't seem to react to her.

She shrugged and moved the staff to her right hand. "Maybe it's broken."

She jiggled it slightly and Simon was about to caution her against doing so when the Eye settled more securely into the headpiece. Suddenly, it came to life. It glowed just as it had in the hotel room all those weeks ago. But it wasn't the only thing—Elizabeth glowed, too. It was as if light was coming from inside her, just like the stone. She glowed like an ethereal golden angel and his stomach dropped.

"Elizabeth," he said, stepping toward her.

Her mouth was open, her eyes wide as the light poured out of her. She shimmered with gold.

In that horrible moment, he realized that *she* was El Dorado—the Golden One. It wasn't a city of gold at all. The original legend of the mythical chieftain of the Muisca had the spark of truth in it, and time and avarice had done the rest. El Dorado wasn't a place, it was a person. And now his wife was the One.

"It's beautiful," she said in voice that was at once her own and yet not her at all.

ELIZABETH FELT THE POWER surge through her. She could feel every nerve in her body, every hair on her head. She was aware of herself in a way she never thought possible. She could even feel the air around her. It was as if she was at one with all. And it felt *good*.

It was beyond anything she'd ever experienced before. It wasn't just a sense of well-being, but of *being* in the truest sense of the word. She was connected to everything in the world and it to her. And it was all so simple and beautiful.

"Elizabeth."

A tiny part of her recognized the voice, so distant and far away.

"It's beautiful," she said, the words like music in her ears. She was beautiful.

The energy of the Eye and the staff didn't run through her, they *were* her now. She was as timeless as they were and as powerful. She could feel them both guiding her, teaching her. Anything she could imagine she could make happen. She could reshape the ground beneath her feet or the skies above her.

"Elizabeth."

She pulled herself from the heavens and into the small space that humans occupied. It was so very small. There were faces looking at her—worried, awed, frightened faces. As they should be.

One of them stepped closer and she looked down at him. He was familiar.

"Elizabeth, can you hear me?"

Simon. It was Simon.

"I can do anything," she told him. "*Anything.*"

"You need to let go of the staff, Elizabeth. Just put it down."

The idea of not being as she was now was impossible to contemplate. She was so much more now. She could *do* so much more. She stepped down from the platform and walked toward him.

"I can fix everything," she said. "I can make it *all* right."

He shook his head. "Please put it down."

"I can save the world with a thought. Just a thought. Isn't that what we do?"

"Not like this." He took a step closer to her, the pain and worry in his eyes reaching some distant part of her. "Remember who you are."

Who she was? The memory of that seemed so far away now, so removed.

"You are Elizabeth Cross," Simon said as if sensing her hesitation. "Outrageous, and funny, and kind. You sing off-key and you don't care. You secretly feed the family of rabbits living in our backyard and you sneeze like a cat. You are the mother to our child and you are my wife."

He came one step closer. "You are not a god. You're human— flawed and wonderful."

He reached out a hand to her. "And I love you. *You, Elizabeth.*"

His words were a lighthouse in the fog. Love. Power still swirled inside of her, lifting her, pulling her away, but Simon kept her from disappearing. Fragments of her life came back to her, pushing against the current of the power of the staff.

She remembered the look of worry in Charlotte's eyes the first time she was old enough to understand what their going away meant, and the relief she tried to hide when they reappeared in front of her. That was love.

Jack rigging the Thanksgiving Day turkey wishbone every year so Charlotte always got the bigger half. That was love.

The anniversary Simon bought out all of Chez Antoine so she could feel what he does, "that there's no one else in the world." That was love.

Whatever the staff and the Eye were giving her, they could never come close to that. She didn't want power. She wanted them. Her family.

Slowly, her mind and her soul came to back to herself.

She wasn't a god. This was wrong; this was all wrong.

With more effort than she wanted to admit, she dragged herself away from promise of unlimited power and back to feeling human again. And loved.

She looked at the staff and shuddered, dropping it like a hot potato.

She shook away the heebie-jeebies with another quivering shudder and then looked down at the staff. "That thing is not safe."

Simon barked out a relieved laugh and took hold of her gently by the shoulders. "Are you all right?"

She nodded, although she could still feel the staff's energy inside her, feel her connection to it, feel it calling to her. And worried for a moment if she'd ever be free of it.

Simon ducked his head to get a look into her eyes. "Elizabeth?"

"I'm all right, just . . .I don't know. That was..."

"Remarkable," Emil said. "Truly remarkable."

As Emil came forward to examine her himself, Alex picked up the staff.

"How did it feel?" Emil asked her. "What did you feel?"

She shook her head; there were no words to express it. "Everything." She looked at Simon. "I think I could feel the blades of grass in our lawn at home. I felt *everything*. The Eye showed me."

"The Eye?"

It was difficult to explain. "It's like a thing, a semi-sort-of-conscious thing."

"The Eye is?"

"The Eye or staff. Both, I don't know. But there was a presence to them. I don't how else to explain it."

"Remarkable."

"Why isn't it working?" Alex said, drawing their attention. He held the staff just as Elizabeth had, but nothing happened.

Emil took the staff and tried as well, but there was no reaction.

"I thought you said that once the staff was removed from the stone that anyone could wield it," Alex asked.

"I thought it would."

"You *thought* it would." Alex snatched the staff away from him. "Well, you were wrong."

Alex's abrupt and rude behavior surprised Elizabeth and the others, judging from the looks on their faces, but they chose to ignore it.

"Not just about that, I'm afraid," Simon said. "El Dorado isn't a place. It's a person."

"Whoever can wield the staff," Emil said with recognition. "The Golden One, of course."

"You mean there's no city of gold?" Alex asked, sounding less and less like himself with every passing moment.

305

She understood being a little disappointed at not finding riches beyond his wildest imagination, but Alex didn't seem the greedy type.

Simon shook his head, watching Alex warily. "Apparently not."

"*I'm* El Dorado?" Elizabeth asked.

"So it seems."

"Wow, well that's one for the Christmas letter."

Emil and Simon couldn't stop from chuckling, but Alex wasn't amused, his expression dark and sullen.

He stared intently at the staff. "You're sure the staff will only work for her?"

The way he said it, as if she wasn't there, sent a chill up her spine.

"It appears so," Emil said. "But what does it matter? What a remarkable—"

"Shut. Up."

The words were so shocking, so unexpected that they all fell completely silent.

Emil recovered himself. "What I mean is that—"

"What *I* mean is SHUT UP!" Alex said, the veins on his neck standing out as he yelled and pulled out his gun, leveling it at Emil.

Aghast and completely caught off guard, Emil put his hands up and stood trembling.

Elizabeth didn't understand what was going on. "Alex?"

His eyes shifted toward her and she hardly recognized him. Gone were the soulful eyes of the poet. He was looking at her with pure hatred. It was so strong, so violent, that she actually took a step back.

306

Simon edged closer to her, but she hardly noticed. She was so shocked by the change that had come over Alex, she didn't know what to think.

His mouth tightened and he shook his head, anger visibly building inside him. He spat out something that sounded like *Verdammt!* And then a litany of other words she didn't recognize except for one thing. And a chill ran through her body.

She might not know what the words meant, but they weren't Portuguese; they were German.

"Alex?"

"Your name isn't Alex Vega, is it?" Simon said, coolly. "You're German," Simon said. "An SS officer unless I'm mistaken."

"What?" Emil blurted out.

The way his eyes shifted coldly to Simon as he paced told her that Simon was right.

"How do you know that?" she asked.

"His tattoo. I saw it at the river. It's small letter A on the underside of his arm. I didn't remember until now what it signified. But it's a type of tattoo given only to officers of the Schutzstaffel."

The SS? He was a Nazi? Alex was a Nazi? Elizabeth felt sick. Absolutely sick. God, she'd actually *liked* him. What an idiot she was. What a fool.

They'd been worried about the Nazis finding the staff and all she'd done was lead one right to it. Her stomach churned at the thought. And Simon had known. He'd known something was wrong with him from the start and she'd *defended* him. She thought Simon was just jealous. She'd been so blind.

She'd always thought herself a pretty good judge of character, but she'd been so far off the mark with him she wasn't even on the map.

"God, what an idiot I am," she said.

307

"I don't understand," Emil said.

"Your benefactor has been working with the Ahnenerbe," Simon replied. "Himmler himself probably."

Alex's eyes shifted from his back and forth toward Simon.

Sweet Christmas, she'd actually helped one of Himmler's men! Himmler. She would never forgive herself for this.

"You're a Nazi?" she asked angrily, wanting to hear from him.

"Nazi?" Emil said, still shocked and uncomprehending.

"Yes!" Alex said, stopping his pacing. "And I am going to bring this staff back to the Reich, to the Führer and be rewarded." His eyes were wild. "And you are going to help me."

Elizabeth shook her head. "No."

It was a simple word, but the result from Alex was explosive. He stepped forward, gun leveled at her head. "Yes, you will," he spat out, and she thought for a moment he was going to shoot her right then and there.

From the look on his face, he thought he might too, but he pulled back and controlled himself slightly. "Yes, you will," he repeated more calmly but no less deadly.

"I had hoped there would be gold as well, but the staff will suffice. With it in our possession, with the power of vril, of our Aryan ancestors, there is nothing that can stop us. It is our destiny," he said sounding every bit the zealot. "It is my destiny."

"But you're not Aryan, are you?" Simon said, with more calmness than anyone had a right to under the circumstances. "Your eyes, your hair, your skin. You're not really one of them."

If Simon was hoping to appeal to some hidden part of Alex, his words had the opposite effect. Enraged, Alex changed his aim, pressing the barrel of the gun to Simon's chest.

Elizabeth held her breath.

"I am that and more." He dared Simon to doubt him again, and thankfully Simon said no more.

He stepped back to put some distance between them again and addressed Elizabeth. "Now, you will come with me."

Elizabeth stood her ground. "No."

"I will kill your husband. Do you doubt I will?"

"I know you won't," she said.

He seemed almost amused and she knew that was her moment. She held out her hand and the staff flew from his hand to hers. The connection she'd felt still hummed inside her. When it hit her palm, her fingers closed around it and the full power surged through her.

CHAPTER TWENTY-FIVE

THE SHOCK OF HER summoning the staff bought Elizabeth the precious seconds she needed and she willed chunks of the ceiling to fall, a large piece striking Alex's arm, knocking the gun out of his hand. Alex cried out in pain and clutched at his forearm. Simon lunged forward and snatched the gun before Alex could recover himself.

Simon kept the gun trained on Alex but shifted his gaze to Elizabeth. "Are you all right?"

The power surged inside her, but for now, she was able to better control it.

"What do we do now?" Emil asked.

Simon glanced at Elizabeth again and she knew what he was thinking. And he was right. Again.

"We have to destroy it," Simon said.

"But the historical significance of such a find, a treasure—"

"Pales in comparison to the danger. Do you want someone like him," Simon said, as he inclined his head toward Alex, "to have it. To give it to the Nazis?"

"No, but surely there's another way."

"The staff isn't a treasure," Elizabeth said. "It's a curse. It can do anything. Anything, right?"

Emil nodded.

"Then where are the people? Where is the civilization that created it? Created this temple? If the staff can do anything, why aren't they still here?"

No one had an answer for that, but Elizabeth knew. The staff showed her everything.

"That painting at the entrance with the man and staff. It looked like he was blessing his people. But he wasn't. He was killing them. It wasn't a tribute, it was a warning."

"What?" Emil gasped.

"It has to be destroyed."

"No!" Alex protested, starting forward a half-step until Simon reminded him that there was a gun trained on him.

"Can you do it?" Simon asked her.

She nodded, but honestly, she wasn't sure. But she had to try now or she'd lose herself again. The control she had was already tenuous.

"You can't destroy it!" Alex cried. "You can't!"

Ignoring him, she closed her eyes and concentrated, but she could feel it resisting her. The staff began to vibrate in her hand. Then the floor began to shake, and then the walls and the ceiling.

"Elizabeth."

"Tryin' to save the world here."

"Sorry."

But the harder she tried, the harder the staff resisted and the more the room began to shake, until more chunks of the ceiling fell away and cracks appeared in the floor.

"Hate to interrupt, but—"

Suddenly, the staff flew from her grip and slammed into the far wall, then ricocheted off it and back across the room, bouncing off wall after wall until it stopped, hovering in mid-air. Then it floated over the pedestal stone and drove itself back into the hole with a bright explosion of light. The shaking of the temple didn't stop.

"I don't think it liked that," she said.

The ground shook so hard then that Elizabeth fell into Simon. It was becoming increasingly clear that the entire underground temple was at risk of collapsing.

"Time to leave?" she said.

"Definitely."

"No!" Alex cried as he stumbled toward the staff. "I've come too far. Himmler will see. They will all see!"

"Get away from that!" Simon shouted.

A huge chunk of ceiling fell and the roar of rock against rock was nearly thunderous.

"We have to go," Elizabeth said, having earthquake flashbacks. "Now."

Emil ran toward the door, but Simon kept his focus on Alex.

"Simon! We have to get out of here."

She knew he was warring with himself over what to do. Alex was a Nazi, but he couldn't kill him in cold blood. Simon stuffed the gun into his pocket and took Elizabeth by the hand.

As they reached the door, Elizabeth turned back to see Alex vainly trying to pull the staff from the rock with his one good arm while the room around him disintegrated. He'd gone completely mad. He ranted to himself as he tried to remove the staff.

"I will be the most powerful man in the Reich. They will all bow to me. Himmler, Hitler, my father. They will all—"

The rest of whatever he was going to say was buried along with him as the ceiling collapsed upon him. Elizabeth watched in horror as he was buried alive.

"Come on!" Simon said, tugging her through the doorway.

They ran through the corridors and rooms, backtracking their path. Bits of wall and ceiling fell around them, narrowly missing them. They made it into the first room with the mural just in time to see it crumble.

"Professor!"

That was Raul's voice.

They followed Emil onto the stairs, which had been scary enough when they weren't shaking beneath her feet. Raul and Bira stood halfway down the steps, clinging to the wall as best they could as the ground beneath them shook. Bira helped steady Emil and passed him along to Raul then reached out for Elizabeth and Simon.

"Go back up!" Simon cried. "Go!"

Bira nodded and started to climb back up. Simon held onto Elizabeth's hand so tightly it hurt, but she wasn't about to ask him to let go. He practically pulled her up the stairs behind him.

Then a strong jolt came and the whole staircase seemed to shift beneath them. About ten feet in front of them Bira lost his balance and plunged over the side. Elizabeth would have followed him if hadn't been for Simon holding her back.

They couldn't pause to take it in, to accept that a man had just died, to process any of it. They had to keep moving.

With each step the earth shook harder and more of the temple fell away. But finally, they emerged into the entry room as Raul helped Emil into a rope harness.

"Agora!"

The men pulled Emil up.

"Where is Bira?" Raul asked. Simon could only shake his head.

Once they had Emil up, the rope came back down.

"Your turn," Simon said to her. "No arguments."

The room gave an extra jolt for emphasis and she didn't argue. The men pulled her up and then Simon and then, finally, Raul. They waited for any sign of Alex as long as they could until the ground near the entrance became unstable and they had to back away.

Then with a deep, horrible rumbling, the entire temple collapsed. The ground fell in on itself, dust and dirt flying up into the air as if a bomb had gone off. And as quickly as it had started the shaking stopped.

The dust lingered in the air like smoke and then slowly settled back down onto the ground. Carefully, they stepped forward as close as they dared. The entire area of the temple, and it was immense, had fallen in on itself like the caldera of a now-dormant volcano. Alex, the staff, and the Eye were buried beneath it all.

THE JUNGLE WAS EERILY silent. The thunderous crash of the collapse of the temple had frightened all the animals. Simon noticed that even the cicadas had ceased to sing. But then slowly, life at the top of the mountain resumed and the birds and the frogs and howler monkeys in the distance sang their songs again.

Elizabeth and Emil stood still staring at the fresh indentation in the plateau, both lost in their own thoughts of what had been and what might have been. Simon's thoughts were simple—get the hell out of here.

He turned to Elizabeth, her eyes still far off. He knew she was hearing Vega's cries, seeing the stones topple onto him, watching as Bira fell, helpless to save him. And perhaps her mind was somewhere he could not comprehend. He'd been as surprised as anyone when she suddenly summoned the staff, yanking it from Vega's hand with only a thought. She was connected to the Eye and it to her. He slipped his hand around hers as if his mere presence could anchor her to this reality.

She held onto his hand tightly and gave him a weak smile before turning back to the sight of the temple. It wasn't much but it was enough to assure him that she was his Elizabeth and always would be.

"What happened to Bira?" Raul asked.

"He fell from the stairs," Simon said.

Raul nodded thoughtfully and Simon was struck by how much older he seemed now than he had just a month ago. He'd thought him a bit feckless, but he'd proven himself to be a man they could rely on, and they would have to if they were to get home.

Of course, they could always use the watch. He and Elizabeth could be home in minutes, but he knew she wouldn't agree to that. Emil needed them. That wasn't part of their mission, but it was part of who they were. They couldn't leave him now.

Raul did his best to communicate with the men who hadn't fled when the shaking started. Without Bira it was difficult. But between pantomime and the few scattered words of Portuguese the men knew, and what Guarani Simon and Raul had picked up during their expedition, they managed to come to an understanding.

The sun hung high in the sky. If they broke camp now, they could make some good progress down the mountain, and Simon wanted to get as far away from this place as soon as he could.

The trip down was even harder than the trip up, but somehow they managed. Elizabeth was uncharacteristically silent that first day, keeping her thoughts to herself. Emil hadn't spoken more than a few words.

That night, he helped Elizabeth into her hammock and began tucking the mosquito netting around her when she stopped him, gently stilling his hand.

"I never did say thank you," she said.

"For?"

She shook her head. "To think what I might have done if you hadn't been there."

"It's all right."

"And you were right about Alex." Her face crinkled in apology. "I was such an idiot."

"I was right for all the wrong reasons."

"At least you were right. I bought his story hook, line, and sinker. Like a big mouth bass."

"You see the best in people. That's a gift."

"Until it isn't."

"I wouldn't change you for the world. Big mouth and all."

Elizabeth laughed, and in that moment he knew she would be all right. He caressed her cheek and she kissed his palm.

"Goodnight," he said and finished tucking her in before climbing into his own hammock and watching her until she fell asleep.

The next morning over a very meager breakfast of canned beans, Emil began to break from his stupor. They explained, as best they could without giving too much away, about what they believed to be the connection between Rasche and Vega. As badly as Elizabeth felt, it didn't hold a candle to Emil's guilt and shame. He'd spent two years with the man and never had the slightest inkling that he was anyone other than who he pretended to be.

"I never suspected him once," Emil confessed.

"He was very good at what he did," Simon said.

Elizabeth put down her tin cup. "Don't feel bad. I was an all-day sucker, too."

Emil smiled kindly at her. "You are a remarkable woman."

"I am an itchy and," she said as she wrinkled her nose, "stinky woman at the moment, who really just wants to get home."

"Yes," Emil said. "I have a great deal to talk about with my wife."

Simon stood. "Then might I suggest we get moving?"

"Right."

They broke camp and continued on. With the help of Vega's detailed notes, their native bearers, and sheer luck, they managed to find Moacir's village on the seventh day. With his help and a few of the men from his tribe they were able to traverse their way back to the village by the lake. The journey took weeks, and they were all one step from collapse when they arrived there, but that night, for the first time in two months, they slept indoors.

Simon woke in the middle of night to find Elizabeth's palette empty. A momentary fear clutched his heart until he saw her silhouette not more than ten feet from the front door of the little house they'd been invited to stay in for the night. She sat on a log by a cold fire pit, petting the little dog, Mancha.

"Elizabeth?"

She looked back at him, gave the dog one last scratch behind the ears and then stood and gazed up at the sky. "I missed it. Being outside. That sounds crazy, doesn't it?"

"Utterly."

She laughed and slipped an arm around his waist as he joined her to look up into the night full of stars.

"Do you still feel it?" he asked. "The Eye?"

"No," she said. "It faded after the first few days. Do you think that means it was destroyed?"

"Possibly. Hopefully."

She only nodded and kept looking up at the stars. "The Council's going to be PO'd about that."

Simon pulled her a little closer to his side. "Good."

"WE LOOK LIKE DEATH warmed over," Simon said as they both looked into the mirror of their hotel room in Rio.

He was right. They looked like hell. They'd both lost at least twenty pounds, gotten far too much sun and not nearly enough sleep. They didn't just have bags under their eyes, they had entire sets of luggage.

Her hair was, well, it was best not to think about it.

"Are you sure you want to stay the night?" he asked.

Elizabeth wanted to go home and see Charlotte more than anything, but they were both beyond exhausted and looked shockingly bad. They were honest with Charlotte about what happened on their trips, as much as they could. Returning looking like they'd both gone full Unibomber might be upsetting.

"You need to at least shave. And I need to …" She inhaled her own special brand of jungle funk and winced. "Oh, they are never going to bottle that."

A tired laugh rumbled in his chest and then he turned on the shower as she began undressing. He looked back into the mirror and scratched at several weeks' worth of beard. Both of them would be happy when it was gone.

Elizabeth had to sit down on the toilet to remove her shoes. She was so tired she nearly fell asleep right there naked with one shoe on.

"Come on," Simon urged her. "You'll feel better after a shower."

"You want to join me?" she asked, trying to be sexy but probably just looking like a dope.

"Under any other circumstances, you know what my answer would be. But I'm just too knackered to enjoy it."

She giggled. "Knackered." He got a little more British when he was tired.

"All right, all right," he said as he helped her into the shower.

She stood under the warm water and felt herself falling asleep again. Only Simon bumping around and cursing as he nicked himself shaving kept her awake.

She climbed out feeling like she'd washed half of Brazil down the drain. She did feel better, but even more tired, if that was possible.

Simon finished shaving, took a shower of his own and joined her in bed. She was nearly asleep as she felt the mattress dip with his weight.

She rolled over into his side and he put his arm around her.

"We can go back now if you want," she said, half-asleep.

"Maybe in just a few minutes," he said softly.

She reached up and caressed his smooth cheek. She lifted her head to kiss him but he was snoring lightly before she got there. She kissed him anyway and he shifted slightly in his sleep, pulling her closer.

"Just a few minutes," she said as she rested her head on his shoulder. The next morning they decided to stay a few hours more and take Emil to the airport on the bay.

"Are you sure you won't come with me?" he asked.

"We need a few days," Simon said. They were both still beyond exhausted. So was Emil, but he'd booked passage on the first flight available. He needed to see his wife in a way he hadn't in many years.

Simon held out his hand. "Safe travels, Emil."

Emil shook it and then turned to Elizabeth. "My dear." Elizabeth stepped forward and pulled him into a hug. He eased her back to get one last look. "You really do remind me of her."

"She'd be very proud of you, I think."

Choked by emotion, Emil only nodded.

They watched him board the Clipper and waited until it had lifted off from the bay.

"We could spend a few days," Simon said. "Rest, if you'd like."

Elizabeth shook her head. "I'm ready to go home."

THE WORLD COALESCED AROUND them as the blue lightning faded, and they stood in the living room of their home. No matter how often they did this, it was always disconcerting. Like returning from any long trip, there was a surreal sense to being back that made one wonder if any of the previous weeks had really happened.

But the blisters on her feet and the ache in every part of her body told her that it had. She'd dreamt of being home so often over the course of the last two months that now that she was here, part of her didn't believe it wasn't just another dream.

She walked over to the window, Simon at her side. He pulled back the curtain; out in the yard, Jack and Charlotte played catch and Elizabeth knew she was finally home.

"I'm glad that's over," she said.

"There's just one more thing to do."

"MR. CROSS!" RHYS SAID as he sprung up from his desk, surprised by Simon's abrupt and unannounced entrance into Travers' outer office.

"Hewitt in?" Simon asked, not breaking stride toward the inner office door.

"Yes, but—"

Simon pulled open the door and stormed inside. Peter Travers sat on the edge of his desk talking to James Hewitt. Both men stood at his sudden appearance.

Simon ignored Travers and fixed his considerable attention on Hewitt.

He jabbed a finger in the air in accusation as he approached him. "You knew. When you gave us the assignment you knew about the Eye, what we'd be forced to do."

Hewitt put his hands out to calm Simon. "Mr. Cross—"

Simon stopped in front of him. "Tell me the truth for once. Did you or did you not know what Elizabeth would face?"

Hewitt gave him a look of Great Patience. "Sometimes it's necessary to withhold certain—"

Simon's right cross broke Hewitt's jaw. He fell to the floor and stayed there, whimpering.

"The next time you lie to me will be your last," Simon said. Then he turned to Travers and greeted him, "Peter."

Travers glanced down at Hewitt, unmoved by what had happened, then back at Simon. "Good to see you, Simon. Give Elizabeth my best."

Simon nodded in return and headed toward the door.

"He bwoke meh jaw," Hewitt wailed.

"You're lucky he didn't break your neck."

Chapter Twenty-Six

1957, Somewhere in the Brazilian Jungle

He'd been looking for so long. He'd lost so much, but he had never stopped. Sweat dripped under his eye patch and he wiped it away with the sleeve of his only remaining arm. He joked with the locals that he'd given an arm and a leg to find the Eye again, but they didn't seem to get the joke.

He hadn't lost an entire leg after all, just a few toes. His arm, however, he thought as he looked at the sleeve pinned at the shoulder, that was long gone.

He didn't remember climbing out of the rubble or even the months that followed. Somehow, he'd lived. It had taken him years to be strong enough to return to the jungle. But he had, again and again. Each time sure this was the one. But this time was different. This time he was sure. He could feel it.

Finally, after twenty years of searching, he would find it. There was no home to return to, but many of his people now called South

America home. With the Eye they could rebuild the Reich and be stronger than ever before.

He hobbled forward using his cane and surveyed the plateau. He'd come to many over the years, but this one was different.

He walked a few paces forward to the edge of a hollow. It was as overgrown as every inch of this damnable place was, but he knew. This was it.

He tapped his cane against the rock. "Here," he said and then turned to his men. "Dig here."

THE END

Don't miss the next adventure! Sign up for Monique's new release newsletter at her website.

If you enjoyed this book, please consider posting a short review.

Have an idea for a time and/or location you'd like to see Simon & Elizabeth visit? Drop me a line or come on by Facebook and let me know. I have quite a few ideas for future adventures, but would love to hear from you! Visit:

moniquemartin.weebly.com

OTHER BOOKS BY MONIQUE MARTIN

Out of Time Series

Out of Time: A Time Travel Mystery (Book #1)
When the Wall Fell (Book #2)
Fragments (Book #3)
The Devils' Due (Book #4)
Thursday's Child (Book #5)
Sands of Time (Book #6)
A Rip in Time (Book #7)
A Time of Shadows (Book #8)
Voyage in Time (Book #9)
Revolution in Time (Book #10)
Expedition in Time (Book #11)

Out of Time Christmas Novellas

In Time for Christmas
Christmas in New York
The Christmas Express - coming winter 2019!

Saving Time Series

Jacks Are Wild (Book #1)
Aloha, Jack (Book #2)
Nairobi Jack (Book #3)
Book #4 - coming soon!

The Blaze Series

The Blaze (Book #1)
Mirror (Book #2)

Hollywood Heroes Series

The Frame (Book #1)
The Curse (Book #2) - *coming soon!*

ABOUT THE AUTHOR

Monique was born in Houston, Texas, but her family soon moved to Southern California. She grew up on both coasts, living in Connecticut and California. She currently resides in Southern California with her naughty Siamese cat, Monkey.

She's currently working on an adaptation of one of her screenplays, several short stories and novels and the next book in the Out of Time series.

Visit moniquemartin.weebly.com to sign up for the new release newsletter and don't miss another of Simon and Elizabeth's adventures.

Have an idea for a time and/or location you'd like to see Simon & Elizabeth visit? Drop me a line or come on by Facebook and let me know. I have quite a few ideas for future adventures, but would love to hear from you! Visit:

moniquemartin.weebly.com

or email

writtenbymonique@gmail.com

Made in the USA
San Bernardino, CA
11 May 2019